UNCONQUERED

A DA CAPO PRESS REPRINT SERIES

China
in the 20th century

UNCONQUERED

Journal of
a Year's Adventures among
the Fighting Peasants
of North China

JAMES BERTRAM

DA CAPO PRESS • NEW YORK • 1975

Library of Congress Cataloging in Publication Data

Bertram, James M
 Unconquered: journal of a year's adventures among the fighting peasants of north China.

(China in the 20th century)
 Reprint of the ed. published by the John Day Co., New York.
 1. China — History — 1937-1945. I. Title.
 DS777.53.B4   1975   951.04'2   74-34456
 ISBN 0-306-70688-1

This Da Capo Press edition of *Unconquered* is an unabridged republication of the first edition published in New York in 1939.

Copyright, 1939, by James Bertram.

Published by Da Capo Press, Inc.
A Subsidiary of Plenum Publishing Corporation
227 West 17th Street, New York, N.Y. 10011

All Rights Reserved

Manufactured in the United States of America

UNCONQUERED

The author on his way to the front in North Shansi.

UNCONQUERED

*Journal of
a Year's Adventures among
the Fighting Peasants
of North China*

JAMES BERTRAM

THE JOHN DAY COMPANY
New York

COPYRIGHT, 1939, BY JAMES BERTRAM

All rights reserved, including the right to reproduce this book or portions thereof in any form.

PRINTED IN THE UNITED STATES OF AMERICA
Van Rees Press · *New York*

For G. M.,

*killed in Spain,
November, 1936.*

"On ne découvre qu'une fois la guerre, mais on découvre plusieurs fois la vie."

ABOUT THE AUTHOR

James Bertram is a young New Zealander, who went to Oxford as a Rhodes Scholar and took top honors in English literature. He had already had political and journalistic experience both in New Zealand and in England. After Oxford he went out to the Orient as a free-lance writer, to investigate social and political developments both in China and in Japan.

He was working at a Chinese university at Peiping in December, 1936, when news came that Chiang Kai-shek had been kidnaped. He made his way to Sian and was the first foreign writer to get the whole story of the mutiny, which was published under the title First Act in China. *He then returned to Peiping and in May, 1937, went to Tokyo and was living there when hostilities began at Marco Polo Bridge. Within a week he set sail again for China and for the adventures described in the present volume.*

CONTENTS

Prologue: JAPAN: APPROACH OF WAR
The Island People, 3
Alarum Off, 10
Midsummer Madness, 16
"Banzai!," 22
Invitation to Death, 27

Chapter One: COLLAPSE IN THE NORTH
Marco Polo Bridge, 34
The Siege of Peiping, 41
Massacre, 49
Triumphal Entry, 53
"Really War," 58

Chapter Two: THE ROAD TO YENAN
Shantung Roundabout, 65
Sian Revisited, 73
Enter the Red Army, 79
The Tomb of Huang Ti, 86
Journey's End, 92

Chapter Three: RED CHINA AT WAR
Inside Yenan, 99
Chinese Lenin, 107
Two Parties, 115
Communist Strategy, 121
"Special District," 125

CONTENTS

Chapter Four: INTO SHANSI

Farewell to Yenan, 134
Yellow River Crossing, 140
The War in Shansi, 143
Chinese Retreat, 147
Political Commissar, 150

Chapter Five: THE EIGHTH ROUTE ARMY

On to Headquarters, 155
Commander-in-chief, 159
Missionary Interlude, 165
Old Friends and New Enemies, 169
Japanese Interlude, 175

Chapter Six: TO THE NORTH

Farewell to Headquarters, 187
Desolation, 190
The Fighting Division, 193
Mass Mobilization, 197
Winter Journey, 202

Chapter Seven: IN THE HILLS WITH HO LUNG

Division Headquarters, 206
By Fire and Flood, 210
Theatrical, 216
Testament of Youth, 221
The New Year, 227

CONTENTS ix

Chapter Eight: THE FRONT OF WAR

Portrait of a Warlord, 232
Mobile Unit, 236
Along the Front, 240
Where the Battle Was, 245
Across the Japanese Lines, 249

Chapter Nine: PARTISAN

Brigade Headquarters, 254
Guerilla Warfare, 258
Portrait of a Hero, 263
They Call It Peace, 267
China's New Great Wall, 272

Chapter Ten: UNITED FRONT

The Return, 277
Christians and Communists, 282
Fifth Column, 287
Hankow Symphony, 292
Hong Kong Discords, 298

Epilogue: THE BLIND INVADER

Second Spring, 305
Peiping in Shadow, 310
The Architects of Empire, 316
May Day in Tokyo, 320
The Unconquered, 325

Reference List of Names, Events, and Phrases Commonly Used

Reference List, 331

ILLUSTRATIONS

The author on his way to the front in North Shansi
Frontispiece

Erosion-scalloped country along the
Wei River in southeast Kansu
Facing page 116

One of the hundreds of old Chinese blockhouses
on the northwest frontier
Facing page 196

Peasants of Shansi
Facing page 266

Soldiers of the Eighth Route Army with antitank
gun captured from the Japanese
Facing page 266

UNCONQUERED

PROLOGUE
JAPAN: APPROACH OF WAR

THE ISLAND PEOPLE

"You have no camera? Good. No pistol? Good. Then we can go ashore." The Passport Officer gathered up his papers, and made me a little bow of welcome to Japan.

He was a sad-faced man in a shabby black suit, with an undernourished look and a mustache like Mr. Chamberlain's. But his formal manner relaxed noticeably now that the interrogation was over, and he apologized for having asked so many questions. It was a matter of routine. . . . He clasped a straw hat and umbrella, and led the way out of the saloon.

At the stairhead, my new guide paused for a moment to admire a big bowl of chrysanthemums. "In England," he said with regret, "you have no such flowers as these."

"Chrysanthemums?" I ventured a mild protest. "Why, yes, they do grow in England."

"But that is not possible." He touched the big blooms with loving fingers. "This is a *Japanese* flower. . . ."

The point did not seem worth disputing, and we strolled amicably down the quay towards the railway station. The narrow harbor was busy with shipping; mist curled delicately along the water, cut by the brown sails of fishing boats. I inhaled the fresh scent of island pine.

"It is a pity," observed my companion, whose mind ran pleasantly on flower themes, "that you have missed the spring blossom. But you will see the irises. Japan"—the name of his country, even in an unfamiliar language, fell like a caress—"is a Land of Flowers. And here it is always green; not like China. In China there are no trees."

4   APPROACH OF WAR

I passed over this surprising last statement without comment. "What do the Japanese people really think about China?"

He sighed deeply, as though I had mentioned a painful subject. "How can we say? Japan wants to be China's friend, but the Chinese do not understand this. Always they make trouble for us." I had a swift vision of China as he saw it: an immense land dark under cloud, where tiny imp-like figures swarmed in a treeless plain, all making rude gestures at the Rising Sun. "We want only to help China; but the Chinese are so unfaithful. It is very difficult..."

We had reached the station, and I thanked my friendly guide. He took his leave with a faint return of the official manner. "That is your train; you are sure you have not got a pistol? And do not forget to visit the Imperial Gardens. In this country there is always something to see."

He was right. It was June, 1937, and I was to reach Tokyo in time to see more than the irises.

In the Far East, one looks back to the spring of 1937—as Europe once looked back to the forgotten summer of 1914—across a gulf of war. It is hard to believe, in retrospect, that those halcyon days were real.

Spring had brought a kind of renaissance to China, with the peaceful settlement of her last grave internal crisis holding out a new hope for national unity. And Japan, rather to the surprise of the Chinese themselves, did not seem to be ill-disposed. A strange lull had fallen in the usual acrimonious exchanges between Tokyo and Nanking. In March, an economic mission of Japanese bankers and industrialists visited China and made favorable reports: it was even said that they had recommended the redress of some of China's more obvious grievances in the North. True, there had been some trouble between this goodwill mission and the Japanese North China Garrison, but it might be possible to get around that. High hopes were based on Japan's new and "moderate" commander in North China, Major-General Tashiro. It was not yet commonly known that the strain of being a moderate Japanese commander had already fatally undermined General Tashiro's health.

THE ISLAND PEOPLE 5

Even in Peiping, where each spring since 1931 had renewed the shadow of war, it would have seemed ungrateful to reject these auspicious omens. The Japanese Army, one knew, did not change its spots overnight. But the swashbuckling tendencies of the Army Premier, General Hayashi, were at this time largely offset at the Foreign Office by the genuinely liberal and enlightened Sato. And Hayashi's days in office were already numbered. It really looked as though the "moderates" in Japan—that inchoate political body always named with desperate optimism by prophets of peace in the Pacific—might yet come into their own.

At least, the time seemed happily chosen for a closer study of relations between two uneasy neighbors in the Far East, and in May 1937 I set out from North China for Japan. But already experienced observers shook their heads. "It's too much like 1931," Owen Lattimore told me before I left Peiping. "Too quiet for comfort. I'm afraid we may be in for another September 18th." A brief interlude of liberal government in Japan, one remembered, and of equally effusive protestations of friendship towards China, had set the stage for the sudden and bloody adventure of Manchuria. Notoriously, even in a decade which nobody can consider remarkable for international sincerity, Japanese diplomacy has had in it the eagle and the dove.

To travel from China to Japan through Manchuria and Korea is an object lesson in history, past and present. For it was over the bridge of the Korean peninsula that Chinese civilization, flowering under the Han and later dynasties, spilled across the straits to the remote and barbarous islands of Japan. In the fifth and sixth centuries, when Korea was an outpost of Chinese culture and a famous Buddhist sanctuary, the tide flowed most strongly. What it took to Japan was nothing less than her whole cultural heritage, now so dearly prized.

China conquered Japan with books fifteen hundred years ago; in our own time, Japan has returned the compliment with tanks and guns. For now the tide has set the other way. And it was over the same bridge through Korea and Manchuria that

Japan set out on her modern "civilizing mission" in East Asia—a progress whose milestones are not libraries and temples, but more solid monuments of concrete and steel.

A growing awareness of this ebb and flow of conquest accompanied us upon that northern journey to Japan. News by the way gave an added point to it. In Dairen, that curiously artificial city of modern docks and ancient droshkies which is the stronghold of the South Manchuria Railway and Japan's northern challenge to Hong Kong, we heard the first rumors of Hayashi's impending downfall. In Seoul—one of the few points in all the Orient where Chinese and Japanese art meet and blend—the fall of the government was confirmed. A new régime, headed by Prince Fumimaro Konoye, was already being acclaimed abroad as a "reform cabinet," destined to carry on the good work of co-operation begun by Foreign Minister Sato.

But some points about the new government, it seemed even then, were rather less than reassuring. Sato himself had given place at the *Gaimushu* to Koki Hirota, author of the famous "Three Points" of 1936 which had become the crystallization of Japan's policy of "permanent peace in East Asia," and effective diplomatic agent in the "Anti-Comintern Pact" concluded with Germany that same year.* Sugiyama at the War Office and Baba—the personification of heavy industry and armaments—at the Home Ministry, were names more than outweighing that of the amiable but politically inexperienced Konoye. The new cabinet, if one might judge from its hybrid composition, was clearly in for squalls.

This was the general political position when I arrived in Japan itself. There was still considerable elation in liberal circles over the defeat of Hayashi, a Japanese Cromwell who had tried to rule without parliament by methods too blatant even for the shadow-show of the Imperial Diet. But the liberals, as liberals are apt to be anywhere, were unorganized and over-

---

* It is noteworthy that this anti-Soviet alliance, later to be strengthened by the inclusion of fascist Italy, was so unpopular with the people of Japan at the time of its announcement that it led to the fall of Hirota's government. Less than a year afterwards, it was to become the official cornerstone of Japan's international policy. This is a graphic illustration of how little a Japanese government may represent the real feeling of the nation as a whole.

optimistic, and their representation in the new government remained an expectation rather than a fulfillment.

Japan is one of those countries, like modern Italy, that welcome the traveler with open arms—provided he remains a tourist or a discreet student of *alta cultura*. Wherever you move within such harmless fields museums, theaters, and university libraries open their doors with quiet efficiency and a charming official courtesy. One could only be grateful for this; and my first weeks in Japan passed pleasantly enough. The cultural approach is the one most of us would choose for the study of any nation, had we but world enough, and time.

But time was the enemy; I had come to Japan in the hope of seeing something more than museums. A few actual and contemporary details could be supplied, of course, by an unconducted tour of the Tokyo slums, or a night visit to the Asakusa, playground of the city proletariat. Even more revealing was a stroll through the cheap licensed quarters, where tiny painted creatures peer like mice through a grating at the passer-by. (It would take a hardy statistician to calculate the total number of prostitutes in this third-largest city of the world. Most of them have been sold into the trade by poor country families.)

But this was still only the fringe of reality. One cannot build up from contrasts, however picturesque. "I want to see the real fabric of this country, not just the decorations," I complained one day to a Japanese professor of economics. "I want to visit factories, to talk with Japanese workers about their own lives. Can't one live in a country village and see something of rural conditions at first hand?"

The shrewd, smiling face conveyed a warning with almost comical suddenness. "A factory is very difficult to see in Japan. Perhaps you could go into the country with a Japanese student, in the vacation. But we would have to choose the district. Then the police would want to know what you were doing...."

This was in the common-room of a Tokyo university. Blue-uniformed students were strolling through the gardens outside with immense decorum and a gravity beyond their years. As usual when baffled, I brought up the name of Freda Utley, whose recent indictment of Japanese society was a convenient if controversial starting point. "Have you read by any chance *Japan's Feet of Clay?*"

Somewhat to my surprise, the economist nodded. "The book is banned, of course; but I had a copy for review. Her facts are true enough, for the most part—I could have given her some that would be even more 'startling.' But it is the interpretation of the facts that is all wrong."

"You admit the facts? About labor conditions, for instance, and the state of the peasants?"

He sucked his teeth in the universal Japanese gesture of polite apology. "We know these things better than any foreigner. But what a foreigner can never understand is the Japanese character. Agreed, that girls work in factories for twelve hours a day, and for very low wages. But these girls are happy in their work. They accept a difficult life, because they know they can serve their country in this way.

"You foreigners cannot realize what patriotism means to a Japanese. It is not just the willingness of the soldier to die on the battlefield. It is also the duty of every citizen to make sacrifices, if need be, for the national good."

This was the fatal paradox one encountered everywhere in Japan. It was for the good of the nation ("nation," I felt, needed a more precise definition) to keep the peasants and farmers, backbone of the whole unstable Japanese economy, in a state of perennial poverty bordering on starvation; to encourage industry by government subsidy and reduced taxation, but at the same time to depress the living standard of the industrial workers.

"The whole trend of economic development in Japan is artificially turned towards the stimulation of industry, at the expense of the farmers. Where does this take you?"

The professor shrugged. "Perhaps to war. It is a wartime economy. Of course, we do not want war ourselves. But Japan has powerful enemies..."

Echoes of 1914. Professors in Germany had talked like that then; they were back again on the same strain nowadays, taking their cue from that economic wizard, General Goering, who had decreed that guns were more than butter, high explosives more than vitamins. It was a crazy world.

There was nothing to be got here. Politics, I very soon found, were not a popular topic of conversation in Japan. But another Japanese economist (to whom I had brought a letter from a foreign friend) was more frank. We talked in the inner room of a Tokyo café, behind closed doors. I knew this man's record; he had been something of a revolutionary, though in a very mild and academic way. But he spoke now in a tone of concentrated bitterness.

"Yes, they are all so hopeful of Prince Konoye.... Konoye is nothing but a figurehead, and everybody knows it. They wanted him to be the leader of the new fascist party; but to give him his due, he's no fascist. The fascist party failed because they couldn't get a popular leader.

"There are only two real powers in Japan—Army and Navy. What do they represent politically? The Army is tied up with heavy industry: this group wants war on the continent, the raw materials and minerals of North China, a base against the Soviet Union. The Navy is backed by the manufacturers and light industrialists, who depend on foreign trade—they want expansion to the south, wider markets, a 'friendly understanding' with the Chinese government, so that they can gradually penetrate the country and dominate China's trade.

"Yes, there is a real contradiction here—a contradiction in the interests of big business. Which is the stronger group? The Army, every time. Ever since the Shanghai War of 1932, the Navy has been in political eclipse. Now they may try to make a comeback, but the Army still controls the government."

"What about the opposition parties—like the Social Mass party?"

His voice was more scornful than ever. "These are some of your potential fascists. There *is* no parliamentary opposition— yet. But now that the political parties feel themselves stronger, since the defeat of Hayashi, something may begin to emerge. The Osaka manufacturers are against the new military budget, and they think that Konoye is with them. But if there is any real danger of the progressives getting power in the cabinet, the War Office will start something. And Konoye will have to do what he's told!"

There seemed to be something in what he said, for during its first month of office the new cabinet was curiously inactive. Most conspicuous of all was the delay in issuing any statement on foreign policy. Newspapermen besieged the spokesmen of the Foreign Office, but without avail. It was a month of stalemate and political face-making.

But something was going on behind the scenes. The liberals, hoping for the best, waited for their champion to declare himself. And the militarists, knowing that time might be short, laid their plans.

ALARUM OFF

The mountain river ran clear and cool between wooded banks. Our boatmen—brown, sturdily-built fishermen whose short jackets and conical hats might have come out of a Hiroshige print—slowly worked the flat punt upstream. Under an awning, we lay on grass mats in that complete stupor of physical well-being that only a punt can induce.

The landscape, too, was like a color-print, with its rounded hills and neat little wooden houses. Dolls' houses, set among miniature rice fields, or perched quaintly on the foothills. A clear, rain-washed air.

In front of our boat, two men waded in midstream with a handnet; a third carried the cormorant that was to do our fishing for us. When the net was lowered across the current, the bird plunged, eager and unbidden, into the green water. It emerged, swallowing greedily, a gleam of silver in its tossing bill. Deftly the fisherman slipped the catch from its throat into his basket. Again the dive and flurry; again the forced disgorgement. The cormorant seemed to be insatiable.

A Japanese parable of Japanese industry, I moralized, idly watching the process infinitely repeated—seldom without success. Did the bird know it was being cheated, that it was catching fish for somebody else to eat? Why didn't it go on strike? But then, its master could soon starve it into the mood for work again.

"This is very beautiful." A musical voice cut into my thoughts. The speaker—a doctor in a Tokyo hospital, whom I had met and admired as a model of efficiency and professional dignity—lay back now in unbuttoned ease, a straw hat tilted across his brow. "To sit and watch the running water." In a burst of confidence, "All Japanese are nature-lovers, you know. For all Japanese are poets at heart."

What is true, is that most Japanese have moments when they like to think themselves a Werther. The novel of "sensibility," which died in Europe with the War, has had a rebirth in Japan; it is one of their most characteristic literary forms. (Later, looking over some Japanese war-diaries, I was to be amazed at the juxtaposition of cynical and realistic details about the fighting, with exquisite touches of natural description. A combination of Rousseau and Remarque.)

A fresh dish of tiny grilled trout was brought from the back of the boat, where two peasant women cooked the catch over a charcoal fire. We washed it down with lukewarm Japanese beer.

"Have all these people come from the city?" I asked. There was a heroic frieze of anglers along the bank, whose costumes varied from complete sports outfits to a jockstrap.

"Most of them. It is always like this in the summer, on a holiday. Some come to fish, some to go walking in the hills. I used to do that, when I was younger—but now I have learned to relax, like your Chinese friends. The Chinese are the real masters of leisure."

Another punt slipped past us, going downstream; it was gay with the colored kimonos of *geisha*. One of the girls was singing plangently; the rest watched us with mingled curiosity and indifference. Two men in city clothes: there must have been a dozen girls.

"And that is another popular holiday amusement," the doctor observed with mild irony. "I think these are not girls of good family...."

It was a sportsmen's train that we took back to Tokyo a couple of hours later. Returning fishermen, nursing their day's catch on their knees; sunburned youths in khaki shorts with heavy nailed shoes; a few young student couples, boy-and-girl summer idylls. Young Japan has certainly taken to the outdoor life. In China, few city dwellers would be found to join in such an excursion. The typical Chinese idea of exercise is still a gentle stroll after a heavy meal.

These young hikers, all elbows and dusty boots, had covered a dozen miles or more of hill country. But they took it all so seriously that it hurt. There was very little fellowship in that crowded carriage; perhaps they had unbent on the hills, but now they all had returned to their city manners. Even my doctor friend sat erect and silent, in his yellow shoes and correct black tie.

The shouting of the newsboys was louder than usual at the city junction where we got out. "What's the excitement?" I asked my companion.

He bought an evening paper. "Trouble on the Soviet border —a Russian gunboat has been sunk." His eyes, so placid and kindly a few hours ago, now looked tired and worried behind his glasses. His sons, I knew, would soon be of military age.

"This is serious, I think. Please excuse me." He took an abrupt farewell.

The "Amur River Incident," which Moscow and the rest of the world rightly regarded as something to be settled promptly with as little fuss as possible, hung during those first days of July like a war cloud across the Far Eastern horizon. It is almost impossible to exaggerate the sensational way in which this very minor affair was handled in the Japanese press. It was the first move of the Tokyo General Staff.

Border incidents have been frequent enough in recent years between "Manchukuo" and the Soviet Union. There is nothing very strange about this, with a disputed boundary line of some hundreds of miles, and a steady refusal on the part of the Japanese authorities to reach a final settlement by arbitration. But such affairs seldom have more than a local significance;

they are blazes, as a rule, giving more light than heat. A general principle of Russo-Japanese relations might even be stated on the basis of these intermittent border clashes. When there is some rattling of the saber on one side, or the other (or on both), you have the norm in northeastern Asia—two vigilant political adversaries, each determined not to be taken by the other at a disadvantage. But when a dead calm falls along this Far Eastern frontier, then is the time to look for trouble. Japan (again, we may cite the disastrous experiences of China) is always most dangerous in her rare moods of diplomatic suavity.

But though the Amur River affair, from the Japanese side, was a molehill of provocation and a mountain of bluff, it was taken seriously enough in Japan itself. One could not easily imagine a better war scare whipped up out of the blue. For two or three days, the atmosphere in Japan was electric. Newspapers brought out special editions; loudspeakers broadcast the latest developments from every shop window. In Tokyo, something not unlike panic was abroad.

"Do you think the communists will bomb the city?" one charming young student asked me with apprehension in her voice, and an involuntary upward glance, as though she half expected to see dark flights of Russian bombers come winging over the Meiji Shrine. I assured her that it did not seem in the least likely to me. But there was clearly something behind all this.

Then, suddenly as it had arisen, the incident was closed, and the vast crop of rumors perished overnight.

In the light of what followed, it is obvious enough now that the whole thing was deliberately manipulated from Tokyo— with two chief ends in view. The first, no doubt, was to test the immediate mood of the Soviet government; and the results, from the Japanese standpoint, were apparently highly satisfactory. The studied calm with which the midnight visits and melodramatic antics of the Japanese ambassador were received in Moscow appears to have been taken as an assurance that the U. S. S. R. was in a particularly peaceable frame of mind. And that was all to the good.

The second and much more important aim of the engineers

of the Amur River scare, was to create a war atmosphere in Japan itself. In this, they were supremely successful.

Japanese newspapers are completely dominated by the War Office, especially by the younger and more aggressive military cliques. That June, they played their part to perfection. There can be little doubt that this war tension was regarded as a necessary preliminary to some further action on the part of the army. That at this stage the Japanese militarists had in mind the general invasion of China that was to follow is unlikely, though by no means impossible: the "Continental Plan," until it turned into a juggernaut, was meant to go by definite stages. What was intended to follow was probably another "incident" in North China, which might yield immediate gains, but whose chief use would be to prove to the nation the indispensability of the army on the mainland, and—on top of the Russian scare —to convince an alarmed Diet of the need for passing without any further quibble the record new military budget.

There was another reason why the army had to make a move at this time. It was less apparent, perhaps, but is sufficiently indicated by one brief announcement that appeared in the current Tokyo newspapers:

"According to a survey by the Social Bureau of the Home Ministry, strikes and industrial disputes in Japan during the first five months of 1937 totaled 1,332, or almost double the number for the same period last year. During May alone there were 280 strikes...."

It was a fact—though one that received little public attention —that industrial discontent was rapidly rising throughout the country, on a wider scale than anything since the rice riots and labor unrest of the 'twenties. The answer to that former stirring of the workers' movement in Japan had been the Manchurian adventure, and a rigid suppression of any labor organization on the familiar cry of "unity in the national crisis." Now, with this new tide of discontent at longer working hours, speeding-up in the factories, and a steadily rising cost of living, the rulers of modern Japan had decided it might be expedient once more to stimulate the patriotism of the nation, and distract the attention of the workers from these unwelcome domestic problems.

It is an old trick of astute statesmanship (which did not originate with fascism, but which fascist and military-fascist governments have made peculiarly their own), to "busy giddy minds with foreign quarrels."

Two scenes remain vividly in my mind from that summer in Japan, with its insistent undertones of war. What followed was to give them a special significance.

The bronze Buddha "to whom the heathen pray" at Kamakura, with its haunting smile and air of ineffable peace, is one of the great monuments of the world, and an enduring symbol of the most creative impulse of Japanese art. But at the other end of this little seaside town, set among lotus ponds and magnificent arching trees, is the vermilion-painted temple of the God of War. Here, on a sunny morning when the sacred pigeons were fluttering overhead, I watched a party of sailors in their white naval uniforms pay an official visit to the God. First the officers, then the men, filed into the open shrine, to take from a kneeling priest a rice-wafer and sacramental wine cup. One by one they knelt, and filed out again—some of the sailors looking more than a little sheepish, wiping their mouths with the back of their hands. But all of them, in this setting of immemorial peace, were re-dedicating themselves to their divine mission of destruction.

Every visitor to Tokyo is taken, sooner or later, to see the "Tomb of the Forty Seven Ronin." This dramatic story of feudal retainers who avenged the death of their lord, and later committed hara-kiri together beside his grave, has never been allowed to grow hackneyed or outworn in modern Japan. The stone tablets stand ranged around a square; none ever lacks its tribute of visiting cards, or the smoke of incense. Droves of school children are continually shepherded by the dusty drive, to the accompaniment of a running lecture on the modern moral of this episode from a world that should long ago have had its day. Now, before the central grave, a young army officer stands rigidly at the salute. His face is taut, blank of all intelligence, irradiated only by a glow of fanatical zeal.

These pictures are on the surface, and no one would suggest that they are all of Japan. But they are one side of it, and the side that is most dangerous and disturbing. For this is the Japan that rules the destinies of ninety million people.

Early in July, I was living in the "Bunka" Apartments in Ochanomizu—a dingy block of flats that had originally been built by an enterprising Tokyo speculator (with the usual government subsidy) for "city-workers"; but which had soon become unashamedly bourgeois, and a kind of cosmopolitan boarding house. On the morning of July 8th, the ancient telephone beside my bed rang unusually early. Taking up the receiver, I recognized the voice of a foreign newspaperman whose insight into Far Eastern affairs was unusual and with whom I had been discussing the Sino-Japanese situation only the day before.

"Oh, hullo. Hope I didn't wake you up. You may be interested to hear that there was a clash last night between Chinese and Japanese troops near Peiping. Lukowchiao, if you know where that is."

Suddenly I became very wide awake. "Is it serious?"

"Not so far. But the War Office here takes an 'unusually grave view.' It may develop into something...."

The General Staff had made their second move.

MIDSUMMER MADNESS

The heat, I was sure, had something to do with it. July and August are always the months when war fever is most catching. And July in Tokyo, when the air is moist and steamy with the rains, and the whole city simmers like a cauldron under a metal sky, would try the temper of a buddhist saint.

For war was in the air. The poison had been laid only too well by the gallant captains and merchants of death who hoped to profit by it. Press, radio, and the Imperial Oracle had all combined to spread the infection a fortnight before, by their monstrous distortion of the affair on the Amur. And in these sultry days the microbe bred fast.

Midsummer Madness 17

I shall never forget the experience of that summer in Tokyo. It is not pleasant to watch a brave but deluded people being stampeded into tragedy. The fighting instinct, glorified by Marinetti and other official poets of fascism, may have some atavistic root in the individual; but only by artificial stimulus can it be made to possess a whole nation. *Man* may once have been a fighting animal, but *men*, in these days when the true face of modern war is sickeningly familiar, are natural lovers of peace. To stir them out of their unheroic apathy, the warmongers of our own time inevitably have recourse to that most powerful instinct of self-preservation —the instinct of fear.

In Japan, the fighting tradition of the samurai, kept alive by those who make war their profession, has very little real hold upon the masses. It is a feudal relic, a banner from a past epoch, cherished only by General Araki and the rest who have embroidered upon it their modern myth of Japanese invincibility. But even in an acquisitive society, dictators have discovered, you cannot get the masses of the people to join in a war that is avowedly a war of conquest. And, by the same token, it would not be easy to get the Japanese peasant to leave his rice fields and shoulder a rifle in a foreign country, merely to uphold the traditions of his own traditional oppressors. The samurai stuff would be useful, no doubt, as war ideology, once the conflict was under way; but in itself it would not start a war.

It is only when drunk with his own eloquence in the heady air of the Rhineland, that Hitler says in so many words that he *wants* the Ukraine, the coal and iron of the Don basin, the oil wells of the Crimea. A more useful justification for the annexation of coveted territories (and generally some British statesman will be found to believe it) is the *defense* of Europe, civilization, or what you will, against the "Red menace." The classical expression of this politic inversion is to be read in the official style of that ring of modern bandits, the "Anti-Comintern Alliance." Mussolini, save the mark, is not in Ethiopia or Spain for what he can get out of it: he is there to preserve "Mediterranean Culture," the "Old Faith," or even—sublimest of paradoxes—the "peace of Europe." This is the most familiar irony of the international anarchy by which we live, that all wars are wars of self-defense, and the peace is only broken to keep the peace.

All of which is no news nowadays. But it has a special bearing in the case of Japan and China. Not even the most cynical Japanese militarist dared pretend openly that in July, 1937, Japan was in danger of Chinese attack—this, on the face of it, would have been a patent absurdity. But what the war party in Japan could do was to exploit the very real fear of the Soviet Union that exists in their country.

This in itself is an artificial creation. For, if anything has been proved by the inglorious history of the League of Nations and the last struggle for a principle of collective security in Europe, it is surely that the U. S. S. R. stands today in the vanguard of the "peace group" of world powers. But, thanks to years of strenuous propaganda by national and local authorities, the Japanese people—and especially those city-dwellers who feel themselves most exposed to air attack—have a genuine conviction that their lives and their country are in continual danger from Vladivostok, which they still regard as the "pistol pointed at the heart of Japan."

From here, it is an easy step to that second myth (later born, but equally direct offspring of the dream of a Japanese Empire of the Far East) of the "Bolsheviks of Asia." For this made it possible to identify China too with the "Red menace."

From sharp experience at home, the rulers of modern Japan knew the power of Marxist ideas—ultimately, and with infinitely better cause, they feared them more than Marshal Bluecher and the Far Eastern Red Army. But it would have been fatal to admit that these ideas had a life of their own, to take root and engender independently in any soil—not least, in the super-fertilized rice fields and sweating factories of the Island Empire. It served the purpose of these builders of Greater Japan very much better to invent and foster this fiction of "Red Imperialism," which they defined in the Far East as the direct extension, by the undermining of the Kuomintang government, by political intrigue and military force, of the U. S. S. R. into China.

Thus there was presented in the liveliest colors to the people of Japan a China torn by internal conflict, where every subversive movement was the work of the agents of Moscow—a vast social ferment pregnant with the direst consequences for Japan and all the nations of the Pacific if "bolshevism" should gain the day. There was this grain of truth in the legend, that if there should ever be a successful social revolution in China, it could only be *after* the defeat of Japanese imperialism: that is, after Japan's "Pan-Asiatic Empire" had ended in shipwreck. But this was a distant perspective of the future, only perhaps unconsciously appreciated by Japan's twentieth-century conquistadors.

Where the picture was most crudely distorted, was in the attribution of "communist" sentiments to every good Chinese bourgeois who ventured on the mildest protest against Japan's rapid encroachment over his own borders. General Chiang Kai-shek, in himself the personification of the landlord-bureaucracy that had ruled China since 1927, the man who for ten years had waged bitter campaigns against the Chinese Red Armies, was accused of being "pro-Soviet." The "Hopei-Chahar Political Council" in Peiping, which had tortured hundreds of students on the mere suspicion of "communist sympathies," and had loosed the machine-guns and bigswords of its Special Police against fifteen-year-old schoolgirls who shouted nationalist slogans in the streets of the old capital, was described as "revolutionary" as well as "anti-Japanese." In short, every manifestation of "anti-Japanese activity"—which the Kuomintang Government up to 1937 had made heroic efforts to suppress by terrorist methods not unworthy of the Imperial Japanese Army itself—was laid to the account of the agents of the Third International.

One did not need to be in Japan long, I had already observed, to discover obvious traces of anti-*Chinese* activity. Even the Children's Hour, on the official radio program, usually contained some moral story about the "brave Japanese soldiers" and the "treacherous Chinese." But I found it impossible, even in discussion with sober professional men in Tokyo, to gain any admission that China might have some legitimate grievance against Japan.

"Why do you suppose this is all the work of Moscow?" I would argue. "A Chinese doesn't need to be a communist to feel resentful about the loss of his own territory. There's 'Manchukuo,' for instance." But it was no use: this was a "settled question," "very delicate." "Japanese people is very sensitive about Manchukuo." There was something suspect, surely, about such excessive sensitivity. And the "Japanese people," it seemed, was even more sensitive about communism. A foreign friend warned me about the open expression of "pro-Chinese" sentiments, hinting darkly at the range of activities of the secret police. "In this country, you have to be careful."

It was with a feeling of utter frustration that I threaded the streets of Tokyo in these July days, trying to read in the faces of passers-by something of their real thoughts. And often, it seemed to me, a general uneasiness was discernible that meant more than any private anxiety. A new oppression weighed upon this city: its name was fear.

The Japanese seldom betray their deeper emotions (except when they are drunk; and then these are apt to have an extravagance out of all proportion to the strength of their beer). Something is there behind the mask, but it is hidden to the stranger. Many of these faces, on streetcars or in subways, were as blank and expressionless as those you might see blurred under cloth caps in a mining district of South Wales, or white at street corners in any Midlands town. Those who were gay—like the *mogi*, those butterflies of modern Japan, brightly dressed in a copy of last year's New York styles—were gay with the inconsequential cheerfulness of marionettes.

But everywhere there ran an undercurrent of apprehension and uncertainty beyond the touch of bodily fatigue.

In a Marunouchi restaurant I talked one afternoon with a young intellectual who bore one of the oldest and most famous names in Japan. He had been educated abroad, and had gained there, if not a foreign point of view, at least a certain detachment from problems as they presented themselves to his countrymen.

"What does it all mean?" I asked him. "Have the newspapers gone mad?"

He nodded gravely. "It looks bad. I am afraid there may be war."

"Does the government want war?"

"Prince Konoye, no. I happen to know that he has been trying hard, these last few days, to moderate the tone of some of the newspapers. But then, his health is delicate"—a smile flitted across his thin lips—"and whenever there is trouble, he is likely to be indisposed. The real decision is already out of his hands."

"But what about all those who must lose by a war—the manufacturers, the chambers of commerce, all who depend on foreign trade? Have they no political influence?"

He made a gesture of impotence with small, graceful hands. "There is no one to speak out—that is the tragedy of the Japanese people today. Many would like to resist the army leaders, but no one has the courage to be spokesman. It would sign his own death warrant." His dark eyes were expressive and mournful.

"What if there *is* a war—will you go to fight in China?"

He shrugged his slight shoulders. "Of course, if I must. I do not want to go. But we Japanese have sometimes very little choice in the ordering of our own lives." He paused a moment, then added with exquisite politeness:

"I may take it, your sympathies are with China?"

"In this case, yes. I have received many kindnesses in Japan, and already I have learned to respect and admire the Japanese people. But I think your foreign policy is abominable. If this goes on, it will be the end of any friendship between Japan and England."

"Yes, that is what many of us fear. We would rather have had England for friend than Germany and Italy. But we are a young nation in the modern world, with our way to make. Who knows were it will end?"

"It will end in a world war, and you will have the honor of having started it."

"*Soit*. If there will be war, there will be war. But believe me, we do not wish it."

His fatalism was gentle but resigned. And there was nothing more to be said.

"Banzai!"

The day that settled it was Sunday, July 11th.

All that morning the cabinet held an emergency meeting, while newshawks fluttered the lobbies and guessed at unimaginable rumors. In the afternoon, the Premier left for the Emperor's summer residence at Hayama, to return bringing peace or war in the folds of his gown. And that night, all Tokyo knew.

Sunday evening in Japan's capital has many attractions. With a friend newly arrived from China, I had gone to hear the Tokyo Symphony Orchestra play in Hibiya Park. In this summer weather they played out of doors, and the amphitheater was crowded.

A widespread appreciation of European music is one of the most interesting features of life in modern Japan. Nowhere in China, I reflected, would you get so many people to come to a symphony concert. And such an orchestra (this was composed entirely of Japanese) would have been unthinkable. I had heard the Tokyo Symphony, at their best under the firm baton of Weingartner, play in indoor concerts, and knew what they were capable of. In China, one is starved for music; in Tokyo there is the whole range, from piano and violin concerts to an orchestra that could hold its own on the platforms of Europe.

Now the regular conductor (another German) took them briskly through a Beethoven Symphony, and then into the Leonora Overture. The music, curiously expressive on that breathless evening, with the dark shadows of the park around us and a last glow of fire in the cloud-streaked sky, seeemed to me ominous and fateful. In the interval, a group of naval officers sitting near us were joined by a friend. They withdrew into the shadow of the wall to talk in whispers.

"I'd give something to understand this language," my friend remarked. "There's been another special edition—listen!" Across the park, we could hear the insistent ringing of a hand-bell that in Tokyo announces an "extra." Coming up from the Ginza, fading into the suburbs. The group of officers had left, I noticed, when we took our seats again.

The second part of the program was light opera and Strauss—it jarred upon my mood. "Let's get out before the crowd." We walked quickly across the park, towards the city lights.

For five sen we bought a flimsy broadsheet, the ink on which was scarcely dry. My friend had a reading knowledge of Chinese; slowly we spelled out those characters that were familiar. It was reading by headlines, but the headlines were what mattered: "JAPAN SENDS AN ARMY TO NORTH CHINA.... Damn this *kana* stuff, I can't read a word of it. Yes, FOUR DIVISIONS TO LEAVE AT ONCE... Well, that means the finish of Peiping. If those troops once reach China, they won't come back empty-handed!"

We strolled on down the boulevard towards the Asahi Building. On the bridge, blocking the street traffic, crowds had gathered to read the electric news sign. How remote from this modern city seemed the quiet countryside around Peiping, the fields of kaoliang and the mud-walled villages that must soon become the arena of war. This crowd was hushed and attentive; in the glow of the lamps, upturned faces were intent but inscrutable. There was very little enthusiasm, it seemed to me; but that would come later.

On the edge of the pavement, a child in a sailor suit, sleepy and impatient at its parents' delay, flapped a paper flag disconsolately. Two young cadets, walking briskly in step, came past along the bridge. The child's eyes brightened, and her flag went up in a sudden salute. *"Banzai!"*

The young officers, with that infinite indulgence towards children that is one of the most amiable traits of every Japanese in his own land, gravely returned the salute, and walked on smiling. The incident, trifling enough, caught my eye like a portent. "It's beginning...."

I turned to my friend. "You leave for America tomorrow. And I'm going back to China, as soon as I can make it. Before it's too late."

At the Japan Tourist Bureau, all was confusion. The owl-like clerk who took my booking was doing his best to remain dignified, but it was an obvious strain. I could sympathize with him, for the office was besieged by discontented travelers. "I've been here for five hours," one melting American lady informed me, "trying to get a berth to Shanghai. And this imbecile says he doesn't know..."

With the air of a wearied Titan, the same clerk had just stamped all my own tickets: express to Shimonoseki, ferry to Fusan, express via Mukden to Peiping. He assured me, after endless telephone calls, that I could leave that night. I had just paid my money and gathered up the tickets, when a red-faced German burst excitedly into the room.

"Cancel my train ticket to Mukden," he gasped. "No use now."

"Why," I said, "aren't the trains running?" He gave me a glassy stare. "No. I have just come from my Embassy; the military have taken over the line. To travel now is impossible." I took his word for it. If a German couldn't travel in Manchukuo, my own chances of getting through were slight.

"Will you please change my booking to the first boat for Tientsin," I asked, handing back the neat little folder of tickets. The clerk looked mutinous. "You'll have to pay a cancellation fee."

"But surely you ought to know about these things, if anybody does?"

He clung to the remains of his dignity. "We only issue tickets..."

"Oh, anything you like then! But I want to get to China."

It was a brief aperçu—trivial in itself, but later to be verified in more significant instances—of something I had already begun to suspect: that Japanese "efficiency" has very definite limitations. The Japanese *are* efficient, infinitely more efficient than the Chinese—up to a certain point. What floors them is the unexpected. And this was to prove true of Japanese staff work in the war. It is excellent, so long as everything is going according to plan. But if the other man makes the wrong move, it can be thrown completely out of gear. In general, the Japanese have this dangerous tendency towards rigidity. The strength—as, so very often, the weakness—of the Chinese is their flexibility.

Confusion reigned in a good many quarters in Japan during those first hectic days, before all was caught up and drowned in the universal war fever. But in foreign circles, even at this stage, there was a curious tendency to make light of the whole affair.

There are two regular news centers for the foreigner in Tokyo. One is the lounge of the Imperial Hotel, where the tongue of rumor is seldom silent; the other is the Dentsu Building, where most of the news agencies have their offices. I had never dared speak out loud in the Imperial Hotel: ever since the regrettable Sansom incident during the February mutiny of 1936, this has seemed a most unhealthy place for revelations. In that cushioned lobby, one felt, there might be a microphone behind every armchair.

But in the Dentsu Building, not far from the white lights of the Ginza, I went in search of a Chinese friend, Tokyo representative of the Central News Agency. The glass door of the office was shut; when I entered, a dozen Chinese students rose conspiratorially from a corner. "Mr. Liu has left—he went back to China two days ago." Their manner, half friendly, half defiant, was a mixture of bravado and apprehension.

We talked about China: was Chiang Kai-shek really going to fight this time? It was an old argument for anyone who came from China, but I found it a relief to meet a point of view that one understood. We are all propagandists nowadays, I suppose, and rival propagandists speak another language. I had never been more conscious of the fact than during those last days in Japan.

"We *must* fight," was the general verdict of these young Chinese. "Now there is no other way." Their own immediate prospects were far from bright; most of them were looking for ways to return to their own country. Even here there was danger, as some Chinese students were to find. To remain in Japan was to face arrest and persecution; to return to Shanghai, and land in the Yangtsepoo area of the International Settlement (soon to be completely under the control of the Japanese military police) might be an even greater risk. When I left the office, one youth with tousled hair called to me: "Better go down the back stair—the main door is watched by the police!" Chinese living in Japan learn to be circumspect.

At length I had completed the details of a hurried departure, and took a brief farewell of my friends. The last day I spent in Tokyo was July 14th. Some time before, I had made an arrangement to meet a well-known Japanese scholar on that date: he was one of the few outspoken opponents of the military regime left in the country, and had not long been released from prison. But a few hours before the appointment was due, a telegram arrived at my lodgings. "Suddenly taken ill; regret cannot meet you today." I could not blame him; the way things were going, everybody would have to be careful.

That evening I walked over the hills past the Sanno barracks, headquarters of the mutineers of February 29th. One ironical feature of this attempted coup d'état (which very nearly developed into an open trial of strength between Army and Navy) was that the young officers who led it claimed to be the representatives of the "oppressed Japanese farmers and peasants." The Japanese peasant, it seemed, was to find salvation from his many troubles by the shortest possible route—a "glorious death" for his country.

Now, in the barracks on the hill, the garrison were rehearsing their evening "hate." This was an extraordinary affair: a hoarse, unrhythmical chorus with a striking resemblance to the least pleasant of jungle noises. Chinese soldiers once used to reinforce their courage by the iteration of similar fierce shouts, but no one—least of all their own commanders—ever took them very seriously. This war chant sounded much more sinister; and the effect, here in the suburbs of a modern city, was both startling and incongruous.

And then, before I knew it, I had come to the Soviet Embassy, a long white building in the factory style, that stands on a height overlooking Tokyo. From the roof, bright against a gray sky, flew the red flag with the hammer and sickle. I had forgotten that this was the anniversary of the fall of the Bastille.

At the railway station, the flag of the Rising Sun had hidden the lamps. Groups of women and children were farewelling officers leaving for China. This was not a military train, but there must have been somebody important aboard it, to judge from the send-off. The Japanese friend who had come to the station with me looked nervous and ill at ease.

"Well, so long.... Perhaps we'll see you in China next summer!"

He grimaced faintly. "I haven't been called up yet. Some people say that the four divisions have not left after all. But you never can tell." He gave us that saddest of all farewells: *"Sayonara!"*

"If it must be so!"

The long train pulled out slowly, past the blur of flags: the crowd on the platform was bowing in unison like a wheat field in the wind. I turned away from it all, trying to bury myself in a book. But the sound of cheering pursued us like an echo all the way to Kobe. At every station—even those we passed at midnight—the same crowds had gathered with their banners. Osaka, in the dim morning light, was a desert of factory chimneys and drifting smoke. But here, too, the red and white flags fluttered shrilly....

Kobe at last; and again it greeted us in a wave: *"Banzai! Banzai! Banzai!"*

I shouldered my rucksack, and set out for the docks. It was time to leave Japan.

INVITATION TO DEATH

The *Nanrei Maru* was an unimpressive little vessel, so light in the water that it was clear she could be taking very little cargo to North China. In Tokyo, I had been told that every cabin was booked; actually I found myself at first the only passenger in the saloon. Here there were no Chinese refugees lining the quay, and very few to be seen about the docks. Only when we were out at sea and beyond the attentions of the shore police, did the steerage disgorge its human freight. Then I realized how many Chinese passengers we had aboard.

We pulled out from Kobe promptly at eleven (Japanese ships and trains, like Mussolini's, are seldom behind time), and slipped down the harbor past the giant dockyards. On the stocks, two or three half-built vessels raised their gaunt beams. Beyond the breakwater, a broad dazzle of light and cloud, lay the Inland Sea.

All that afternoon we threaded our way gently through a maze of islands, most of them wooded to the water's edge. It was pleasant sailing, but nowhere could you get a long view: everything, it seemed, was in miniature, except what modern industry had built. These islands wore perpetual mist like a cloak. I found myself longing for the clear air and wide horizons of North China. But the Japanese—more indefatigable beauty-lovers than Germans on a Rhine cruise—stayed on deck, drinking in the scenery with their beer, until the last glow of a picture-postcard sunset had faded in green and purple.

Some time that night we reached Moji. I woke to the rhythmical chant of the coolies who were coaling our vessel. This is one of the sights of Japan (only less celebrated than Mount Fuji, and more easily visible). It is a reminder, in case the Mitsui Building and the taxis of Tokyo should make you forget it, that you are still in the East, where human labor is the cheapest of all commodities.

Every basket of coal was loaded by hand, through a living chain of workers, from an open barge. The heaviest task— that of swinging the loaded baskets up a wooden gangplank— was done by men; "lighter" jobs were done by women. The dexterity and precision with which the whole human machine worked was amazing. But what appalled me was the tempo at which it worked. Was it really "patriotism," duty to their country, that kept this slave-gang in such automatic and heartbreaking motion? Another explanation suggested itself, when I saw in the red-rimmed eyes of the nearest coolie an expression I had seen once before in the face of a Chinese miner in the British-owned mines at Mentowkow. This is the most profound and moving sign one may read upon any features: the look of human despair.

With a few hours in hand before we sailed, I took the ferry across to Shimonoseki. It was filled with khaki uniforms, and the railway terminus was thronged with eager crowds, welcoming and farewelling troops bound for China. There could not be much doubt about it, I reflected gloomily; the four divisions were certainly on their way.

Never in Japan had I felt so complete an alien as now, in this hour of leaving. I found myself caught up for a moment in a crowd of breathless schoolgirls, all waving flags and shouting "Banzai!" with the frenzy of hysteria. Tomorrow, perhaps, they would be standing at street corners, holding out to passers-by the "thousand-stitch garments" which were to protect Japan's soldiers in their sacred mission of "establishing permanent peace in East Asia."

The harbor still echoed with the sound of cheering as we weighed anchor and nosed our way out into the channel. A number of new passengers had come aboard, several Japanese officers among them. Our Chinese passengers had again vanished below.

One new arrival was a Russian merchant from Tientsin, who had just been placing orders in Japan for the China trade—they would be a bad investment now, he informed me philosophically. We stood together beside the rail as the ship moved down the harbor. Then, "See those gunboats," he said suddenly. A couple of modern destroyers lay at anchor across the channel; they had the indubitable marks of a Japanese shipyard about them, but the ensign—a gaudy affair that hung like a banner—was new to me.

"What are they?"

"Siamese—just built to order in Japan. That's one way"—he dropped his voice—"these people are moving."

It was another straw in the wind. Not long ago, Siam bought her warships in Britain; she had found new friends since then. Small nations, perhaps, have little choice in these matters.

Further downstream, we passed a Soviet freighter. She was

filthy, streaked with rust and soot, with a tattered flag flapping from the jack staff. Two or three members of the crew leaned across the rail and watched us as we passed. One, stripped to the waist, was a copper-colored giant; the muscles of his shoulders rippled as he moved.

"An old ship," remarked my companion with a strange wistfulness, "but the crew looks well enough fed." I guessed that he was one of those Russians—so common in exile—whom a name, or some chance association, had barred from return to his native land.

There are two distinct camps among Russians who live abroad, especially Russians in the East. Most familiar, because most vocal, are the "irreconcilables," disgruntled white-guardists who gather beneath the portrait of the last of the Tsars to keep alive an implacable hatred of those that dispossessed them. These are the authentic exiles of history, dying off one by one of drugs or vodka: the remnants of a class that in its own land has ceased to exist. Theirs is a necessary tragedy.

But there is a younger generation of Russians now growing up in exile who keep little of the rancor their fathers nourished. Rather, they are repelled by the futility they discern in the lives of their own parents, the tawdry dreams of a forever vanished splendor. All they know of Russia is the tale of the growing strength of the Soviet Union among the nations of the world: they read a smuggled copy of *Pravda* much more eagerly than the pathetic sheetful of rubbish that may be published locally among their own community. Many of these younger Russians have already returned to the U. S. S. R. from the Far East. But, in general, it is harder for them to return than it was for their fathers to leave.

It is from the first group that Japanese agents recruit their private gangsters, the "Iron Crusaders" and the rest who may be useful to do Japan's dirty work in China inside those foreign concessions where it is still a certain advantage to be a European. For these people will do anything to be revenged on "communism." But the younger generation, even though they may feel themselves caught between two fires, keep an unbroken front. If Japan should ever attack the Soviet Union, they know well enough which side they would be on.

By July 19, we were off Shantung. The atmosphere aboard seemed easier, though the silhouette of a Japanese cruiser at dawn was a reminder of the constant threat that hung over the China coast. That night, however, when the wireless had been busier than usual, there was a noticeable change. The Japanese officers were definitely more aggressive: they had discarded their comfortable kimonos, and now sat stiffly about the saloon with the air of men of destiny.

I went in search of the Russian, who had all the tongues. "What's the news?"

"Chiang Kai-shek has made a speech at Kuling," he told me, "and it seems to be pretty strong. It looks as though he's going to defend North China after all."

In the steerage, groups of Chinese students talked excitedly in whispers. Tomorrow we would know better how things stood.

At seven in the morning we were off Taku Bar, in the center of a small Japanese fleet. There were seven or eight warships, and a number of military transports waiting for the tide. Ahead —a flat, seemingly boundless shoreline—was China.

A salvage tug came alongside as we rode at anchor, with a redheaded figure on the bridge demanding our skipper in broad Scots. It was an urgent demand for cement to line the plates of a leaking Japanese freighter.

"How are things ashore?" I asked the new arrival. He responded cheerfully, "O ay, there was firing last night at Tangku. And they're still at it near Peiping—it'll come to a real scrap this time, as like as not. Well, it's no white man's war—we're out, and we stay out." He took aboard his sacks of cement, and waved a casual farewell. Half an hour later, our own lightly-laden vessel was leading the line across the bar and up the Haiho.

We made our berth with some difficulty, in a sudden blinding squall that blew the *Nanrei Maru* half across the river. Two Japanese cruisers held the port, and there were no Customs officers to be seen. When the express came in from Shanhaikwan it was crowded with Chinese refugees. But with it all, my spirits rose steadily as we ran through the summer countryside, where the kaoliang stood ten feet high in the fields, and the willows (I thought of my Customs Officer) were a fresher green than any trees in Japan. For this was a familiar world.

Tientsin, the commercial heart of North China, was restless under the shadow of war. At the East Station, Japanese troops and foreign guards were very much in evidence (since Boxer days, this line from Peiping to the sea has been under "international" control). But the Japanese were clearly resentful of the other foreign troops, and one could easily guess at that ill-feeling which was later to result in several brushes, and the deliberate sniping by the Japanese of Sergeant Chrétien of the French Guard.

All the railway sidings were filled with Japanese armored trains and cars: it was like the preparation for a military maneuver, that only waits the dropping of the umpire's flag. Where else in the world, I wondered, could a "friendly nation" so easily, and as a matter of course, make all the preparations for military invasion actually *inside* the territory of its intended victim? China, whose gates had been forced by the foreigner a century ago, has been at a fatal disadvantage ever since in matters of her own defense.

In Tientsin, too, a number of Japanese *ronin* boarded the train. These—the unimpressive descendants of their "lordless" ancestors—are the irregular militia that have always had very definite duties in Chinese cities, co-operating with landing parties or with the regular Japanese troops. In the dress of merchants or tourists, with automatic at hip or a sword for a walking-stick, they did their best to look like civilians. But it was a transparent disguise, and all had the walk of conquerors.

Late that afternoon we reached Fengtai, the military *point d'appui* that the Japanese had already carved out only a few miles southwest of Peiping. And here, as though they had reached the temporary border of their home ground, every Japanese left the train. For the first time one heard Chinese

INVITATION TO DEATH

voices raised freely. It was as if a hundred tongues had been loosed at once.

Slowly, and with many stops, we made our way on towards the old capital. Not until Yungtingmen, the south gate in the outer walls of Peiping, did we meet with the Chinese troops. And here guards from the 29th Route Army—sturdy North China peasants, but with deplorably inadequate arms—searched the train, thrusting their bayonets under the seats to see if any Japanese were lurking there. Their resolute air was encouraging; properly led, these troops could still be effective.

We passed slowly beneath the walls, and the steel gates clanged to across the track. That was the last regular train to enter Peiping before the real fighting began.

We had arrived in a city under siege. As the train, moving freely at last, swept round the magnificent curve that brings to view first the cedars and blue-tiled roofs of the Temple of Heaven, then the gaily-painted Fox Tower, finally the great main gate of Ch'ien Men, bigswords and bayonets were glittering all the way along the battlements. In Japan, I had been an unwilling witness of the prologue to this latest Chinese drama. And now, when the stage was set for action, I had arrived at the theater of war.

CHAPTER ONE
COLLAPSE IN THE NORTH

MARCO POLO BRIDGE

Peiping—that Florence of the East, whose "fatal beauty" subdued two dynasties of alien conquerors—retained all its fair and floral air. This city lost in memories, where only a few students had fed a little life with songs and banners, was really the last place in China to look for serious resistance to any invader. It had been too long a palace of Sans Souci. But, like an old beauty always ready to take the stage, Peiping played with surprising verve, in those July days, her last role of defiance.

When I arrived, there had been desultory fighting going on in the neighborhood of the city for a fortnight. So far we had heard only the Japanese side of things; now at last one could get, from foreign observers, a more or less reasonable account of how it had all begun.

On the night of July 7th, Japanese troops on midnight maneuvers near Lukowchiao (the old marble bridge mentioned in Marco Polo's Travels, and familiar to all foreign residents of Peiping as a favorite rendezvous for summer excursions and winter riding parties) had missed one of their men. As this was just outside the walled town of Wanping, on the northern bank of the Hun Ho, the Japanese commander decided that his missing soldier had been spirited within the walls. He demanded that the gates be opened, and his men allowed to search the town. Not unnaturally, the Chinese garrison refused to open the gates to foreign troops at such an hour.

Subsequent developments are shrouded in mystery. The Chinese claim that the missing soldier rejoined his troop within a couple of hours; they suggested that he had in fact been making a quick visit to a local bordel. (This need not have been merely a spiteful invention; anyone who cares to consult the long record of incidents caused in China by "missing Japanese," can easily verify the fact that it is in such places as these that the "victims" usually turn up.) The Japanese version, of course, is that the Chinese troops opened fire without warning, and "treacherously attacked" their column.

The details are unimportant, for they do not really affect the issue. In plain terms, the Japanese were asking for trouble by holding night maneuvers at all in this area; and knew it. But, for once, the troops of the 29th Route Army were not to be bluffed into submission. The Japanese settled down outside Wanping, called up reinforcements, and began to shell the town. The Chinese, flourishing their bigswords and making insulting remarks, manned the walls and were unusually full of fight.

General Sung Cheh-yuan, Chairman of the Hopei-Chahar Political Council and commander of the 29th Route Army, was at this time away on a visit to his native town. (Chinese officials have always had a happy knack of remembering their ancestors when they get into political difficulties.) Perhaps as a result, the Chinese troops were given a little more rope than usual. General Feng Chih-an, Sung's second-in-command, was a much younger man, and very much more resolutely "anti-Japanese" than his wily old chief. The rank and file of the army, who for years had been smarting under orders to avoid any kind of incident with the Japanese, whatever provocations they might have to swallow, knew this well enough.

In general, then, we may say that the Japanese North China Garrison, after one more high-handed action of the kind they had been accustomed to carry off in the past without fear of reprisals, were met at Lukowchiao not with the smooth language of officials, but with the blunt response of the rank and file of the Chinese armies. This was not an answer of policy; it was the answer of the common people of China to Japanese imperialism.

For a couple of weeks, finesse and bluff were tried by the representatives of both sides, with "terms of peace" that were advanced, considered, rejected, and taken up again like the pieces in a game of Chinese chess. Meanwhile, hardly a day passed without fighting of some sort. But the significant point —the only point that really mattered—was that during this interim for "negotiations," the Japanese army command ordered mobilization at home, rushed in reinforcements, and launched the war campaign in the press that was in full swing by the time I had left Japan. The Chinese were surprisingly confident, but the 29th Route Army, one of the weakest technically of all the regular Chinese group armies, received in the meantime nothing whatsoever in the way of reinforcements or fresh supplies from the south.

Into a situation already critical, Chiang Kai-shek's Kuling speech of July 19th fell like a bombshell. This was a forthright and deliberate statement from the leader of the National Government, outlining four essential points on which China must insist in any settlement—her territorial integrity and sovereign rights in the north, her direct interest in the Peiping government as a Chinese authority, and her firm determination to allow no Japanese dictation either to the Hopei-Chahar Political Council or to the 29th Route Army.

"The four Northeastern provinces have already been lost to us for six years," declared the Generalissimo.

"Now the point of conflict—Lukowchiao—has reached the very gates of Peiping. If we allow Lukowchiao to be occupied by force ... the Peiping of today would become a second Mukden; the Hopei and Chahar provinces would share the fate of the four Northeastern Provinces.... *We seek for peace, but we do not seek for peace at any cost. We do not want war, but we may be forced to defend ourselves.*"

It was just what the northern soldiers had been waiting for— an unequivocal pledge of support from Nanking. General Chiang had committed himself at last to the defense of North

China. From this time on, there was very little question of what must happen.

Perhaps the local officials in North China did not really know what they were up against, though there was little excuse for such eleventh-hour ignorance. Perhaps the Japanese militarists thought his Kuling speech was the last shaft in Chiang's diplomatic quiver, and that swift action would soon bankrupt all his solemn assurances. But, stripped to its essentials, the situation in North China was clear enough. On one side was the familiar "active" factor, the Imperial Japanese Army, well-trained instrument of the controlling group of Japanese expansionists who had only been waiting for this day. And against it, strong in little but his feelings of outrage, was the peasant soldier of China, who for a dollar a month and his own most inadequate keep, was yet prepared to fight in the defense of his country.

In the opening stages, it was bound to be an unequal match.

The events of that fourth week of July may be briefly summarized. On the 21st, it was announced that "troops were withdrawing" on both sides. On the 22nd, it was discovered that the Japanese had not withdrawn, after all. Sung Chehyuan, who had returned in haste from Loling, and ordered the replacement of the "anti-Japanese" 31st Division by the 132nd (it made very little difference, as the Japanese were not slow to point out), seems to have been playing for time rather than for "peace at any cost." It appeared later that Nanking at this stage was prepared to send reinforcements to the north; but that Sung was not yet prepared to welcome them in his province if they came. The Japanese, however, left him no loophole: on July 23rd they presented their first "ultimatum."

Two days followed, during which the most sensational incident occurred in the South, with the alleged "kidnaping" of a Japanese sailor in Shanghai. This time the missing Japanese, a certain Miyazaki, had by his own confession been visiting an "unruly house"; after an amazing series of adventures, in the course of which he jumped into the Yangtse from a Chinese steamer, swam ashore, was picked up by the Chinese police and succored with tea and cakes, he was finally restored to the bosom of his own most ungrateful command. After which, one imagines, hara-kiri would be about all that was left for him.

But on July 26th, the real prelude to action began with the entry of the Japanese air force. The Chinese, it was claimed, had been interfering with the Japanese telegraph lines to Tientsin; again, it is hardly worth while to attempt to sift the conflicting evidence. In revenge, the Japanese launched a surprise air raid on the village of Lanfang, and effectively reduced it to a ruin. There were an unknown number of deaths, largely among the civilian populace. The same day, army officials in Peiping presented Sung with a "second ultimatum," which amounted to a demand for the withdrawal of all Chinese forces to the south of Hopei.

Sung took a day to think about it, and then announced that he rejected the Japanese demands as "unreasonable." He seems to have given a general order to his army to "resist any further attack." With this, apparently, he felt his duty was at an end. It was the last positive step he took in the whole brief tragedy of Peiping.

These events are recalled, not for their intrinsic interest, but because they were destined to become the preliminaries to a much wider military action. The story of Marco Polo Bridge might be made picturesque enough, if one were to sketch it against a background of crumbling walls and kaoliang fields, and include a few details of those night sorties against the small besieging force in which the famous Chinese bigswords for once became something more than a decoration. But after all, the local issue at Lukowchiao was nothing.

Under other conditions—at the same time a year before—it would have been just one more drop in the cup of China's national humiliation. Actually, Lukowchiao became the prelude to the long-awaited trial of strength between China and Japan. *Why?*

The reasons are to be sought, not in anything that had changed in Japan (though the attempt has already been made to suggest just how it was the Japanese people were so easily stampeded into war at this time); but in what had happened inside China in the preceding nine months. The signal for the outbreak of the Great War was a pistol shot in the streets of Sarajevo; but no one today would be likely to maintain seriously that this was what caused it. In the same way, only the shallowest view of history could see the beginning of the present Sino-Japanese conflict at Lukowchiao in the summer of 1937.

To begin with, we must accept the phenomenon of Japanese imperialism (and even yet, many people are trying to delude themselves about its real nature and intentions). The aim of the present rulers of Japan, so admirably summarized by Baron Tanaka in the famous "memorial" he presented to the Mikado just ten years before Lukowchiao,* is nothing less than the conquest of China and the ultimate overlordship of Asia. It is an ambition not unworthy of Tamerlane; but none of the historical Asiatic conquerors has ever set out armed with such deadly weapons. If we accept this as a starting point, the question is simplified. It is not so much, "Why did Japan attack?" as "Why did China—this time—resist?"

Confronted with Japanese imperialism in its advanced, expansionist stage, the Chinese people had only two real courses of action: submission or struggle. Traditionally, the Chinese government tried to choose a "middle way," and for some years succeeded in persuading its own people that such a course was possible. But as Jehol followed Manchuria, and the Ho-Umetsu Agreement followed the Tangku Truce, it became overwhelmingly clear to all classes in China that this middle way was a fiction, and that what it amounted to was simply delayed surrender.

General Chiang Kai-shek, one of the shrewdest diplomats at the head of any nation, found himself in that most uncomfortable of all dilemmas for a political leader—when there is no longer any chance to placate either one of two opposing forces. For years, he had hoped that the struggle with Japan might be avoided; that another power—the most likely, of course, seemed

---

* "In order to conquer China, we must first conquer Manchuria and Mongolia. In order to conquer the world, we must first conquer China."—*Tanaka Memorandum, July 1927.*

to be the Soviet Union—might take it off his hands. But the U. S. S. R. grew stronger, and Japan was not yet ready to challenge the Far Eastern Red Army. More and more, it became clear that China was her immediate goal.

Two specific statements of Japanese policy, the "Amau Doctrine" of 1934 and the "Three Points" of Premier Hirota in 1936, were direct warnings to the Chinese that they had better accept the inevitable. Then, in December, 1936, when Japan was once more active in Inner Mongolia, a most dramatic interruption occurred. The "coup d'état" of the Young Marshal Chang Hsueh-liang in Sianfu, and the forced detention of the Generalissimo by a part of his own armies, was one of those rare single episodes that determine the fate of nations. The sequel to the Sian coup, which was the first understanding in ten years between the Kuomintang and the Chinese Communist Party, the termination of civil war in China, and the rapid consolidation of a "National United Front," was decisive for the future policy of the Chinese Government. A politically united China had emerged at last, as the direct result of Japanese aggression. And this was the one thing that Japan's military leaders were afraid of.

Foreshortening the history of the last seven years, we might say that the first shots in the present Japanese invasion of China were fired at Mukden on the night of September 18th, 1931. And the first shots in the Chinese war of national resistance were fired, not on the Manchurian or the Shanghai or the North China fronts, but outside the snowbound pavilions of Huachingkung on the morning of December 12th, 1936. To miss the causal connection between Mukden, Sian, and Lukowchiao, would be to miss the real movement of social forces in the Far East.

This is not to say—as was said at the time by some of Japan's apologists—that it was Chinese "extremists" and "aggressive elements" who provoked the war. Any charge of Chinese "aggressiveness" is, of course, ludicrous: it is as much as to say that it was the truculence of Haile Selassie that "provoked" the Italian invasion of Ethiopia. Those who are so opposed to any resort to violence should distinguish clearly where violence begins. What had happened in China in 1937 was that, for the first time in years, the feeling of the vast majority of people was being to some extent reflected in government policy. And just as, in Spain, it was a United Front government, openly elected by the Spanish people, which "provoked" the fascist rebellion of July 1936, so—a year later almost to the day—the growth of a National United Front in China was the signal for this new and final phase of Japanese invasion.

This time, Japanese imperialism would not be content with a "local" incident and a "local" settlement. As soon as the Chinese resistance, once tested, had proved real, Japan had to stake everything on the big throw, and play for China or nothing. "At last," as the President of the South Manchuria Railway declared breezily not long afterward, "Nippon is in for the final, for a knockout decision.... Japan has taken up her scalpel. She will permit no foreign interference whatsoever here."

For twenty days from July 8th, the Lukowchiao affair— dramatized as the defense of this ancient bridge, sadly decayed from the days of its glory, but still a symbol of the old cultural tradition of North China—had engrossed the attention of most people in the Far East. To the Chinese, it was summed up in that popular photograph, reproduced in innumerable illustrated weeklies, of a soldier of the 29th Route Army, in gray cotton uniform, leaning with his bigsword against a carved marble parapet. If you look in the Japanese weeklies of the same period, you will see other—and very much more artistic— camera studies of steel-helmeted troops taking cover in the kaoliang, while the field guns come into play behind them; of squadrons of Japanese planes black against a North China sky. It is a fair measure of the difference in the odds.

And on the morning of July 28th, the attack on Peiping, thoroughly rehearsed in the combined Japanese maneuvers of the autumn before, began in real earnest.

THE SIEGE OF PEIPING

In these summer months, the foreign community of Peiping was somewhat thinned. But the usual round of dinner parties, with the guest lanterns glowing in Chinese courtyards, and a distant rumble of gunfire to drown the shrilling of the cicadas, found now an unfailing new topic of conversation, "Was there going to be a siege?"

The Japanese Embassy seemed to think so, to judge from the mountain of sandbags and barbed wire that had appeared outside its gates. But these fortifications, and the guns and military trucks assembled inside the Japanese barracks, might have another significance. The Japanese had never shown any hesitation about using the International Settlement in Shanghai as a military base; might they not do the same with the Legation Quarter in Peiping, if it came to fighting inside the city?

The British Embassy, just across the road from the Japanese sandbags, retained its traditional air of masterly inactivity, though some old residents at the Club recalled gloomily the Boxer days, hinting at the unknown dangers of a "Chinese mob." The American authorities, with the first sign of a nervousness that was to be generally characteristic of the policy of their government in China in the months that immediately followed, were issuing complicated instructions to their nationals almost daily. A gala display of lights on the American wireless mast was to be the alarm-signal for all foreigners to seek shelter inside the walled Legation Quarter.

There was some justification for all this. Chinese troops had built barricades at a number of street-corners (showing that they, at any rate, expected attack from inside the walls as well as from without); and there were patrols in the streets at night. Some students I talked with were full of enthusiasm, and saw Peiping becoming another Madrid. It was by no means impossible.

The main defense of the city was in the hands of the 29th Route Army. This force, part of the old Kuominchun once under the command of Feng Yu-hsiang, had been virtually independent for some years: it was one of the most poorly equipped of all the Chinese armies, but its fighting quality—as it had proved at the Great Wall in 1933—was far from negligible. The rank and file and the younger officers, in particular, were resolutely "anti-Japanese," with a long history of insults and humiliation to avenge.

THE SIEGE OF PEIPING 43

Though it would almost certainly have proved impossible to hold Peiping against the Japanese if the latter brought all their resources to bear upon it, there was no reason why the city, resolutely defended, might not have held out for weeks and even for months. It was not, like Shanghai, under the direct fire of the big guns of the Japanese navy. And even if the attackers should succeed in making a breach in the walls, the example of the street fighting in Chapei in 1932 had shown that, under such conditions, the lightly-armed Chinese troops could be very effective indeed.

Such speculations may seem vain enough now, when everyone knows what actually happened. After one day's serious fighting, the regular army evacuated the city, which fell without further resistance into the hands of the enemy. But it may be useful to suggest here some of the reasons for this ignominious collapse; for they are a good illustration of some of the weaknesses at first only too apparent in the general Chinese resistance.

In the home of a Chinese friend, shortly after my return to Peiping, I was introduced to a big man in a white gown, with the shoulders of a professional boxer. He was "very high up," I had been told, in the *Ko Lao Hui* * and several more of those secret societies that play so important a part behind the scenes of Chinese life. He was completely "unpolitical" in any modern sense; but he was a representative Chinese.

Now—he told us very simply—he had organized ten thousand peasants, all of them members of these old societies, in southern Hopei. They were already marching north "to fight the Japanese dwarfs." But they had no arms. For weeks, in Peiping, he had been trying to get arms from Sung and other local officials, but without result. Now he was going to Nanking, to see what could be done there.

Many leaders of popular organizations had made the same demand, and been refused in the same way. Mobile units in the villages, partisans organized along the railway, might have made a world of difference in the strength of the Chinese de-

---
* The "Elder Brothers' Society," one of the oldest and most powerful underground organizations in China.

fense. But at that stage, no official assistance of any kind was forthcoming for the arming of local volunteers.

Madrid, in the first hectic days of Franco's assault, held out against technically superior forces because the people of Madrid and of the whole countryside were organized and armed in their own defense. Peiping (and later, Nanking) fell so easily, largely because they were defended only by regular troops. It was not until both the old and the new capital of China had been lost, that the Chinese government learned this very necessary lesson: that the war of resistance against Japan must be a mass war of the whole Chinese people.

Before long, it was evident the storm that now muttered beneath the very walls of the city must break in earnest. But the Peiping authorities continued to underestimate the seriousness of the situation. On the evening of July 26th, some three hundred Japanese troops tried to force an entry through the Chang Yi gate. They claimed to be a part of the Japanese Legation Guard (already swollen far beyond the numbers prescribed under the Boxer Treaty). The Chinese on the wall, with some presence of mind, opened the main gate to the Japanese, then closed it quickly behind them. The small enemy force was thus trapped between the outer and inner gates, and soon found itself surrounded and hopelessly outnumbered.

There were real possibilities in such a situation. For a time, the Chinese amused themselves by firing trench mortars and throwing hand grenades from the wall; the Japanese had sought cover in a little temple, and replied very ineffectively with machine guns. In the morning, it was clear that nothing could save them but surrender.

But again the Chinese command showed the fatal indecision that was to prove its undoing. With a heaven-sent opportunity to disarm this enemy troop, they not only accepted a truce, but allowed the Japanese to march with their arms into the Legation Quarter. "They deserve to lose," was the comment of the American journalist—an eyewitness—who described this affair to me. If the Chinese had been the defenders at the siege of Troy, the Greeks, one imagined, would have had no need of a wooden horse.

It was on the next day that Sung rejected the "second ultimatum" of the Japanese. That afternoon, I was in the house of a visiting Cambridge professor, who—like most of us—was finding it hard to regard recent developments with academic calm. We talked of the tragic death of Julian Bell in Spain: I recalled the last cloudless days I had spent with him in Wuhan, sailing in his tiny yacht among Chinese lakes.

"It seems such a waste; but he felt he had to do something. And if he had stayed in China, it might have been the same. This is the same war. It will find us out...."

A new arrival—a Frenchman—joined the group, fingering a flimsy sheet of notepaper. "We have all been summoned to our Embassy. Yes, by tonight at the latest."

"Are you going?"

He shrugged. "Naturally." The French were realists, and always well-informed in North China. If they were calling in their people, that meant something.

Conversation flowed more freely, though everyone was a little distracted. "The Eve of Waterloo...." "Yes, but to *think* of the Japanese in Peiping, and what they'll make of this city. A Little Tokyo...." "The trouble with China, is that it's too old...."

"Well, I shan't leave my temple," one usually cynical American teacher asserted. "And I hope the Chinese make a fight of it." He was so much in earnest that he nearly spilt his cocktail.

This was Tuesday evening. Next morning, all Peiping was rudely wakened by the thunder of bombardment just outside the south wall.

Sung had a few troops inside the city; but his two main concentrations were in barracks south and west of the main walls—the Nanyuan and Hsiyuan respectively, in the outlying suburbs of Peiping. It was against these that the first Japanese attack was directed. Both barracks were death traps, and it is no reflection on the defenders that the Hsiyuan was promptly abandoned. But at Nanyuan, completely exposed to aerial attack and armed with nothing more effective than trench mortars and machine guns, the Chinese held their position all that day.

Inside the city, from the first alarm we knew little enough of what was going on. Cars and trucks had been hastily dispatched to gather foreign residents into the Legation Quarter. Many went with a bad grace; but if street fighting had developed, it would be very easy to get cut off in the narrow Peiping *hutung*.

The "Quarter" exchanged its usual diplomatic calm for the bedlam of a continental bank holiday. No one had guessed that there were so many foreign nationals in the city. Tents were pitched on ambassadorial lawns that never before had seen so strange a garden party; informal summer dress lent to the scene something of the air of a bathing parade. Harassed missionaries appeared with enormous families, and Russian dancing girls—basing their claims for protection, no doubt, on past associations—ogled the American marines (who, with the children, seemed to be about the only people who were really enjoying themselves). Even the most famous recluse of all Peiping emerged after many years to the light of day, in an Edwardian straw hat. The number of Chinese, natives of Hong Kong or Hawaii, who could claim British or American citizenship, was another surprise. Probably never since Boxer times had so picturesque an assortment of races and professions been gathered within these walls.

All that day, and most of the night that followed, fighting continued around the city. The gates of the Legation Quarter were closed at sunset, but up to this time it was still possible to come and go. The air, of course, was thick with unverifiable rumors; and the Chinese saw a Kuomintang sun on the wings of every high-flying aeroplane. It was already clear that the air factor would probably be decisive.

That evening, the Chinese had their first real encouragement. Official radio broadcasts from the Peiping station announced that Fengtai, military base of the Japanese at the railway junction, and Tungchow, capital of the Japanese puppet-government in East Hopei, had been captured by Chinese troops. The news sounded almost too good to be true; but it was by no means impossible, if the Chinese had been resolutely led, and had taken the initiative on all sides. At this stage, their numbers were still overwhelmingly superior.

The high spot of that Wednesday, for a number of us who had gathered in the office of a local correspondent to sift the crop of rumors, was when an official entered, known to be a representative of the Nanking Government. His face wore a smile of triumph. "Good news!" he announced exultantly. "General Chiang Kai-shek is in Paotingfu! He has ordered up a hundred Chinese planes from the south!"

Something like a cheer went up all around. If this was true, the Japanese might find their latest conquest more difficult than they had supposed. That was the highwater mark of Chinese optimism, in these days only too ready to mount mercurially. We retired to our respective embassies, to a sleep punctuated by the stutter of machine guns and the flame of trench mortars. But next day, we knew better.

For on Thursday the city woke to an unnatural calm. All sounds of firing had ceased, except a distant thudding of guns across the river towards Changhsingtien. Coming early out of the Legation Quarter, I saw that the gray army uniforms had vanished from the wall. The city gates were open, and a thin stream of rickshaws passed in and out.

Then we got the papers: the last issue of the *Peiping News* that was to appear. Sung—leaving "with tears in his eyes"—had evacuated the city. Chang Tze-chung, one of these figures whose loyalty, in the shifting North China scene, is most difficult to fix, but who was at this time mayor of Tientsin and notoriously "pro-Japanese," * was to take over leadership of the Hopei-Chahar Political Council.

The "siege" of the old capital had lasted just twenty-four

---

* General Chang later redeemed himself by deserting the puppet Peiping government and rejoining his command in Shantung.

hours. Once more, in its long history of surrender and betrayal, Peiping had been sold out.

MASSACRE

It was all over in Peiping. But that same Thursday—July 29th—was eventful enough in other parts of the province. The two chief centers of action were Tungchow and Tientsin.

Tungchow, the old terminus of the Grand Canal about twelve miles east of Peiping, had gained a certain notoriety since 1935 as the "capital" of the "East Hopei Anti-Communist Autonomous Government" under Yin Ju-keng—a Chinese who had earned, if anyone had, that most opprobrious epithet of *hanchien*.* This puppet régime, the pure creation of the Kwantung Army, came into being in twenty-two *hsien* of Eastern Hopei shortly after the Ho-Umetsu agreement in the summer of 1935 had cleared the way for a new "North China Autonomy" drive by the Japanese.

Within the "demilitarized zone" established after the Tangku Truce, the new state had had from its inception a strong Japanese garrison, with its center at Tungchow. But the maintenance of order was officially entrusted to an overgrown Chinese force of *paoantui* ("Peace Preservation Corps"), who were recruited locally, trained by Japanese officers, and given regular "anti-Communist" education. This was a beginning in North China of the "Anti-Red Army" which the Japanese militarists hoped to use later in their far-reaching schemes of conquest.

The chief fame of the East Hopei régime in its brief and checkered history was as a base for smuggling operations on the grand scale, carried on not so much with the connivance as under the direction of the puppet government. The North China Customs was quite unable to cope with the situation, for Japanese goods unloaded on the beach below Shanhaikwan could be transported overland through Yin Ju-keng's territory to Tientsin and Peiping. One of the most profitable lines for the smugglers was narcotics: heroin, manufactured at Manchukuo and brought in bulk to Tungchow, was distributed throughout North China by the ronin and Korean dope-peddlers

---
* "Chinese traitor."

MASSACRE 49

who are the familiar vanguard of the Imperial Japanese Army. Yin Ju-keng (this was another of those delightful anomalies of North China, before it came openly under the control of the Japanese army) lived in Peiping in some state with his Japanese wife, and kept only office hours in his "capital." Though the Nanking government had issued a warrant for his arrest, Sung Cheh-yuan was much too politic an official to attempt to execute it. But Sung had a contingent of his own 39th Brigade stationed just outside the walls of Tungchow, on the western border of Yin's domain. And here, on the main highway to Peiping, Chinese and Japanese troops had faced each other across the road for several months.

On July 27th, things began to happen around Tungchow. In anticipation, no doubt, of the general attack on Peiping, the commander of the Japanese garrison gave the Chinese troops three hours in which to give up their arms. The latter refused, and an eight-hour action ensued, the Japanese artillery playing havoc with the lightly-armed Chinese. Sung sent no reinforcements from Peiping, and from the shattered Chinese force only about a hundred survivors are reported to have made their escape. This was the first act in the drama of Tungchow.

With the situation well in hand, the Japanese left only a skeleton garrison in Tungchow, and turned to the major action of the next day—the attack on Sung's main positions around Peiping. By Thursday morning, as we have seen, the city was at their mercy. But on that same Thursday morning—it was the most dramatic and unexpected reversal of this brief opening campaign—Tungchow was once more in the hands of the Chinese.

Encouraged by the mischievous reports of Chinese successes elsewhere that we had heard in Peiping on Wednesday afternoon, the *paoantui* rose in revolt throughout East Hopei. In Tungchow, led by their own Chinese commander Chang Ch'ing-yu, they surprised and completely wiped out the small Japanese garrison, and made short work of most of the Japanese and Koreans (some three hundred in number) who had remained in the town. All Japanese buildings and offices of the bogus government were sacked and burned to the ground. The great column of smoke which rose from the ruin was clearly visible all that day from the walls of Peiping. This was the famous "Tungchow Massacre" which has become a "black day" in Japanese history, gathering around it such associations as the names of Delhi and Cawnpore had in Britain in years after the Indian Mutiny.

It is perhaps impossible to comment impartially on the events of that Thursday morning. No one—least of all this writer—is likely to defend the slaughter of women and civilians, whatever the provocation. But there is still a good deal of misunderstanding about the revolt at Tungchow, which was described in official Japanese reports as the work of "monsters and animals." What has been carefully left out of the Japanese accounts is all that led up to this rising of desperate men.

It must be remembered that all Japanese nationals in Tungchow were employed, openly or indirectly, by the hated "East Hopei" régime. The Koreans were for the most part smugglers and dope-peddlers; the Korean women were unfortunate, and perhaps unwilling camp-followers. The whole "Japanese colony" in East Hopei might be described without injustice as consisting of Army agents and their families, and shady adventurers. It was this foreign minority, backed by the Japanese North China Garrison and aided by Chinese traitors, that had been able to dominate the whole district for two years, and impose upon it a degrading and (through the unlicensed and officially sponsored drug traffic) debasing alien rule.

The depth of resentment against the whole puppet régime may be accurately measured by the violence of the revolt—when it came. And it must not be forgotten that the signal for it had been a devastating attack on the local Chinese garrison, with no more warning than a sudden demand for unconditional surrender.

Those Japanese who escaped the holocaust of Thursday morning at Tungchow owe their lives to the curious devotion of

MASSACRE 51

Chinese servants, who smuggled them out of the town in disguise, and here again—as so often in the past, most notably in the Boxer days—remained faithful to foreign masters at the risk of their own lives. But among "Government" officials, only one—and that the least-deserving—survived. This was the wretched Yin Ju-keng, who had sought undignified cover in the upper room of a friend's house. Run to earth by the *paoantui*, he was immediately arrested (the fact that he was not shot out of hand shows that there was discipline among the mutineers); when all was over at Tungchow, he was brought back a prisoner in his own car to Peiping.

Here a rude shock awaited the leaders of the revolt. They had naturally expected to find the old capital still in the possession of the 29th Route Army, and intended to hand over the arch-traitor to Sung Cheh-yuan for court-martial. Instead, they arrived at the East Gate to find it held by the Chinese city police acting under Japanese orders, who refused to allow them inside the walls. In the confusion only Yin himself (whose least desert was a bullet) slipped through the gates; and the mutineers, menaced by the guns of their own countrymen, were either disarmed or left to disappear into the fields in the attempt to rejoin the Chinese army.

It was a most tragic anticlimax to an enterprise which—however bloody the issue—was at least boldly conceived and carried out. As a crowning irony, the petrified head of the puppet government, who may have flattered himself that once inside the walls of Peiping he was safe, soon found himself a prisoner once more in the Japanese Embassy, charged with failure to control his own police force. His subsequent fate remains a mystery.

In Tientsin, too, much had been happening on that fateful Thursday. The Japanese were already well entrenched in this key city, and with a "friendly" Mayor (Chang Tze-chung, who took over in Peiping after Sung Cheh-yuan's sudden departure, was concurrently commander of the 38th Division of the 29th Route Army) they had expected little positive resistance in the immediate neighborhood. But here again they made a grave miscalculation.

For in Tientsin the story of Tungchow was repeated. The Chinese *paoantui*, fighting shoulder to shoulder with individual units of Chang's troops, voluntarily joined the struggle, and put in a heroic day's work. They captured the West Railway Station, came within an ace of storming the main East Station; and fought their way within two hundred yards of the Japanese military airdrome, center of all the bombing operations of the last two days. Japanese control of Tientsin—a vital military base—hung in the balance.

On Thursday night, by the admission of an official Japanese spokesman in Tientsin, the position of the Japanese North China Garrison was critical. They had lost connection with their scattered units (who had pressed on too eagerly for the attack on Peiping), and this sudden blow in the rear had taken them almost completely by surprise. The railway was cut by the Chinese, and if the latter had only pressed their advantage, they might well at this stage have rolled the Japanese back to Tangku.

But once again, a desperate effort by the rank and file was betrayed from above. The old weaknesses—a disunited command and no political solidarity—were only too apparent. After one day of reckless fighting which held out the promise of undreamt-of success for the Chinese, the regular army units in Tientsin (like those at Peiping the night before) were withdrawn to the south. The *paoantui*, exhausted in the street fighting and demoralized by lack of support, scattered into the country or gave up their arms.

Within twenty-four hours, the whole picture had changed. The Japanese were once more masters of the railway and could bring in the reinforcements which had already been rushed down from Manchuria. The Chinese city of Tientsin, devastated by aerial bombardment and concentrated artillery fire, was a smoldering ruin. All that remained for the invaders around Tientsin and Tungchow was that operation pleasantly described in Tokyo dispatches as "mopping up." This is to be distinguished from such "outrages" as the massacre at Tungchow only by the greater scope afforded to those carrying it out.

Today a marble monument in the center of Tungchow commemorates 280 Japanese nationals who lost their lives in the East Hopei revolt. The *paoantui* of Tungchow and Tientsin—coolies in uniform who turned their arms against the enemy of their country, and whose reckless bravery is almost the only redeeming feature of the parody of resistance put up by Sung Cheh-yuan in the north—these have no memorial, unless it is in the hearts and minds of their fellow-countrymen. Abandoned by the army command, betrayed by their own comrades in Peiping, they were hunted down like rats in the kaoliang fields, and their graves are nameless.

They took the risk that their own government was still unwilling to take, and only too many of them paid for that indiscretion with their lives. But it was they, along with the rank and file of the 29th Route Army, who were the true vanguard of the Chinese people in the greater struggle that was soon to develop.

And the real significance of the part they played on that bloody Thursday—if the Japanese could only realize it—was shattering. For it was in the two "safe" areas of Tungchow and Tientsin, and from the very groups of Chinese that they had already taken under their benevolent "protection," that the invaders encountered the fiercest resistance of those July days. In other words, *where the Japanese had been longest established in Hopei the opposition of the Chinese was most resolute and determined*.

It was hardly a favorable augury for the new rulers of Peiping.

TRIUMPHAL ENTRY

What had happened to cause Sung Cheh-yuan's sudden defection, after his firm stand of only two days before? It is probable that the inside story of those last days of July, and the exact nature of the military assurances that passed between Nanking and Peiping, will never be known in full. The official Chinese version is that Sung's original orders were to evacuate the old capital without a struggle. When he disregarded this by his rejection of the Japanese "ultimatum," he committed himself to independent action. But even at this stage, Chiang Kai-shek promised support if Sung could hold out for forty-eight hours.

It seems that Sung Cheh-yuan trusted neither Nanking nor his own judgment. Having begun on a bold course, he developed the fatal "last-minute panic" of the old-style Chinese warlord as soon as he saw where it was leading him, and deserted his post. The 29th Route Army paid the price of his indecision.

What that price was, one saw on Thursday morning, going outside the south wall of the city.

The garrison at Nanyuan had been smashed to pieces by the Japanese attack. Exposed, their lines of communication cut, with no further orders than the original command to "resist," they had remained all Wednesday within their mud walls under the concentrated fire of heavy artillery and aerial bombardment. It is impossible to calculate the total of their losses, but it was probably in the neighborhood of five thousand killed, and of the wounded few can have survived.

Two division commanders were killed, Generals Chao Teng-yu and Tung Lin-keh—this was the sacrifice to reputation that Sung had wanted. Nearly a thousand Peiping students quartered in the Nanyuan barracks, raw volunteers in arms who had joined the army that summer for their first two months of military training, received a rude baptism of fire: only a handful survived it. Among the victims was the son of Feng Yu-hsiang, a young captain in the regulars. The most tragic aspect of the Nanyuan fighting was its futility. Without anti-aircraft guns, the Chinese were defending an airdrome that held no planes. For no planes came from the South.

The Japanese plan of attack, to be used again on many North China cities, was to surround the Chinese position on three sides but leave one apparent way out, along which they could lay an ambush. They had done this on the road from Nanyuan to Yungtingmen. Pulverized by a day's bombardment, with no further direction from the army command, the Chinese had at last abandoned Nanyuan. Cars and military trucks loaded with troops, retreating blindly from the charnel-house behind them, had been caught by the enfilading fire of machine-gun nests on either side of the road; in one spot there were eight hundred

Chinese bodies. No veteran of the World War could remember such a slaughter. For even in the War, the worst military tactics of either command could not compare with what Sung had done to his army.

Japanese losses at Nanyuan were given as fifty or so, and for once this was probably correct. To talk later with Chinese soldiers who had been in this engagement was to hear a heartbreaking story. Most of them had not seen a single soldier to shoot at. Airplanes, long-range bombardment, and tanks are weapons against which the stoutest heart can do little with a rifle or a hand grenade. All that was left to do was to slip away into the fields under cover of night and try to escape to the hills.

There were single instances where the retreating 29th Route Army put up a better showing. To the west, Chinese batteries held up the Japanese long enough for the remnants of the army to get across the river. The withdrawal from Tientsin was well-conducted, with few casualties. But in general, the whole action was lamentable from a military point of view. Honors of this first round of hostilities in the north were overwhelmingly with the Japanese.

It has seemed worth while to describe at some length this débâcle of Peiping, if only to point a contrast with all that the Chinese later learned from it. The mistakes of military strategy, of course, are obvious; but it was to be some months yet before regular commanders learned not to mass their lightly armed troops in vulnerable and exposed positions. And it is significant that at this stage, though Sung had deserted his command and forfeited any claim he might ever have had to responsibility, he was still able to face it out, and not long afterward was appointed to a chief command of the Chinese front in Shantung.

On the political side, the lessons of Peiping were already convincing—though these again were not truly learned until after the greater catastrophe at Nanking. The local Chinese authorities had no real will to resist—they had discouraged every effort that had been made to organize the people of Hopei in their own defense, and when the hour came, shamelessly abandoned them to their fate. That there was a will to resistance among the rank and file is proved by the example of the *paoantui* in Tungchow and Tientsin; if the peasants and workers of the north had had any kind of backing from their leaders, if they had even been given a part of the arms and supplies at the disposal of the provincial government, the results of those few days might have been very different.

As it was, resistance in the north during this first phase was given no opportunity to gather a mass basis. From the suspense of the last few weeks, Peiping relapsed into its traditional mood of *"meiyu fa-tze"*—the phrase of resigned or cynical acceptance that has for many years expressed the basic philosophy of the North China peasant. Only in the months to come, under such influences as had molded the determination of the people of East Hopei, and with fresh heart from the growth of guerilla units that began to make their appearance in the first weeks after the collapse, was this mood to undergo any decisive change.

On Sunday, August 7th, after a week in which "mopping-up" had gone on briskly in the outlying districts and the main Chinese line had been pushed back to the strategic pass of Nankow, the Japanese army made its official entry into the city of Peiping. It was a curious ceremony.

All morning, police and armed guards had cleared the route for the Japanese column. It entered from the southwest, through streets where no single Chinese was to be seen, where every house had been searched in advance. The grand parade was to be held in the *Tung Ch'ang An Chieh*—eastern section of that "Avenue of Everlasting Peace" which Chinese emperors planned to run east and west before the gates of their Forbidden City. No other capital in the world, perhaps, could offer to a conqueror so magnificent a *Siegesallee*.

And here had gathered, along the walls of the old Austrian Legation and across the glacis that the Boxer Treaty conveniently expanded into a polo-field for "foreign devils," the entire Japanese population of Peiping. Merchants and café proprietors, high-booted ronin and "barmaids" in gaudy kimonos—it was a full local turnout, if not a very impressive one. Perhaps a thousand in all, they were there to celebrate with paper flags and shrill "banzais" one of the most notable of time's revenges. Only one man in history has ever led an invasion against the islands of Japan. That was the "Great Khan" Kublai, Emperor of China and Korea, and ruler in his day over one of the widest dominions the world has ever known. Now, after the lapse of nearly seven centuries, the island people were marching as conquerors into the old capital of Kublai Khan. Once before—in the days after the lifting of the Boxer siege—Japanese soldiers had marched in triumph with the Allied Forces through these streets. But that had been a hollow victory. Now it was the day of Japan alone. And this time—if they knew anything about it—the armies of Nippon had come to stay.

Slowly the parade took shape. First came the tanks and armored cars, plowing up the warm asphalt as they ground their way along the tree-lined avenue. (I remembered the Japanese maneuvers of the year before, that might have been a rehearsal for this. A Chinese schoolgirl had been crushed beneath the advancing tanks....) Then cavalry units, the big Australian walers, lean and ugly, looking strangely out of place in a Chinese setting. The troops themselves arrived in American-built trucks, which backed up to form an extended line beneath the trees. At the end of the line was the inevitable Asahi Beer wagon.

It was a naked display of military force; and nothing is uglier than the panoply of modern war. These drab-painted tanks and howitzers were an insult to the carved marble bridges, the faded-pink palace walls, against which they now stood ranged. Japanese reporters, wearing the bright armband of the rising sun and busy with their complicated cameras, might see this as a pageant of victory; to any but a Japanese eye, it could only appear a kind of defilement.

I had been standing with a little group of Europeans at the corner of Morrison Street: we had watched the troops march in with very mixed feelings. But now a bearded Japanese sergeant moved us on. General Kawabe was coming to address the parade; we must stand further off. Foreigners, on such occasions, were notably lacking in a proper respect to the Emperor's representatives.

"What are we here for anyhow?" one of the group demanded. "At least, the Chinese had the sense to boycott this show."

"Oh, I don't know. Somebody *might* have thrown a bomb...."

"In Peiping? Not a hope. Come on, let's get out of this."

There were no bombs. Peiping was too old, too vulnerable, too unprepared. The people of the north had found no answer—yet—to this line of tanks and guns. In time, they would find an answer.

But it did seem as though Peiping, in this hour of humiliation, had fallen back upon those immemorial weapons of her defense: beauty and indifference. Too weak to repel the latest of her invaders, at least in the moment of their triumph she could ignore them.

Over the amazing roofs of the Forbidden City (as we turned away) came a power-diving Japanese plane, a trail of colored leaflets in its wake. *"Peace and Harmony between the Peoples of East Asia..."*

In the streets, only a few rickshaw coolies gaze up with impressive faces. The peaceful and harmonious missives drifted down unattended on to the golden tiles.

"REALLY WAR"

In the bar of the Hotel du Nord, the usual group of Germans at the center table were playing dice. In one discreet corner, a corporal of the French guard sat over a vermouth with a Russian dancing-girl from the Alkazar. In another—rather surprisingly—a group of blue-gowned Chinese talked in whispers. They had come here for safety, not from preference.

The doors swung open on the summer evening, to admit half a dozen Japanese ronin. Automatics at their hips, they were in high good humor.

"Beer!" called their leader loudly. The Number One Boy, stately as a prince of eunuchs, filled the glasses. The Chinese had left their corner, and the new arrivals promptly occupied it. Already they dominated the whole room.

"This used to be a good quiet pub," my friend remarked peevishly. "But I don't like the present company. Finished?"

"Wait and see the news," I suggested. "It won't be long now." A few minutes later, we had the typewritten Reuter sheets.

"I say, things are looking up in Shanghai! 'Chinese planes attempted to bomb the Japanese flagship. . . .' That's the first time Nanking has ever used its air force against the Japanese! This is bigger stuff than '32. If Chiang starts using his planes—"

"—And how!" An American newspaperman had just come in with the latest despatches. "Cast an eye over that!"

It was the account of the disastrous dropping of Chinese bombs inside the International Settlement of Shanghai, by which nearly two thousand civilians had been killed and wounded. The barroom was all agog.

"So like the Chinese!" one of the Germans maintained to the world at large. "They drop their bombs just two miles away from the target! *Menschmeyer,* what clumsy fools."

"But if it was an accident . . . the bomb racks hit by shrapnel?"

"*Ach!* If the bomb rack was hit, the bombs explode, *nicht?*"

"Not necessarily. . . ."

"—For the love of Pete, don't start an argument. Can't you see he's tight?"

"Oh, all right. . . ." What with the war and what with the sweat, tempers were getting a little frayed on all sides. We followed the excellent example of the Chinese, and slipped out into the courtyard.

The general feeling of foreigners in China, while deploring this most inauspicious début of the young and inexperienced Chinese air force, remained sympathetic. The bombing in the Shanghai Settlement caused no such universal resentment as the deliberate Japanese attack on the car of the British Ambassador which followed so closely upon it, or the bombing and machine-gunning of a train filled with Chinese refugees at the South Station of Shanghai not long afterwards. But perhaps the most vivid impression it made on all of us was a new realization of what modern weapons of destruction could do. A single bomb claimed a thousand victims. And China, one of the most densely populated countries in the world, lay wide open to aerial attack. We knew now what we were in for.

Reuter, for once, had the appropriate comment: "...Discussing the afternoon's events, a grinning Japanese spokesman observed: 'Now it's really war.'"

The Japanese landing at Woosung on August 12th and the rapid development of hostilities around Shanghai during the third week of August, swiftly and effectively drew most people's attention away from the North China front. This was natural enough, for Shanghai is the main focus of foreign interests in China, and the spectacular fighting there brought into action land, air, and naval forces. From the midsummer of 1937 until late November, when the Chinese defenders were at last dislodged from the positions they had held so grimly, Shanghai held pretty constantly the center of the picture in the Far Eastern war.

To experienced military observers, however, and to anyone who had made a study of the lines of Japanese encroachment into China, the Shanghai hostilities could only appear as a diversion. It was formidable enough diversion, a direct blow at the economic base of the National Government in the rich adjoining provinces of Kiangsu, Chekiang, and Anhwei. And no doubt the Japanese hoped that, by terrifying the bankers, industrialists, and great commercial interests of Shanghai, they might undermine the resistance of Chiang Kai-shek's government and accelerate a general Chinese collapse. But this did not alter the fact that Japan's immediate objectives, in 1937 as in 1931, remained in the North.

The "Man-Mon" policy of the Kwantung Army, which insists on the occupation of Mongolia after Manchuria, and the driving of a wedge deep into northwestern China as a safeguard against Soviet Russia had not been abandoned. (To the orthodox Japanese military mind, the whole China campaign is still only a prelude to the "inevitable" war with the Soviet Union.) The early occupation of Tientsin and Peiping had given the Japanese armies a convenient base for further operations in the North. The next step must be an assault upon the strategic Nankow Pass, gateway to Inner Mongolia, and an advance westwards along the Peiping-Suiyan railway. No time was lost in getting these operations under way, and General Terauchi, one of the ablest and most experienced of Japanese commanders, was entrusted with the task.

But the Nankow Pass, a superb natural feature for defense, might—and indeed did—prove a tough nut to crack. If at this time General Chiang Kai-shek had been left free to send more of his best divisions north, the flank of the whole Japanese Hopei-Chahar-Suiyuan wedge might have been threatened. The Japanese knew this well enough; they knew too that they could not secure their position until they had occupied most of the North China plain—at least as far south as the Yellow River, the first natural defensive line. This meant the investment of Shansi, Shantung, and a part at least of Honan: a pretty ambitious program, if the Chinese should be able to put their full strength in the field.

The one thing Japan must provide against at this stage was a Chinese counteroffensive in the north. Hence, with an obvious military logic, the extension of hostilities to Shanghai.

And the Shanghai diversion that August worked to the direct advantage of the invaders (a point overlooked at the time by those who argued that the fighting at Shanghai was a subtle Chinese countermove, made in the hope of embroiling Japan with other Western powers in this "international" port). By landing a small mixed force in Shanghai, under the cover of a naval squadron and naval planes, the Japanese were able to draw the main fighting and technical resources of the National Government into this sector, and keep them there while the northern offensive proceeded according to plan. This strategy was well-conceived; by mid-September, more than 300,000 of Chiang Kai-shek's best troops were immobilized in the Shanghai area, and the apparent failure of the Japanese landing party to make ground there was more than outweighed by rapid and sweeping gains in the north.

The main outline of this Japanese plan was already clear by the end of August. Whatever happened in Central China (and it was generally conceded that neither Shanghai nor Nanking could be held indefinitely) the fighting in the north was still of primary strategic significance. Until Japan consolidated her hold upon North China, any gains further south might prove to be illusory.

And one key area was formed by those Chinese provinces adjacent to Mongolia and Chinese Turkestan—a region of plateau and loess highland, of uneven economic development, and with a most diversified population, known traditionally as the old home of Chinese civilization and destined, in this twentieth century, to regain something of its former importance. This was China's Northwest, her overland bridge to the Soviet Union. So long as this bridge remained open, military supplies could continue to reach the province of Shensi, and the Northwest remain as a firm base of resistance against Japan in North China.

Something else besides its strategic importance gave the Northwest a special interest at this time. For it was here, in the barren mountains of Northern Shensi, that the Chinese Communists had established their position after the historic "Long March" from the South. The "Chinese Soviet Republic" was now a Special District under the National Government, the old Red Army that for ten years defied Chiang Kai-shek had become officially one part of the Chinese National forces, under the new and unfamiliar name of the "Eighth Route Army." But for Japan these significant changes of status meant nothing. The Northwest was "Red China," a political as well as a strategic objective. Inevitably, as Japanese columns pushed on from Peiping to the conquest of the North, they must come up against these redoubtable antagonists, once characterized by a Japanese general as the "chief enemy of the Empire." It would be an interesting trial of strength.

The war had passed by Peiping, and left us all stranded overnight behind the Japanese lines. Nothing was to be gained from staying on here, unless one wished to make a study of the peculiar modern art of creating puppet governments. Besides, before long the Japanese police might start asking awkward questions. There had been a magazine called *Democracy* to

"REALLY WAR" 63

which I had been a contributor, along with Edgar Snow and a group of foreign and Chinese liberals. It had been a modest little magazine, and had died a very sudden death when the Japanese troops entered the walls of Peiping. But the Japanese, we gathered, did not like democracy. . . .

In Snow's house with its pleasant rambling garden beneath the South Wall, we discussed the latest turn of events. The summer afternoon was broken by the rumble of gunfire; in the Western Hills, scattered units of the 29th Route Army were still putting up a stand. Further north, the Japanese were pounding away at Nankow, where steel-helmeted Chinese troops under General Tang En-po manned once more the ancient ramparts of the Great Wall. The war was on, and at last China was making a fight of it. But we were on the wrong side of the guns.

"Where do we go from here?" I wanted to know.

"Shanghai for me, I suppose," Ed responded without much enthusiasm. Most of the correspondents were already trekking south; in New York and London, only Shanghai meant headlines. "But I know where I'd like to be now."

"Northwest?"

Snow nodded. I knew what he was thinking; reports had come through to Peiping that the Eighth Route Army had been ordered up to the northern front. Once more the Red Army was marching, this time against Japan. It was the last stage of a march that had begun four years ago in Kiangsi.

"It isn't a big story yet," Ed was saying. "But it's going to be one. Anyhow, I'd like to get up to Sian. There's been no word from Peg"—his wife, I knew, was away at this time on a trip to North Shensi—"and that's another reason. What do you say?"

To go up into the interior now meant taking a chance on being cut off there. Communications in China were being steadily disrupted by the war; even to get out of Peiping was not going to be easy, with the Japanese in control of the railways west and south. The only open road was through Shantung, which could still be reached by sea from Tientsin. It was by this roundabout route that thousands of Chinese refugees were daily crowding out of Peiping and Tientsin on their way to the South.

But the railway held to Sian, and Sian was the rendezvous for the Northwest. It did not take long to decide. If I was to see anything more of the war in the north (that had begun so disastrously for China) it would be with the Eighth Route Army.

"I'm coming along," I said. "After all, someone ought to write 'Red Star against Japan'..."

CHAPTER TWO

THE ROAD TO YENAN

SHANTUNG ROUNDABOUT

August was ended, the summer rains were over, when we set out from Peiping on our way to the Northwest. The rains that year had been prodigious throughout North China: it was as though the heavens wept in sympathy at the fall of the old capital. For the Chinese, it meant a most welcome respite. The Japanese advance, bogged down along those roads that vanished emperors had built to be "good for ten years and bad for ten centuries," came to an unexpected standstill. Whole mechanized columns stuck fast in the yellow mud, an object of wonder to the few peasants who emerged, greatly daring, to salvage something of their ruined crops. Around the Grand Canal, the retreating Chinese armies had taken to the water and gained a new mobility in junks.

The railway remained the only effective "feeder" for the Japanese, and they used it to the full. With the multiple resources of the S. M. R. to aid them (besides what they had taken over of the Chinese rolling-stock), they had an overwhelming advantage in this matter of transport. Troop trains, supply trains and hospital trains arrived with disconcerting regularity from the north—and in broad daylight, for at this time not a single Chinese plane had visited the northern front. A formidable reserve of cannon, horses, and brand-new American motor trucks accumulated round Peiping in preparation for the North China offensive.

As against all this military activity, there was only one passenger train a day from Peiping to Tientsin. It left at daybreak, and with luck might make Tientsin—normally reached in two hours or so—by nightfall. While it lasted, it was probably the most crowded train in the world.

We arrived at the station early (as we thought) and prepared for a strenuous journey; but a first survey of the "Tientsin Express" was not encouraging. Half Peiping seemed to be there before us. "Why did we buy first-class tickets?" Snow asked disgustedly. There was one first-class car, but that was reserved for Japanese. The rest of the train contained already about two thousand travelers, and the number was mounting rapidly.

"It *was* a little unnecessary.... Well, there's still the buffers and the roof. There's more room on the roof, but it's going to be hot."

We chose the buffers, and hoisted ourselves into a strategic position between two third-class coaches. Both of the platforms were already occupied by Chinese refugees who had settled in with their household bundles. One of them laid a sack of flour across the coupling for us to sit on. "That is a bad place," he warned us. "Very dangerous when the train starts." He illustrated in lively pantomime what might happen to our legs, and then, as if in consolation, offered us a handful of melon seeds.

The station might already have been Mukden. A braying loudspeaker addressed us now in Japanese, apparently for the benefit of the stout uniformed officers and gentlemen with briefcases who had begun to make their appearance. These were the new rulers of Peiping, active as ants about the business of empire.

We pulled out from Ch'ienyangmen on time, an event which raised our hopes unduly. Five minutes later the train ground to the first of what proved to be a series of agonizing stops. Over a complicated maze of points, a lone engine was rehearsing the approach to Peiping. Or it may have been that the two Japanese soldiers who drove it were just playing trains. After an hour they got tired of the fun; the engine shunted off, and we moved slowly on.

It grew very hot on our crowded platform. But at least we were better off than the people inside, and at every halt we got off and strolled along the line. We had discovered that there was a sealed carriage at the end of the train, mysteriously guarded by Chinese police; a communicative trainboy informed us that it contained a certain Chinese general with his family. This privileged traveler, it appeared, had a position in the Chinese National Railways. We observed with some satisfaction that when a group of Japanese soldiers later boarded the train, they showed scant respect for the general's private car.

It was a deserted countryside through which we passed, the green fields stretching wide and empty under a glare of sun. But every station had its garrison of Japanese troops, usually with a lookout posted on the roof. Then *"Ta mati!"* * ejaculated one of our fellow-passengers, and pointed down the track. We saw where all the peasants had gone.

Labor gangs of Chinese coolies, directed by armed Japanese guards, were hard at work cutting down the kaoliang on either side of the railway. This is a regular measure of precaution taken by a Japanese army of occupation; the standing crops, in midsummer, afford a perfect protection for bands of guerillas and snipers. For the peasants of Hopei, it was a first taste of the new rule they had come under. Menaced by Japanese bayonets, they were being forced to level miles of their own crops just before the harvest ripened. This countryside had escaped the devastation of war, only to come under a new devastation of "peace."

Tientsin we approached at dusk through a fringe of ruined schools and factories. Most melancholy sight in all this desolation was the wreck of Nankai University, once famous as a center of liberal economic studies. Here the invaders had not been content with shelling the buildings in the brief action around Tientsin; what survived the bombardment had been worked over by a demolition party. With a number of outstanding grudges to settle, the Japanese had made a thorough job of Nankai.

The East Station, too, bore the scars of battle. And here, when our trainload of exhausted humanity emptied out on to a barricaded platform, every passenger had to pass the scrutiny of a posse of detectives. Only a couple of hundred yards separate the

* An impolite Chinese expression.

railway terminal at Tientsin from the foreign Concessions; but that narrow strip of enemy territory, as we knew, had proved the undoing of many Peiping refugees. Now, as we watched the station entrance, Japanese guards emerged with a group of youthful Chinese. Boys and girls in rough country clothes, they still kept the unmistakable air of intellectuals. Students probably.... They were marched off under escort. They had been unlucky. We felt sorry for the girls.

The impressive façade of heavy foreign-style buildings along the Tientsin Bund—the Banks, Corporations, Trading and Shipping Companies of five nations—looked stable and prosperous as ever. Inside a Foreign Concession one is within a citadel of Western imperialism, and it gives a convenient sense of security in times of crisis. But how long, I wondered, could this citadel hold out against the new pressure of Japan? These walls might soon become as idle as the moated palaces of Peiping.

Outside the shipping office where we had gone to check our passages to Tsingtao, I was hailed effusively by a shirt-sleeved student, who wrung my hand and led me to a warehouse that sheltered several hundred refugees from the universities and high schools of Peiping. Many of them were in desperate plight; they had very little money, and the compradores who farmed out steerage accommodation on ships going south were charging fantastic rates even for a deck ticket.

"What are you going to do when you get south?" I asked them. There were a dozen different answers. Some planned to join the army; but the boldest spirits among these had already made contact with the first mobile units operating in the hills west of Peiping. One group—it was the most enterprising thing the Chinese had done since the Japanese occupation of Peiping—had broken into the city jail near Hsichihmen, released some four hundred political prisoners, armed them from the prison magazine, and escaped under cover of night into the hills. This was the kind of action the students yearned after, though few of them were resolute enough to undertake it on their own initiative.

For some years, the Chinese students had been one of the most vocal elements in the country demanding active resistance to Japan: it was a common charge against them that they did little more than talk about it. But in general, it must be conceded that the students responded pretty well to the war situation. With a greater sense of responsibility than any other section of Chinese society, their chief problem, at this stage of hostilities, was to find some practical expression for their passionate beliefs. And increasingly, in these next months, they were to find it.

This group in Tientsin was typical. About half of them were making their way to the "emergency university" center in Changsha, or to new establishments set up in the interior, where they could continue their studies. This westward movement of schools and colleges would bring a new intellectual life to remote Chinese provinces; it could not fail to stimulate the political awakening of the vast hinterland of China. But many had already decided that they had had enough of their books, and were looking for ways to engage directly in war work. The great task of mobilizing the Chinese people for the final struggle against Japan lay ahead of them. It had given these ardent young propagandists a new opening, a chance to work among the masses of their countrymen that had not existed since the revolutionary years of the 'twenties.

Among this band was one thin and nervous youth I had known before as an active member of the old Students' Union in Peiping. Already he was twice an exile, for his home—before 1931—had been Manchuria. His face was prematurely lined, and there was a fanatical look about his eyes, but his voice now was controlled and steady. I asked him where he was going.

"First to Shantung," he said. "I shall try to work in mass mobilization there. And then perhaps to Shansi. You are going south?"

"Somewhere behind the Chinese lines," I told him. "We may meet again."

I did not know then how much I was to see of Wu in the months to come.

"Heaven send us no hurricane," breathed the young missionary beside me, "or there'll be more souls lost at sea." He had once been mate in a China coaster himself, so should have known what he was talking about. "Have you ever read Conrad's *Typhoon?*"

From behind the spiked iron grille that protected the cabin class from pirates and vulgar deck passengers, we looked down on to the hatches of the S.S. *Hoihow*. It was a human maelstrom that eddied beneath us, where hundreds of refugees sought room among derricks and winches to unroll their pitiful bedding, or erect a matting shelter against the wind. Whole families sat disconsolately on the single bundle that contained all their household belongings; energetic old women with bound feet bargained vociferously for points of vantage. For every yard of deck space had been auctioned.

"*Lao Chungkuo*," my companion was saying. "Old China— the worst of her faults. You'd think the compradores, or the deckhands at least, would have some sympathy for these poor wretches. But not they, if there's the chance of a few more dollars! When the Chinese learn to think communally, instead of just for themselves, they'll be the greatest people in the world."

He was returning, I knew, to a country station in Hopei directly in the path of the Japanese advance, to give what protection he could to his own Chinese friends. It was the kind of action for which some foreign missionaries at Paotingfu were to pay with their lives.

"But surely these things must change, in a crisis like this?"
"Perhaps they will. It's China's only hope...."

Chefoo in normal times is a sleepy little town on the north coast of the Shantung peninsula, and a summer base of the U. S. Asiatic Fleet. Here we went ashore for a couple of hours, to eat American ice cream in the "Navy Y" and see how Shantung was responding to the war.

It was something to see the Chinese flag flying again; but we were unimpressed by Chefoo's defenses. Magnificent sandbags had been erected along the promenade, but it was unlikely that the Japanese or anyone else would want to land conveniently just below them. Meantime, the local troops sat around in the sun and scratched themselves with supreme indifference. They had not been paid for months.

"The commander here got $200,000 to defend Chefoo," one foreign resident informed us. "He farmed out the job to a friend of his for a hundred thousand, and retired with his cut. I think his friend must have been a building contractor, hence all the sandbags and cement. But then, it makes a good show...."

"Have they got any guns?"

"There are some fine old antiques in the fort, but they were rusted up years ago. Then there are supposed to be two antiaircraft guns, but someone found out that the sights cost almost as much as the guns, so they economized by just buying the guns. Without the sights, of course, the guns are useless."

"Old China again. Han Fu-chu, governor and military despot of Shantung, was supposed to have a fairly effective army, but this was not a very promising sample of it. General Han, like his old crony Sung Cheh-yuan in Peiping, had played off the Japanese for years by relying on his native wit; but that would not serve him much longer. At this time, Shantung had still escaped any serious invasion. Han Fu-chu was clever enough to gain himself this temporary reprieve, but in the end his cleverness proved too much for all concerned. He was to meet the death of a traitor, *pour encourager les autres*.

From the sea, Tsingtao has nothing Chinese about it. Redtiled villas suggest South Germany; the twin towers of a Marienkirche dominate the skyline. Once this flourishing port was to all intents and purposes German, an answer to Russian-leased Port Arthur and British Weihaiwei. The Germans built Tsingtao and the railway into the rich province behind it; but Japan took over during the World War, and the Tsingtao-Tsinan line had been a Japanese sphere of influence ever since.

All Japanese nationals had already been evacuated from Shantung when the *Hoihow* deposited us on a cobbled quay, pleasantly shaded by acacia trees. We took a horse-carriage, and clattered along to our hotel through streets lined with Japanese shops, all closely shuttered and officially sealed by the Chinese authorities. Japanese property in Tsingtao alone was valued at some three hundred million yen: it was the largest Japanese investment in China, outside of Shanghai. And the burning question of the hour was then, what were the Chinese going to do about it?

We asked this question next day of Admiral Shen Hung-lieh, Mayor of Tsingtao, as he sat blandly in a reception-room of his Municipal Offices overlooking the bay. Chinese admirals are rarer than Chinese generals, and they are apt to be more experienced in political than in naval maneuvers. Shen Hung-lieh was no exception: this plump, smooth-faced official in a palm-beach suit and silk shirt had little of the air of a mariner, though he had once done a period of naval training in England. But as a diplomat he was superb.

"Japan is invading China," Snow insisted bluntly, "both in the north and in Shanghai. Does the Chinese Government intend to confiscate this enemy property or not?"

But we got no change out of Admiral Shen, who stalled politely and evasively for a couple of hours. "War has not been declared between China and Japan," was the burden of his replies. "In the meantime, we have guaranteed the safety of foreign investments. Of course, we cannot say what might happen if the Japanese were to attack Tsingtao. . . ." He sat back comfortably and sipped his excellent tea.

Four months later, shortly after the fall of Nanking, Tsingtao leapt into the headlines with the news that the valuable Japanese mills had been blown up and destroyed by "Chinese irregulars." Not many days elapsed before a Japanese squadron sailed into the bay, and a naval landing-party made a "bloodless occupation" of the Shantung port. The Mayor of Tsingtao had disappeared; that, after all, was to be expected.

I was to hear the news of the final destruction of Japanese property at Tsingtao over the Japanese radio, from a remote army headquarters in the hills of North Shansi. The voice of the Tokyo announcer quivered with indignation as he described this latest "Chinese outrage." And I thought then of smooth old Admiral Shen, and his discreet official assurances. In any situation where they still held bargaining power, the Chinese could never be at a total disadvantage.

SIAN REVISITED

But Shantung, that September, was about as depressing as it could be. For in those months of respite, while the Japanese armies pushed on in Hopei and Shansi, this province should have been the most active base of war preparations in the North. Instead, Han Fu-chu swore solemn pledges of loyalty, and did nothing.

This mood of procrastination, and even of deliberate obstruction, was reflected in the provincial capital of Tsinan. Han had stacked the cards pretty evenly; he had a line out with both Nanking and the Japanese, though the one thing to which he could ever be really faithful was his own interest. And he had gathered around him in Tsinan a choice selection of the discredited champions of the North. Most of them, in one way or another, were his own relatives.

There was Sung Cheh-yuan, of course; but there was also Sung's successor in office, the protean Chang Tze-chung, who after a week in Peiping with the Japanese had found the pace too hot, and had made his humble escape on a bicycle. Shih Yu-san, former commander of the Peiping police, belonged by right in the same galley. The only resolute "anti-Japanese" leader in the capital was General Yu Hsueh-chung, once a prime mover in the Sian coup under the Young Marshal, now returned to Shantung with a full command from the Central Government. Yu was maneuvering desperately to get his own troops into a key position at the front, in the hope of forcing Han Fu-chu's hand. But it was a forlorn hope: the one thing Han was determined *not* to do was fight.

The odds were too heavy here, as they had been in Peiping. The whole atmosphere reeked with treachery and pusillanimity on the part of responsible authorities; only when the "old gang" at the capital had been cleaned out, could any real front of popular opposition be built. When the final débâcle came in Shantung, and the Japanese armies rolled (it seemed, irresistibly) down the railway from Tsinan, Han Fu-chu made a last desperate bid for power. He took a large part of his army westwards out of Shantung, hoping to carve out a new sphere of influence for himself somewhere in the interior of China. But he was betrayed to the Central Command by his own officers, court-martialed, found guilty of disobeying orders, and shot. The only pity was that more of his kind were not sent the same way, and more promptly.

All this was yet to come, when we passed through Shantung that summer. But it was clear enough which way the wind was blowing. Somewhere in China—it was all we could hope—things must be taking a different course.

We had almost forgotten the war, in the pleasant autumnal sleepiness of Shantung; but we met it again at Hsüchow, junction of the Tientsin-Pukow railway with the east-west Lung-Hai line. The station had been bombed that day by Japanese planes, and more raids were expected. At least, in this strategic town for which one of the major battles of the war was soon to be fought, there was a new briskness of military activity. And the steel-helmeted, khaki-clad Central troops looked alert and well-equipped.

The whole Lung-Hai railway zone was a fortified area. It was here that Chiang Kai-shek, behind modern defenses prepared on the advice of his German experts (and every detail of which was known to the Japanese), expected to make his major stand in Central China. And the country we ran through next day—Kweiteh, Kaifeng, Chengchow—was to be the scene of the heaviest fighting in the whole North China campaign, before the Japanese finally broke through the Lung-Hai front. At this time, the Chinese were confident of their ability to hold the Lung-Hai indefinitely. Certainly they were better prepared here than anywhere else in China to meet the full strength of a Japanese attack.

Our train was leisurely enough, and stopped once or twice next day at an air-alarm. But it had not yet developed that addiction for hour-long halts in every cutting and tunnel that was to characterize all Chinese trains at a later stage of the war. On the morning of the second day, we drew in to the

SIAN REVISITED 75

neat little modern station of Sianfu. The first stage of our journey was over.

A year before, Sian had been a name known to few people outside of China. Late in 1936, it had gained a brief world-notoriety as the scene of the capture and detention of Chiang Kai-shek by one part of his own armies. But even before that time, as the largest city in the Northwest and one of the projected "inland capitals" of China, Sian had already emerged from the sleep of centuries. It was given increasing attention from the National Government, and had been to a very considerable extent modernized and "improved." Now, as the terminus of the long overland route from the U. S. S. R. through Sinkiang and Kansu, it had become an extremely important military base.

For both Snow and myself, as we stepped out on to the well-guarded platform, Sian had memories. It was from the Shensi capital that Snow had set out on his pioneer trip to "Red China," the *terra incognita* of the Northwest, some eighteen months before. And over the critical winter of 1936-37, I had spent two months here with the "rebels" of Sian while the city stood a virtual siege from the massed armies of the Nanking government. At that time, the American writer Agnes Smedley and I had been the only foreign journalists in Sian; and some of our efforts to tell the outside world what was happening there—in particular, an association in amateur broadcasting—had won us a very undeserved reputation for conspiracy. Snow, of course, after his visit to the Soviet district, had become a very suspicious character indeed in orthodox Kuomintang circles. And Sian, with the notable exception of those forty-four days of revolt, had always been a very good Kuomintang town.

I wondered what sort of welcome we should get this time. We were not left long in doubt. As we emerged from the train, a smart young officer in a steel helmet saluted and demanded our papers.

As luck would have it, I had a visa endorsed for Sian by the old Hopei-Chahar Political Council. The fact that this régime was now defunct did not seem to matter; I was passed with flying colors. But Ed, who had acquired a new and virgin passport before he left Peiping, had no Sian visa. The young officer drew his attention to the fact.

"No," Snow said patiently. "You see, we've just come from Peiping. And I couldn't get a visa there."

"Why not?"

"Because there was no Chinese government to issue one."

This obvious explanation, with the production of an official press card, got us past the military. But it was the civil authorities I was afraid of; and sure enough, these descended upon us at the barrier in the shape of a young and very conscientious member of the Special Police. Here press cards, eloquence, and bluff all failed. My worthless visa, it seemed, would let me into the city; but Snow was informed that he must leave without delay by the next train.

This was a complication, of the kind that is only too frequent in China. We stood on that familiar platform and looked helplessly at the walls of Sian. Ed for once was beginning to get ruffled out of his customary good humor. Then he had an inspiration. "When does the next train go?" he demanded. There was none, it seemed, until late afternoon. Admitting the point, the detective at last consented to allow us both to go to the hotel inside the walls, provided that he and a couple of his men accompanied us.

We made a triumphal entry through the gate in rickshaws, the police escort riding beside us on bicycles in a neat formation. Once inside the city, we counted on official assistance from the Eighth Route Army.

The Sian Guesthouse was familiar too. Here where all Chiang Kai-shek's staff had been arrested on that December morning nine months before, I had come to meet the young leaders of that amazing revolt, and listen to their confused and glowing plans for a united "war of national resistance" against Japan. For more than ten weeks I had lived in this hotel: the very corridors seemed peopled with ghosts. It was here, for the first time, that I had been conscious of a new determination in the Chinese people. And it was a good deal clearer, now, how much

Sian Revisited 77

had really hung upon the outcome of those December days of revolt.

As we entered the lounge, the manager greeted me like a long lost friend. "Welcome back to Sian!" There was an unaffected cordiality in his handshake; the war had brought us all closer together. "Have you come to meet Mrs. Sze?" he demanded.

"What, is she here?" For this was Agnes Smedley's Chinese name. The past was renewing itself with a vengeance; my last sight of Agnes Smedley had been in this hotel lobby, when she had gone off to join the Red Army. I had thought she was still up north in the "Special District."

"Not in the hotel. But she is in Sian—she arrived two days ago with Mrs. Snow."

This was the news Ed had been waiting for; his wife, then, was back from Yenan. "And Mrs. Snow?" Mr. Chow's face expressed his regret. "She left this morning by the express."

Our trains had crossed just a few hours outside Sian. But there was still time to send a wire to Tungkwan, and Peg could be back that night. "Can you send a message to Miss Smedley?" I asked, while all this was being arranged.

The friendly manager was all smiles. Out of those Sian days, it seemed, a real United Front had emerged. "Sure," he said. "She's staying at Eighth Route Army quarters. I'll ring up and ask her to come right over."

In the hotel lounge that had seen so many dramatic happenings the year before, we lit cigarettes and tentatively discussed plans. Ed was here, it seemed, only on sufferance; but at least he had got in touch with his wife, and they could travel back together to Shanghai. From the Eighth Route Army people we could get some general information about military and political developments. I was still uncertain about my next move, until we heard more from Yenan.

At that moment the door swung open, and a familiar figure, curiously attired in raincoat and sou'wester, strode across the threshold, followed by a uniformed bodyguard with swinging

Mauser. It was Agnes Smedley. Under the astonished gaze of the hotel clerks and our own official watchdogs, we exchanged greetings.

"Why the raincoat?"

"Well, I don't want to advertise this," Agnes responded. Beneath the waterproof, she wore a regulation Red Army uniform. "Let's go somewhere where we can talk!"

We moved to a hotel room; our detectives had vanished, at least for the time being, at the sight of the army guard. After all, he was a member of the National forces.

"You've just come down from the north?"

Agnes nodded. "Peg and I came with some of Liu Pei-che'ng's division. We rode horseback all the way—it rained six weeks here, and the roads were terrible. None of the trucks can get through." She was staying a few days in Sian, and then going on by train to Taiyuan, where Chu Teh had his field headquarters.

"And how is Yenan?" I wanted to know.

"Fine. But the army's all left by now. Are you going up there?"

"If I can make it."

"Well, you'll have to wait till the weather clears to get a truck. And I can tell you, you'll have some trouble getting out of Sian! We aren't popular here."

Everything pointed to further difficulties if I should try to make the trip north. Next day, when Peg Snow had returned, we all gathered at a reunion dinner. She was a picturesque figure too, in a blue Chinese gown such as foreign missionaries often wear in the interior.

"How do you like my traveling outfit?" she had demanded.

"You make a very charming missionary. But why?"

Peg wrinkled her nose disdainfully. "Sian! They don't like foreigners who make trips to the Northwest." She had only got through the cordon by climbing out of her hotel window in the middle of the night, to dodge the waiting detectives. Now she had returned as a missionary, with her guard—a hulking Hunan youth, who had made the Long March with the Red

ENTER THE RED ARMY 79

Army—most inadequately disguised as a middle school student. Travel in the interior of China, especially on the borders of the "Red" Northwest, is always a bit of a masquerade.

We saw the Snows off next day at the railway station, to the infinite relief of the Special Police, who still followed our every move. Peg's guard, sheepish in his middle school uniform, with a great bulge in his hip pocket where he kept his gun, was profoundly affected by this second parting.

"I hope you get up to Yenan," Ed told me from the carriage window. "It's really important to have a statement from Mao just now. But get across to Shansi as soon as you can. As the war develops, North China—and the Eighth Route Army—will come more and more into the picture."

He was going back to the Shanghai front, to the "big story," where two armies were locked in a desperate struggle for control of the largest city on the mainland. But one thing we both were sure of: Shanghai could not hold. And it might well prove to be in the hills of the north, where I was going, that the next stage of this war would be fought out.

ENTER THE RED ARMY

The uneasy state of the United Front at this time caused many difficulties. In Sian, perhaps, it was inevitable that there should still be considerable suspicion of the communists. The Eighth Route Army had been formally constituted by the Central Government in August, and shortly afterwards had opened a branch office in the Shensi capital. But the legality of the Chinese Communist Party was not officially recognized until late in September, with the open publication of a letter from General Chiang Kai-shek. I had arrived at Sian during this interim, when the hostility of the local authorities towards the communists and all their doings was scarcely veiled.

To shake off my private detective (who was really becoming rather a nuisance) I shifted across from the hotel to the Army Office. This was a modern building with an immense bomb-proof cellar, presided over by an eminently respectable old man with white hair who looked like a Kuomintang official. His name was Lin Pai-ch'u, and he was indeed an "Old Revolutionary"—an original member of Sun Yat-sen's party * in the early days. Trained as a civil servant, Lin had become a communist after the split with the Kuomintang in 1927, and for many years had been Finance Commissioner of the Chinese Soviet Republic. With his benevolent air and gentle, rather formal manners, he was an excellent ambassador of political unity in a situation which certainly called for diplomacy.

Comrade Lin's office was emblematic of the whole political imbroglio of 1937. The Eighth Route Army (whatever the newspapers might say about "*ex*-communists") was still a communist army, organized and controlled by the Chinese Communist Party, under the military command of the National Government. Thus, on the walls, Lenin and Stalin held the place of honor. But there was a large photograph of Chiang Kai-shek, flanked by a black-and-white poster of Chu Teh—a curious juxtaposition of army commanders who had fought each other with bitter determination for nearly ten years. From the opposite wall, the enigmatic features of Mao Tse-tung, former Chairman of the Chinese Soviets, gazed calmly with shrewdly narrowed eyes. And over all, infallible political solvent in China, the one figure to whom all groups and parties paid unreserved homage, was the portrait of the founder of the Republic, Dr. Sun Yat-sen.

"But the United Front is making progress," Lin Pai-ch'u assured me, "and it is only some of the old-style officials who will not work with us now. Since the army left for the front in Shansi, everywhere the common people have welcomed our march."

He gave me a few routine details of the mobilization of the newly-named "Eighth Route Army." Immediately on the outbreak of hostilities at Lukowchiao, the Reds had begun their preparations for this new and greater war. The Communist forces at that time comprised three main groups, the First Front, Second Front, and Fourth Front Red Armies of civil war days. Each of these units had been accustomed to operate independently; indeed, it was only towards the end of 1936, with the "grand reunion" of the Red forces after the Long March from

* The *Tung Meng Hui,* predecessor of the Kuomintang.

ENTER THE RED ARMY 81

the South, that they had come together for the first time in the Northwest. Thus each unit had its own individual staff, besides the main army command headed by Chu Teh.

When official sanction was at last forthcoming from Nanking, three new regular divisions—the 115th, 120th, and 129th—were formed on the basis of the old "front armies." The whole made up what was to be known as the "Eighteenth Group Army," or (in the current and more popular designation) the Eighth Route Army of the National Revolutionary forces.

As was only natural, Chu Teh, former commander-in-chief of the Chinese Red Army, was finally confirmed in his position as Commander of the new National Corps. P'eng Teh-huai, famous in his own right as one of the most experienced and belligerent of Red leaders, and for long a close associate with Chu Teh in Kiangsi, Hunan, and on the Long March, became vice-commander. The new division leaders corresponded closely to the arrangement of the old Red Army command. Lin Piao, youthful president of the Red Military Academy, author of the famous "short attack" which the Chinese Communists had perfected in the civil wars, and one of their ablest strategists, was given the 115th Division, with Nieh Jung-chen as second-in-command. This was perhaps the most experienced unit of all; it contained the nucleus of the old First Red Army led so brilliantly by Chu Teh and Mao Tse-tung in the years after 1927, and later commanded by Lin in person with no less striking success.

The 120th Division, chiefly made up of the old Second Front Red Army from Hunan, remained under the redoubtable Ho Lung, with Hsiao K'eh as his lieutenant. This was a combination which suggested unorthodox tactics and swift movement: Ho Lung, even in this most mobile of Chinese armies, had a reputation for lightning thrust and recovery. Finally, the 129th Division, comprising the old Fourth Army of Szechwan together with some more recently-recruited troops, was entrusted to Liu Pei-ch'eng—one of the most promising younger commanders—with the able assistance of the experienced Hsu Hsiang-ch'ien. Each division had a war time strength of 20,000 men. There were two brigades to a division, two regiments to a brigade.

Such was the force that Chu Teh was prepared to throw across the Yellow River to strengthen the Chinese resistance in the north. But marching orders from Nanking were unaccountably delayed until the end of August, when Chiang Kai-shek ordered his new command into Shansi, to co-operate in the "Second War Area" with other forces under the direction of General Yen Hsi-shan, aged governor of that province. The delay was unfortunate, for the presence of these experienced guerilla troops in the North Shansi hills during the month of August might have seriously impeded the Japanese advance.

Now, in September, when the Japanese had already taken Tatung and were beginning to come down into Shansi through the northern and northeastern passes, two divisions of the Eighth Route Army (the 115th and 120th) had at last reached the war zone, and found themselves for the first time within striking distance of the invaders. "At any time now," Lin informed me pleasantly, "we expect to hear news of the first engagement."

I was to spend nearly a week in Sian, for the rains continued for another three days, and there could be no question of a truck to the north. The Army Station, in addition to its regular staff, housed at this time some fifty students on their way to the new "Anti-Japanese University" in Yenan: since the opening of the gates to the Northwest, many thousands of young politically-minded Chinese had flocked from all parts of the country to this bare northern province. The numbers, in fact, were far too great for Yenan's scanty resources, and a system of elimination had been devised by which a stiff preliminary examination weeded out the most likely candidates. These were "finalists," who would pass the last tests in a little country town further north on the border of the "Special District." Most of them filled in the hours of waiting earnestly reading Lenin.

Then one evening—it was Saturday, September 25th—I was returning from a greasy game of tennis with a one-armed, thirty-year-old veteran of the Long March, when we were met by an ecstatic *hsiao kwei* * from headquarters. His red little face was

---

* Literally, "small devil"—a member of the "Young Vanguard" of the Eighth Route Army.

puckered with emotion. *"Ta yinchang! Ta yinchang!"*, he was chanting. "Great victory!" His account of it was a little incoherent, but there had been a radio message from Chu Teh: the Japanese had been defeated in North Shansi. "Three thousand killed," he repeated with obvious relish.

"That will be Lin Piao," said one-armed Tsai with quiet satisfaction. "Let us go quickly." He led off at a jog-trot across the muddy park.

In the army station, a jubilant crowd was milling around the bulletin board. There were few details; an enemy force had been surprised and routed near Pinhsingkwan, one of the smaller passes in northeastern Shansi, just below the Great Wall. The Chinese had occupied the pass. The news, if true, was certainly interesting: it meant the first real defeat suffered by a Japanese column in two months of war. But the *hsiao kwęi* who were running wild about the courtyard had no doubts. "Their" Red Army had met the Japanese, and beaten them, as they had always known it would.

The battle of Pinhsingkwan, in that last week of September, 1937, is notable in several respects, and not merely as the first encounter between the Eighth Route Army and the Japanese. It was an object lesson in tactics to the other Chinese forces in the north.

The Reds had always maintained the futility of a "passive" strategy of "simple defense" against superior enemy equipment. This war, they maintained, apart from the attempt to hold vital positions as long as possible, should be largely a war of maneuver, in which surprise attacks on the flank or rear of a moving enemy could reduce the defenders' disadvantage in technical equipment, and bring the Chinese, who were at their best in close fighting, to immediate grips with the Japanese infantry. In positional or long-range fighting, the Japanese would always have the advantage. But the Chinese, as the defenders, could have their choice of terrain, and the superior mobility of their lightly armed troops was their greatest asset.

At Pinhsing Pass, they had found ideal country to work in. And the enemy was formidable enough: the 5th Division, under

General Itagaki (later to become Minister of War in the Konoye Cabinet) was one of the crack regular forces of the Japanese Army. This division had arrived in Chahar after the storming of the Nankow Pass, and advanced with supreme confidence into Shansi, encountering practically no resistance from the demoralized provincial troops of Yen Hsi-shan.

While one part of the Chinese troops under General Kao Kwei-tze blocked the main route of their advance, two brigades of the Eighth Route Army secretly worked round to the Japanese rear, and launched a surprise attack on Itagaki's column. Not realizing that their communications had been cut, the Japanese rushed up reinforcements along the highway: these were intercepted by overwhelmingly superior Chinese forces, who trapped them in a narrow curving valley and demolished them at close quarters with hand grenades. Having destroyed the enemy reserves, the Chinese turned their main forces against the Japanese positions in the pass itself. In this running fight among the hills, the Japanese were unable to make any use of their artillery or mechanized equipment. Itagaki's headquarters was captured, the pass completely occupied, and the Japanese retreated in disorder, having lost a third of their numbers, and almost all their transport and supplies.

Such a battle, of course, could be in no way decisive; and it was unlikely that any Japanese commander, after so disastrous an experience, would advance in quite the same reckless manner into hill country. But the importance of Pinhsingkwan at this stage can hardly be exaggerated. It vindicated the communist tactics, put new heart into the Chinese resistance in Shansi, and altogether gave the Japanese a much better idea of what they were up against. With the development of positive, offensive tactics a new factor had entered into the Chinese resistance. And the Eighth Route Army had won its spurs in the anti-Japanese war.

The Sian police had begun to renew their interest in my movements, and it seemed that I had better be on my way, unless I wished to be forcibly deported. Agnes was leaving by train; with a military pass, there would be no difficulty about this. But

I had had a radio invitation and welcome from Mao Tse-tung in Yenan, and though the roads were still impassable further north, a provision truck was leaving next morning, taking some of the students to Yünyang. It seemed my best chance to get out of Sian.

That night, there was an impromptu concert in the army station. It was partly to celebrate the news from Shansi, partly a meeting called to hear a long report on the war from Lin Pai-ch'u. Everyone gathered in the largest room of the building, from Mrs. Chou En-lai down to the smallest and dirtiest *hsiao kwei*, and squatted on the wooden floor—in itself, an unaccustomed luxury. When the reports were finished, the concert, an informal and high-spirited affair, began.

Even in so scratch an assembly, the variety of items was amazing. For here, it seemed, all sections and dialects of China met. One Peiping student sang a complicated classical aria from an old opera; another strummed modern tunes on a guitar. A Cantonese worker sang husky river-songs, and was followed by a pock-marked army veteran who played plaintive Kiangsi airs on a bamboo flute. One-armed Tsai broke in with a spirited account of the famous "Crossing of the Tatu Bridge"—perhaps the most celebrated single episode in the ten-year history of the Chinese Red Army. He told it in the ample manner of the professional Chinese story-teller, and the *hsiao kwei* and students hung round-eyed upon every word. There were dances by the children, and an expressive monologue (mostly grunts, and entirely unintelligible to everybody present) from a dark-skinned Miao * girl.

The two foreign guests, of course, were called upon for an item. Agnes, who had enough of a voice, sang American cowboy ballads. I fell back upon a souvenir of football days, and contributed a New Zealand Maori *haka*, which was militant enough to be received with great enthusiasm. I explained it, perhaps not unjustly, as an anti-imperialist war dance. The last song, appropriately enough, was a "Ballad of the Long March." Based on one of the oldest and most beautiful of Chinese folk-songs, this tells, in each successive stanza, of one month in the progress of

---
* A member of one of the aboriginal races of southwestern China.

the Red Army on its year-long trek from the south. It was the living tradition of a modern epic.

Most Chinese armies—this is one legacy of the old war-lord regionalism—are drawn from separate provinces, and their commanders have always sought to preserve this local character of their troops. The weakness of the "old-style" provincial armies had already become only too apparent in the fighting in Hopei, Shansi, and Shantung. But the Red Army, in its wanderings across half China, from many-rivered Kiangsi, through the red earth of Szechwan and the "great snows" of Sikang, to the loess hills of the Northwest, had recruited peasants and workers, "anti-Japanese fighters," from a dozen Chinese provinces along its march. In this sense, then, more than any other force at that time, it was a representative army of the Chinese people.

Here in the north, it seemed to me, the influence of this "people's army" might change the whole course of Chinese resistance. For it was not by regular troops (as the Central Government was slowly beginning to realize) but only by the armed strength of the whole Chinese people, that China could ever hope to win this war.

THE TOMB OF HUANG TI

"Halt!" The crisp challenge rang out from the West Gate. "What truck is that?"

It was early morning, in that first hour after dawn when trees are black against a bare sky, and sentries' tempers are apt to be short. I could hear, but not see what was going on, for I was wedged firmly down in the body of the truck among a pile of rice sacks. Around and on top of the sacks were some twenty students, so I felt I might pass in the crowd.

"Eighth Route Army for Yünyang," our military escort answered from the cab. He must have handed over his papers, for there followed a lengthy pause. I was afraid the guards might want to search the truck, in which case I should have to do a lot of explaining; but from the outside little could have been visible except the heads of the students. And these, whatever revolutionary thoughts they may have harbored, looked innocent enough.

"All right." At length the guards seemed satisfied. "Open the gates..." The big truck lurched into gear, and sky vanished under a vaulted arch of stone. Then a glimpse of iron-studded gates, and the curving roofs of the gate tower as the truck swung clear. I stretched my cramped limbs, and came up gratefully for air. The students, settling down amid their bundles for a long ride, chattered enthusiastically as we gathered speed along the highway. We were outside the walls of Sian, on the open road to Shenpei.*

But the "open road" was a myth. We had set off in a burst of exhilaration unsuited to country travel in China, and especially at that time of year. It did not last long: at the first ferry crossing, our back wheels skidded on the greasy bank and ended up in the Wei river. We salvaged the truck, but it took a whole afternoon to do it. And across the river it was worse. On an average we stuck in the mud and dug ourselves out again two or three times in every mile. Yünyang—a sprawling, rather decrepit district town which should have been only a few hours run from Sian—we reached, in very chastened mood, only at the end of the second day.

Here, where our students remained to prepare for their "political finals," I was to spend another three days waiting for the roads to improve. By that time I had developed a proper fatalism, and did not regret the delay so much. It gave me a chance to get used to the daily round of army life that was to become so familiar in the next few months. And here, in a little farmhouse where we shared a loft together, I met my traveling companions to Yenan.

There were four of them, and they made a curiously assorted group. Two were party members, returning to report from "outside." One of these was a young graduate of the Sun Yat-sen Institute in Moscow, who now held a secretarial post in a provincial government. With the tight-lipped manner and self-contained air of a professional diplomat, he was dressed in a black official uniform and dark overcoat, and never seemed to look untidy. Comrade Sun thawed out a little as we advanced

* "North Shensi," the communist Special District.

our journey by progressive stages of dirt and discomfort, but he never lost for long his intense and brooding preoccupation with political affairs. He struck me as a first-class brain under considerable tension, who would probably benefit from a month or two of "holiday" in Yenan.

Much more picturesque and approachable was the second communist, who had been a Red Army commander under P'eng Teh-huai, and was certainly a man of action rather than a politician. His name—though I doubt if it was his real one—was Chang Min, and what he had been doing in Shanghai I never discovered. He was a bold, restless figure in a shabby leather jacket and tweed cap, and carried a gun in an open holster in the best cowboy tradition. He had an amazing fund of anecdotes, a highly inventive and practical mind, and was (as we discovered on several notable occasions) a cook of something like genius.

The other two were considerably older, and were visiting Yenan as political delegates from southern provinces. One was a university professor, a comfortable little man with a thin Chinese beard, who wore the conventional blue silk scholar's gown. He was an authority on Japan, and carried about with him constantly a black leather portfolio which he never let out of his sight. Of us all, he seemed to suffer most from the primitive living conditions we encountered. He made no secret of his distaste for plain living, and embraced Chang Min as a brother when that resourceful campaigner, from the one unpromising local restaurant, produced a magnificent *latze chi*.*

The fourth man was the most difficult of all to place. In plus-fours and a distinguished beret, he had a pleasantly cosmopolitan air; and had indeed traveled, it appeared, in most of the countries of Europe. His manner was almost excessively refined, and his conversation ran most naturally on art and letters. At first, I had supposed him the director of some learned institute; but he had an erect carriage and a physical vigor uncharacteristic of the Chinese scholar. He turned out to be a provincial general and a millionaire. Yenan, it seemed, had some strange visitors.

* Chicken cooked with pepper and spices in the Szechwan style.

The Tomb of Huang Ti

From Yünyang, we were told mysteriously, we could go north in the "little car." This proved to be a modern American limousine, originally a gift from the "Young Marshal" Chang Hsueh-liang, and a very strange apparition in the mud-walled barn of a Shensi farmhouse. But a brief inspection of this low-slung vehicle, and the already parlous state of its springs, convinced me that it would be useless on the sort of roads we would have to cover. Fortunately the driver shared the same point of view. We set out at last from Yünyang in one of the big Dodge army trucks, loaded (most uncomfortably for us) with second-hand sewing machines for the Yenan uniform factory.

The gateway to North Shensi is Chintzekwan, or "Gold Lock Pass": from here on to the northern bend of the Yellow River and Mongolia, there is nothing but hills. The pass itself is a famous haunt of bandits, and there, of course, we stuck again for several hours. We worked furiously to dig out the truck, with an armed guard scanning the hillcrests; but nothing more dangerous appeared in view than an occasional mountain hawk, drifting superbly across the pillared clouds. Before we cleared Chintzekwan, the rain broke again; and we spent another night upon the road.

The morning dawned fine and windy. We were off the plains, and the upland road dried more rapidly. Chang Min snuffed the air with an expert nostril. "There will be no more rain," he prophesied, "this year."

"You know this country?"

He grinned. "I've fought over most of it." To some effect, it seemed, for he knew the name of every town and village. And he was an accurate weather-prophet; there was to be no more rain before the November snows.

Over the first range, the country grew wilder, and villages were sparsely scattered along our way. Rare fortresses, sometimes no more than crumbling ruins, thrust up gauntly along the dark ridges; the peasants we met were swarthy mountaineers, who walked with a loose highland stride. And at Chichun, a little mountain town whose gray walls climbed abruptly to a watchtower and a gold-tiled temple, we met our first army garrison.

This was the old "Red Army"—both men and women wore still the black uniform with red collar tabs, and the black peaked cap with the red star, that had once been the terror of landlord and tax-collector over the length and breadth of China. For there had not been enough new "National" uniforms as yet to fit out more than those troops who had left for the front, and meantime these peasant-soldiers clung to the familiar emblems with the habit of years. Sun told me that in their fondness for the red star under which they had fought so long, many of the Eighth Route Army regulars still wore their old caps, *inside out,* beneath the new blue regulation headgear with the white Kuomintang sun. Here, I noticed, the rank and file still spoke of *"womenti Hung Chün"*—"our Red Army"; in Yenan, and at the front, I was to hear nothing but the new name, *"Ti Pa Lu."* *

These barren hills had their own wild beauty; but even to the undiscerning eye, they told besides a tale of history. I had noticed a look of great age about some of the temples and stone *p'ailous* we had passed; but Chinese architecture in general has found few enduring materials, and there are not many buildings that antedate the T'ang dynasty. On the plains near Sian remain still the ribbed outlines of the walls of the old Han capital of Ch'ang An, and I had supposed these, with the grave-mounds of the later Han emperors, to be the oldest authenticated monuments in China. But now, as we crossed a river into another dusty little town, with the inevitable crumbling temple set up against a ledge of hills, the professor started out of the lethargy into which traveling usually plunged him.

"This is Ch'eng P'u?" His eyes lit up with the true archaeologist's zeal, and he examined the scene with unfeigned interest. "See," he said to me, pointing. "There is the oldest tomb in China—the Tomb of Huang Ti!"

Behind the temple roofs and shattered stone arches, rose a steep conical hill fledged with mountain pines. Its lines were roughly symmetrical, suggesting the shape of a huge grave-mound. Traditionally, this is the spot recognized by the Chinese as the burial place of their first emperor.

---

* "Eighth Route (Army)."

THE TOMB OF HUANG TI 91

Yao and Shun and Huang Ti, the shadowy "First Three Kings of China," have long been familiar in literature as heroic figures on the threshold of Chinese history. Recent researches have called back from the shadows something more than the names of a saga, and have surprisingly vindicated the written records. Of these mythical "three kings," Huang Ti is perhaps the most substantial; and there is considerable evidence to support the localization of his legend. If we may accept it, then the gravemound at Ch'eng P'u must be one of the oldest surviving monuments, dating back some five thousand years.

It was from these northwestern highlands that the first great Chinese migration, moving south along the Yellow River into the fertile plains of Honan, and east across the hills to Shansi, spread that indigenous Chinese culture which flowered in the earliest known dynasties.* By a strange trick of history it is in the shelter of these immemorial hills that the Chinese Communists—vanguard of the new China of the twentieth century, one of the latest-born of modern republics—have found their present home.

The oldest records of the first phase of Chinese civilization survive today in oracle bones, inscribed with the same ideographic characters that have persisted in China for forty centuries. But in the shadow of Huang Ti's mound, I took from the hands of a Shensi peasant, one of the millions in China who could never find time or teaching to master the intricate classical characters, a copy of the only Chinese newspaper that is regularly printed in latinized alphabet. It was the *Shin Dzunghwa Bao*, the "New China Press," published in Yenan.

"Can you read this?" I asked him. His weathered features creased in a ready smile.

"Of course! I learned to read in the Army School. This is about the Japanese imperialist robbers who invade our country, and the new United Front of the Chinese people."

A peasant can learn to read in "Latin hwa" in two months; it would take him two years or more to gain the same grasp of the classical characters. A new learning, it seemed, was flowing

* *Hsia* (c. 3000 B.C.) and *Shang* (c. 1500 B.C.).

out of the old Northwest; and it was planned to reach more than a few thousand long-robed scholars.

JOURNEY'S END

Not all of northern Shensi is barren moorland. Beyond the first ranges we crossed with such difficulty, our road led out upon a fertile plateau, with smooth well-tilled fields shaded by immense trees. It was a pleasant landscape in the soft afternoon light, patterned with contrasting shadows where deep ravines gashed the yellow loess. In the distance could be seen the walls and towers of a considerable city.

"Lochwan," Chang observed with satisfaction. "At last we can have a comfortable night. For my friend is now commander here."

Center of a favored agricultural region, Lochwan is the biggest city between Sian and the "Special District" of Shenpei. For some months after the Red Army reached the Northwest, it served as a kind of unofficial boundary between "White" and "Red" territory. It was here that Chang Hsueh-liang held his first conversations with Red leaders, in the summer before the Sian coup. Now Lochwan was one of the so-called "United Front" districts, jointly administered by the Shensi provincial authorities and the Communists. But the city—like other towns we had already passed through—was garrisoned by communist troops.

Chang Min's friend—"Comrade Chen!"—turned out to be a young Brigade Commander in the 129th Division, with dancing eyes and the swift, impulsive manner of the south. He made us free of his headquarters with informal hospitality, explaining that he had expected us three days before. Brigadier Chen, I noticed, wore the regulation blue Chinese army uniform, without any marks of rank. But he also wore at his breast pocket a five-pointed metal star, white enameled, with the gilt figure of a horseman and the dates "1927-1937." It was the first time I had seen this star—the only decoration in the Eighth Route Army. Before long, I learned to associate it always with positions of responsibility, whatever the youth of the wearer. It signified ten years' active service with the old Red Armies.

"Do you know *Shih-lou?*" had been Chen's first question. This was Edgar Snow's Chinese name; and when I answered in the affirmative, the young brigadier was delighted. Snow, I was to discover, was far and away the most popular foreigner in the Northwest; other journalists from "outside" had visited Shenpei after him, but none had made such an impression. Snow—and Agnes Smedley, who had stayed even longer in the Red capital —were the only "foreign friends" whom everyone knew by name. Later visitors were referred to by various circumlocutions, not always flattering. I was to become *"Yingkuo chich'e'rh,"* "the English journalist," (which was at least distinctive, for most of my predecessors had been American: I was the first British visitor to reach Yenan).

In that brigade headquarters, the accent was emphatically on youth. None of the officers, it seemed to me, could be much above thirty; and every room was thronged with *hsiao kwei,* those diminutive recruits who are to be found wherever this army travels. The "little devils" in this brigade were more than usually curious, and my appearance (like that of any other *"Ta pitze"* or "Big-nose") seemed to fascinate them. It was not surprising, perhaps, for I was wearing shorts, and had not shaved for a week.

"How old are you?" one youngster asked me seriously, after I had already overheard him discussing this interesting question with his companions.

"Twenty-eight," I replied, adding an extra year in the Chinese fashion.

"That's the same as Commander Chen," he informed me with interest. He was fourteen himself, I discovered, and had been in the army for three years. And he had done the Long March, so had reason to consider himself a veteran.

Everyone who has come in contact with the Chinese Red Army (or the Eighth Route Army, for the same organization continues under the new banners) has found something to say in praise of the *hsiao kwei,* "Young Vanguards," to give them their official designation. They are unique: to meet them is rather like meeting in real life those improbable bugle boys and powder monkeys of fiction whose juvenile exploits were so dear to a more adventurous world than ours.

These youngsters in uniform, of all ages from ten to sixteen, are to be found in every branch of the army. Many are orphans; more have run away from home, or from the factories to which they have been apprenticed or sold by their impoverished families. Though their unfailing cheerfulness does much to encourage the general high spirits of the army, they are far from being just mascots. They have their regular duties as messengers and orderlies, and are often organized into special service units to do intelligence or propaganda work. In the traveling theater companies they are always well represented, and their education is never neglected for long. When they have earned the right to carry a gun of their own they may take part in actual fighting; and here they have proved themselves utterly fearless, with the annihilating and unself-conscious devotion of the very young.

It is only when one knows something of the old China, with its universal ruthless exploitation of juvenile labor in city sweatshops and rural industry, that one can really appreciate the miracle that freedom and a sense of responsibility have worked in the lives of these youngest fighters in the National Revolution. Their reckless gaiety, their gamin independence, are a new phenomenon in a Confucian society. For the first time, children born into the most oppressed class of the most oppressed country on earth have chosen for themselves what their lives shall become, and have identified themselves with a movement reaching far beyond the old ties of family or village. They belong to the new China they are helping to build: Old China can never reclaim them now.

Lochwan refreshed us, but again the roads undid us. We had left in high hopes of reaching Yenan the same day, but in a tiny cave-village we learned that a landslide had brought down heavy boulders across the way ahead. Nothing on wheels could get through until these had been cleared with dynamite. It was checkmate at last. We would have to abandon the truck.

Chang Min—always the most enterprising member of the party—found out the nearest army station, and telephoned to

Yenan for horses. We arranged to meet these next day at Kanchwan, a town some fifty *li* to the north. We could hire mules to carry our baggage, and walk the intervening stretch.

It was rather a relief to get rid of the truck, I reflected as we took the road next morning. At least we were reasonably sure of reaching our destination on our own legs. The machine, at best, is fallible; in China it is very fallible, for it has much to contend with. And the real pleasure of travel here, as in any Asiatic country, is to be on the road, a part of that endless procession of humanity that ebbs and flows, summer or winter, along these dusty or frozen highways.

For the roads of China are seldom deserted. Carriers, muleteers, peddlers, itinerant tinkers and knife-grinders form one part of a constant stream: to these must be added commonly priests, bandits, vagabonds, and mere peaceful travelers. But the road to Yenan, in these days, was a kind of pilgrimage, with its own special company of wayfarers. We fell in with one group of students who had walked all the way from Sian to attend the new Shenpei University. Girls in flannel slacks and blue denims strode along manfully, with all their baggage in a single bundle; one sunburnt youth who accompanied them told me that this was part of the process of "hardening themselves" for the "anti-Japanese struggle." They were counting (accurately enough) on few comforts in Yenan, once they had arrived.

"Are you a communist?" I asked this young student, who had introduced himself as a graduate from a Christian college in the north.

"No," he said frankly. "Before, I belonged to no political organization. But now that we wage the sacred war of national liberation, many of us feel that we can learn best from the Eighth Route Army. The leaders in Yenan have great political experience, and they know especially about partisan tactics and mass mobilization. We come to learn these things in the Northwest."

"Where were you at the time of Lukowchiao?"

"I was in Shanghai; and at once I went to Nanking to volunteer my services. But in Nanking there was nothing—only the old officials, the old bureaucrats. Always we were told to wait in an office, then come back the next day. Many were turned away like this. Such methods cannot help China: we all wanted to have practical training, to work among the people. Then my friend who is in the Party School in Yenan wrote to me and told me of the new *Shenpei Kunghsueh*,* where many students have come since the United Front. I did not tell my family where I was going, but took the train for Sian."

There was a desperate earnestness about this brief narrative, and the tone in which it was delivered. And there was good human material among these young political pilgrims. It was not because they were afraid to take a rifle and go into the front lines that they were here; they could not get the rifle anywhere else. And most of them were only too painfully aware of the shortcomings in their training.

"Before, our lives were much too sheltered," my young informant continued. "We trained our minds, but not our bodies. Now in Yenan we will get another kind of training, and find some work that will be really useful for the war."

It was certainly one of the weaknesses of the Chinese National Government in the first months after Lukowchiao, that it took so long to adopt a realistic approach to the problem of war mobilization. One result had been that many volunteers, especially those with radical sympathies, had turned naturally to the Northwest when they had met discouragement in other places. Paradoxically enough, in the big cities and in the "revolutionary" south the mass movement lagged. It was in the more primitive, politically backward northern provinces, that were the first affected by the war, and where the communists had the chance to work most freely, that a genuine popular resistance to the invaders first developed.

Kanchwan, a bleak windblown town guarded by a massive citadel, was reached in good time: and we found that the horses had already arrived there. We put up at the only decent inn, ate heartily of noodles and one of Chang Min's triumphant improvisations, and spent the evening watching a traveling theater company play old Shansi drama in the marketplace. A

* "North Shensi (Anti-Japanese) Academy."

sound night's sleep restored everyone's good temper—even that of the unathletic professor, whose feet had suffered on the day's march, and who had twice fallen off his mule. In the morning, we were all a little excited, for Yenan was only sixty *li* away. After one look at the horses, however, the provincial general decided to wait for the arrival of the truck: perhaps he felt he would lose too much face by being seen on such a screw. They were certainly not handsome—a string of scrubby little ponies, with a most nondescript assortment of saddles and bridles. The guard who had ridden over with them apologized profusely for his mounts; all the good horses, he said, were already at the front. These were the best that were left. But all of them—he assured us—"could gallop."

And so it proved. The appearance of these northern ponies is highly deceptive: they are hardy little beasts with almost incredible stamina. Their best pace is not so much a gallop as an animated scurry, and they can keep it up for hours. With Chang Min in the lead on a wicked-looking sorrel, we lost no time on the road. There was one more range to cross, and we took a short cut over it. Beyond, the many-folded hills opened out into a narrow valley, running straight to a pass. Crowning the pass, a watchtower and sentinel pagoda were outlined against the blue.

It was Yenan at last, and our ponies, headed for home, needed no urging. We swept down the valley in the best Mongol style, splashing through the shallow fords. On either hand, rocky outcrops were bold with painted slogans: here the very hills seemed instinct with life, and we passed several groups of armed peasants practicing extended order drill in this ideal guerilla terrain. From a narrow ravine echoed suddenly the rat-tat of a machine gun; and the sorrel pony shot ahead.

"*Man tsou, man tsou!*" the professor pleaded vainly; he was still clutching his precious portfolio, which he had slung over one shoulder with a cord. But it was no use. The last half-mile was an open race, with the guard yelling wildly to clear the road, and delighted peasant children waving us on. I had a brief impression of a wide playing field beside the river, where soldiers in faded blue uniforms were playing tennis and basket ball; of high cliffs overhung by temple roofs. Then we bucketed over a ditch, pounded up the last slope, and arrived—more or less together, and with about as much noise as a cavalry charge—underneath the battlements of Yenan.

Ready hands took the horses' reins, as we stamped our feet and beat clouds of yellow dust from our clothes. Chang Min had vanished within the walls, but through the gathering crowd a young officer came running. He halted to give us a sweeping inclusive salute, along with a broad grin of welcome. "Welcome, comrades! You must be tired, if you ride so fast. Come in and drink some tea!"

Counting delays, the journey of a mere 200 miles from Sian had taken us ten full days. But we had already forgotten that, as we followed our guide through the gates of the Red capital.

CHAPTER THREE
RED CHINA AT WAR

INSIDE YENAN

I had never seen a more picturesque Chinese city. Yenan at first sight is as fantastic as a Sung painting. It lies in a pass where two rivers meet, at the base of precipitous cliffs. On the west side, battlemented walls climb steeply to a jutting crest, with a watchtower that dominates the sea of hills beyond. The town itself is compactly built across the valley floor, the eastern walls rising directly from the water's edge. And across the river the cliffs rise again, crowned with ruined temples and a lone pagoda.

Centuries ago, this city played a not insignificant rôle in Chinese history. The present walls date from the Sung dynasty, when Yenan was an outpost of the old empire against the "northern barbarians" who so often swept down south of the Wall from the Mongolian plateau. But like many other towns in the Northwest, Yenan had suffered continuously in more recent times from the ravages of incessant civil and religious wars; and it was the mere shell of a mountain capital that the communists entered peacefully early in 1937, to set up here the government of what was to become "The Special Border District of Shensi, Kansu, and Ninghsia."

Before this time, Yenan had been garrisoned by the troops of Marshall Chang Hsueh-liang, in the days when the Chinese Reds were "bandits," and the Young Marshal an unenthusiastic "Bandit-Suppressor." Then the Red capital had been in Pao An, a *hsien* city more than a hundred *li* to the west. It was in Pao An, in the summer of 1936, that Edgar Snow met and interviewed for the first time Mao Tse-tung and other Red leaders.

At the time of Snow's visit, Yenan was still under a communist blockade.

The garrison of those days—"Tungpei" troops of the Young Marshal—must have been very apprehensive of their formidable neighbors, for they had labored prodigiously to strengthen the city defenses, had repaired the old Sung walls, and thrown up many earthworks on the outlying hills. But the Reds never tried to storm Yenan (as one of their commanders told me later, "a regiment could hold that town against an army"). Few citadels in that strategic region could be more favored in the way of natural protection. It was only when the long truce between the Tungpei troops and the Red Army reached its climax in the peaceful settlement of the Sian revolt, that Chiang Hsueh-liang's men withdrew to the south of the province and the communists formally occupied Yenan.

When we arrived, Yenan had been capital of the "Special District" for nearly eight months, and the town had been galvanized into a new life. The population had trebled (it was at this time around 40,000) and trade had boomed—as was evident from the line of merchants' booths which reinforced the local shops along both sides of the curving main street. Soldiers, cadets from the military academy, men and women students from the new university, all mingled their gray-blue uniforms with the padded cotton jackets and bulging sheepskins of the Shensi countryfolk. Small as it was, Yenan had the authentic air of a capital. And politically, as the center of the Chinese Communist Party, now exercising an increasing influence within the United Front, it was perhaps the second city of China.

We were billeted in modest style in the "Guesthouse" of Yenan's *Waichiaopu,* or "Foreign Office"—surely the least pretentious building in the world to be dignified by so impressive a title. There were three guest rooms enclosing a tiny court, and the beds consisted of the usual brick *k'ang* in each room, covered with rush matting. But the place was scrupulously clean, and the white-painted walls were decorated with the now familiar portraits of Lenin and Stalin, and with colored scrolls bearing revolutionary slogans in several languages. An armed sentry posted at the gate soon after we arrived was, I felt, a friendly concession to "face" for the benefit of the southern delegates.

My own letters of introduction I presented to the "Commissar for Foreign Affairs," Wu Liang-p'ing, a young man who seemed to have a thoroughly diplomatic command of languages. In fluent English, he apologized for the "poor accommodation" Yenan could offer us; and invited me to dine with the other delegates and a group of officials at the co-operative restaurant. Here we were feasted in traditional Chinese style, with a wealth of dishes that seemed to belie the reports I had heard of Yenan's scanty fare.

"Do you often have meals like this?" I wanted to know. Wu shook his head, and addressed me in a confidential whisper. "No, of course not: this is only for our guests! While you are here, you will have the best food we can provide—that is the custom of Chinese hospitality. But we do not eat such food ourselves." Later, when I was more familiar with day-to-day life in Yenan, I realized that this was strictly true. These communists were no ascetics, and enjoyed as much as any Chinese (which means, rather more than most people) good food whenever they could get it. But the resources of Shenpei were severely restricted, and regulation diet in Yenan was unleavened Chinese bread or millet, with cabbage and perhaps an occasional meat dish thrown in. This was the standard ration for all, government officials included, unless there was good reason for a banquet.

Our first morning in Yenan happened to be graduation day and "opening of term" at the Military Academy, and to this we received a formal invitation. Comrade Wu called early to remind me of it.

"Mao Tse-tung is to speak," he told me. "It is one of the rare occasions when he gets up as early as this." I had heard before of Mao's nocturnal habits; as a rule he works late at night, and seldom rises much before noon.

The Red Academy, military and political training school for all ranks in the army, is one of the oldest regular establishments of the Chinese Communists. Its first fixed location had been in Juichin, the old Soviet capital in Kiangsu; but both before this, and later, when the Reds were dislodged from Kiangsu, it had continued as a "traveling school" with the army on the march. With the possible exception of the "Party School," it represented the most intensive training effort to produce cadres of leadership that the Chinese Red Army had developed.

At this time, the Military Academy was housed in a large and rather decrepit temple-building that had once been a middle school. The gates were gay with banners and anti-Japanese slogans, and there were several posters with inscriptions in English. One of these was headed "Welcome to the Foreign Friends of China!" and was illustrated by a macabre sketch of two individuals in foreign dress, one in a bowler hat smoking a cigar, the other with a check cap and what I could only believe was meant for an eye-glass.

"You see, you are expected," Wu said slyly, as I stopped to examine this masterpiece.

"Thanks. But I think your artist got his experience drawing caricatures of imperialists. Do I have to make a speech?"

"We should like you to. Something about the international position..."

Inside the wide court, some fifteen hundred cadets and officers squatted in rows on the stone paving. Above their heads—an epiphenomenon of the United Front—waved in unwonted proximity the twin banners of the Kuomintang sun and the red flag with the hammer and sickle. The speakers' platform was draped impressively, with inscriptions in several languages including Esperanto (for which Chinese revolutionaries have a curious fondness). "Long live the International Peace Front against Fascist Aggression!" the main banner exhorted us.

The meeting had not yet begun, and we made our way to the front through a smiling group of girl-cadets, smart and workmanlike in their belted uniforms. Room was made for me on a wooden bench, and someone passed the inevitable tea in a cracked enamel mug. Beside me, a tall, slightly stooping figure rose and extended a hand. I looked into shrewdly puckered eyes, under the brim of a faded blue cloth cap.

"Chairman Mao," said Wu.

Mao Tse-tung is no longer such a man of mystery as he used

to be when foreign writers, drawing recklessly upon hearsay, described this most famous of Chinese Communist leaders as a brain-crazed idealist, a fanatical invalid "suffering from an incurable disease," and the rest. But perhaps some remnant of the legend had left me unprepared for this first impression of the man himself. It was not easy to reconcile these smooth, unlined features, the still-youthful figure with a slight student's stoop, above all that boyish, mischievous, completely infectious good humor, with all one had heard of the "iron bolshevik" and fighting leader of China's Red Armies.

"Sit down, won't you?" Mao said in his thick, rather pleasant Hunan dialect, "and have a cigarette." He fished in the pockets of his unbuttoned cotton jacket, and produced a crumpled packet of "Pirates." "We can talk after the meeting."

At that moment a bugle band struck up the call for assembly. The cadets sprang to rigid attention; I looked across the rows of eager young faces to the blue cliffs beyond the river, still wreathed in morning mist, and the sun-flushed pagoda thrusting up above them. No film director could have designed a more picturesque revolutionary setting. Over our heads, the red flag with the yellow hammer and sickle was bright against the blue.

> *"Chi lai, chi han chao p'o ti nu li,*
> *Chi lai, chuan shih chieh ti tsui jen..."*

The men's voices blended with the hard metallic voices of the girls. Since I had been in China, it was the first time that I had heard the *Internationale* sung out loud.

After a brief introduction, Lo Hsueh-ching, hard-bitten Dean of the Academy, called on Mao Tse-tung to speak. Mao abandoned his cigarette with obvious regret, and climbed without ceremony on to the platform. He saluted briefly, and began to speak very quietly and naturally, with his cap pushed up from his forehead, hands clasped behind his back.

I watched for the oratorical tricks of the demagogue, but they did not come. Instead Mao spoke, in his homely dialect and with a continual lively play of peasant humor, in direct and concrete terms, intelligible even to the twelve-year-old *hsiao kwei* who refilled our mugs with tea. It was characteristic of him, I learned, that he never talked above the level of his audience. And while it is probably impossible to translate the tone and idiom of Mao's speaking style (for his stock of *t'uhwa* and "common expressions" was inexhaustible), with Wu's help I made enough notes to connect the main ideas of his speech.

"Comrades," he said, "for more than four hundred years, China has faced no such life-and-death struggle against foreign aggression as the present struggle of our people against Japanese imperialism. It is in such a time of crisis that the thirteenth class of the Red Academy now graduates, and the new term begins.

"Every effort we can make in this Academy must be directed towards this struggle. And though there are many armies in China, among them all our own People's Revolutionary Army has had in the past special experience to prepare it for this anti-Japanese war. To overcome Japanese imperialism, we must have a real revolutionary program! Such a program has not been realized as yet by all the Chinese armies.

"We need one army at least which has such a program, to serve as a model and example to the rest. The Eighth Route Army should be such a model army. We must set a friendly example to the other Chinese forces, not only by our heroism and discipline, but by our work among the masses, by organizing the Chinese people for the revolutionary war...

"We need, too, a new kind of strategy. The old kind of strategy means that an army has a rear, with military support and lines of communication. But if we have the full co-operation of the people, we do not need to have a rear. That is why our army has already been successful against the Japanese in North Shansi. And the more territory the Japanese robbers try to take, the more room there will be for us to work in!

"The Japanese armies have many more tanks and big guns and aeroplanes than we have; but this does not mean that we cannot fight them. We hope in time to get tanks and big guns and planes ourselves, but we can fight without these. Even if we had no rifles, so long as we have the full co-operation of the Chinese masses we can fight with sticks and stones!

"There never was an army yet, however well-equipped, that did not have its weaknesses. Our task is to find out in practice the weaknesses of the Japanese army. Then, if we are resourceful and determined, we shall be able to destroy it piece by piece."

Mao went on to describe the "three disciplines" of this communist army—to act strictly under orders; never in any way to violate the interests of the peasants and workers; to confiscate the property only of traitors and "pro-Japanese elements." "Remember," he said, "that you must not take even one potato from the peasants, for if you take one you will want to take more! This has been a weakness of some of the old-style Chinese armies, that they did not always respect the rights of the common people, and so did not always have a good relation with the people. Without such a close relationship, these armies cannot fight effectively.

"We remember the Last Will of Dr. Sun Yat-sen, where he said that, after forty years, the revolution had not yet succeeded; and that the reason why it had not succeeded was that the whole of the people had not yet been roused. That is the true spirit of Sun Yat-senism, of Marxism, of any revolutionary party! Now our Party and our army must have these two guiding principles: *first*, to concentrate our army to fight the enemy in the most effective way; *second*, to disperse our political forces to work among the Chinese masses, and rouse them thoroughly to join the struggle for national liberation and the democratic revolution.

"In order to rouse the masses to support us, we must improve their own livelihood. We must abolish heavy taxes, and lighten the economic burden of the masses. The Chinese people must be given arms to form partisan and mobile units, to co-operate with the regular armies. If all this is done, then we shall be able to operate against the enemy from all sides. And even if the Japanese enclose China by a blockade, we will always be able to enclose the Japanese armies, to cut off their rear and destroy their individual units.

"If only we can organize such a mass war as this, then very soon the Japanese armies will have no spirit left for fighting, and will begin to turn against their own commanders. So that is our task now—to allow no talk of compromise or surrender, but to work to prolong the war, to achieve the full co-operation of the whole Chinese people!"

When other speeches had brought the meeting to a close, we moved into the next court for an open-air banquet. This, the Dean of the Academy had already announced, was costing the District Government two hundred dollars; he justified such extravagance (it averaged about twenty cents per head!) by the fact that the graduating class would be leaving for the front almost immediately, and deserved some sort of send-off. There would be a special theater performance that night in their honor. . . .

I found myself seated with the rest of our group at a round table with Mao Tse-tung and Lo Fu, a spectacled ex-teacher, secretary to the Central Executive Committee of the Chinese Communist Party. Before the food arrived, Mao helped himself liberally to red pepper, which he ate "straight," licking it off his chopsticks with immense relish. "Do you eat this in England?" he asked me. And to my emphatic negative, "That's a pity—no food tastes good to a Hunanese without it!"

It was a friendly and informal meal. Clearly there was nothing wrong with the appetites of the Red Academy, though such fiery diet should have ruined their digestions years ago. Mao asked many questions about the international position; this was just after President Roosevelt's celebrated "quarantine-the-aggressor" speech at Chicago, when there had seemed for a moment to be some chance of Anglo-American action to restrain Japan. "What about the British labor movement?" he wanted to know. I told him of mass meetings in London, of resolutions of sympathy with China. "Yes, but can they force the British Government to take a more positive policy?" I found these political leaders in Yenan, remote as they were geographically, to be exceptionally well-informed about world affairs. "We get all the regular radio news," Lo Fu told me. "And of course, the Japanese military reports."

Mao smoked incessantly, even during the meal. This—and his inordinate love of pepper—seem to be his only vices: he had a special allowance from the District Government for cigarettes, "Pirates" being his favorite brand. When we had finished eating, and sat back with that sense of repletion that always follows a large Chinese meal, Mao drew a piece of paper towards him, and began to write in English, with some prompting from Wu Liang-p'ing.

"Promise to pay," he enjoined me, "five hundred dollars. *After* one hundred years." I initialed the bill he presented, which Mao folded up and placed carefully in his pocket as he rose to go. "If anyone ever claims this bill," he warned me solemnly, "there won't be enough money in the British Treasury to meet it—*at Chinese rates of interest!*"

CHINESE LENIN

No single commanding figure, no "Lenin in October," dominates the confused and troubled course of the Chinese Revolution. But each succeeding phase of this complicated historical process has produced its own representative leaders; and it may be convenient to list a few of these here, in order to gain some picture of the social forces at work in China today. For it is upon the co-operation of these social forces that the strength of China's resistance to Japan, and indeed the whole future of the Chinese people, must ultimately depend.

As the founder of the National Revolutionary Party of the Kuomintang, the visionary who never lost sight of his goal of a "free, democratic Chinese Republic," Sun Yat-sen earns with full justice the title of "Father of the Chinese Revolution." Across the stormy years which saw the final collapse of the Manchu Empire, down to the verge of the great "anti-imperialist" movement of 1925, the figure of this inspired and restless dreamer, whose life was spent with selfless devotion for a cause his own party was to betray, emerges with a startling and tragic distinctness. The strange blend of social idealism and political expediency which met in Sun Yat-sen was perhaps characteristic of a period in which a ferment of revolutionary ideas was only beginning to find expression in mass action. But "Sun Yat-senism," with its "Three People's Principles" of Nationalism, Democracy, and the People's Livelihood, at least charted the outline of the revolution in terms which common Chinese understood.

The National Revolution, however, triumphantly launched after Sun Yat-sen's death with the Northern Expedition of 1926, was arrested in mid-career early in 1927, with the developing split between the Right Kuomintang, led by Chiang-Kai-shek, and the Left (which included the Chinese Communists). Chiang established himself in power at Nanking, turned against the legally-elected government at Wuhan, and rapidly destroyed it. The Kuomintang, forgetting the bright hope it had at the outset of the great revolutionary movement that carried it into power, became frankly a party of reaction. It made its peace with foreign imperialism, and devoted the next nine years largely to the attempt to destroy by force all "opposition elements" remaining within the country.

If Sun Yat-sen was an idealist, Chiang Kai-shek was most emphatically a realist. By nature a conservative, with the training of a soldier and with military ideas of discipline, his policy for the "unification of China" meant above all consolidation of military power. But the political and economic base upon which the Nanking government rested was a very narrow one, and objectively the nine-year term of Kuomintang dictatorship was a disastrous period for the Chinese people. It was a period of unbroken civil war; and, coinciding with the new imperialist offensive of Japan, it resulted in a steady loss of Chinese territory with no attempt at serious resistance.

What had happened to the old revolutionary leadership during this interlude of political reaction? One by one the "heirs of Sun Yat-sen" had come over to join the Nanking government, or had sought the futility of exile in some center of disaffection. Only one group, the communists, remained in active opposition to what they considered the "betrayal" of the Kuomintang; and they were driven by the counter-revolutionary offensive of Chiang Kai-shek into the "Red Army phase" and the movement for Chinese Soviets.

The Soviet movement in China, restricted to the interior provinces, and fighting for its existence against overwhelmingly superior forces, achieved some astonishing successes. But the communists themselves had no illusions about the incomplete nature of anything they might achieve in isolation. By their own theory, there were two main revolutionary stages ahead before any transition to socialism could ever become possible: the "anti-imperialist" and the "bourgeois-democratic" revolutions. Both of these, they considered, had been interrupted in 1927, with the defection of the Right Kuomintang. Not until the Kuomintang itself, or a re-united National Government, could be persuaded to take up the struggle for national liberation where it had been left off, could there be any complete or enduring advance over China as a whole.

In the end, Japanese pressure proved more convincing than any political arguments could have been; and in 1937 the Kuomintang and the Communist Party came together again with the common aim of resistance to Japan. The Kuomintang, as the preponderant government party, naturally took the lead, and the whole nation rallied swiftly behind the commanding figure of the Generalissimo. But it must be remembered that in the opening months of the war, the political character of the Kuomintang was still conservative—it remained largely a party of landlord-officialdom. Chiang Kai-shek, as the leader of a government of national defense, had returned to something of the old revolutionary position he had occupied ten years before as commander of the Northern Expedition; and once the die was cast in favor of final resistance to Japan, he knew he might have to depend increasingly on the more advanced political elements for mass support. But many members of his own party had followed him reluctantly into the United Front, which was bound to be subjected to considerable strain in the storm and stress of the war period.

The curiously indirect (and very Chinese!) way in which the "reunion" of the Kuomintang and the communists had been effected, left a good many unanswered questions—especially after the development of hostilities with Japan. What did the Chinese Communists think of the war? What was their own wartime program and how did it differ from that of the Kuomintang? What degree of co-operation was to be expected between these two reunited allies, foes for ten years? What was to be the strategy and tactics of the communist armies, and how would they work together with the main body of the Chinese forces?

It was to get a full answer to such questions as these from the communists themselves that I had come to Yenan: and I had the answers, in a series of midnight interviews, from Mao Tse-tung, certainly the most authoritative possible spokesman for the Chinese Communist Party. In the pages that follow, I shall quote very extensively from these interviews, for they represent an analysis of the whole political and military situation in China shortly after the outbreak of the war that deserves close attention. For better or worse, the communists form one considerable and important element in the China of today, and their influence is likely to be an increasing one.

And whatever role they play, Mao Tse-tung will have a leading part in it.

I had my interview with "Chairman Mao" in his own house —a roomy cave-dwelling sheltered beneath Yenan's towering cliffs. We would begin talking early in the evening, and often carry on far into the night, with the candles guttering on the table between us, throwing grotesque shadows across the curving roof. The room was piled with iron despatch boxes, and radio messages arrived constantly, which Mao read in the intervals between answering questions. Wu Liang-p'ing acted as interpreter, and Mao—with his usual care over details—insisted that everything I wrote should be translated back later into Chinese, so that he might check his statements.

"What is the general attitude of the Chinese Communists towards the present war?" was my first question.

"Before the actual outbreak of hostilities," Mao began, "the Communist Party had repeatedly warned the country that war with Japan was inevitable, and that all Japan's talk of 'peaceful settlements,' all the beautiful phrases of Japanese diplomats, were only so much camouflage to screen Japan's preparations for war. We repeatedly pointed out the necessity of strengthening the National United Front and realizing a revolutionary policy, in order to wage a victorious war of national liberation.

"The most important thing of all, we insisted, was the adoption by the Chinese Government of a democratic system, so that the masses of the people might be mobilized for active participation.... The outbreak and development of the war have proved that this analysis was correct." Mao went on to quote from a number of recent communist manifestoes, all of which concentrated on one central point: the realization of a "nationwide, inclusive war of resistance" against Japan.

"What do you think should be the foreign policy of China at the present time?"

"One principle," Mao stated, "should determine all our foreign policy—to work towards an international Peace Front of all nations opposed to Japanese aggression. Morally, the international situation is not unfavorable to China: but the program of such a Peace Front as this must be decided not only by words, but also by action.

"Most important, for China, is the policy of Great Britain and the U. S. A. These two countries are especially endangered by the fascist aggressors both East and West. And hitherto England and America, notwithstanding their friendly words, have in fact by their policies aided the fascist aggressors. This was because they spoke, but did not act. Words without action to support them have in reality let the fascist countries have a free hand, and have thus objectively favored the fascists. Now the fascist powers of the world are endangering the very existence of the democratic powers; it is all the more necessary to have unity of action in order to meet this challenge. A united Peace Front of the kind we propose is very necessary not only for China in her present struggle, but also for the safety and continued existence of the democratic powers."

Mao's conception of the Japanese objectives in China was, quite simply, the "liquidation" of China as a whole. He considered North China and the Yangtse Valley the immediate military objectives, but was sure that the Japanese would never make more than a temporary halt until they had reduced all China to the status of a Japanese colony.

"How effective has the Chinese resistance proved so far?" I asked him.

Mao divided his answer into two sections, positive and negative.

"On the one hand," he observed, "we may say that the Chinese resistance so far has been effective, to a very considerable degree. In the first place, the present war is of a kind that has never occurred since China was first penetrated by foreign imperialism—a war of genuinely revolutionary character. In the second place, this war has brought about the political unification of China, which for so long was divided and disunited. Thirdly, China's war of resistance has aroused international sympathy—throughout the world, the past contempt at China's nonresistance in the face of Japanese aggression has been changed into a new respect for the China of today.

"On the other hand, certain weaknesses have appeared in the Chinese resistance during the last few months...." These weaknesses Mao summarized as political backwardness on the part of some elements within the nation, the lack of a common program agreed upon by all parties, and certain vital errors of military strategy. His critique of the early conduct of the war was advanced very frankly, and with complete sincerity. It was obvious that he thought less of scoring political "points" than of advocating what he believed to be a more effective general policy. And he was not wanting in constructive suggestions, as I found when I asked my next question.

"What, in your opinion, are the necessary conditions for successful resistance to Japan?"

Mao again divided his answer into two sections, political and military.

"On the political side," he said, "first of all we must modify the present government into a real United Front government, in which representatives of all sections of the people will participate. This government should be democratic, and at the same time centralized. The people must be given freedom of speech, assembly and organization, and the right to arm themselves against the enemy, so that the war may have a mass character.

Not only is it necessary for the people to have democratic freedom, but there must be a real improvement in the people's livelihood.... Only by such measures can the people be induced to support the government unanimously.

"On the military side," he continued, "we must realize a general modification of the existing system. Most important is the change of strategy from 'simple defense' to active attack upon the enemy. Old-style armies must be changed to new-style armies. Compulsory mobilization must be replaced by political mobilization. Disunited command must give way to a united command. Any conditions of indiscipline and estrangement from the common people must be changed by the adoption of a conscious discipline and a principle of non-violation of the interests of the people. The situation of a war of regular armies must be changed into a situation where the fighting of the regular armies is more and more combined with the partisan warfare of the people."

Mao had very much more to say about the "Ten Point Program" of his own party; but the main outline is sufficiently clear from the statements quoted here. And perhaps the most interesting thing about these eminently practical suggestions, put forward with all appearance of sincerity by a man whom the Kuomintang had long regarded as their mortal enemy, was that every one of them could be reinforced by a text from Sun Yat-sen. What the Chinese Communists were demanding, in fact, was that the Kuomintang should begin to put into practice some parts of its own original program which it had long neglected.

"The Kuomintang has partly realized the principle of Nationalism," Mao summed up. "This has already appeared in the realization of the anti-Japanese war. But the principle of Democracy has not yet been realized, and neither has the principle of the People's Livelihood. Because of this, a serious crisis has appeared in the present war.

"Now, in the critical war period, is the time for the Kuomintang to recognize their own Sun Yat-senism, and put it into practice. If they do not put it into practice now, it will be too late afterwards for them to change their minds."

The hour was late; and the yawning *hsiao kwei* who filled our tea cups was almost as sleepy as I was. But Mao seemed tireless, and only excused himself because a sheaf of telegrams claimed his attention. He walked out into the court with us, as Wu and I took our departure.

"You must come again, and we will talk more together. Do you know the password? Then I will send a guard to go back with you."

We shook hands in the dark courtyard. Mao stood for a moment, a tall, impassive figure, looking up at the cliffs that cut the stars. Then he turned back without a hint of weariness to his all-night vigil.

On parting from Mao Tse-tung after this first long interview, I tried to note down a few impressions of the man that might stand against any future developments of a complex and changing situation. This leader of the communist movement in China has so often been described (though never by those who have met him) as an "extremist," an embittered "class-revolutionary," that I had half expected to find a brilliant fanatic. This is a notion that might even be gathered from some published photographs, for Mao's long hair and careless dress seem points to support the legend.

The briefest acquaintance with the man, however, with his warm humanity and unfailing sense of humor, is enough to dispel any suggestions of this kind. In plain fact, Mao Tse-tung struck me as having incomparably the coolest and most balanced mind I had encountered in China. Talking to him, one is immediately aware of an immense intellectual force, a brain moving easily and surely along orderly lines of thought. This penetrating intelligence is combined with an essentially practical approach to any problem, and with a deep understanding of his own countrymen.

Mao Tse-tung is thoroughly Chinese; he has never been out of China, and has lived always in the closest possible contact with his own people, especially with Chinese peasants and workers. His command of political theory is something he owes, no doubt, to natural gifts, a well-trained mind, and an amazingly retentive memory. He is an omnivorous reader, and a man of many interests. But what is un-Chinese about him (or at least, untypical of the Chinese intellectual) is his extraordinary grasp of detail, his capacity for sustained mental effort, and his obvious power of concentration on the task in hand without losing sight of ultimate objectives.

I would say that Mao Tse-tung has in an unusual degree the subtlety and flexibility characteristic of the Chinese mind at its best—this is what makes him a successful strategist, in a country that has never been lacking in political acrobats. But dominating and controlling this (and it is a much rarer phenomenon in China) is a disciplined, relentlessly-driving human will. It is a formidable combination. The Chinese Revolution has no Lenin; but if any one man stands in the same relation to the Chinese masses as Lenin appeared in his lifetime to the workers of Europe, that man is Mao Tse-tung.

TWO PARTIES

On another October night, Wu and I sat together opposite the same table. It was chilly in the unheated cave, and I had wrapped a blanket round my shoulders. Wu sat cupping his hands around the china teapot. "Chairman Mao" lay stretched out in a canvas deckchair; it was the only luxury he had acquired for himself in all the months since the end of the civil war. I wondered if he kept warm by smoking his innumerable cigarettes.

The bare simplicity of the scene reminded me (if only by contrast) of that other capital of Nanking, where over ten years a one-party dictatorship had built up so impressive a façade of National Government. At this moment, perhaps, in Nanking sirens were sounding the alarm, searchlights sweeping the sky to pick out the night raiders.... But much of that Nanking, the capital, had been a pretense; and I for one did not regret the grandiose buildings crumbling beneath the Japanese attack, if only the old face-saving bureaucracy and red tape were to go with them. From now on, China would have to be governed from dugouts. And the return to reality might prove no bad thing: the dugout atmosphere, the urgency of crisis, were what had long been needed to bring out a real leadership for China.

The best of Nanking would remain; the worst, one hoped, was buried in the ruins of pseudo-European public buildings.

In our cave in Yenan, we were talking about the problem of government in wartime. "All wars in history," Mao was saying (sometimes he could sound very professorial) "can be divided into two kinds—revolutionary wars, and counter-revolutionary. The World War of 1914-1918 was a counter-revolutionary war, a war between imperialists. Imperialist nations forced the people to fight against their own interests, and so an absolute centralism of government was found necessary. The same thing is true of the Japanese government today.

"But there have been revolutionary wars in history, such as the American War of Independence, the first wars of the French Revolution, the war of the Soviet Union against foreign intervention, the present war of the Spanish people. The purpose of this kind of war is the same for the government and for the people, for these wars are based on the full support and sympathy of the masses. So the government is not afraid of the people, but must arouse them and encourage them to express their opinions, so that they can take an active and positive part in the war.

"The Chinese war of national liberation is completely supported by the people. Both government and people have the same purpose in the war. Hence, the more democratic the government, the more successful the war organization will be. The government need not fear any opposition from the people against the war: on the contrary, what it has most to fear is the apathy or 'non-rising' of the people.... That is why we must have a really democratic system of government in China today."

"What do you think are the chances of realizing such a system of government in China?"

Mao stroked his forehead with his fingertips in a characteristic gesture. "This depends, of course, on the co-operation between the Kuomintang and the Communist Party. The relation between these two parties has been a decisive factor in the Chinese political situation during the last fifteen years. Co-operation between

James Thorp; courtesy of ASIA Magazine
Erosion-scalloped country along the Wei River in southeast Kansu.

the Kuomintang and the Communist Party from 1925-27 created the victory of the first revolution: the split of the two parties in 1927 created the unfortunate situation of the past decade. Now we enter the third stage, when co-operation has been reestablished. For resistance to Japan and national liberation we must have agreement on a common program; and an important part of that program is the establishment of a democratic political system in China."

Everything came back in the end to this fundamental question of co-operation between political parties. But so long as the war continued, the Chinese Communists were in a very strong position indeed. Certain elements remained within the Kuomintang who were still bitterly opposed to them, and might become jealous of their growing influence. But Chiang Kai-shek—who had good reason to know what their military and political co-operation was worth in the war crisis—could probably be relied upon to prevent any open clash with reactionary elements. It was an ironical position, for the man who broke the "National bloc" of 1926 had now become something like the guardian of the United Front against Japan.

"Is there any guarantee," I asked Mao, "that there may not be another split—a repetition of 1927 at some future date?"

"There are four chief factors," he replied, "to safeguard the present National United Front. First of all, the Chinese people have learned many lessons in the last ten years. They remember what they have suffered in this time—all the bitterness, unhappiness and economic hardship that resulted from the fact that the National Revolutionary Front was broken after 1927. They remember nearly ten years of civil war between the Kuomintang and the Red Armies. The Chinese people will not let this happen again; they will not allow the National United Front to be broken by one small section of the community. If certain elements try once more to destroy the United Front, the majority of the people will refuse to support them. The people will fight for the United Front, because they know that only through it can the principles of national salvation be achieved.

"Second, those elements which broke the United Front in

1927 have also learned the lessons of the last ten years. They must know that the violation of the United Front in 1927 did serious harm to the Chinese nation; and they know that they have had a warning from the Chinese people, that a similar betrayal of the national revolution will never be allowed again.

"Thirdly, we communists have also learned many lessons and experiences from these last years. The Communist Party will use every effort to maintain and strengthen the National United Front, with a consistent and democratic program to encourage the full participation of the Chinese masses.

"Fourthly, the present international situation is very different from 1927, and will not allow a National Front in China to be broken again so easily. Rather, the international situation demands now a strengthening and widening of the United anti-Japanese Front, to bring it into line with the world peace front against fascist aggression."

What was most impressive to me about Mao's whole analysis of the war was his supreme confidence in the Chinese people, and in the future of the Chinese revolution. And there could be no question of the loyalty of the Chinese Communists to the leadership of Chiang Kai-shek; it was a loyalty that had already been sealed in blood along the northern battlefronts. Mao, and every other communist leader I talked to, had this same conception of a United Front that was no mere wartime improvisation, but was destined to carry the Chinese people successfully through the war to the establishment of the "democratic republic" that had been Sun Yat-sen's most cherished dream.

And they were not looking for any short cuts, as I found when I asked Mao Tse-tung how long he thought the war might last.

"We believe the war will be prolonged," he said, "because it will take time to mobilize the Japanese people against their own fascist cliques; it will take time for the international situation to be changed in favor of China's success; above all, it will take time to change the internal political situation in China itself.

"This last is part of a long process, in which the Chinese people will learn the lessons of their first defeats, will modify obsolete military and political systems, and organize on a mass basis for the victorious war. And while this process is going on, the Japanese fascists and militarists will be preparing the way for their own overthrow.

"So we will not despair after losing battles in this first period; we will never allow an atmosphere of pessimism or defeatism to grow up in China. We will accept the fact of a prolonged war, and steadily and fearlessly prepare the conditions for final victory. We are confident that, within two years or more, the conditions of Chinese success will be established, and we will reach a point where Japanese imperialism must be defeated."

"What do you think is the likelihood of a revolution occurring in Japan?" I asked. Mao nodded briefly.

"The severe oppression of the Japanese fascist cliques and the Japanese militarists has in recent years limited any activity on the part of the revolutionary forces within Japan. On the surface, it might appear that there is little opposition to the war, and that the Japanese nation in general supports it.

"But in reality the Japanese fascists are preparing their own destruction. The more bitter the oppression of the Japanese people—and this oppression must increase, the longer the war lasts—the greater the strength of the revolutionary opposition must become. So the revolutionary movement in Japan will grow steadily as the war progresses. But to overthrow Japanese imperialism, the first condition still remains the defeat of the Japanese armies, and the victorious struggle of the Chinese people."

Just how closely all this would correspond to Chiang Kai-shek's perspective of the war, it might be difficult to say. But the important thing was the agreement on essentials that had made it possible for China to present an unbroken fighting front. And there is a story told of General Chiang after his safe return from the hazardous episode of Sian, which may well be apocryphal, but which—if there is any truth in it at all—shows a very keen appreciation of character on the part of China's Generalissimo. Friends were congratulating Chiang upon his lucky escape, and themselves upon his return to the leadership of the nation. The Generalissimo reminded them that, after all, no one man could remain indefinitely at the head of the government.

"If I should be removed from office," he is reported to have said, half in jest and half in earnest, "either by illness or by some worse misfortune, whom do you think I should advise as my successor?"

With the usual polite demurrals, and very reluctantly, a number of names were at last put forward. The favorite guess was Ch'en Ch'ien, one of Chiang's younger and most active generals; but there were votes for Wang Ching-wei, H. H. Kung, and other veterans of the Kuomintang.

"No," Chiang replied to each of these in turn. "As my successor, I myself would choose—*General Pai Chung-hsi!*"

This was interesting, for General Pai (formerly Chiang's chief-of-staff on the Northern Expedition, and unquestionably one of the ablest commanders and organizers in the country) had quarreled bitterly with the Generalissimo shortly after the Nanking government was formed, and had remained aloof in his own province of Kwangsi, more or less in opposition, ever since.

But if Pai's name came as a surprise, it was nothing to what followed.

"For a second choice?" Chiang urged. No one could improve on earlier suggestions. "For a second choice," the Generalissimo said calmly, *"I would suggest Mao Tse-tung."*

I certainly do not vouch for the whole truth of this story; but it has a keen political point. If Chiang, in naming the two Chinese leaders for whose abilities he had the greatest respect, should have hit upon his two outstanding opponents over the last decade, that might well be the recognition of one master strategist for the two rivals (both former associates) whom he had most conspicuously failed to subdue.

But what was significant was that now, less than a year later, Pai Chung-hsi had already brought his troops north from Kwangsi, and was holding the chief field command under Chiang Kai-shek in Central China. And Mao Tse-tung, from his vantage point in Yenan, was directing the strategy of the Communist armies, with an official commission from Nanking for the defense of the vital Northwest, and for the major task of prolonging the war in North China.

COMMUNIST STRATEGY

What was the reason for the striking success of the Chinese Communist forces, that had already been shown at Pinhsingkwan and in the fighting in North Shansi? This army, it was true, had had an astonishing record during the civil war. But some military observers had always been inclined to put this down to lack of determination on the part of the Kuomintang troops, rather than to any special fighting qualities of the Chinese Red Army. What the Chinese Reds had done against halfhearted "punitive expeditions," it was argued, they could never hope to do against a well-equipped, well-trained modern army such as the Japanese.

Yet the very first months of the war had proved the contrary. The Eighth Route Army was then in much worse plight, from the point of view of technical equipment and military supplies, than even the northern provincial armies. Yet while the latter had suffered continuous defeats and had been obliged to fall back steadily before the invaders, the communist troops, from their first entry into the war, had been able to win victories.

There was no mystery about this, of course: the explanation was to be sought, not only in the remarkable fighting spirit of this peasant-and-worker army, but in a fundamentally different conception of the strategy of a defensive war held by the Chinese Communist commanders. This strategy had been outlined by Mao Tse-tung a year before the outbreak of hostilities at Lukowchiao.* But now that it was actually being tried out against the Japanese, it had ceased to be merely an interesting theory, and had become one of the vital factors affecting the course of the war.

"Can you tell me something about the Eighth Route Army," I asked Mao Tse-tung that October, "now that it has already gone into action against the Japanese?"

"On the question of strategy and tactics," Mao replied, "we may say in general that the Eighth Route Army undertakes actions that cannot at present be undertaken by other Chinese troops. We fight on the flanks and in the rear of the enemy.

* See Edgar Snow's *Red Star Over China*, Part Three, Chapter 3.

Such a style of fighting is altogether different from that of simple frontal defense.... Only by such tactics can we preserve our forces, and destroy those of the enemy in detached units. Moreover, forces operating in the rear of the enemy are especially dangerous, because they can destroy enemy bases and lines of communication.

"On the general military situation at this stage of the war, we can make one observation. The situation is *less favorable* than it was for the heavy concentration and centralization of Chinese forces; and *more favorable* for the division of our forces into mobile units. This is necessary, for now that the war covers so wide a territory, we must make as many sudden attacks as possible on the flank and rear of the extended enemy.

"The first principle in any war is to preserve your own forces, and liquidate the forces of the enemy. To achieve this end at the present time, we should make use of a mobile warfare of independent initiative, combined with the fullest possible use of partisan tactics. Every kind of immobile, passive, mechanical fighting should be abandoned. If a sufficient number of the Chinese armies wage such a war, and the Eighth Route Army helps them with guerilla fighting, then victory may be in our hands."

In later months, one was to hear a great deal more talk in China of the possibilities of this "mobile warfare"; at that time, when the best of Chiang Kai-shek's troops were still being held in deep-line formation around Shanghai, and were suffering daily four or five times the losses of the Japanese opposed to them, it was still a novel idea. Mao's theory, he was careful to explain, did not involve the abandonment of important Chinese positions so long as they might be defended. But I know he considered the gallant Chinese defense at Shanghai, with the attempt to hold an extended line right under the guns of the Japanese fleet, a mistake from a military point of view. And in this, most foreign observers would probably agree with him.

"Another very important and significant feature of the Eighth Route Army," Mao went on, "is its political work. There are three fundamental principles underlying this.

"First, *unity of the officers and soldiers*. This implies the liquidation of any remaining traces of feudalism, the establishment of conscious discipline, and the realization of a manner of life in the army whereby all share alike together both bitter and sweet. In this way, our army has achieved a unique degree of solidarity.

"Second, *unity of the army and the people.* This is an unfailing principle with our army. We must keep the closest possible relation with the common people, and never in any way violate their interests. Then the people will support us, work with us, take messages, keep military secrets. Co-operation with the people is an important factor in our military success.... And we get new recruits not by compulsory draft, but by agitation and political organization of the people—a method which is very much more effective.

"Third, *propaganda among the enemy armies, and special treatment of prisoners of war.* In this work, victory does not depend entirely upon the fighting quality of our armies: it depends also on the deterioration of the armies of the enemy. Though this effect is not yet so significant, in the future it will assume ever greater proportions."

"Could the style and strategy of the Eighth Route Army be profitably adopted by other Chinese armies?"

"Though our army has the special features outlined above, which make it particularly dangerous for the Japanese," Mao replied, "still it cannot, of course, play the decisive role in the anti-Japanese war. Numerically it is still limited; and at present the Kuomintang armies are still playing the decisive role in the Chinese resistance.

"But there is no reason why some of the good points of the Eighth Route Army should not be adopted by other Chinese group armies. The Kuomintang troops originally had a revolutionary spirit similar to that of the present Eighth Route Army —that was in 1925-27. And in the period of the Great Revolution the war tactics and strategy of the new troops matched their political spirit. This was not a passive and mechanical strategy, but positive, active and offensive. Because of this, victories were gained in the Northern Expedition.

"The present anti-Japanese war needs a similar kind of army."

In the "Red Army" period, one of the strongest weapons of the Chinese Communists had always been propaganda among the "White" forces. Against foreign troops, one supposed, this kind of activity would be very much limited. But the Chinese Reds were indefatigable propagandists, and one could be sure they would never neglect any opportunities in this direction.

"What *is* your policy towards prisoners of war?" I asked Mao Tse-tung. "And towards the Japanese rank and file?"

"Essentially the same," he replied, "as the policy we have followed in the Red Army during the last ten years. Prisoners are disarmed, but are not insulted or ill-treated in any way. We explain to them the common interests of the peoples of China and Japan, and then release them.

"Of course, we make a certain distinction between soldiers and officers, and between officers of lower and higher rank. Common soldiers, those from the oppressed classes, and especially those Mongol and Manchurian peoples who are compelled by Japanese imperialists to fight against us, we greet as friends and comrades. Any who, with us, oppose Japanese imperialism, are welcomed within our ranks; those who do not wish to stay with us are at liberty to return to their old units. Officers are treated in the same way; but those higher officers who have directed the war against us and helped to form the present policy of Japanese militarism, we keep with us in China for a while, so that they may have time to understand and appreciate their errors. Then, if they recognize their own mistakes, we will release them too."

"But in view of the discipline and traditions of the Japanese army," I argued, "is this policy likely to achieve any results? Released prisoners will be killed by their commanders if they return to their regiments, and the Japanese army as a whole will not understand the purpose of your policy."

"The more released prisoners the Japanese kill," Mao stated confidently, "the more the sympathy of the Japanese soldiers towards the Chinese troops is roused. We have already followed our announced policy with those prisoners captured in the recent

"Special District" 125

Shansi fighting, and we will continue with it. It is one way of making clear the real enemy that we are fighting—Japanese imperialism, and not the Japanese people.

"We have no quarrel with the Japanese people, with members of the oppressed colonial peoples, even though they are sent to fight against us. These people are our friends; and those who do not wish to return to their troops can always join for service with our own army. If in the future an international column should appear on the field of the anti-Japanese war, they can join this column, taking up arms to fight against Japanese imperialism."

At the time, this all sounded so improbable to me that I was inclined to regard it as one of Mao's rare excursions in wish-fulfillment. Later, when I met and talked with Japanese prisoners in the Eighth Route Army, I began to change my mind. And by the time I left China, Mongol, Manchurian, and even Japanese troops, under communist commanders, were already organized in the north, and were actually fighting shoulder to shoulder with the Chinese guerillas.

"SPECIAL DISTRICT"

Altogether, I stayed in Yenan for nearly a month—which was about three weeks longer than I had intended. But it was hard to resist an almost overwhelming hospitality, and there were many points of interest, for the foreign visitor, in this busy little mountain capital. For Yenan—even though the army had left—was a hive of wartime activity.

There were certain significant changes to distinguish the "Special District" from the former "Soviet Region." Politically, this was expressed by the fact that all classes had now the right to vote and participate in the government. A general election for the whole district had just been completed that September: it had been conducted on a basis of universal suffrage, working upwards from the village councils, through the divisions of county and shire, to the District Government itself.* There was

* The village councils are directly elected; and these elect delegates for the county council, more or less on the soviet principle. The ratio is *hsiang* (village),

no longer any discrimination against landlords, nor any confiscation of property. The Special District at this time could fairly claim to be the nearest thing to a complete democracy in China.

But it was a wartime government: the extension of political privileges was in accordance with the formula that "all sections and classes of the people should take part in the anti-Japanese struggle." Taxation had been revised on a war level, and there was now a universal *"Chiu-kuo kungliang"* or "National Salvation Fund," which worked as a kind of single-tax, assessed according to the annual income of the individual. "It varies from 1 per cent to 5 per cent of the total yearly income," the Chairman of the District Government told me. "Very poor peasants who have just enough to live on are exempt from taxation, but most peasants pay a rate of 1 per cent. Those who are better off pay 2-3 per cent; this is the average for the 'middle peasant.' Anyone with an annual income of over 100 dollars pays 5 per cent. Any peasants who still rent their land pay only one half of the tax; any landlords who still hold all their estates pay double." * It was a rough-and-ready revenue system, but it was adequate for the purposes of local government; and the army—which had, of course, been the chief expense of the Old Soviet District—was now supported directly by the National Government.

Both politically and economically, then, the Special District represented something like a "progressive experimental area" within the Chinese Republic. And though the economic level of these northwestern provinces was low, the living-standard of the peasants had already been considerably improved. The great majority of them owned their own land; rural co-operatives were extensively organized, rates of interest were fixed by the government, and though trade seemed brisk enough, no one was making excess profits. The communists regarded their district as a "model area" for the rest of China in a war situation: and where

---

1 delegate from approximately 20 voters; *ch'u* (county), 1 for every 50; *hsien* (shire), 1 for every 200. So that for the District Government, each delegate represents approximately 1,500 voters.

* Landlordism had practically ceased to exist within the "Border District" proper, before the change of status. But there were still landlords with large estates in some of the "United Front" districts administered by the communists.

the force of example seemed strongest, was in matters of education, mass organization, and political training.* It was here that Yenan shone, especially by contrast with some other parts of China that I had seen during the war months. In the little capital alone there were, besides the Military Academy and the Party School, the *Shenpei Kunghsueh* (ranking as a university, for students who had passed high-school stage), a Normal School, a radio and engineering school, and a large girls' school. In Yenchwan, the main District Normal School was training teachers for the "thousand schools" covered by the general Education Plan: this was an ambitious effort paralleling what the communists had accomplished in other years in Kiangsi. In all these and in all existing schools throughout the district (which included many short-term classes for peasants) a general "anti-Japanese" educational program was in full swing, with the emphasis on emergency defense training. Shortage of materials was a constant problem, but all educational facilities, from the smallest village school to the anti-Japanese University, were provided free of charge.

Mass mobilization had been carried out on a universal scale, and with a spirit which defied the scanty material resources of Shenpei. Young and old, women and children, were organized, trained, and armed in different ways to prepare for the coming struggle. Men and women were formed into "anti-Japanese Self-Defense Guards," youths had their "Young Vanguards," even children were brought into *Erh Tung Tuan,* or "Boys' and Girls' Groups." Every kind of weapon was in evidence, from modern rifles to old-fashioned swords and spears; and the primitive arsenals and factories were working day and night. "With all its military forces," I heard Mao Tse-tung declare at one mass peasant meeting, "we do not think Japan can conquer this district."

It is impossible here to give a detailed account of the communist district in the Northwest; it has already been described in many aspects (under the old Soviet régime) by Edgar Snow,

---

* The same model of a "reformed democratic system" has been followed by those Chinese governments set up in North China, with the assistance of the Eighth Route Army, in such districts as the "Border Regions of Shansi, Hopei, and Chahar" —partisan areas behind the Japanese lines.

and I have only tried here to suggest a few of the most notable changes in the war situation under the United Front. But I cannot leave Yenan without attempting to jot down a few impressions of the life that went on within and without its walls—something so novel and stimulating, by contrast with the Old China, that it is hard to write of it without undue enthusiasm.

If one were to believe the Japanese commentator, Yenan—home of the "Bolsheviks of Asia"—is the source of contamination for most of China today. Yet I can only describe what I saw as a place where most people seemed to be working hard and contentedly, where nearly everybody seemed to be young, and where the most enthusiastic could find something to do to work off their enthusiasm. Life was plain and frugal enough, even by Chinese standards; but Yenan seemed to me a good place to be in.

Sunday was the general "rest day," the day for inviting friends. (It was perhaps the only time in the week some hard-working communists would be able to spend with their wives.) In the co-operative restaurant, every room is filled at noon. As we go in, a diminutive figure in a Red Army cap sprawls in the center of the courtyard. This is the two-year-old son of Mao Tse-tung (the only person in Yenan, so far as I could see, who was in any danger of being spoiled). From the kitchen window, the chief cook offers him a prawn, at the end of a pair of greasy chopsticks. Young Mao accepts with delight....

We are invited to join one of the dinner groups—here are young cadets from the Military Academy, and girl students from the University. At first sight, it is not easy to distinguish between them. The uniform is identical; the girls have short cropped hair and wear the same cloth caps. Skirts, or the long Chinese gown, are unknown in Shenpei.

"What do you think of Chinese women?" one obvious feminist demands of me. She is a graduate of the Sun Yat-sen Institute in Moscow, and now an instructor in the Party School. "Don't listen to her," says a burly man on the other side of the table, in French. He is a member of the Politburo, and—as I happen to know—her husband. "She only wants to be flattered."

But the first questioner is not to be put off with light answers. She goes on to talk of the position of women in the interior of China, of child brides and bound feet....

Chinese women have always had a considerable influence in society, and even today they are very much more "emancipated" than women, say, in Japan. But in Yenan it is not just the domestic influence of the *lao tai-tai,* or the fabulous Chinese mother-in-law (a constant reminder that China was once a matriarchy) that makes women a social force. Here there are women in the army, in the government, in education. They have found other careers, now, besides marriage.

Few country towns in districts as poor as North Shensi have a bookshop. But here in Yenan there is one, down a side street. It even has glass windows. There is not quite the range you might have found in Shanghai along the Foochow Road; but the stock, the young manager assures us, is "select."

On tables are ranged the standard Chinese periodicals, most of them a month out of date; but after all there is a war on, and communications in China were never too reliable. Modern Chinese novels, textbooks and atlases, a few foreign volumes in English, German, or Russian. On one table are the paper-backed issues of the "New China Press" in Yenan: for the most part, translations of the standard works of Marx-Leninism. Among the magazines I notice a familiar cover: *Democracy.* "We've been waiting for the latest copies," says the manager. "The magazine was very popular with the students."

I tell him he will wait a long time: *Democracy* had died in Peiping when the Japanese arrived.

Outside the East Gate, an impressive arch of stone has been built, leading to the athletic field. Here the grand annual sports meeting of the Red Army had been interrupted three months before by marching orders. There is a running track, broad- and high-jump, half a dozen basketball courts. In that crisp October weather, games were especially popular. I played many sets with the staff of the Military Academy, veteran commanders of the civil war who rarely discarded more of their uniforms than the belt, and were probably more expert with a bigsword or a cavalry saber than with a tennis racket. But what they lacked in finesse they more than made up in concentration. Given another year, tennis in Yenan would probably reach middling country-house form....

The Young Pioneers had sent us an invitation to an evening at the Young Men's Club. The club, we find, is housed in the quarters of the Baptist Mission: the church, built in Chinese style with a campanile that dominates this end of the town, is the main concert hall. "What about the missionaries?" I ask.

"They won't come back, though we have asked them to several times. So we use the buildings. We put a new roof on the church last winter, the old one was leaking."

Now the earthen floor, between wooden pillars, is crowded with peasant children, and a platoon of soldiers who will soon be leaving for the front. The program features the Children's Group in peasant dances: they wear colored smocks, with red kerchiefs tied around their heads. There is one play presented by the Military Academy Drama Unit, in which a strikingly beautiful girl (her silk gown belongs to another world) takes the main singing part. With bound hands, a symbol of China, she sings of the suffering of the whole people, in a voice superbly trained for the old Chinese drama....

"The Modernist Group wanted to ban this play," Kim—the Korean revolutionary who is my guide—whispers across to me. "They said it was old-fashioned, and bourgeois. But Mao Tse-tung liked it, and so it's been kept on." The whole room is hushed while the girl is singing. I feel that even the vanished pastor might have approved.

Along the river valley, under a glare of sun, a whole hillside is in motion. These are the shock-brigadiers of the Red Academy, digging the hundreds of caves in the yellow loess that will be their new home. (Japanese planes have been over scouting, and all Yenan is going underground.) Lo Hsueh-ching, who can only speak through his clenched teeth because his head was nearly hacked off once in a forgotten battle in Kiangsi, shows us with

some pride over this scene of intense activity; he outlines his latest plan for the construction of a bomb-proof base hospital. Girls are here, working as hard as the men to advance their flag beyond that of the rival squad. Chinese Stakhanovites....
A slim, dark-haired figure in uniform passes us with flushed and perspiring face. "Do you recognize her?" Kim asks me.
"No, I don't think so...."
"She was the girl who sang in the play last night."

I could write enthusiastically about many things in Yenan, critically about some others. I have tried not to disguise the material hardships and shortcomings of life in the "Special District"; but it did seem to me that they were more than made up for by omnipresent qualities of enthusiasm and initiative that are only too rare in China. Perhaps I have exaggerated the carefree atmosphere of the place, though that would be difficult.

But one episode may suffice to show another side of the picture. No charge was more frequent against the Reds in the old days, than the well-worn taunt of their fondness for "communizing women." I remember being shown once, in Kiangsi, a "divorce certificate" from the former Soviet district, in which the grounds for separation were noted curtly as "husband—*different class.*" The woman had married again on the same day, a fact which served as text for a discourse on "communist immorality" by the good Kuomintang official who showed me the documents.

One afternoon, with Kim I was climbing the hills above the University compound. In the open space behind the buildings a crowd of perhaps two thousand blue-uniformed figures had gathered around a platform. "What is it?" I asked, "mass meeting?"
"No," said my companion, hesitating for a moment, "*mass trial.*" He told me the story. At that time it was being kept out of the papers; next day, by a decision of the Central Committee, it was published in full in the *New China Daily.*
A week or so before, the river besides the university had been the scene of tragedy. A young girl student who had recently

come to Shenpei had been—it was the worst anyone could find to say of her—something of a coquette. She was pretty, and had before long a number of suitors. The most persistent of these had been a graduate of the Military Academy, a thirty-year-old regimental commander who was a "veteran" of the Red Army, with ten years' fighting service, and an exemplary revolutionary record.

For some months the affair had run a stormy course. The officer had repeatedly asked the student to marry him; but the girl—she was only seventeen—remained fancy free, and seemed on the whole to be rather enjoying the situation. One night he had called for her, and they had gone out together. Next morning her body was found beside the river.

It was a *crime passionnel*, if ever there was one; but serious enough. The young colonel was immediately suspected. At first he denied any knowledge of the incident, inventing an alibi which was easily disproved. His gun, recently cleaned, told its own story. When he was arrested he broke down and confessed that there had been a quarrel. He had demanded a definite answer from the girl: yes or no. She would not give it, and in a rage he had shot her.

The facts were clear enough; it was a story, in another setting, that one might read in any American newspaper headlines. What interested me was the Shenpei method of dealing with the case.

The offender was held under arrest, and students of the academy and of the university were given a day off to study every detail of the affair. Then—on the afternoon we looked down on the scene from the hills—the case was tried by the fellow-students of the dead girl and her lover.

It had been a very near thing, I learned afterwards. The university group, and some who had been the girl's closest friends, argued that she too had been to blame, urged the revolutionary record of the young colonel in favor of a light sentence. On the whole the Red Academy group demanded a death penalty. The man had been a communist, his responsibility was all the greater. Elected advocates spoke on both sides.

What finally settled it was the man's first denial of the crime. If he had made a frank confession, it seems that he might have got off, perhaps with nothing more than a warning or demotion. But he had been guilty of disloyalty. It was put to the vote, and the mass vote was decisive. Sentence was formally passed by the judges of the High Court; and an hour or so after we had crossed those hills, the young commander had been shot.

"It was hard on him," Kim told me ruefully; I knew where his personal sympathies had lain. "But there was the Party discipline to consider."

CHAPTER FOUR
INTO SHANSI

FAREWELL TO YENAN

It was early November, and the first snow had already fallen in Yenan, when I set out on the second stage of my journey to the front.

Our most obvious destination should have been Taiyuan, the capital of Shansi province. But at this time Taiyuan was threatened by a Japanese column which had pushed southward from Paotingfu, occupied the railway junction of Shihkiachwang, and had just succeeded in storming the commanding mountain pass of Niangtzekwan, on the eastern Shansi border. The loss of Niangtzekwan had opened the Chinese flank in North Shansi, and a retreat from Taiyuan might soon become inevitable.

The safest way to travel, it seemed, was to move east over the Yellow River directly into Shansi, and let the developing war situation determine future movements. This meant a cross-country trip; but the autumn weather was ideal for it, and the army had connections to the ferry, and on as far as headquarters. I discussed the details of my plan with Comrade Wu Liang-p'ing.

"We can give you horses and an escort," he said, "and letters to Chu Teh at headquarters." He scribbled a chit to the chief of staff in Yenan. "They'll look after you."

The chief of staff was pleasantly efficient. "One horse and one mule," he said, making notes as he spoke. "You can ride whichever you like—I should advise the mule. Have you got a uniform? No? Then take this order to the uniform factory. You'll need a greatcoat too; it will be cold in the hills this winter." He was right, of course, and foreign clothes are hardly the safest wear in a Chinese war zone. For foreigners are uncommon travelers in the interior, and I did not want to be taken for a Japanese.

I went to a sun-filled courtyard, loud with the rattle of second-hand sewing machines. In long rooms, women in overalls —many of them released political prisoners—were hard at work clothing the army. A union assistant took my measurements. "Your uniform will be ready tonight." To my astonishment, it was.

Next morning, outside Yenan's modest *Waichiaopu*, we gathered for the start. My escort consisted of a dozen infantrymen, who were on regular patrol duty, and in addition, I had been assigned a couple of personal bodyguards from the local G. P. U. These were Shenpei youths, whose dialect was almost unintelligible; they were more at home with their Mausers than with polite conversation. The soldiers came from all over China— Kiangsi, Kweichow, Szechwan; the leader of the troop was a twenty-five-year-old veteran from Hunan.

The Eighth Route Army, as I was to discover, never travels without full fighting gear. All our party had been issued with excellent winter uniforms, had spare socks and two spare pairs of shoes—though some preferred to march in the bark sandals they were more accustomed to. Each man had two hand grenades, and they wore the longest bandoliers I had ever seen. They had rifles, but no bayonets.

It was interesting to compare this equipment with that of the Japanese troops I had seen in the north. The Japanese soldier carries a pack that is heavy even by western standards, in these days when infantry march by motor-truck. He has more gadgets strung about him than a Chinese knife-grinder. He marches in leather boots, usually studded with nails, and invariably carries a steel helmet. The general effect is workmanlike; and no doubt he is the better figure of a modern soldier, on parade, or column of march along a graded road.

But I tried to imagine him in the hills of North Shansi, or in the kind of country through which we were going. Then the pack he carried—useful as each individual item might be— would become an intolerable burden. His boots would slip on the loess hill paths, especially when winter brought frost and ice to the northern uplands. I was not surprised later to hear a comment on this from an officer who had been in the fighting at Yenmenkwan, when the Chinese and Japanese forces were struggling for command of the pass. "If both sides started even for the same hilltop," he said cheerfully, "we would be at the top before the Japanese had got halfway!"

In open warfare, of course, or in a battle of positions, such lightly-armed troops would be at a fatal disadvantage against the superior Japanese technical equipment. But that was just the kind of fighting that the former Red Armies—unlike other Chinese forces in the north—had been careful to avoid. They traveled light, with a mobility that was worth more than field batteries.

Across the new bridge that was the pride of the Red Engineering School, I shook hands with the last comrades from Yenan. "I wish you could stay for the November 7 celebrations," Kim said regretfully. "But there's more to see in Shansi." An organizer of the Canton Commune, I knew that he fretted secretly against the fate that kept him in Yenan translating Japanese telegrams when he longed to be at the front.

I bade farewell to Yenan with real regret. I had found a warm welcome there, and a hospitality it would not be easy to forget. To many young Chinese, I knew, this little city in the mountains of Shenpei had a value far beyond any mere regional significance. It was the symbol of a leadership that had held intact through years of almost incredible difficulty and privation. And it was this kind of leadership China needed now.

East from Yenan is easy going, through the river valley. Providentially, a threatening sky had cleared before we started, and a clear morning in North Shensi is a delight. With the sun well up, the air was almost warm.

On the road, our little party at once assumed a military formation. Three men went ahead as scouts, taking short cuts over spurs and through water-courses. I came with the main group, riding the gray pony, and the mule came behind with the baggage. I had decided to ride the pony, against good advice, largely out of *amour propre*. The horse is a nobler animal than the mule;

FAREWELL TO YENAN   137

and this mule was a particularly sullen beast. My bodyguards dogged my heels like shadows, and a hundred yards behind, two soldiers with unslung rifles made a miniature rearguard.

At first I had been amused by these precautions. "Are you afraid of bandits?" I asked the leader of this troop, (themselves known to the outside world as "bandits" only a few months before). But he took the question very seriously. "There *are* bandits in these hills," he told me. "You know they ambushed Chou En-lai's truck only ten miles from Yenan? We rounded up that band, but there may still be more around. Besides, this is a matter of discipline." Later, when I had seen how some other Chinese troops moved in Shansi, I saw what he meant.

And indeed, we sighted several groups of mountaineers on the road, armed with swords and rifles. But it was by no means uncommon in Shenpei to see peasants go armed, for partisan forces had been organized over the whole Special District. If there were any real bandits about, they were taking no chances with our compact little escort.

By this first week in November, all the crops were in except the cotton, and in the farmsteads peasants were busy thrashing the grain. In spite of the immoderate rains, the crops had been good, and there would be no shortage of food that winter. These northern hills are barren enough, to the eye that longs for the lush green of rice fields, or tree-shaded pasture; but they provide a living for the hardy farmers who plow their impossible fields on the mountain slopes, or on the verge of loess ravines. And in the river valleys, there is pasture of a sort for sheep and cattle.

The ubiquitous brown bullock of North Shensi is quite impressive. He is used for every kind of labor, and is as accustomed to the pack saddle as to the plow. Poor as it may be in other respects, this district has probably a higher percentage of livestock to the population than most other parts of China. Mules, donkeys, and camels are common on the roads; and if there were not more horses, it was again because (my guides assured me) they had nearly all been requisitioned for the front.

It is almost impossible to see a North Shensi village until you are right on top of it, for most of them burrow into the loess hillsides. The great majority of the population live in these loess caves, which in wartime gives them a unique security against bombing from the air. I do not know if it is still necessary to say a word in defense of these maligned cave-dwellings; having slept in a good many of them, I can vouch for the fact that they are infinitely superior to the average North China farmhouse. They are cleaner, cooler in summer, and incomparably warmer in winter, when the *k'ang*, which runs most of the length of the cave, is heated by flues from the cooking-fires. Besides this, with their one wide window they are surprisingly light.

The first night out we spent in such a village, and I had the chance to see what the communists meant by their slogan of "non-violation of the interests of the people." Though this was within the Special District, where a military party might easily have demaded a billet, rooms (or rather caves) were rented with the consent of their owners, and paid for in national currency. That evening scene was typical. Though they had covered a day's march that would have prostrated regular troops of most countries, with no food since early morning, as soon as our quarters were decided upon it was the soldiers themselves who set to work, sweeping out the rooms, cooking the evening meal, cutting chaff for the horses—all with invincible good humor. As soon as the word of their arrival got around, half the village gathered in the courtyard—some of them come to gaze with unconcealed dismay at the first foreigner they had ever seen; but more to mingle with the soldiers, talk with them about the war, and pass the time of day. And always someone came with gifts: old men would bring tobacco, and offer a communal pipe; or small boys would shyly offer fruit. In the morning, cave and court were scrupulously swept out, and the reckoning—not without traditional bargaining—paid in full.

What it means from a purely military point of view to have a countryside solidly behind your armies, only those who have learned to depend upon the support of the masses really know. I had seen the fatal effects of a lack of co-operation between the peasants and the Chinese armies in Hopei, when the Japanese in their first occupation of the north ran open lines of communication across a densely populated country without the slightest interference. They would have met with a different reception here.

Cutting across loess highlands to avoid a bend in the river, we came upon the city of Yenchang, as picturesquely situated as Yenan itself, with walls that on one side climb the mountains, and on the other are swept by the same waters at Yenan. We spent the best part of a day in Yenchang, where I visited what was then the only operating oil well in China. We were greeted at the wells by a group of husky workers who had not yet (like the army) put off their black caps with the red star. The machinery was primitive, but it worked, and supplied oil for the lamps of Shenpei.

From Yenchang, for one day more we followed the river, which here ran deep and swift through stone gorges, with some splendid pools and waterfalls. At times the path was almost a tunnel through the face of the cliff. Bridges were logs precariously spanning the torrent. Fortunately, the gray pony was as sure-footed as a mountain goat: the only thing that bothered him was frost or ice, and one developed an uncanny anticipation for icicles hanging from the rocks—a sure danger signal.

Always, as they marched, the soldiers would sing, and they had a varied repertoire. This army has always made its own songs, and some of them, based on local airs from the various provinces the Red Army had traversed, have a real musical as well as historical interest. Others were the staccato marching songs of "National Salvation" that one had heard in Shanghai and Sian. But sometimes it would be a tune more familiar to Western ears, and it was a curious experience to hear these mountain gorges ringing with the *Internationale,* or the *Marseillaise,* or a theme-song from a Russian film—all rendered, with a difference, in throaty Chinese dialect.

Then, after a night in a little walled fortress on a crag above the river, we struck up again into the hills. Despite the morning chill, and the hoar-frost white on every blade of grass, we were all drenched with sweat when, after a long climb, we came out on a wide loess plateau. It was another clear morning; and the view from the heights was superb. To the east, range on range of hills were lost to view; south of these, a line of higher mountains showed dark against the sun.

"You see?" my guard said, pointing. "Over there is Shansi."

YELLOW RIVER CROSSING

Somewhere ahead of us, cutting a deep cleft through this wilderness of hills, was the Yellow River. It should be a day's march to the ferry, the troop commander reckoned, consulting his map. We set out across the loess highlands.

From its head waters in the mountains of Tibet, to the flat coast of Shantung, the Yellow River divides a continent. "China's Sorrow" or (as it was to prove at a later stage of the war) China's unlooked-for ally, the Huang Ho, remains an incalculable factor of history. It is the most characteristically Chinese of all China's great rivers, alike in its work of beneficence and destruction. No foreign gunboats thread its shifting channels: there is something primitive and implacably hostile about that muddy current. Summer or winter, it has no gentle moods.

Nearly a year before I had crossed this river, traveling from a Shansi still at peace into a Shensi under the shadow of civil war. Now, more than a hundred miles to the north of the windy pass of Yümenk'ow where then we had scrambled on foot over its frozen waters, I was to cross the Huang Ho once again—this time into a Shansi already overrun by foreign armies.

All that day, alternately burned by a sun that beat fiercely even in November, and chilled by a cold wind from the north, we followed a trail that wound alarmingly round loess cliffs, and crossed ravines on natural bridges barely a yard wide. I had never seen wilder country; it had all the appearance of desolation, though it was far from uninhabited, for dipping down into the valleys, we would find tiny villages sunk like rabbit warrens into the face of the cliffs. We made for the highest point ahead, where the walls and towers of what might have been a medieval fortress jutted from a height.

But a closer approach discovered it a ruin; a couple of soldiers, peering curiously from the ramparts, shouted to us that there was not even food enough to give our party a meal. From this point of vantage, the Shansi hills were plain in view, and great

Yellow River Crossing

spurs ran down from the plateau we had crossed to a vaguely defined valley where, hidden as yet from sight, the river ran between two provinces.

It was another twenty *li*, they told us; and the day was already drawing in.

"We can't cross the river tonight," the commander decided. It had been a hard day, and even those tough campaigners were weary. For the first time since we left Yenan, the pony had begun to stumble, and it took all the *mafoo's* vocabulary to persuade the mule to budge after this brief halt. We decided to stop at the first village; and about an hour later we came to it, suddenly rounding a cliff and finding ourselves in a sheltered hollow where some twenty farmsteads clustered. Again, we met with the same friendly welcome; and we passed the most comfortable night of the trip.

Next morning the hills were shrouded in mist, and the wind had shifted to the south. But we got away to a good start, and now it was downhill going. The sun was struggling through a cloudbank when at last, coming out on the foot of the spur, we looked down on a broad stretch of water that cut through the brown hills like a sword. It was the Huang Ho.

Scrambling down the last fall of hills, we came out on the bank, by a straggling village of caves and stone huts. The river here ran straight for two or three miles, keeping an even width of perhaps a quarter of a mile. It was running full and fast, and the absence of noise with which so vast a body of water traveled was disconcerting. Three streaks, parallel to the banks, of what had looked from above like ripples, appeared now like an ocean surf; the regularity of these great rounded billows, which occurred where the riverbed was shallower, and which—unlike an ocean surf—did not advance, created a curious impression of immobility. Only the speed with which the current was running could have preserved their unbroken smoothness.

This was not a regular crossing, and the boat we took was manned by a military patrol. It was newly built, but on the immemorial model of a boat in China, that must date from the Chinese Great Flood. It was subjected to a lengthy process of baling and overhaul, before we took the towline, and began to work it upstream.

Not until we had covered nearly two miles of towing was the head boatman content, and we anchored the unwieldy craft to a stone for the embarkation. This was a long process, but at last our own party, in the closest of company with about a dozen mules and some twenty passengers, was sandwiched into the body of the ark. Four sturdy soldiers manned the sweeps, two boatmen stood by with immense poles, and we cast off.

Not until the boat was fairly launched on the current, which whirled it away like a leaf, did I realize what we were in for. The bank we had just left slipped past like something seen from the window of a train. The rowers were grunting rhythmically at the great sweeps, but though we were going downstream fast enough, we seemed to be making painfully little headway across it.

Then we struck the first waves, and the heavy boat, broadside on to the current, began to rock like an eighteen-footer in a choppy sea. I was holding the pony's head down, but the mules —many of them still with their packs—became first restive, and then wildly alarmed. Fortunately we were so tightly jammed in that there was no room for any movement except overboard. We were shipping water steadily, and every time we hit a wave the wind, now blowing strongly upstream, whipped the icy spray about our ears.

It was the craziest trip I have ever made on fresh water. The first impulse of the mules was to kick, and for a moment I was afraid they would kick the planks out. Three times, crossing the three stretches of rough water, we had the same paralyzing experience. The whole thing lasted perhaps a quarter of an hour, but it seemed an eternity. We hit the far bank (again with a shock that might have sunk the boat) just in time to avoid the bend in the river.

"Were you afraid?" my guard asked cheerfully, helping me out of the chaos. "*Very* afraid," I said emphatically. Yet this was a regular army crossing, by which supplies were normally transshipped into Shansi. My respect for the Chinese army transport was enormously increased.

On the Shansi bank, the hills rose no less steeply; and they were decorated here and there with block-houses, built by Yen Hsi-shan to repel (a year before) just the people with whom I was now traveling. There was a certain irony in this situation, not lost on the troop commander as he pointed out these fortifications to me. The army which had been characterized as a "bandit horde"—some of the anti-communist slogans still remained on the walls of the forts—when it pushed across the Yellow River early in 1936, was the army that Yen and his generals now looked to to save Shansi.

Certain indications remained, however, to remind us that we were now under another administration. While we were resting in a little inn a local official called to ask for my card and my destination. When I said I came from Yenan (a remark which, in Sian, would still have invited deep and dark suspicions), he smiled as though it were the most natural thing in the world, and said, "Ah yes, the Eighth Route Army are our very good friends." And he invited me to drink tea with him to seal our good relations.

I was eager for news, but he had very little to give me. The situation in the north was bad, he said, and the government had already moved to the south of the province. It looked as though nothing could save Taiyuan.

Taiyuan fell—I learned later—on that very day we crossed the Yellow River.

THE WAR IN SHANSI

We heard of the loss of Taiyuan in the first Eighth Route Army base we reached in Shansi. This was some days later; and, for obvious reasons, I shall have to be a little more reticent about place names and routes from now on. The war in Shansi is not yet over.

It altered my own plans considerably. When we had left Yenan, I had hoped to go direct to Taiyuan, and connect with Chu Teh and P'eng Teh-huei at Army Headquarters. Now it was not so simple.

"What has been happening here?" I asked the base commander.

I knew the general outlines of the fighting up to the beginning of November. The Japanese plan had been clear enough: it was to occupy Taiyuan as rapidly as possible, consolidate a base there, and push on to the south, cutting through the heart of the province along the broad Fen River valley. The first part of this program had been accomplished in a remarkably short time. The only serious opposition the Japanese had met in Shansi so far was from the Eighth Route Army in the north, and from General Wei Li-huang at Hsinkow.

In September, before they had occupied Shihkiachwang and cut off the Cheng-Tai railway, the Japanese columns had advanced from the north along four separate routes, converging north of Taiyuan. This was where the Eighth Route Army came into the picture; and in the spectacular engagements at Pinhsingkwan and Yenmenkwan they had inflicted on these invading columns the first defeats the Japanese forces had yet suffered in the course of the war. By the middle of October they had cut three of the four lines of communication with the north; and a Japanese force of some fifty thousand men was strategically surrounded north of Taiyuan.

There should have been enough Chinese troops in North Shansi to annihilate this isolated force; and the only hope for the Japanese was to rush through reinforcements from the east and establish a new connection. The vital point for the Chinese was to hold the Cheng-Tai railway, or failing this, to keep Niangtzekwan—one of the strongest natural passes in China. If Niangtzekwan once fell, the Japanese troops in the north would be relieved, and could come down swiftly on Taiyuan. Then much of the effect of the good work the Eighth Route Army had done in the mountains would be wasted.

In reply to my question, the commander grinned broadly, and said "Not very good," which was putting it mildly. He was a pock-marked veteran, wearing on his breast pocket the five-pointed metal star of the Red Army.

"You know, Niangtzekwan has never before been taken by force in Chinese history," he said. "Our own army urged Nanking to send fresh troops to the north; we asked for four divisions, to hold Shansi and save Taiyuan. We heard that two divisions of Kwangsi troops were being sent, but they never came. Instead, the troops from the Ping-Han line, who had already had several weeks of stiff fighting, were transferred to Niangtzekwan. So we had no fresh troops there. And when the enemy made a determined drive, the Chinese armies fell back."

"So there was no chance to hold Taiyuan?"

"Not very much. The fighting strength of some of the Chinese armies in Shansi is not very great." I felt he was being very diplomatic in his manner of statement.

"You see," he went on, "the Japanese do not worry to secure their communications, relying on the strength of their attack to force their way through to their objective. If they are only held up somewhere, the Eighth Route Army can cut off their rear and attack from behind. We have succeeded in doing this many times already.

"It is very easy to attack the Japanese in the rear. You have heard how we destroyed twenty-four enemy aeroplanes at Yangminpao? Our army had watched the airfield for several days, from the top of a high mountain—the Japanese never troubled to reconnoiter. One day, we saw that many aeroplanes came—more than twenty. That night we attacked.

"We sent one regiment; one battalion to cut off the Japanese base on either side, one battalion to attack. They had one battalion guarding the airfield. We were shown how to cross the river by the peasants, took them by surprise, and destroyed the planes very easily. That sort of action is possible when the enemy disregarded their own rear."

"Has the Eighth Route Army had any heavy fighting?" I asked. "I mean, in massed positions?"

"Not since the first engagements," he told me. "That was when it was still possible to hold up the Japanese advance. Now we do not concentrate our army, but operate in mobile units, doing the maximum amount of damage to the enemy by sudden surprise attacks.

"Even in the fighting at Yenmenkwan, we did not keep simple positions, but withdrew in the daytime to deceive the enemy, and then attacked at night. We found in our first experience of fighting the Japanese in positions that the enemy would first use bombing planes, then artillery; finally tanks and armored cars. To resist such an attack with inferior technique is to invite heavy losses.

"Now the Eighth Route Army never takes a fixed position, but keeps its mobility. And our tactics now are to operate deep in the rear of the enemy. Because of the good relations between our army and the people, we never have any difficulty about food or communications; but everywhere the people co-operate with us and help us. So we are able to occupy many cities in the Japanese rear, and strike sudden blows, surrounding and destroying enemy units; or if we cannot destroy them, withdrawing again before reinforcements can arrive."

"What will happen, now that Taiyuan is lost?"

He shrugged his shoulders. "The Chinese armies are retreating to the south. Perhaps they can still make a stand at Lingshih or some other place; but I do not think they can stop the main Japanese advance. It is very likely that most of the fighting in Shansi now will be guerilla and partisan war."

Later, I heard details of the condition of some of the provincial troops in Shansi that were illuminating. Many of them had no winter uniforms, and no shoes. Their regular pay was about six dollars a month, and five dollars of this went for food, so that what they actually received was usually a matter of sixty or seventy cents. It is not an inducement for which many would be prepared to risk their lives. And before long, I was to see for myself how demoralized some of them had become.

But the army I was with seemed cheerful enough. Without any false optimism, they were quietly preparing for a long-protracted war. For them, the real struggle was just beginning.

And I knew that the fighting in Shansi would not be over when (if ever they did) the Japanese reached Tungkwan. For the Eighth Route Army had had time enough to organize their bases, and make full preparations for partisan warfare all over the province. Already in thirty *hsien* they were mobilizing and arming the peasants, and this meant a new kind of resistance in Shansi.

"You are going to the front?" the base commander had asked me. "Well, we'll send you south for a start, so that you can make a connection with the mass organizations. Our 'front' now is all Shansi, and soon the Japanese will find that out!"

CHINESE RETREAT

There was only one restaurant in the little mountain town, and I went there to snatch an early breakfast, before our truck left for the south. The inner room, poorly lighted by a couple of candles, was cold and gloomy. One other man sat by himself at an enormous round table, obviously dedicated to rural feast-making. He was a Chinese officer, whose uniform had suffered badly; and he was shoveling *mien* into his mouth as though he had not had a square meal for a week.

He looked up furtively as we entered; but was reassured by the sight of my bodyguard, who was never shy of introducing himself as "Ti Pa Lu Chün." "Ah, the Eighth Route Army. Your people fought well in the north."

He had just come from Taiyuan, and was the first man I had seen who had been in the recent fighting. But he had not come out of it too well himself, from the look of things.

"I tell you, it was terrible. We never saw the Japanese. The planes came, again and again—*bom, bom!* and the big guns; they killed thousands of us. And the tanks, and the armored cars..." His eyes reflected horrors.

"Where are *they* now?"

"They've got Pingyao—it was bombed worse than Taiyuan. And they're probably in Fenyang. I tell you, we haven't a chance against those devils." He finished his third bowl of *mien*, belched disconsolately, and went out without a greeting. Obviously, he was pretty badly shaken.

"What do you think of that?" I asked my guard, who had sat listening solemnly, his Mauser clasped on his knees.

"Oh, he's all right, really. Only he's got the 'fear-of-Japan sickness.' The Red Army doesn't mind the Japanese tanks and guns; we know how to fight them."

His seventeen-year-old mastery of the situation was superb.

But the pale unshaven face and haggard eyes of the young officer haunted me all that day.

Once we got on to the main road, I saw plentiful evidences of tragedy. We were still well behind the Chinese lines, and the troops that were moving south had nothing to fear from Japanese howitzers, or from the air. But higher up they had been bombed and machine-gunned for hours on end, and what should have been an orderly withdrawal looked—even here—suspiciously like a rout.

The road was choked with every manner of conveyance, and the dust rose in clouds. Military trucks, like our own, were moving both north and south; but the general flow of traffic, in carts, on mule-back, or afoot, had set south like a tide. Single units were orderly—a mule train with mountain guns, a group of officers on pony-back, a battery of seventy-fives (though why were they moving south, unless it was because their caissons were empty?). But the great majority trudged along aimlessly, or flogged wretched animals that dragged carts loaded with twenty men.

There was every kind of uniform to be seen, and every kind of headgear. Some wore the regulation steel helmets of German pattern with the Kuomintang sun on one side, others shallow "tin hats" after the American army style; some wore fur caps, some field caps, and some marched bareheaded. Many had hooded greatcoats, but others were still in summer uniforms, or had only a tattered blanket across their shoulders. Blood-soaked puttees trailed in the dust; I did not see any seriously wounded men on the road, but many were in the last stages of exhaustion.

There was no attempt to rally the march, or put any order into these dispirited stragglers. It was a welcome relief to see at last one party camped by the roadside for a morning meal, their rifles neatly piled with a man on guard. "Some of ours," the driver informed me, as the truck sped past, and they waved a friendly salute. They were going north.

Worst of all were those poor wretches—deserters from the northern front who had lost touch with their units—who limped along in tattered uniforms, with a bayonet perhaps, or a bandolier, as all that remained of their equipment. But some still had their rifles, and were in an ugly mood. Our truck, with its twenty-odd soldiers, did not seem overloaded. There was a reason for this (not apparent to the uninitiated) in that four leaves of one front spring were broken. If we had taken one more man on board, we should soon have had twenty, and the truck would have foundered within a hundred yards.

It is not easy to explain a technical point in a hurry, and the best thing would have been to drive fast and save explanations. But it was impossible to drive fast all the time on that road. Whenever we slowed down, someone would demand a lift. Once a sturdy intransigent leaped on to the running-board, and would not be dislodged. The driver tried passive resistance, and refused to start the truck. In the ensuing argument, I had got out with some vague idea of acting as a mediator, when a shot was fired just behind us, and the bullet whistled past our ears. One of the trouble-maker's friends was expressing his feelings a little too positively for our liking.

In a moment, two of our party sprang from the truck, and the man who had fired was disarmed. "Drive on!" someone shouted; my guards had their Mausers out. It looked like an unpleasant incident.

But the troop commander intervened. "No, comrades," he insisted. "We can't take his gun, or he may get into trouble." He took the rifle, shot the bolt to make sure it was unloaded, and handed it back over the side of the truck. "That gun was given you to use against the Japanese, not against your fellow-countrymen," he remarked succinctly. "We would take you with us if we could." And then in a lower voice, to the chauffeur, "Drive on—*fast!*"

This little outburst surprised me, for even in the confusion on the road, I fancied, most people retained their patient good humor. But there was a woeful lack of discipline, and it seemed to me that many of the officers, themselves well-mounted, had lost touch completely with their men. I was getting the most unfavorable possible introduction to the Shansi troops. And the point I had heard made so often in Yenan—the need for a thorough reorganization of the Chinese army system—was clearer now. Many things would have to be changed in the provincial armies before that result could be secured; not least, the troops would have to be given a decent living and something worth fighting for.

All that day we drove southwards, much of the way through hills. Here a truck had gone over the bank and piled up a useless wreck; there an abandoned cart would stand with a broken axle. Once the driver leaped down to investigate a pile of battered gasoline cans, and gleefully salvaged two half-full of lubricating oil. For a long time, a small car kept ahead of us, absurdly overloaded with civilian refugees; suddenly, on the crest of a hill, passengers sprang out like alarmed cats from both sides, and the little car burst into flames.

It was already dusk when we crossed the river over a bridge of boats, and came in sight of the walls and towers of Pingyang. It looked peaceful enough on the open plain; but once inside the walls, I had never seen a city so crowded. Through a welter of troops, mules, refugees, and camels, we made our way at last to the Eighth Route Army quarters.

At first I thought there must be some mistake. The slim, youthful commander to whom I was introduced, in the comfortable room of a private house, was spruce in a tailored khaki uniform, with an ornamental "Chiang Kai-shek" smallsword at his hip. I had first met the Eighth Route Army in Yenan, and had grown used to Mao Tse-tung's faded blue-cotton uniform, or the trim but weather-stained garb of the staff of the Red Academy. Only the frank and unceremonious greeting, and the familiar cluster of *hsiao kwei* about the doorway, finally reassured me. This was the Eighth Route Army, in the full glory of its metamorphosis. I would have to get used to it.

POLITICAL COMMISSAR

Until a few days before, Pingyang, or Linfen, as it was called locally, had been the center of the provincial government. But this had just left "for an unknown destination" to the south. No one knew where Yen Hsi-shan—that rusé old politician who seemed at last to have met his Waterloo—had gone; the city at this time was virtually under control of the military and the "patriotic movement."

"You will want to see something of the mass organization here," the young commander at Eighth Route Army quarters had suggested. "But first, you must see Chou En-lai."

I had never met "The Insurrectionist," as Edgar Snow had called him, though we had once been together in Sian at a time when Chou En-lai's eloquence, backed up by the "peace line" of the Communist Party, had been chiefly responsible for saving the life of Chiang Kai-shek. Chou was usually to be found at a focus of political tension, and I knew that in the past weeks he had been active in mass organization in Shansi.

The man who came briskly into the room, dressed in a plain black "Sun Yat-sen" uniform, was certainly a compelling personality. The short hair and beard gave him a strange resemblance to the self-portrait of D. H. Lawrence, an impression which was heightened by Chou's intense nervous vitality. This was a man, one felt, who would have been an artist, if he had not been a revolutionary.

His manner was lively, almost gay; and he moved his hands in deft, sudden gestures. He spoke current English with perfect ease, but with an occasional French turn of phrase, or a French word to help out a sentence.* Dark eyes were youthful and animated, and lit up as soon as he began to talk. He had an unaffected charm, and the power to convince of the born orator.

"How is the work going?" I asked him, for he was so busy at this time that I felt I might not get another opportunity.

"Political mobilization? It is not so bad. You know, in North Shansi we had a very good chance to work among the masses. Always it is like that—when there is real danger, they give us freedom to organize the people. But then it is too late—the Japanese come down and occupy the districts where we have begun to work! Now we must extend the people's movement all over Shansi, so that we will be really prepared for the Japanese when they come."

---

* Chou En-lai studied for two years in Paris, and was one of the founders of the Chinese Communist Party there in 1921 (some months before the founding of the Party in China).

"How is it here, since the fall of Taiyuan?"

"Yes, that is a real crisis—the capture of Taiyuan, and the capture of Shanghai. Now the Japanese hope to drive the Chinese armies south of the Yellow River, and then to declare that the fighting in North China is over. You know of the terms for a 'peace settlement' that they have proposed already through the German Ambassador? Some elements in China, who are dismayed at the Japanese advance, and who had relied too much on help from England and America, think now that we cannot resist the Japanese in the north."

"What are the chances for continuing the war here?"

Chou made a wry face. "Of course, we must try to keep some of the regular armies north of the river; and Generalissimo Chiang is in favor of this—he has just sent some more Central troops into Shansi. But most important is the strengthening of the Chinese armies, and the development of the mass movement. Some of the armies here are very discouraged—they have suffered severely, and because the people did not rise to support them, there are already many deserters.

"We must improve the livelihood of the Chinese soldiers, and organize and train the masses of North China. This is where the Government must help us, by giving us support and arms. The armies complain that the people do not rise—but this is not the people's fault; it is the fault of the local authorities, who will not permit the free mobilization of the people. Partly, too, it is the fault of the old-style army regulations. You have seen what some of the armies here are like; how can they expect the people to welcome them?

"But there are many points in favor of continuing the war of resistance in North China. For one thing, the general topography is suitable for guerilla fighting. And then, the Japanese have not enough troops to occupy the whole territory, even if they could. It is a matter of simple arithmetic. There are more than 300 *hsien* cities in North China; the Japanese can never hold all of these, even if they put one company of troops in each city. And if they did, that would be fine for us—we could destroy each separate company in turn!

"As I say, we hope that some of the Central armies will

remain north of the Yellow River, so that the war in the north will not become *merely* partisan fighting. But if it does, the Eighth Route Army can be the backbone of the Chinese resistance. And if we can only mobilize and arm the people to cooperate with them, the Japanese will find the war in North China will not be 'finished' so soon as they thought!"

It was already clear that the main task of organizing popular resistance throughout the North would devolve upon the Eighth Route Army. But much was to be expected from the local and provincial governments, and in Linfen—the largest city of Shansi remaining in Chinese hands—the official patriotic organizations were increasingly co-operative. The degree of co-operation, as Chou En-lai had said, was in direct proportion to the immediate danger of Japanese advance.

"I will introduce you to a student who can take you round the patriotic organizations," Chou told me. I welcomed the idea of an interpreter, for my own Chinese was certainly inadequate for the securing of detailed information; and I had already decided that I must find an English-speaking companion for the rest of the trip. In Yenan, the political base of the communists, language had been no difficulty; but there were few linguists with the army. In Linfen I had hoped there might be the chance of picking up a student who could travel with me to the front.

What happened was a pure stroke of luck. For the guide Chou En-lai had recommended turned out to be the same young Tungpei student whom I had last seen two months before in the British Concession in Tientsin. He was thinner and more harassed-looking than ever; but he greeted me with immense enthusiasm. Along with a group of friends from Peiping, he had formed in Linfen a branch of the old Student Union, and they were now editing the only daily newspaper in the city.

Wu took me to the local headquarters of the chief popular organizations, which were functioning in these days with unusual activity. All were of an official or semi-official nature, which meant—in Shansi—that they had the open or indirect support of Yen Hsi-shan. There were the "War Zone People's

Revolutionary Mobilization Committee," the "National Salvation League of Sacrifice," the inevitable "Dare-to-Die's"; and the *Shaonien Hsienfengtui,* or "Youth Vanguard." All were volunteer movements, with political as well as military training departments.

The high-sounding names were very familiar, and I knew enough of the mushroom growth of such movements in China, which only too often perished as swiftly as they were born, to be a little skeptical about any results they might achieve. But, as Wu lost no time in telling me, "all these groups had Eighth Route Army advisers and instructors." And that made a great difference. Under such teachers, volunteer and partisan training would not be merely textbook and theory; the unrivaled experience of the communists in popular organization had given them a mastery of this difficult technique which no one else in China at this time possessed.

The war emergency had produced in Shansi a situation where inevitably the most determined and experienced elements took the lead. And there could be no two minds about who these elements were. Every day in Linfen or surrounding districts Chou En-lai addressed mass meetings; every day, organizers left for the country villages where, even more than in cities where the old officialdom lingered, the work of political mobilization was to be continued. One could see this movement growing and reaching out to those remote mountain valleys where, as far as Manchuria but with infinitely better organization and preparation than the Manchurian Volunteers had ever known, the war of resistance would be carried on to the end.

Linfen gave us an idea of what was already being done. And Wu, I found, was only too eager to accept my invitation to come along as interpreter and translator on the next stage of the journey. Someone else could take his place on the paper; he exchanged the last of his civilian clothes—his only possessions—for a padded cotton uniform and greatcoat. And a couple of days later, through a frozen drizzle that soon would turn to snow, we were moving northwards towards Eighth Route Army headquarters.

CHAPTER FIVE
THE EIGHTH ROUTE ARMY

ON TO HEADQUARTERS

By day, the Tung-Pu railway, a narrow-gauge line which runs north and south through Shansi, was silent and deserted. But nightfall and the evening star that called the Japanese bomber back to its base, awoke it to a new activity.

The little station where our party had arrived was bitterly cold, swept by a wind that came from snow-covered hills. Storm-lanterns, electric torches, and a red glow from the cab of an engine, were the only lights on the scene. To make up a train under these conditions, and from the confusion of rolling stock that spilled over three or four sidings, was a task almost as intricate as Chinese chess. As if in protest, from time to time a locomotive hooted dismally.

For nearly an hour we had played hide-and-seek with the moving cars, trying to find the carriage that was to take us north. It was a tantalizing game, for I had my own pile of baggage, and others had piles of maps and papers that were destined for the Army Staff. A shout from one of our men, to announce that he had located the carriage, would be the signal for all of us to plunge off the platform into a dangerous labyrinth of points and rails. When we reached the spot, it was usually to find an empty stretch of siding, and the soldier shouting fluent Hunanese after the carriage as it disappeared into the night. Five minutes later, it would come back on a different line, and we would start all over again.

At last we had all scrambled aboard, into a blessed shelter from the icy wind, and settled down for the night. Outside, the moving silhouette of cars that were still being shunted up and down continued like a fantastic shadow show. Muffled to the eyes, refugees for the south clung precariously to open trucks; every boxcar was loaded with half-frozen humanity. How many hours had they been there already, I wondered; and how many hours more would it be until they had reached Tungkwan, to pay fantastic prices for a place in the crowded ferry over the Yellow River into safety?

Our own third-class carriage, with its military markings and guards posted at the doors, was continually besieged by these unfortunates. Clasping all that they had salvaged of their precious belongings, they would hammer at the windows: "Where is this train going?" "Going north," the sentry would answer briefly; and inevitably would come the startled response, "Going *north?*" in a tone that spoke volumes.

North meant Taiyuan, the armies, and the front; above all, north meant the Japanese. These new invaders, who "did not make war on the Chinese people, but only on the Chinese armies," had chosen methods of expressing their friendship which at last were clear and unequivocal. Already from the mouths of refugees I had heard tales of whole villages burned to the ground in northern Shansi, of groups of young men "selected" and shot by the Japanese in "hostile" districts. These were not rumors and atrocity scare-mongering, but sober tales of reality from those who themselves had seen these things.

And the effect of all this, in the war zone, was unmistakable. Further south, I had asked one old peasant what he thought of the war. "Yes, we know there is a war," he had grumbled, "because there are so many soldiers about. Either it is a war with the communists, or with the Nanking Government!" No such confusion remained in the minds of those who had seen the khaki uniforms of the invaders, or the bombers with the red sun on their wings.

In the narrow aisle, Chou En-lai paced restlessly up and down. The political commissar I had seen in Linfen, with his dark beard and plain black uniform, now appeared in the role of Vice-Chairman of the Military Council—clean-shaven, in the blue uniform of the Kuomintang armies. The change, in so versatile a personality, was not surprising. Chou looked younger, less picturesque perhaps, but none the less a man of action.

"What do you think of this lull in the fighting?" I asked him. For several days, there had been no Japanese advance, and very little bombing.

"Perhaps the Japanese are taking a rest," he remarked. "They want to consolidate their position at Taiyuan, of course; and this cold weather they do not like at all. Then perhaps their aeroplanes are afraid of the new concentration of Chinese planes in Sian."

"But you don't think they're likely to call a halt at Taiyuan?"

"Not in the least! Once they have secured their communications, and the weather clears, we shall have them down here. Of course, there may be some trouble inside their own armies."

I was curious about this, for if anyone knew of the condition of the enemy troops, it was the Eighth Route Army. Chou began to tell me of some of the "finds" they had made.

"At Pinhsingkwan, some of the dead Japanese troops had manifestos of the Japanese Communist Party in their pockets, calling on them to resist the war against China that their own militarists were making. You know, we captured many diaries and records from the Japanese troops, and some of these show quite clearly their opposition to the war. The rank and file do not know why they are here in China. They hate the country and the climate. They cannot eat the local food; and wherever their armies come, the countryside is deserted. They have had some hard fighting—much harder than they expected—and they really do not know what it is all about."

"How do you manage to make any contact with the Japanese troops?" I asked him.

"Of course, we have taken some prisoners, and we are eager to explain to them our policy of friendship towards the Japanese people. It is not easy to take the Japanese prisoner, for they have heard that the Chinese kill all their captives, and so they will fight to the last, even when they are wounded. But the special policy of the Eighth Route Army towards prisoners of war is gradually having an effect. We have one section of our political department, which prepares material and slogans in

Japanese, to be distributed among the enemy troops. And now we are beginning to teach our soldiers Japanese songs!"

We talked of other things—of Paris, and of London, where Chou had been fifteen years before—in this bare little third-class carriage, with only a couple of guttering candles to show the pattern of frost upon the windowpanes. Like many of his countrymen, Chou had preferred living in France to England. But he was full of curiosity about English customs, and had—it seemed to me—a very shrewd understanding of British policy in the Far East. "Even yet," he said, "your Government does not see the real danger of Japan in China. But in time they must see it." I noticed that he made a very clear distinction between such "incidents" as the wounding of the British Minister, and the direct threat of Japanese encroachment into British spheres of influence like the Yangtse and South China.

The little town we reached at last, sheltering beneath the hills, was dark and lifeless except for an occasional patrol. It was Chou who led the way to Army headquarters, discreetly placed in a cotton-merchant's house down a back street. The court we entered was wide and bare, with a covered goldfish pool. In a room with walls as thick as a dungeon, and about as cold, we found places on a brick *k'ang* to snatch a few hours of sleep.

My guard woke me, when the court was filled already with pale winter sunshine and the clatter of horses' hooves. In the room across the way (that had been empty the night before) voices and laughter now resounded. Lathered horses were being led through to the back courtyard; they had traveled all night. Chou En-lai, greeting me cheerfully across the goldfish pool, beckoned us into a room where half a dozen men in uniform, gathered around a table, were doing full justice to a simple Chinese meal.

"Let me introduce you," he said. "This . . ."—a short, unassuming figure rose from the table; I was conscious of a friendly handshake, and of an incredibly wrinkled brown face with very bright eyes—"is Comrade Chu, our commander." Across the room, a big man waved his chopsticks, and boomed informal salutation. "And that is Comrade P'eng Teh-huai."

For ten years, the names of these two Red Army commanders —Chu Teh, who led the Nanchang uprising of 1927, and with Mao Tse-tung formed the first Chinese Soviet; P'eng Teh-huai, reputedly the fiercest and most *"lihai"* of all the communist leaders—had struck terror into the hearts of the Chinese bourgeoisie. Now, as commander and vice-commander respectively of the Eighth Route Army, they were leaders of the most effective resistance to the Japanese in North China, and popular national heroes.

In this period, I flattered myself, I was probably the first Englishman to shake hands with either of them. "Please sit down," said General Chu politely through a mouthful of millet, "and have some breakfast!"

COMMANDER-IN-CHIEF

Chinese generals, with the notable exception of Feng Yu-hsiang, are not usually shy in the matter of uniforms. And even Marshel Feng, whose field garb was always that of a common soldier, has blossomed out of recent years into gold braid and epaulettes. But Chu Teh, in his plain blue padded-cotton uniform, with a woolen lumber-jacket buttoned around his throat and a blue cloth army cap, looked what he was—the leader of a peasants' and workers' army.

Since 1937, much has been written about this extraordinary man, who was once a successful southern warlord, an opium-smoker with his private fortune and his concubines, before he cured himself of the opium habit by a magnificent effort of will, went to Germany, became a communist and returned to China to lead a Red Army for ten years with such amazing success. Inevitably, in such a man one looks to find a Garibaldi, a figure to pose on horseback as the leader of one of the greatest marches any army in the world has ever made. But no army commander can ever have had less to do with heroics than Chu Teh.

His unassuming appearance is the expression of a personal modesty that is completely natural and unaffected. In this, it seemed to me, Chu Teh made an interesting contrast with Mao

Tse-tung. Mao, with all his indifference to form and ceremony, has an intellectual force and an immense dignity which would mark him out in any assembly; Chu Teh (it is one of the things he likes to do, and that has proved extremely convenient on several occasions in his surprising career) could lose himself in a crowd in a moment. His favorite reply to the common reproach at his bad habit of exposing himself to danger in advanced positions, is that if ever his headquarters were taken by surprise he could disappear in coolie clothes and "nobody would know him." This complete identity of the commander with the rank and file of his own army is something that is rare in any country (Feng Yu-hsiang gives us the classic example of the strength of it in China, even in the old militarist wars). It is this that has made Chu Teh perhaps the best-loved of all Chinese leaders among the common people.

Yet it would be a dangerous error to suppose that Chu Teh's modest exterior was any indication of mediocrity. His own record, and the scope of his achievement, should be the readiest answer to that. But it is true that his outstanding qualities, as an army commander and a political leader, do not show on the surface: one reads them first in the implicit confidence which all his subordinates (including brilliant young graduates from Russian military academies) have in his judgment and experience. I was to spend long enough, on other occasions, with Chu Teh to realize just why this quiet, ugly little man with the gentle manner and disarming smile held the position that he did. It would be hard to imagine anyone at first sight less like a revolutionary; I never saw Chu Teh lose for a moment his even temper, or his quiet acceptance of heartbreaking obstacles in the work in which he was engaged. But when one had seen him in action, and realized that nothing could shake his patience or his iron resolution, one began to understand why legends had gathered around his name.

On that first morning, an hour after breakfast, Chu Teh came into my room and sat down on one corner of the bed. "Would you like to talk with me?" he asked modestly. "I have a little time to spare."

His invitation was so frank that I abandoned any pretense at formalities. "Tell me something about the war in the north," I said, "and your own Army."

Chu beamed contentedly now that we had made a start. "As you know," he began, "the Japanese want to occupy all of Shansi, and some of the heaviest fighting in the north has been in this province. After they had occupied the Ping-Sui railway, the enemy moved very swiftly to Tatung; and then lost no time in coming down on Shansi through the northern and northeastern passes. On this front, the Japanese used their North China army, part of the Kwantung army, and their crack Fifth Division. In our sector—that is, to attack Shansi—they had at this time between fifty and sixty thousand men.

"They had several lines of advance from the north; but the Fifth Division made the first big attack late in September, on Pinhsingkwan. Here one division of our army advanced to the rear of the Japanese column without their knowledge, and we were able to take them completely by surprise. We captured their headquarters, many maps and documents, with a great deal of military material; destroyed two companies of a relieving force, and advanced on Pinhsingkwan. The Japanese withdrew to the north, losing more than three thousand men."

"Tell me something more about the fighting here," I suggested.

Chu Teh looked embarrassed. "There were two main reasons for our success," he said. "First, it was hill fighting, so that the enemy could not use their tanks and planes: and then, it was a surprise attack. Second, we had the co-operation and assistance of other Chinese regular armies.

"We engaged the enemy infantry right at the start, so that they had no chance to use their artillery; they could not even use their machine guns. It was a running fight in the hills, and our troops, of course, are much more mobile than theirs. The Japanese, we found, do not like this kind of fighting. They had learned to rely on their tanks and on their heavy artillery in all the fighting so far, and they were very uncomfortable without them. We killed many of them here with hand grenades.

"But even though they were defeated, they fought to the

last, and none of them would surrender. Why? Because they knew that, if they lost their arms, they would be killed by their own commanders; this is a rule of the Fifth Division, and it applies also to the Manchurian and Mongol troops that are fighting with the Japanese. Partly, too, it was because they were afraid of being killed by the Chinese if they were taken prisoner. The Japanese themselves usually kill wounded Chinese, and they have killed so many villagers in their advance that they are afraid of the Chinese people taking their revenge.

"Our soldiers do not speak Japanese, and so we were unable to move them by propaganda, when they would not surrender. We were very sorry about this, and since then we have made special efforts to explain our policy towards prisoners of war and enemy captives."

"Was this the heaviest fighting the Eighth Route Army has had?"

"No, other engagements have been heavier than this. But this was the most clear-cut victory that we have yet had against the Japanese."

So the first Japanese invasion of Shansi had resulted in a check. "What was the next stage in the fighting?" I asked.

"The enemy had already begun to advance along another route, directly from the north. Now they pushed strongly down on Hsinkow, where the Central and Shansi troops were holding the pass. There was severe fighting here, and the Nanking troops did very well against the Japanese—they held out stubbornly for three weeks. We admired very much General Wei Li-huang's resistance at Hsinkow.

"Meantime, our army moved rapidly northeast, to cut the enemy lines of communication. As you know, we succeeded in reoccupying Yenmenkwan, and before long our troops, operating independently, had cut three of the main Japanese lines of communication. At this time, the Japanese troops who had advanced from the north suffered very severely. They could get no supplies, for we held the roads, and trucks and munition trains had to turn back. They had no supplies of petrol, so could not use their mechanized units. For a while, this invading Japanese force was in a really desperate position."

This was the main outline of the Shansi campaign, as I knew it already. But it gained a new reality as Chu Teh retold it, a nicotine-stained finger pointing out the movements of troops on an outspread map.

"But then," Chu went on, "the Japanese advanced south along the Ping-Han railway, and occupied Shihkiachwang. Here their Twentieth Division branched off, and advanced swiftly along the Cheng-Tai railway towards Niangtzekwan. At this time, we hoped again to cut off their rear, but we moved a little too slowly. One important strategic town before Niangtzekwan unaccountably fell with scarcely any resistance; and so it proved difficult for the Chinese troops to hold the eastern pass.

"But near Niangtzekwan, our army again had some heavy fighting with this Twentieth Division, which was about twenty- to thirty-thousand strong. We had a much smaller force, and no support at all: the other Chinese troops had withdrawn on Taiyuan. But south of Niangtzekwan, we again defeated a large force of Japanese infantry, and captured a great deal of munitions and supplies. While we were still fighting here, the Japanese advanced along the railway on Taiyuan, which fell shortly afterwards.

"Altogether, we estimate that so far the enemy have had at least thirty thousand casualties in the fighting in Shansi.* The Chinese losses have been very heavy; but at present their strategic position is not unfavorable. The Japanese now must wait for more supplies and munitions from the north; and remember that the north and northeast of Shansi are now well covered by our guerilla units."

"What is your opinion of the fighting quality of the Japanese army?" I asked. Chu nodded pleasantly.

"Very good," he said. "They are well-trained, and very much better armed than our troops. They use their mechanical arms —tanks, armored cars, and planes—to great advantage when they get the opportunity. They are good at taking cover, shoot well, and keep their arms in good condition." This frank tribute to enemy efficiency rather surprised me.

"But"—Chu went on—"they have very definite weaknesses.

* i.e., after three months of fighting.

One weak point is their infantry. The Japanese infantry, we have found, are not very good at independent action. They depend entirely on mechanical means of transport for communications and supply. If these are cut off, they are at a real disadvantage. They cannot use animal transport, or human labor, as our armies can. They cannot take advantage of the hill country, but must follow the easiest and most level route.

"When we fight the Japanese, we try to avoid their strong points, and select their weak points for attack. So we always fight in the hills, not in open country. And we have the assistance of the people, whom we organize and train into partisan units, to harass the enemy lines of communication."

Chu went on to show me the position of the scattered Chinese forces at that time in Shansi, Hopei, and Chahar. "You see," he chuckled, as his finger moved from one *hsien* city to another, "outside of their main lines of advance, the Japanese hold nothing. Our troops are deep in their rear, and—in co-operation with the volunteer mobile units in Hopei, and the partisans— occupy practically the whole of the territory through which they have advanced. *We* have no rear to worry about, for we are fighting in our own country, and everywhere the people support us, give us food and assistance. If necessary, we can rely on the Japanese themselves for ammunition, for their cartridges fit our rifles. So you see there are very good prospects for continuing the war in North China."

He folded his maps, and rose to go. I knew how busy he was, and could not offer to detain him. But there was one more question I wanted to ask. "Is there anything that you, as commander of the former Chinese Red Armies, would like to tell the foreign countries?"

Chu's genial expression for the first time became serious. "Yes," he said, "there is this. You know the Japanese excuse for their present military action in China—that they are fighting 'communism.' They use this propaganda to justify what is, quite simply, the invasion of our country.

"You know how false this propaganda is. You know the Eighth Route Army is not fighting for communism in China, but is joining with all the other Chinese armies to fight for

China's national independence. Along with the armies of the Kuomintang, we are fighting for a free and democratic Chinese Republic. Tell all the friendly foreign nations the truth about this, so that no one can any longer believe the 'anti-Red' inventions of the Japanese propagandists."

I am convinced that Chu Teh was sincere in this, as he said it. And all that I had seen of the Chinese Communists, in their own district and in the army, fully supported the claim. From their side, at least, there would be no danger to the United Front. It was this kind of political unity that was new in China: and if it could only prove enduring, then it might not have been bought at too great a cost.

MISSIONARY INTERLUDE

Headquarters were shifted again that day to an outlying village, where part of the army was due to arrive from the front. It was abominably cold in our temporary lodging, and when Wu told me that there were some English missionaries in the little town, I suggested a visit. In Linfen, at the China Inland Mission hospital, I had already made my first contact with Europeans in over a month. Most of the mission workers there had already evacuated: one Canadian doctor remained with a staff of nurses, doing heroic service in the hospital, and treating many wounded soldiers as out-patients.

It was something of a surprise to learn that another group of missionaries were still at their posts further north. With Wu, I made my way through narrow streets to the compound. My guard was very suspicious of the whole proceedings, and took up his stand outside the gate, with ready Mauser. He knew all about the "united front" with the foreigners, but was taking no chances.

At the little chapel we made a discovery: it was Sunday. (With the army all days were alike, and I had been keeping my diary by dates, not by days of the week.) The morning service was nearly finished, and we waited in the snow-filled court, listening to the sound of singing. It was a curious experience, in this wintry, war-harassed countryside, to hear the strains of "*Adeste, fideles!*" with their promise of Christmas peace. I wondered how much peace there would be that winter for the peasants of Shansi. . . .

The service over, we introduced ourselves, and were given the friendliest possible welcome from a gray-haired veteran missionary, his wife and sister. I expressed my surprise at finding them still there. "Why not?" the stout-hearted evangelist responded. "We've been in this province for forty years, and we don't intend to quit because of the Japanese." His gray eyes twinkled. "Mind you, we've a Union Jack over the compound, to educate their bombers—who seem to need it! For the rest, we have faith. . . ."

I had come, a little uncertain about the reception I should get, to put in a request for English newspapers. But there was nothing uncertain about their hospitality. And our host was only too eager to talk.

"Of course you'll stay to lunch, and your friend too. . . . So you're with the Eighth Route Army? Those are the people that shut us up here last year; they gave us a good scare then, I can tell you! But come in out of the cold."

In the late winter and spring of 1936, the Red Army had crossed the Yellow River, and overrun most of Shansi; by the margin of a few hours only, Nanking troops had arrived in time to relieve the capital. This "bandit incursion" had been regarded at the time as a national disaster (though, as one young officer had told me with some justice, "If we had taken Taiyuan then, and held it, the Japanese wouldn't be there now"). But times had changed.

"You're not afraid of the 'Reds' now?" I asked our host, when we were seated before a substantial Sunday dinner of roast mutton and vegetables. I had been living on army rations —two meals a day of Chinese bread and cabbage—and had forgotten that there was so much food left in the world.

"Bless my soul, no. We'd rather have them here than some of these other Chinese troops; they have real discipline in their army. These other fellows are the bandits, who go looting the common people. Why, that communist general, Chu Teh—"

"Did you know that he was living just down the street from you, yesterday?"

"We certainly did not! But when the communists—or the 'Eighth Route Army' I suppose I must call them—came into Shansi this summer, on their way to the front, you know they stayed for a while at Hou Ma?" I nodded. "Well, we have a little mission there, and that's where Chu Teh had his quarters. Our Christian folk called him 'Brother Chu'—*they* didn't know who he was—and were delighted to have him. Only when he left, did they discover who they'd been entertaining unawares!"

When one remembers that, for many years, Christian missionaries in China had been perhaps the most vocal and hostile element in the country against the "Red bandits," one can appreciate the full strength of this tribute. In Sian, during the 1936 revolt, I had seen the beginning of a change of attitude on the part of those missionaries who had met and talked with communist leaders, and had seen something of the Red Army in their own district. The change of policy announced by the Chinese Communists earlier that year, when they renounced any indiscriminate enmity towards "foreign imperialists," and declared their intention of respecting the safety and property rights of all foreigners except the Japanese, had been proved by demonstration, and was beginning to have its effect.

The good opinion of the missionaries is worth having, for they are the only considerable section of the foreign population who are in China for other reasons than profit. And just as most of them had outspokenly condemned the barbarous methods of the Japanese militarists in China, so now I was to find the missionaries in Shansi united in their praise of the discipline and exemplary conduct towards the common people of the Eighth Route Army. And they were under no illusions about their fighting quality.

"Yes, the communists know the right way to tackle the Japanese," my host informed me roundly. "And we have no quarrel with their program of improving the livelihood of the peasants. If only they weren't against religion, we would have much in common...."

"But *are* they against religion?" I suggested. For—fresh from

Yenan—I found myself something of an interpreter of the communist policy, as I understood it. "Now there is a United Front in China, things look rather different. The communists have announced a change of policy, and it seems to me they're keeping to it. Certainly there is no discrimination against Mohammedans in the Northwest; and you admit there has been none against the Chinese Christians here...."

But on this point, my host was unshakable. He recalled chapters of past history from the south, kidnaping and maltreatment of missionaries by the "Reds." This was familiar ground, and I had no wish to cover it once again. My own belief was that many of these stories had been exaggerated, though some unquestionably had a basis in fact. But during the "Red Army" period, the communists were outlaws at open war with landlord-officialdom: and the missionaries had generally sided with the landlords. In such a situation there was bound to be trouble. But now, with the same "Reds" recognized members of Chinese society, there need be no further cause for misunderstanding. A common danger and a common cause erase the memory of old hostilities more swiftly, perhaps, than peaceful overtures can ever do.

In this friendly mission station I saw my first foreign newspapers in many weeks, and learned something of the reaction in Britain and America to the war—above all, to the Japanese bombing of open towns in China. Here, at least, we could all agree; and I found my hosts pretty obviously disgusted with the weakness of British policy in the Far East. Strangely enough (or perhaps not so strangely) missionary opinion in China was a good deal less conciliatory towards the Japanese than were Messrs. Jardine Matheson or the Hong Kong and Shanghai Bank....

We parted from these new friends with real regret. "You must come again," they assured us, "if you're ever back in this part of the country."

"We'd love to, if the Japanese aren't here before us...."

Wu, I noticed, was presented on leaving with a number of tracts: the United Front, it seemed, had opened the way for propaganda on both sides. But I knew that the real reason why this group of "foreigners"—no longer young—remained at their station right in the path of the Japanese advance, was to give what protection they could to several hundreds of young Chinese students in their mission schools. New ties of gratitude and loyalty were being formed in this hour of China's crisis, and they would surely not be forgotten in the years ahead.

A few hours later, at the head of a troop of cavalry (as a mark of special honor I was riding Chu Teh's horse—a bad-tempered animal with an astonishing turn of speed) we were galloping across country towards our new headquarters.

OLD FRIENDS AND NEW ENEMIES

Just in front of me rode Jen Pi-shih, head of the Political Department, in a khaki Japanese greatcoat with flying hood. Our whole troop, in fact, had drawn heavily upon the Japanese for their cavalry sabers and much other useful equipment: there were even a number of "enemy" chargers, tall raking beasts that looked like giants amongst the little Mongol ponies. I felt a certain affection for these big raw-boned captives—like myself, some of them had probably been raised under the Southern Cross. But the Chinese had a very poor opinion of "foreign horses," considering them clumsy and difficult to ride. Most of them, indeed, were in terrible shape after the hard fare of the northern hills, and were no match for the hardy China ponies.

We were the advance party to establish headquarters, and the troops who had crossed the mountains would arrive some time after midnight. We rode fast to reach our village before nightfall, threading the intricate bypaths and sunken roads of these terraced loess fields. But it was already dusk when we clattered under a stone archway into the streets of what looked like a small country town.

It was a wealthy village, and the house we entered belonged to the headman—who had probably trembled for its safety a year before, when the Red Army occupied all this countryside. Now his son, a Taiyuan student and member of the Young Vanguard, welcomed us with immense enthusiasm. Jen's first words: "This is the Eighth Route Army; tell the people they needn't be afraid!" were hardly necessary here. The schoolteacher came smiling to offer billets, and there was no mistaking the welcome the villagers gave to the troops.

Wu, my guard, and I shared a room in the headman's house. It was the most comfortable lodging we had yet had, for we were given what Wu called "the bridal suite." This was a handsome room with the red-paper squares across the windows that mark off the living quarters of a newly-married couple in a Chinese house. On the wall was a rather alarming painting of a Chinese matron nursing a generous family, all set about with pomegranates. In each corner of the room was a tiny bow and arrow, fastened high up against the wall by a red-paper strip. These, I learned, were to ward off the spirits of conjugal infelicity—an apt commentary on the mentality of a household where the sons were getting a modern education, and which boasted (unheard of luxury in a Chinese village!) a radio set in the back parlor.

The main body of troops arrived that night. Tso Chuan, a wiry young Hunanese who had been an honor graduate of the Red Military Academy in Moscow and was now acting chief-of-staff of the Eighth Route Army, came in time for the evening meal. We sat together beneath the Goddess of Fertility and ate steaming *mien* that the villagers offered to us, for the army cooks had been delayed. Then, between mouthfuls, Tso Chuan broke a piece of news. "*Sze-mo-teh-lai,*" the "American journalist," would arrive with the main column of troops late that night, to be billeted in the neighboring village.

This was the first news I had heard of Agnes Smedley since she left Sian. And now, when I was still on my way to the front, Agnes had just returned from it, after a journey that would certainly have prostrated any less hardened campaigner. Those who know the North China country are perhaps in the best position to appreciate what it means for an American woman to keep up day by day with a Chinese army; no wonder these first reports described the "foreign comrade" as feeling "tired."

OLD FRIENDS AND NEW ENEMIES 171

There were few signs of exhaustion, however, about the businesslike figure we discovered next morning, hammering away at a typewriter in a little farmhouse where half the neighborhood seemed to have gathered around the doorway, or glued its nose to the foot of glass in the window. "You seem to be one of the sights," I remarked, after we had exchanged greetings.

"I know," said Agnes disgustedly. "They think I'm a Japanese captive"—she wore a plain khaki uniform—"or a Russian staff officer, or part of a traveling circus: anything but a journalist, and a woman! Still, I've gotten used to it."

She had traveled up with the army to Taiyuan, had been with Lin Piao's division in the fighting south of Niangtzekwan, and had marched back across the mountains with the troops who had arrived in our village the night before. With her was a Chinese journalist and interpreter, picturesquely named Li Po; and the young Manchurian novelist Hsü Chun, whose *Children Without a Country* is a prose epic of the exiles of the Northeast. These two young Chinese intellectuals had marched all of the way on foot with the army.

In this smoky farmhouse I read the manuscript of Agnes Smedley's diary of those last two months—"Days of Warfare" *
—a glowing record of the heroism and endurance of these peasant soldiers who with the poorest of arms and most inadequate supplies, had yet achieved such amazing success against the Japanese military machine. It was a fitting sequel to the story of the "Long March," and the past record of China's Red Army. Only this time communists and Kuomintang were fighting shoulder to shoulder against a common enemy. And the last chapters of that struggle had yet to be written.

In Yenan I had heard a good deal about the "special policy" of the Eighth Route Army towards prisoners of war, and here at headquarters one had a good opportunity to see how it worked out in practice. On Agnes' advice I went round to call on the "Enemy Department"—a special propaganda bureau made up of students and political workers who spoke Japanese.

* Published in America under the title *China Fights Back* (Vanguard, 1938).

In China, the technique of using a loudspeaker on the battlefront to convert the enemy rank and file that was used so dramatically by the Spanish Loyalists at Guadalajara had not yet been called into play; the only reason probably being, that the Chinese had not got a portable loudspeaker. The next best thing was to teach Chinese soldiers simple slogans in Japanese, which they could call across the lines in night attacks. This, and all means of influencing the enemy rank and file, were the special studies of the Enemy Department.

"Do you want to interview some of our prisoners?" the propaganda officer asked me. There were two, he said, in a neighboring farmhouse, who had responded particularly well to "political education." I followed my guide into a courtyard where there was indeed a guard lounging at the gateway; but he had not even removed the red woollen tassel from the muzzle of his gun. Inside, two prisoners, still wearing their full Japanese uniforms, sat cross-legged on the *k'ang* facing each other across a little table. The straw mats showed a sad falling-off in cleanliness from Japanese standards, and the greatest discomfort of all captives, I was told, was the impossibility of getting a hot bath. (Shansi peasants have a sturdy distrust of hot or cold water, and I had not seen even an approximation to a bathroom since leaving Yenan.) But with it all, these prisoners looked cheerful enough. They cooked their own food—rice, which was a great luxury in these parts, and more than the Chinese soldiers had seen for many a day—and seemed well enough supplied with cigarettes. They talked freely and with obvious pleasure to anyone who spoke their language.

One had been an officer with the rank of captain in the Kwantung Army; he had already done two years of service in Manchuria before the war. This man had been almost desperate at the time of his capture, and had made several attempts at suicide; only very slowly had he begun to yield to the persuasive tactics of the "Enemy Department." But as I talked to him now through an interpreter, he was friendly enough, and after a little volunteered some surprising comments.

When the war began (he said) he had been in complete sympathy with the Japanese army leaders. "The regular army was

Old Friends and New Enemies 173

always trained and prepared for war in North China, and so we welcomed the war when it came." But he had soon noticed that the new recruits who were drafted to North China from Japan in the first months of the war had a very different point of view. "Many were openly dissatisfied with the war when they first arrived in China. This was a great shock to us in the regular forces, for we had never heard the policy of the Army Command criticized in this way." Though he had fought against such dangerous opinions himself up to the time of his capture, this officer, it seemed, had since come around to sharing something like the attitude of those young Japanese recruits. "The Army policy now is not good for Japan," he told me earnestly. "We can only hope that some international movement will restrain the Army leaders before our country is ruined."

This seemed to me a pretty fair response to a few weeks of "treatment," for an officer and property-owner—this man had been a merchant in Osaka before he joined the army—must have proved intractable enough material to work on. The other prisoner in the same room, a radio-worker by trade, had been in no two minds about it from the start. He had admitted on capture that only a mobilization order brought him to China; and he had already spoken against the war and against the "Japanese imperialists" at public meetings in Shansi. He was being sent on to Yenan.

It is hard to make such interviews as these sound convincing. I can only say that I paid several visits to Japanese prisoners at headquarters, none of which was in any way prearranged; and that each time I was satisfied, from the eager and friendly manner of the prisoners themselves, that they meant everything they said. All assured us with touching sincerity of the "kindness" of the Chinese. It was clear enough that they had expected a very different reception. And after I had examined a few of the Japanese relics and documents collected by the propaganda department, I realized why.

Here a miscellaneous assortment of maps, military reports, political documents, diaries, trophies, was offered for my inspection. The personal relics were especially curious, and revealed a new side of the "invincible armies" of Nippon. Along with their faith in the "thousand-stitch garments" made for them by their womenfolk, the Japanese seem to have infinite faith in the power of charms. Here were all kinds of lockets, satchels, and amulets, generally made to be worn on a string around the neck, and containing inscriptions, prayers for peace or protection, drawings of Buddhist deities. Most of them had been taken from dead bodies; one, with a bullet hole through the cover, was a mute witness to its own inefficacy. Altogether, they afforded convincing evidence of that fear complex ("earthquake-psychology," it has been called—the outlook of a people living always on the brink of natural disaster) which is probably responsible for much of the recurrent uneasiness and melancholy of the Japanese mind; and must certainly be held accountable for many of its more abrupt and unpleasing manifestations.

But the documents were even more revealing. Many of these had been captured from the enemy headquarters at Pinhsingkwan, and had not yet been fully worked over. But my interpreter pointed out a number of passages in military reports that had been marked in pencil. One entry described the capture of thirty Chinese soldiers at Hweilai: five of them had been chosen "after examination" and sent on to headquarters; the remaining twenty-five, it was noted with soldierly brevity, "had been beheaded." Another report was on the occupation of Ch'i Ken Chun, a village in northwestern Shansi. "Because the population had been unfriendly" (the report ran) "thirty young men were selected from the village and publicly executed." There were many similar reports, from these files of one Japanese division, all signed and countersigned by the responsible authorities.

The Japanese military have made no secret of their policy of deliberate intimidation; they are not alone in it today. The Kwantung Army has pursued this line for years in Manchuria, and holds that it is justified by results—it has been proved, indeed, the only possible counter to large-scale partisan warfare. But its most conspicuous result in Manchuria, when all is said, had been the heroic five-year history of the Manchurian Volunteers; now, in North China, I was already beginning to see similar results in the sudden and spontaneous growth of a new Chinese "people's army." And intimidation, whether justified on military grounds or frankly preferred as the choice of the terrorist, is a two-edged weapon: it reacts upon the agent as surely as upon the victim. No army can pursue such a policy for long without degradation of its own morale.

"This is the biggest single advantage we have over the Japanese," the young head of the Enemy Department assured me. "The *social factor*. It may take time to work, but it is worth more to us than many guns."

His meaning was clear enough. The mechanic who drives a Japanese tank or loads the bomb rack of an aeroplane is not invulnerable to propaganda, though he may escape enemy bullets. The most venomous technique of modern warfare is no more ruthless than the skilled hand that controls it. This was the weakest link in the chain of Japan's military strength; and the Eighth Route Army had not been slow to find it out.

JAPANESE INTERLUDE

Among all these documents, there was one which seemed to me of special interest. It was the diary—beautifully kept and illustrated with maps and sketches—of the bodyguard of General Itagaki, commander of the Japanese forces at Pinhsingkwan. With the help of a translator, I spent the best part of a day making an English version of it. That word-for-word translation is reproduced below.

Most war diaries are best left in decent privacy to the friends and relatives of those who wrote them. But this brief document does give, I think, a representative picture of the mind of the Japanese soldier fighting in China; and for this reason I insert it here, suppressing only the diarist's name. Essentially, it is the sincere expression of a loyal and sensitive Japanese brought face to face with the fact of war made by his own rulers in a foreign country.

The deep appreciation of natural beauty, the thrilling sensibility and conviction of the "holiness of the heart's affections" so apparent in these brief entries, will surprise no one who has lived even for a little in Japan. They are characteristic of a nation that is trained (at home) to love the principle of beauty in all things. But there is not much beauty in a modern war of conquest, as the writer of this diary soon found. And there can be little doubt that his disillusionment must have steadily grown, if the war which he welcomed so resolutely had not claimed him as one of its earlier victims.

The first entries of the diary were made in Japan (apparently in Yamaguchi, where the 5th Division was recruited). The year, of course, is 1937.

August 2.—A clear day. Got up at 5:30.

For long I have waited, and looked forward to the time when a man may prove himself before the world. Such a day has come at last. I bear the fate of my country on my two shoulders. The place I go to is North China, dark under wind and cloud—a land thousands of *li* wide. Fighting, and again fighting. Although I do not expect to come back alive, yet when I think of my parents, of my wife who will be left after my death, I cannot help feeling sad at heart.

It was 9:30; time for me to leave my home. O my parents, my wife! Although we said, "Do not look for my return," I could not hide my own distress. There is the saying, "A mother's heart is heavier than a son's." With what thoughts did you send me on my way?

11:10—A steam whistle sounded; the train began to move, carrying our several souls. Many of our fellow-countrymen had come to see us off. Amid their cheerful shouting we left at last.

My wife's hands were trembling as they held the five-colored paper streamers. Her face was like that of one who awaits the coming of the God of Death. It made her more beautiful. O my wife, perhaps this is the last time I shall ever see you!

When I said, "Take care of yourself; I entrust our baby to you," our eyes met—our cheeks touched— But then her face was lost to view among the crowd. The shouting of *"Banzai!"* still came faintly to our ears. The long flags became smaller and smaller as the train entered the valley. The tense heart relaxes; I sit down with a deep breath.

5 P.M.—We arrive at Hiroshima. I leave the crowd. 6:30, I reach my lodgings.

August 3.—A clear day. At 10 A.M. I went to 5th Division Headquarters to begin my duties. I am in General Itagaki's bodyguard. We are bodyguards in the Headquarters of the 30,000 troops leaving for China. If a single officer at Headquarters should meet with danger, the action of the whole division might be impaired, for without organization the soldiers could not fight. When I think of such things as this, I feel my duty in going to China is very important.

August 4.—Clear day. Weapons and uniform issued.

August 5.—A rainy day. Officers inspect uniforms and equipment.

August 6.—Rainy again. I got up at 3 A.M., and thanked the host whom I have disturbed for four days.

3:50—Left our billet. 4 A.M., concentrated at the Military Training Square, West Hiroshima. 7:30, left, passing through the road along the tramcar-tracks.

6:30 P.M.—Arrived at Port Ujina. 7 P.M., went aboard the transport *Miziho Maru.*

August 7.—Showers today. 5 A.M., the ship is about to start. Probably this is the last time I leave my mother country. The wide sea was shining in the sunlight. Across the way, where water and sky looked alike, floated the shadow of sails. All around us were the blue mountains; and the water, so beautiful! When we left Ujina, crowds waved our flag—the flag of the Rising Sun. And the shouting of "Banzai" was a brave sound to remember.

But, after crossing the channel, the blue ocean in the night looks lonesome. Nothing to be seen. I entered the cabin, and heard the noise of the engines thudding beneath us. My heart flew far away toward my home. I could not sleep, and went out on deck. The ship was struck by dark waves; she sailed to the west without a sound. The cold wind touched my hot, red cheeks. Dully I looked at the night sky: the stars seemed to fall down. Despite myself, I felt my eyes were wet.

August 8.—A clear day. At 12:10 A.M., entered Fusan Harbor [Korea]. 8:30, began to disembark. 6 P.M., began my work as bodyguard—military police.

August 9-12.—In Fusan.

August 13.—Clear day. Up at 8:30, to transport materials to Fusan station.

5:15 P.M.—To the sound of the steam whistle, the long line of the military train moved off.

August 14, 6 A.M.—Left Antung station [Manchuria]. Slowly the sorrowful clouds become light. The sky is a piece of blue. Everywhere beautiful clouds float; the sky is lovely today. I saw the sun rise up from the wild land.

11:30—We passed through the Chikwan mountains. The sun is flying in the blue sky, the landscape a moving panorama outside the window. But from a clear sky the sun shot down strong hate; it burned the iron walls of our car. The air grew very bad, and inside the car the heat was stifling.

7 P.M.—We passed through Mukden station. Had supper. It grew dark; the light of the oil lamp in our car looked lonely. The hot air dissolved, and gradually we felt cold. It became another world.

August 15.—The train did not care about anything; it carried the hot air and the soldiers in its crowded freight-cars. At noon, it stopped at the gates of the enemy—Shanhaikwan [North China]!

In the brief halt, I sent a telegram to my home, "Shanhaikwan safely passed." Ten minutes later, the train was off again. Immediately a military song was struck up along the line of cars. One stage more, and we shall have entered enemy territory —the center of the war, and of the victory of our armies.

JAPANESE INTERLUDE 179

August 16.—Today the train continued to run. I did not know where I was going. The great plain of North China was smooth, shaped like a wave—I could not see the edge of it. Open country stretching on forever. Near the railway line, here and there were flowers and willow trees. Amongst the trees, small birds were calling. Their song is not so sad as the cuckoo's, but they sing as if they would burst their throats—the only music in the forest.

August 17, 11:30 A.M.—Arrived Tientsin station. Had breakfast. 1 P.M., started again from Tientsin. This station, bombed by Japanese airplanes, evidenced its miserable fate. There were steel rails twisted like noodles, and the skeletons of burnt-out trains.

6 P.M.—Arrived at Lo Fa station, which looked like a beehive. A vivid impression of the dignity of our Japanese army. Here were the graves of two First-Class Japanese soldiers, killed in the fighting. 9:30 P.M., left this station.

August 18, 3 A.M.—Arrived at Fengtai; had breakfast. 8 A.M., started again.

9 A.M.—Came to Hsichihmen station [Peiping]. On the right-hand side stretched the great wall of the city. In the stations northwest of Tientsin, there are no Chinese clerks or officials. The train was directed by our own railway company.

6 P.M.—We came to Changping station [near Nankow]. In this long week's trip in a freight car, conditions have been very bad. For a whole week I had not touched the ground. Now that both my feet stand on solid earth I am very glad, but I dare not tell my companions of my joy.

August 19.—We marched to our division in Changping, and arrived at 10 A.M. Today is very hot. As we were in enemy country, we could collect things by force. So we did not eat our lunch, but went out to make "compulsory collection." We got twelve chickens, and one *kwan* of onions, two *kwan* of potatoes.

2 P.M.—Some one got water, and others killed the chickens. This is a fine soldiers' life!

3:30.—We finished our good food, and jumped into a small stream behind Headquarters. We took a bath—the first in a week. The dirt dropped from my body like scraps of paper. After the bath, I was very much surprised—everyone looked so cheerful. Grown men looked like children. We went on along the railway bank, and discovered the dead bodies of horses, and five or six Chinese.

August 20.—My turn on duty as bodyguard.

August 21.—Came off duty at 6 A.M.
I helped transport fifty or sixty thousand *yen* to the Yokohama Specie Bank in Peiping. As there was no train back, stay the night in Peiping.

August 22, 8 A.M.—Thought to leave Peiping, and came to the Hsichihmen station, for a train to Nankow. Waited eight hours and, as no train came, returned and stayed in the former 29th Route Army barracks.

August 23, 8 A.M.—Left the barracks.
1 P.M.—Reached Nankow station.
4 P.M.—I serve as bodyguard to two Representatives of the Diet who are visiting the army.

August 24, 11:50 A.M.—The Division Commander left by airplane to inspect the front. Went with him as guard to the airfield in Nankow. 12:40, came back and off duty.

August 25, 4 P.M.—Take my turn as bodyguard.
There are many mountain peaks in this part of North China, bare in the sunlight. Halfway up the mountain, some red clouds float; the peaks stand up toward the blue sky. A cold wind blows from the mountain side to the camp. Those thousands of soldiers who suffered in the heat of the day now are revived.

August 26.—As the Headquarters will move forward tomorrow, I left by truck to inspect the road. Our route was from Nankow, through the village, and over Pataling to Hweilai.
In the mountains (which are about eighty *li* across) the truck

moved on and on along the stony road. After half an hour, we passed through a place where there was a most unpleasant smell. I got out, and by the light of the headlamps discovered the corpses of many Chinese soldiers; among them were the bodies of eight of our men, their steel helmets fastened round their chins.

We went on into the mountains. Here and there were the walls of enemy towns that had been shelled by our artillery, sadly bathed in moonlight. At 9 P.M. we came to Chuyungkwan; but as the road was blocked by our motor column, we turned back.

As we came to Nankow village, about thirty Chinese soldiers suddenly appeared on the right side of the road and opened fire on our truck. We fought with them, and after about thirty minutes they disappeared. It was 11:15, and the moon was about to sink along the enemy front. We took a rest, and twenty minutes later continued along the broken road to Nankow. We got back at 12:30.

Our comrades sat in the dim light of the lamps. When they saw we were back safely they were very glad, and got out some beer to drink our health. That time, it was touch and go with our lives.

August 27.—At 8 A.M., the whole division left Nankow. In the village where the Chinese soldiers had surprised us the night before, all was quiet. There were many cars on the road, and our trucks moved with difficulty—move, stop, move, stop. We passed safely over the dangerous pass at Pataling and reached Hweilai at 9:30 P.M.

After the capture of Chuyungkwan—a very important place strategically—our army had continued to advance, like splitting bamboo. One column had gone over the left side of the Great Wall, and reached Hweilai. (From the time when we attacked Nankow, for two weeks our army had kept their lines along the Great Wall.) This was why our Headquarters removed to-day to Hweilai.

September 2.—To attend a military conference, the Division Commander took a plane to Changchiak'ou. At 8 o'clock, the

Chief Bodyguard and I (ten persons in all) accompanied him by truck to the airdrome. At 9:40, we reached the plane, and at 9:50 the Commander got aboard. With roaring engines, the plane with the red sun painted on its wings took off, and flew to the south until it could not be seen.

As the Commander would not be back until 3 P.M., I and my friends rode on in the truck to collect some grapes. We came to a place where grapes were abundant, and jumped into the fields. Two Chinese farmers made signs with their hands, saying, "Don't pick the grapes!" But some one beat them back—"*Pick!*" The color was purple; the saliva ran from our mouths.

In an hour, we had collected two or three petrol cases full of grapes, and we came back about noon.

Today, because we had eaten so many grapes, we could not eat our supper.

September 3, 6 A.M.—Took my turn with a scouting party.

September 4.—Came back at 8 A.M. My friend K——, who left with me from Hiroshima, accompanied me on the beach by the blue sea, in the hot and stifling train, and in the dangerous place we passed through on August 26, is sick and sent to hospital.

Oh, as a soldier he came here to the war zone, but now he is in a sick-bed! He must be disgusted about it himself. I have been very lucky; since we left Japan, I have not taken a drop of medicine. How lucky I am. (My wife, you should be happy, too!)

September 5.—In the crisp morning air, I have an apple between my teeth. Went for a short walk.

From 11 o'clock, a meeting in honor of those killed in battle was held in the open space in front of Headquarters. At the sound of the bugles, all the soldiers in the meeting shed tears.

Oh, to protect their country they joined the army and came to North China! And, fighting in the Nankow Pass, they left us their glorious fame, the foundation of our Empire.

But, though it was a glorious death, the corpse is soon only pitiful white bones in the small coffin. O brave friends, you sleep eternally! But when I compared myself with these, and thought of the state of mind of my parents if they should lose their son, I could not help shedding a tear.

September 6, 10 A.M.—I took my turn on guard. Oh, I had today a letter from my wife, who was thinking of me!

September 7, 11 A.M.—Started out from Hweilai, acting as a guard for 350,000 *yen* we were sending to Suanhwa by train. Passed through Siahwayuan station; left and right was sandy plain. I thought of the great sandy plains of Mongolia. In every station, I saw some Chinese come to welcome our train with Japanese flags. The first time I saw this, I thought how much oppressed they must have been by the Chinese war lords.

2 P.M.—Came to Suanhwa; we brought the money safe inside the walls by motor truck.

6 P.M.—Rested at Headquarters in Suanhwa Middle School. Took a bath, but there was so little water that it barely covered my feet. Oh, but now I hope to return home as soon as possible, and be with my wife again! Then I could lean my head to the water, and my wife would wash my back with her soft hands.

September 9.—Came off duty, and was instructed by T—— in "communication with airplanes."

At 6:30 P.M. took another bath. Some of us sang, and some talked about what we would do after our military service—back to our wives! This was a happy interlude in our war life. At 7, we were given Japanese wine. After bathing, every one drank one cup.

September 10.—Among the bodyguards, I and nine others have been made guards for the Staff. At 8 this morning, we left by truck from Suanhwa for Hwashaoying. Leaving Suanhwa, we crossed a river about 300 yards wide and two feet deep. The division baggage cars advanced through the muddy water. Looking down from the truck, we could see the tired horses drinking the reddish, muddy water; and the Chinese guide, with a Japanese flag in his hand. Coming toward us were wounded horses, and wounded men. From our truck, some newspaper men took photographs. We could not watch this scene without our eyes blurring with tears. Oh, *for whom* should we suffer such pain as this?

After crossing the river, our car advanced along the ravaged road. The road itself is like a river, curving around the mountain, with the loud noise of whirring machinery. We keep on, through the corpses of Chinese soldiers.

3 P.M.—We came to Hwashaoying. I went out with three friends to make "compulsory collection." After a while, we had eight chickens and some vegetables. We made food for eleven; and then we attacked our food as fiercely as if it had been the enemy!

Oh, I remember the tenth of September is my birthday! Now I use the good food in my stomach to bless my birthday in my heart.

September 11.—Today was again a good day.

In the sunshine, I went out with a friend, and collected one bushel of beans and one bag of white sugar. We ordered five Chinese to carry the things back for us. In a big pan we boiled the beans; some one went to get water. Once more, our barracks became a battle-ground! Yesterday we ate chicken meat; today, bean soup. This is, after all, the most cheerful thing in a soldier's life—when he sits in the camp after fighting, beside the warm stove, and talks with his friends about things at home.

September 12.—At 2 P.M., we left Hwashaoying for Yuhsien, by truck. Reached Yuhsien by 7:30 in the evening. Threatened by our guns, the enemy retreated yesterday to Tatung.

O my Chinese soldiers, sooner or later you must die! Why did you retreat? I cannot understand the minds of troops like these. I heard that in this place there were men of the 29th Route Army.

September 13.—Went out at 8 A.M. to collect things. By 11, had got ten chickens, and came back. Under any conditions, a soldier can always get something to eat! Besides the bearer, the others soon ate all this. From their faces, it seemed that they wanted more.

September 17.—The Commander left by truck for Kwangling to visit the 21st Brigade; I went as guard.

There was only one road, with willow trees on both sides, and pines. Beyond these trees, we could see kaoliang fields. But the ears of grain were black. The sky was clear and bright; one or two wisps of cloud floated slowly.

Some one said, "In Japan, it should be autumn too." The other soldiers looked up at the sky. At that moment, in the hearts of these brave soldiers who had marched against the enemy grew again the thought of home, and how they longed to return there.

Suddenly, "Pong! Pong!"—the sound of rifle fire broke the clear air. "Oh!" cried a journalist with us, "what is that? The soldiers must be shooting sparrows, mustn't they?" He seemed to be reassured, and screwed his head around. It was 11 A.M., when some one said, "Soon we'll get to Kwangling." As we entered Kwangling city, I saw many soldiers of the 42nd and 21st regiments; and among the 42nd regiment I found some very intimate friends.

September 22.—I work as bodyguard at the airfield. At 6 P.M., I flew from Yuhsien to another air base farther north. The moon was at the fifteenth ("full moon," by the old calendar), and shone brightly in the sky. The airplane flew in the moonlight— splashes of light were reflected like the ray of a pistol-flare. It was a beautiful sight to see.

September 23.—At noon, Headquarters moved from Yuhsien. We took a motor truck to go to Lingch'u. Arrived Lingch'u 5 P.M. Direct from here, the Division Commander, who wanted to inspect the 21st regiment at the front, went on with his bodyguard to Tayingchen. We arrived there at 9 P.M. There was heavy fighting at Tayingchen when we arrived. The sound of gunfire and rifle fire hurt the ears. At that time, the moon came out from the clouds and shone on the tops of the mountains—

the enemy troops were moving there, and we could see them very clearly. Under this mountain was the Headquarters of the 21st regiment. Bullets were flying over our head, and we felt very uncomfortable. Twenty minutes past midnight on the twenty-fourth we came back.

Today at noon we left Yuhsien, and went on to Tayingchen in the front line. Then came back to Lingch'u. The whole twelve hours I was on the truck, and we hurried back without a halt. I have not had a moment's rest.

Took my turn as bodyguard.

It was on September 24 that the Japanese began their advance on Pinhsingkwan; next day, the writer of this diary was killed in action defending his division headquarters. Who is to write his epitaph, and the epitaph of his generation? For the vision was already beginning to fade, the splendid vision of General Matsui:

> *Where arises the Yangtse River I fail to see,*
> *But all the mountains of China in dream I see;*
> *How noisy is the League of Nations?*
> *We have a fine road for kings to follow...*

The end of that royal road, for this young Japanese as for so many of his comrades, had been a shallow grave in the North China hills. Not the least part of his tragedy was that he died before his eyes were fully opened. But after him, others would see more clearly.

CHAPTER SIX

TO THE NORTH

FAREWELL TO HEADQUARTERS

In the rambling farmhouse, enmeshed with telephone wires and the antennae of a radio transmitter, where Chu Teh had his headquarters, we had just finished lunch. The Japanese had started heavy bombing of Linfen and other points in southern Shansi that week; their intelligence service had been good, for they had secured direct hits on General Wei Li-huang's headquarters, and one Shansi army commander had been killed. But the Eighth Route Army staff was always located in a village, never in a city, and it shifted its ground every few days. "So far," Tso Chuan told me with satisfaction, "their bombers have never caught up with us!"

We had washed down our millet and cabbage with captured Japanese coffee—it was the only table luxury Chu Teh's staff enjoyed—when I brought up the question of my own next move. More than a month had passed since I had left Yenan, and the first stage of the journey planned there was completed. I had reached the war zone, and met the chief military and political leaders in the army. It remained to see the army itself in action.

"When can we go north to the front?" I wanted to know.

"Where do you want to go?" Chu asked with mild curiosity. Unlike most Chinese authorities, the communists never made unnecessary difficulties for an "accepted" traveler. "We can send you to any of our division headquarters in the field."

I knew the general location of the three main divisions, two of which were now well behind the Japanese lines. It was not going to be especially easy to get to any of them, and with an army as mobile as this, "division headquarters" might be a shifting and very elusive point. Agnes Smedley had just come back from Lin Piao's division, however; so, from my point of view, that disposed of the 115th. There remained the 120th Division under Ho Lung, which was already operating as far north as Suiyuan.

And Ho Lung—the man of whom it is said that if he were set down in any province of China, he could raise an army within a month—was perhaps the most picturesque of all the old Red Army leaders. He had built up the Fourth Front Red Army in Hunan, starting out with four rifles; tales were told of him in half a dozen southern provinces that made him into a sort of modern Chinese Robin Hood. His second-in-command, Hsiao K'eh, was another almost legendary figure. The combination sounded promising.

"I'd like to go with Ho Lung," I said, "if we can do it." This meant a long trek northwest, but it should be worth it.

"All right," said the chief-of-staff. "We're sending some supplies up there—you can go part of the way by truck. But you'll need your interpreter, unless you can learn to speak *Fulan hua!*" Hunan dialect is notoriously difficult for a northerner. "And once you start, you'll probably have to stay up there all winter."

I was prepared for that, for I knew the difficulties of travel in this region; and Wu was only too eager to come along. Chu Teh beamed paternally at our decision. "When you see Ho Lung," he chuckled, "ask him from me how many lice he has in his beard!" It was a standing joke at headquarters that Ho Lung's veterans were the "lousiest fighters" in the army. I began to think seriously of having my own head shaved.

Next morning the bugles woke us before dawn; headquarters was already on the move, with signalers taking down telephone wires and preparing for the march. In the frozen courtyard waited a troop of half a dozen cavalrymen, who would escort us to the main road where we were to pick up a truck for the north. They were a tough-looking lot, with their slung carbines and shaggy mountain ponies.

Jen Pi-shih waved to us from the gateway of the Political Department, as our horses clattered down the paved street. "*Lengte hen!*" he shouted cheerfully, and the soldiers grinned at his broad southern dialect. But it would be colder than this in the hills with Ho Lung.

The first glow of sunlight on the snow-peaks of the Luliang-shan was another reminder of it.

In the early morning we rode along the foothills, towards the supply depot where we were to pick up the truck. A light mist covered the base of the mountains, and spread in a winter haze across the plain, broken here and there by an island of trees, or the watch tower that announced a village. The mist was not unwelcome, for it offered some sort of protection against enemy aircraft.

Six planes had passed over in formation shortly after dawn, flying north. They should have been Chinese, but the Nanking air force had not as yet been very much in evidence on the northern front, and I had my doubts. The troop commander—a stocky cavalryman from Szechwan—announced that they were Soviet planes, come to "fight against Japanese imperialism." At that time, the air was thick with rumors of war between Japan and the Soviet Union, for a speech by Marshal Bluecher of the Far Eastern Red Army had sounded a note of ominous warning, and the Japanese were certainly withdrawing some of their troops to the north. There might be other explanations for that: the Fifth Division which had just left Taiyuan had suffered particularly heavily in the Shansi fighting. All the same, I wished I could know what was happening in Manchuria. We would learn more at Ho Lung's headquarters.

Our way was marked from village to village by slips of paper pasted on stone archways, or pinned against the loess terraces. Organizers were active all over this area in political mobilization, and continually we passed groups of soldiers, or heard the beating of a gong, muffled through the mist, which called the villagers to a mass meeting. Once we passed a long straggling column of newly-raised recruits—burly peasants in their black padded winter clothes, youngsters carrying with pride spoils of war in the shape of Japanese leather wallets or water-bottles.

About noon we reached our destination—a cave village set against the hills, with half a dozen camouflaged trucks concealed beneath a clump of trees. And an hour or so later I found myself, clinging precariously to the topmost bale of a load of winter greatcoats, bumping northwards along the main road to Fenyang.

DESOLATION

It was just a fortnight since I had come south along this same road, then blocked with the main Chinese army retreating from Taiyuan. They were still coming now, scattered bands of troops and mule trains, but in much better order than before, and without the same desperate urgency. For the Japanese had called a halt at Pingyao—though whether to await reinforcements, or because of some international complication, was another of those mysteries.

The Shansi armies seemed to be using this unexpected respite to get as far away from the enemy as possible. In the two days we were on the road, we found ourselves the only party going north. To me, it lent a touch of zest to the whole business. Our trucks, with their load of winter uniforms and half a dozen guards, were heading towards the front and the fighting. These others—whole regiments on the march, with supply-carts and batteries of light artillery—may have been executing a masterly strategic movement; but it did not look particularly threatening to the Japanese.

Traveling by open truck in December through the hills of Shansi is exhilarating, but has its discomforts. At first we had been drowned in a sea of yellow dust, that caked most unpleasantly in the eyes and nostrils. But the cold—once we had crossed the main range, and were following a frozen river between snowbanked hills—was worse than the dust. The billet we reached after dark on that first day was humble enough (to the uninitiated western eye, it would have appeared indescribably mean and filthy) but it was warm; and that positive advantage was the only one that counted. And when the owner of the hut found that we were "Ti Pa Lu Chün," he insisted on our taking the *k'ang*, and slept himself with his family on straw mats on the floor.

Next day we dropped a woman passenger, and I found a place

DESOLATION   191

inside the cab of one of the trucks. The driver was an old friend, the same with whom we had traveled to Yenan two months before. He was a tousled youth, whose skill on these mountain roads, and at starting his engine in winter dawns when all the world was frozen, had already won my unqualified admiration. I had reason to renew it now, for the road we were traveling had hazards enough. Many of the bridges had been washed out, and others partially destroyed by the retreating Chinese troops.

All that morning we threaded our way northwards, skidding around the brink of ravines on the frozen snow, or laboring along stony river beds. We were climbing steadily, and in these barren hills one did not look for many people on the roads. But it struck me as curious that we had met only soldiers for so long, when we halted for a few minutes in a mountain village garrisoned by the 3rd (Shansi) Brigade. Again, nothing but blue uniforms in sight.

"What's happened to the countrypeople?" I asked, when we took the road again, having discovered that there was no food to be bought. "Have the Japanese been here?" The truck driver shook his head; his usually cheerful features had set grimly. "Not the Japanese, but the 3rd Brigade! We shall get no food tonight unless we can reach some of our own people."

At first I thought he was joking. Then I began to understand.

For another five hours, we drove through a deserted countryside. We had crossed a divide, and were coming down into what should have been a prosperous valley. It was beautiful enough, in the yellow afternoon light, but the fields stretched empty between the hills, and no smoke rose from the clustered villages. Houses that we passed had gaping doorways and windows; every plank had been torn down to serve as fuel. The villagers had left as one man, and taken with them what they could save of their provender. There was indeed no food to be had here, unless it was the pheasants that thronged the open fields, pecking freely at the freshly-sown grain.

It was a scene of complete desolation, all the more dismal when one realized that it was the work of a Chinese army.

We came to one such deserted village, and stopped to ask

again about the road. In the main street, only the purr of our motors broke the silence. Fragments of earthenware were strewn around; curved grotesquely across the road the skeleton of a mule, with the bones stripped clean to the hoofs, announced eloquently on what strange flesh the last passers-by had fed.

"*Lao hsiung!* Countryman!" our guards shouted loudly, and the indignation was plain in their voices. At last one old man came quavering—the only inhabitant of this ruin—and squatted in the snow before us.

"Don't be afraid; *this* is the Eighth Route Army," said the leader of our party. The old man grinned toothlessly, and wagged his head. Someone gave him a cigarette, which he lit with obvious delight, though the first puff racked his lungs with coughing. In a few sentences, he told us all he knew. It was another fifty *li* to the first village where our own army was stationed.

On the road, we met the rearguard of the retreating army that had wrought this havoc. The men were typical Shansi peasants, well enough armed—many of them had automatic rifles; they were the raw material of a real fighting army, if only they could be properly led and trained. But the officers rode apart from their men, swinging incongruous walking sticks, and the fur coats they wore made an unpleasing contrast with the soldiers' cotton uniforms. "It's bad going from here," one of them told us. "The people have all cleared out, and you can't buy a thing to eat."

"Yes, but *why* have the people gone?" our commander could not help replying. "It's the way your army treats them." He could have said much more, but refrained; and the officer rode on without a word.

We covered the last stretch of road at breakneck speed, for we would have cold comfort that night unless we reached our own outposts. The last we saw of the 3rd Brigade was a couple of sentries guarding a tunnel in the road; it was with some difficulty that the trucks got through. Then at last, through the night that had fallen, a friendly light. We had reached our billet.

Good food at a restaurant, a cheerful village welcome, and a warm room for the night—the light meant all of these things, and we were not disappointed. I had already discovered that the words *"Ti Pa Lu"*—"Eighth Route"—were a magic formula throughout the Shansi countryside. But never before had I seen it work so clearly.

One should emphasize, perhaps, the fact that this 3rd Brigade was an independent provincial force, not incorporated with any of the National divisions; by all accounts, they were the worst-trained and least-disciplined body of troops in Shansi. But I had seen dramatized so vividly that I could not forget it that most familiar weakness of the old-style Chinese armies—their callous disregard of the welfare of the common people.

"This is one of the things," Wu told me ruefully, "that we are fighting against."

Before long, we were to see how differently another system worked.

THE FIGHTING DIVISION

The nearer we came to the front (Fenyang at this time was a Chinese outpost) the worse grew the condition of the road. I had never seen so many wrecks of trucks and motor cars—the spent debris of war was strewn all about us along the highway. Our own drivers and mechanics descended upon each ruin like ghouls, seeking spare parts to salvage, but in most cases the engine had been removed. Nothing of any value is abandoned for very long in China.

The guards kept a close lookout for enemy aeroplanes, for we were traveling in broad daylight, and in open country. But the sky was clear; not even a cloud broke its blue. And our driver seemed to have few cares: he sang all the time under his breath, and always the same song. The first line was something about "My little Soochow girl," but I never understood the rest, and perhaps it was just as well.

We cut across to the western road through a maze of villages, where only the friendly guides who voluntarily came with us could have shown us the way. Although this district was much nearer the war front than the deserted countryside we had passed through the day before, every village was occupied. And the first place we stopped at, where a company of soldiers was stationed, was thronged with peasants—men, women, and girls. Many of them carried baskets of provisions.

"Is it a *chi*—a Chinese fair?" I asked in astonishment. Wu grinned involuntarily. "No! They have heard the Eighth Route Army is here, and they know now that they will be safe." It was the simple truth, and the confidence these Shansi peasants had in the army was the most heartening thing we had seen since leaving headquarters.

In this village, I made my first acquaintance with the 120th Division. Ordered west after the fighting at Yenmenkwan, this force now occupied a district perhaps a thousand *li* from north to south, and they were hard at work mobilizing the countryside. Through the crowded streets passed many peasants already organized, wearing the red-and-blue armbands of the volunteer mobile units. Their rifles, I was told, had mostly come from those the Eighth Route Army had collected in the northern mountains, where they had been abandoned by some of the provincial troops.

The company commander who entertained us at lunch was a slim youth from Hunan, very erect in his old black uniform (but without the Red Army collar tabs) that had seen service in other wars than this. For Ho Lung's division, ordered to the front after the fall of Tatung, had not waited for the new uniforms that all other units of the army I had seen hitherto had worn. Our trucks were bringing new outfits for some; but many had already found their winter overcoats from another source, and were comfortable enough in the woolen khaki of the Mikado's armies.

"What do you think of this?" our host asked, offering for my examination a Japanese automatic pistol. "And these?"—he took down from the wall an excellent pair of German field-glasses, and a periscope in a fine leather case. Given time, it appeared, the 120th Division might be able to re-equip themselves entirely from the enemy. These particular trophies were only a week old, and had come from a Japanese cavalry troop that had unwarily ventured too far south of Pingyao.

"How do you find the people here?" I asked the young commander. His response was enthusiastic. "Very good! We have a hundred partisans in this place alone, and they've already begun independent action—yesterday they arrested a traitor in the village, who was trying to prepare a welcome for the Japanese. In our Army District"—this meant, for all practical purposes, northwestern Shansi—"we have now ten thousand men organized in partisan units; and we can soon double that. If only we get enough arms!"

That was the great problem, as ever, for the Eighth Route Army. I could not help thinking of all the weapons that I had seen on the road going south—often one man carrying two light machine guns. Perhaps they would be put to some use later on; but the crying need was here, where the question of arms supply might become increasingly difficult. If necessary, new units could be furnished with captured war materials, for in the mountains of North Shansi this army was quite capable of making the enemy its "munition-carriers," as it had always done during the civil wars. But much valuable time might be lost in the process.

We took the road again that afternoon, for the last stage that would be possible by truck. And crossing a high divide, I had a glimpse of the sort of country over which this partisan and guerilla warfare would be continued. Range on range of hills extended north and west—hills now covered with snow, and frozen hard for the next three months at least. It was an ideal terrain for mobile units who knew the country, and had no need to worry about their food supply. And, by the same token, it offered immense difficulties for a modern army like the Japanese, dependent on mechanical transport. The only advantage the latter could have would be their aircraft. But the villages were scattered, most of them consisted of caves, and there was cover enough in the folds of these hills for whole armies.

The Japanese were busy widening the narrow-gauge railway to Taiyuan, so that they might bring in troops and supplies direct from the north. But they would need a force the size of the Kwantung army to hold their gains, let alone make the attempt to subdue the whole countryside.

At another village in the hills—a windblown spot where the

cave-dwellings were ranked in tiers in the mountain side—our trucks deposited their load, and us. We spent that night at a regimental headquarters. Colonel Ho Ping-ying was a brisk little man who always wore a leather helmet and a blue sleeveless cape; only when I offered to shake hands did I discover that his right arm was missing. His conversation—like that of his officers, and most of his men—was brusque and explosive, with the characteristic intonation of Hunan. These were all "veterans" of the Red Army, who had seen ten years service in the civil wars, though none of them except the Colonel was over thirty. Their food was as fiery as their manner. I could see I would have to get used to that too, if I was going to stay any length of time with this division.

The one-armed colonel, with a picturesque vocabulary and meridional gestures of his left hand, described for us some of the fighting at Yenmenkwan. "Here's what we did at one place," he said, stabbing his finger on a wall-map. "There was a bend in the road, on an uphill grade, between high banks. First we ambushed forty Japanese trucks there, and destroyed many of them with hand grenades—killed about three hundred of the enemy. We got out when their planes arrived.

"Next time, about sixty trucks came, with three tanks leading. But the night before we had destroyed the bridges, so that the whole column jammed. Then we attacked from above and below, and destroyed about half of the trucks. After that, they sent out their next column with five hundred infantry as escort. But we ambushed the escort, and attacked all along their line with machine guns. Altogether, we killed five hundred Japanese in under a week—that's their own hospital report! And we had less than one hundred casualties."

It was a typical example of guerilla tactics—to attack the enemy at a disadvantage, inflict as much damage as possible, and disappear into the hills before support arrived for the Japanese. And the same sort of thing was being continued indefinitely along the Japanese lines of communication.

After an early supper, we played basketball in the snow, with the one-armed colonel acting as referee. I was struck by the way

Howard A. Smith; courtesy of ASIA Magazine

One of the hundreds of old Chinese blockhouses on the northwest frontier.

in which this regiment—most of the men, and all the "cadres" were southerners—adapted themselves so readily to the wintry conditions of North China. But on the Long March, they had come through the snows and over the mountains of Sikang, and a Shansi winter had no terrors for them. The mountain pass they were holding here was one of the coldest posts in this area, but they accepted it cheerfully, as men who had known a worse life than this. And their fighting quality was unmistakable.

Next morning we left again for the west; a long line of mules, loaded down with winter uniforms. It was bitterly cold as we moved along in the shadow of the hills, but we were grateful for that shadow when a Japanese scouting plane droned slowly overhead, the red sun gleaming on its wings. In sunlight, against the snow, our mule train would have made a perfect mark. Not until well after noon, when the sun had thawed the road a little, did we dare to ride our ponies at more than a walk. And it seemed to me that I had never seen a more welcome sight than the walls of Lishih, the prosperous *hsien* city where we arrived at last.

Here Nanking troops formed the garrison. But the 120th Division had a supply station in an old temple building, and there, for the first time in days, we could be really warm.

MASS MOBILIZATION

Anyone who undertakes a journey in the interior of China gets used to delays, and—sooner or later—learns to accept them with the easy bohemian philosophy, that it is better to travel than to arrive. Because of a shortage of carts and pack animals, we stayed on in this *hsien* city for four days.

Within Lishih's medieval walls—a stage-setting for *Hamlet*, against a backdrop of snow-covered hills—the normal life of a Shansi country town was interrupted, a little against its will, by the intrusion of the war. The only concrete evidence of Japanese invasion was an occasional plane, flying high; and an alarming fluctuation in the local currency. But patriotic activity of every kind, from bill-posting to community singing, was very much in evidence. For this was a center of mass mobilization, to which a number of popular committees had lately removed from Taiyuan.

From early morning, the narrow stone-paved streets were thronged with a bewildering medley of costumes and uniforms. The regular troops stationed here were one Nanking division, and some of Yang Hu-cheng's Shansi army, reorganized after their part in the Sian incident. But there were numbers of volunteer units, variously attired, and invariably accompanied by student organizers trying to look like political commissars in fur caps and leather jackets. Girl volunteers, even more picturesque than their Spanish prototypes, wore their blue slacks and carried their slung rifles with easy nonchalance.

Wherever I went with my bodyguard, I was greeted with an embarrassing reiteration of salutes, and the humor like a breeze of *"O Kuo jen"*—"Russian!" I believe I could have passed for General Bluecher, and perhaps I did, in the reports of the Japanese intelligence service. The only foreigners ever seen in these parts had been the black-gowned priests and missionaries; not even the enterprising agents of the British-American Tobacco Company ever penetrated here, for Yen Hsi-shan had a virtual monopoly of cigarettes in his "model province." In view of the prevalent hopes for Russian aid, it was not surprising that a foreigner in a military greatcoat should appear to the more credulous as a Soviet staff officer.

"Do you want to see something of the partisans?" they asked me one morning in our temple quarters. "We can pay a visit to the office of the Mass Armament Committee in a village just near here." I accepted the invitation, and set out with my interpreter along the river valley. The cold spell had broken suddenly, and the air, between these loess hills, was mild and warm like spring. Snow dripped from the terraced fields like icing on a layer cake. Faintly, along the furrows, showed the first green of the winter wheat. We followed a telephone wire up into the hills, past a temple where a squad of peasants were drilling; and dropped down to a village where every wall and gateway bore a colored slogan. Here, in a roomy cave-dwelling, we were welcomed by the chief organizer of the "People's Armament Committee."

A slight figure in a badly-fitting gray cotton uniform, he wore on one sleeve the improvised badge of the Volunteer Army. "Comrade Chen"—as I had expected, he came from Yenan. But both the hands that were reached to me in greeting were crippled by rifle bullets, and the wrists showed thin as sticks under the frayed cuffs. I thought of the one-armed colonel I had met in the mountains, holding one of the most exposed posts in this whole region: something besides physical disablement linked him with this young political worker. These people, one knew, whatever they suffered, would never give up the struggle.

"How long have you been working here?" I asked, for I soon discovered that this was not a local but a provincial headquarters.

"Not so long—about three weeks! After the evacuation of Taiyuan, Yen Hsi-shan wanted us to go south; but it seemed to us much better to stay and organize the people in the war zone. So when General Yen disappeared, we came here."

Chen gave me some further details of volunteer organization in the northwest. There was no lack of human material; the chief trouble was to get rifles. "In Taiyuan, General Yen helped us at first, and gave us one thousand guns. But these were not enough for the mobile units we had already organized. We could use ten thousand rifles in this district alone."

"How do you manage now?"

"At present, we have three ways of getting arms. First, there are the private arms of the people themselves—and there are more of these than you might suppose! Then there are the thousands of *shanping* (deserters from Chinese armies) in the hills here; we are steadily collecting arms from them. Finally, wherever we find local authorities who are willing to help us, we get arms from their reserves."

"How do you find the magistrates, generally?" For this was one of the great difficulties of the United Front: old-style Chinese officials did not always find it easy to accept with equanimity the arming of the peasants in their own districts.

He grimaced, without bitterness. "They vary a lot! Best of all, for us, are the areas where there are no officials left. We never have any difficulty with the people themselves. But the local police always join our volunteer units, and sometimes the magistrates freely help us with arms and supplies.

"In this city, for example, we had at first very good relations with the local authorities. But when the Japanese withdrew some of their troops from Taiyuan, and did not immediately continue their advance in Shansi, the officials here became less friendly, and even made some obstruction for us in our work."

It was the old story of the difficulty of carrying through a "United Front" program without a United Front government. The peasants and volunteer units I watched later, drilling and practicing partisan tactics, were only too willing to fight for their own homes and families against the invader. These were the vast potential reserves of China, infinitely more effective fighting material, in these hills they knew so well, than any regular troops. And yet some local authorities, it seemed, were still unwilling to put rifles into the hands of the only people who could save North China.

"But if you would like to see how things are here," Chen had said, "come to the mass meeting in the city tomorrow." All the patriotic organizations, official and semi-official, would be represented. It was to be a full-dress anti-Japanese demonstration.

Noon that next day found some five thousand persons gathered in the clear winter sunlight in an open square before the city yamen. Perhaps half of these were armed—the Nanking troops with brand-new equipment; volunteers, some in uniform, with women soldiers here and there among their ranks; peasants with a few battered rifles, pikes, and hoes. The civilians were mostly peasants and farmers, with a few long-gowned gentry and shopkeepers in sober black. As a foreign journalist, I was given a seat on the platform, next to General Kao Kweitze, the ranking Nanking commander. After the formal opening ceremony, with the rather depressing Kuomintang hymn, "*San Min Chu I*," and the three bows before the portrait of Sun Yatsen, the meeting began.

The speakers were as varied as their audience. First on the list was General Kao—a genial little man, who spoke affably but without great emphasis. He was followed by one of Yang Hucheng's officers, and by the local *hsien chang*, or magistrate. This was, so to say, the "official" part of the program. Followed the representatives of the volunteers and the popular organizations.

Here, I could not help feeling, we were getting down to business. Chen Chih-hua, speaking for the Mass Armament Committee, made a modest figure on the platform; but he had a voice that rang across the crowd into the streets beyond and drew fresh listeners to their ranks. Simply and directly, with a few stark gestures of his crippled hands, he spoke of the crisis in the war, and the need for all groups and sections of the people to unite and defend Shansi. There is a style of popular speaking—with none of the tricks of demagogy—that can only be learned among the masses, and this man was a master of it.

But the outstanding speech of the day was made by a Shansi peasant who found himself on a platform for the first time in his life. At first there was some laughter at his manner, and his throaty dialect, but the common people hung upon every word, for this was a language they understood. There was no subtlety about this orator. "The invaders have come here to take our land and burn our homes," he roared. "Who says that we cannot fight the Japanese dwarfs and their running-dogs? *Down with Japanese imperialism! Down with the Chinese traitors!*" The sweat dripped from his gray shock of hair as he raised a clenched fist, and the crowd shouted the slogans after him with unrehearsed spontaneity.

The speeches were followed by open-air drama, vivid and effective propaganda. Between the plays, I found myself in polite conversation with General Kao. "What do you think of the meeting?" he asked me.

I was enjoying a certain irony in the situation which was probably lost on the general. More than anything else, this meeting reminded me of mass demonstrations held in Sian less than a year before, after the kidnaping of Chiang Kai-shek had made such gatherings possible in the Northwest. At that time General Kao, along with other Nanking commanders, had been massing his troops on the borders of Shensi to attack the "rebels."

"It's fine," I told him. "If you can keep this United Front of the Government and the people, China can resist any invasion." But upon that "if," it was already clear, the whole future of the war must depend.

WINTER JOURNEY

The road to Ho Lung's headquarters lay through frozen hills, filled at this time with scattered bands of *shanping*—deserters from the regular armies, many of whom perforce had turned bandit. Our load of winter uniforms and greatcoats would be a tempting bait to such ragged adventurers, and a strong escort was advisable for the supply train of mule carts and oxcarts. We took the road at last with an advance guard of Eighth Route Army men, and a platoon of local volunteers marching beside the carts. It would be slow going, I thought, watching the long convoy wind its way along the river valley from the town. The mule carts made pretty good time, but the oxen advanced with grave deliberation—*"ohne Hast, ohne Rast."* The only thing slower than an ox is a camel; but before we had finished, we were to rely on these unhurrying beasts as the best transport of all for a heavy pack under winter conditions. They were slow but sure, and could do a nine-hour march without a break.

Wu, my bodyguard, and I had found seats on top of a pile of uniforms on one of the carts. It was pleasant enough to lie with the sun in your eyes (for the clear weather continued), and watch the line of terraced hills slowly unfold along the valley. So long as the wind kept down, it was not even cold.

All that day we advanced through a landscape that was perfect Breughel, with snow-blue hills in the distance, and bare willow trees fringing the frozen river. At nightfall, we reached a district town, and found a billet in the house of a local wine merchant. The room was dark, and smelt powerfully of *paika'rh* —one of the strongest and most questionable of Chinese liquors. But our host was friendly enough, and heated for us some of his most potent vintage. "The poorer the district, the better the wine," observed the Transport Officer who was in charge of our convoy, tossing off a good measure. In general, we found it true: in some of these mountain villages, *paika'rh* was about the only thing the peasants could find to warm themselves with. This white spirit and red pepper with every dish were certainly stout fortifiers against the cold.

That night, two young cadets came to our lodging. I was struck by their keen and intelligent expression, but was not surprised when I learned that they belonged to the "9th (Educational) Regiment," a special political-training unit in the Shansi armies. They had come to talk over the problem of the *shanping*, and few reputations were spared in the frank discussion that followed. "It was a mistake to move all the regular troops to the south," someone remarked, referring to the sudden withdrawal of the Chinese armies from the strong mountain position north of Taiyuan that had been held for three weeks against the Japanese attack. "Even if Taiyuan fell, several regiments could have remained in the hills. But the way some of the Shansi troops retreated without any order and command was criminal."

It was in this retreat that most of the deserters had broken away from their units and begun to plunder the countryside. "You can hardly blame them," one of the young officers defended the rank and file. "They have no political training, and none of their own officers cares what happens to them. They were used to looting even when they were in the provincial army—why shouldn't they loot now, when they have no food to eat? We have found, with those groups of them that we have reorganized, how quickly they respond to political training when they get it."

"Yes," said the Transport Officer. "When the Red Army came to Sian last year, many of the people were afraid at first. But when the soldiers helped them to harvest the crops and thrash the grain, they realized that we were their friends. So this year, when we came through that same district on our way to the front, all the countrypeople thronged to our army, bringing presents of food, and offering to carry our baggage."

The young Shansi officers nodded emphatically. "The Eighth Route Army is the 'Teacher of the People,'" one said, using a phrase that had become common in the last few months. "We need the same kind of training in all our fighting forces." *

The third day out, we were in higher country, and the road became worse and worse—soon it was a mere hill track. We had managed to hire more mules, and had sent some of the carts back: those that remained were continually getting stuck in frozen ruts, or in the half-frozen mountain streams. The thaw —which made traveling so much pleasanter for us—had not improved the state of the road. Then, "Camels!" said the adjutant, as if suddenly inspired, when we came upon a string of these ungainly animals in one little mountain town. At last we were in "camel country"; I felt we were really getting to the north. No time was lost in hiring a new pack-train.

There is a curious attraction, to the westerner at least, about a camel caravan. These beasts had their long winter coats, which gave them a certain dignity; two were white camels, of a particularly malevolent disposition, but undeniably handsome. Bawling protest, they submitted to the immense bales that were loaded on their backs, and we continued our way with only three mule carts left.

But those three carts proved our undoing. One foundered in a river-crossing; another had shaky wheels that did not look as though they would stand a further ten miles. In this impasse, while the carters shook their heads gloomily, and the Transport Officer (in this, at least, like his fellows in any army) swore with great eloquence, a shot sounded from the advance guard. Coming towards us over the snow was a long line of troops and mules.

"*Shanping*," said Wu dramatically, and I nerved myself for a possible encounter. But my guard looked keenly at the gray-clad line, and said scornfully, "No, those are some of ours!" "And they've got mules," said the Transport Officer, so gratefully that he forgot to swear. Division Headquarters had come to the rescue. Now it would be plain sailing.

---

* In January, 1938, a Political Training Department was at last set up by the Chinese Government for all armies. It was headed by General Chen Ch'eng, with Chou En-lai as Vice-Director.

But it was dusk before we had loaded the whole train, and set out once more. On the ponies that had been sent "with General Ho Lung's compliments," we rode on by moonlight to reach our billet in advance. Ahead was the range we must cross the next day, shadowy and mysterious in the half-light. We were right up among the hills, which glimmered whitely all around us. Overhead, the stars were magnificent in the winter night.

At last we clattered into a little mountain village, challenged by a peasant with ready rifle. This was an Eighth Route Army district, and the mobile units were very much in evidence. Inside the gate, I had a glimpse of armed peasants sitting round a fire of sticks. Where the countrypeople were organized and armed, the *shanping* were no longer a serious problem. In front of us, a youth with the volunteer armband ran to show us our lodging for the night.

"Well, *this* is the last day!" the convoy commander assured us next morning, when we assembled in the narrow street just after dawn. The worst stretch of road was still in front of us, but with all the load on single animals, and with a string of spare mules, we were well prepared for it. We stood on a bank to review the caravan as it passed. First came the mules, with tinkling bells on their harness; then the stately camels, the slow deep note of their bells sounding rhythmically. The long line wound up the ravine into the hills.

"Ready? *Tsou-la!*" We set out along the frozen road, leading our ponies. "Tonight you'll be in Ho Lung's headquarters." It was about time, I reflected. Counting delays, we had been two weeks on the road. Two weeks without news—surely something must have been happening in the south!

It had. We arrived at division headquarters just in time to hear of the fall of Nanking.

CHAPTER SEVEN
IN THE HILLS WITH HO LUNG

DIVISION HEADQUARTERS

In the narrow doorway, the Transport Officer surprisingly achieved a salute worthy of a guardsman. He was greeted with a genial roar of welcome. "Go in," whispered Wu behind me. I found myself shaking hands with Ho Lung.

For once, a Red Army commander justified my liveliest expectations. "Chapayev" was the name that had already suggested itself to me from what I knew of Ho Lung's record; but here was a veritable Chapayev in the flesh. A round bullet head, close-cropped, set on powerful shoulders; eyes strangely hooded and almost mournful in repose, that lit up now with infectious gaiety; a generous mouth with a dark line of mustache. The whole figure expressed a restless energy that betrayed itself in abrupt southern gestures and the stride of a caged panther up and down the room (Ho Lung could never sit still for very long). This man looked what he was: a born peasant leader and a master of partisan warfare.

I sat down to the inevitable glass of tea, and Ho Lung pushed a tobacco container towards me—it was beautifully made of aluminum. "Japanese!" he said with a broad grin, lighting up his own pipe and puffing with obvious enjoyment. "We can show you a lot more things like that. See!" From a corner he produced the case of a thermite incendiary bomb, and handed it over for my inspection. On the metal cylinder was the mark of the swastika.

"We've prepared some food for you," Ho said; and before long the other members of his staff had gathered for the meal. Chinese introductions are always baffling when they contain unfamiliar titles, but at last I had sorted out the company. They offered some strange contrasts.

Hsiao K'eh, second-in-command of this division, and formerly a "red bandit" hardly less notorious than his present chief, I had pictured as something like Ho Lung himself: a man of forty or so, with the obvious marks of the *condottiere*. Instead, I found myself greeted shyly by a slim youth of 28 (who in Europe would easily have passed for 20). With his long eyelashes and delicate features, he looked like a poet in uniform. It was hard to believe that this was the veteran commander of ten years of civil war whose "death" I had seen several times reported in the newspapers.

Head of political work in the division was Kwan Hsiang-ying, another slight and youthful figure, with unruly hair and a small mustache. He came from Manchuria, and had something of the quick temper of the exiles of Tungpei. With him was the other "political commissar," Kan Sze-ch'i, who introduced himself with a flourish as "Comrade Gansky." Broad features and a face like a full moon radiated good humor, but beneath this manner of a buffoon was the shrewd intelligence of a mind trained by years of political study in Russia. To complete the party there was Chou Shih-ti, chief-of-staff—a Cantonese, and formerly the commander of a division in the 19th Route Army. Tall, with a deep voice and imperturbable calm, his was—I suspected—the coolest head in the division.

Curiously sorted as they were, Hunan was in the majority; and the conversation that developed was swift, explosive, and full of strange oaths. After a couple of weeks, traveling with this division of southerners, I had begun to get accustomed to their speech and fiery ways. But at division headquarters we lived in an atmosphere charged with electricity. And always, it seemed, somebody was singing at the top of his voice.

That first afternoon, when we had washed down our food with *paika'rh* (there was even an approximation to foreign bread, prepared in my honor), Ho Lung sprang up before the meal was properly finished, and ordered a guard to bring horses. "You can ride? Good." I had been riding most of the day, in a wind that whipped yellow dust and powdered snow into my eyes. But that did not seem to matter. "You must come and see my horses, anyway," Ho insisted. We strolled in a group along a narrow street into the open fields. The wind had dropped, and the air was clear and cold between the loess hills. Behind us, the crumbling walls of the town flushed pink in an early winter sunset.

Ho Lung ran like a schoolboy along the frozen stream to see if it would bear his not inconsiderable weight; fortunately there was no catastrophe. "Do the rivers freeze in England?" he demanded.

"Sometimes. But not like this." There must have been three feet of ice vaulted above the current.

Mafoos came then with the horses, which Ho scanned with a critical eye. They were two "Japanese captives," foreign-bred in a warmer climate than this, and clearly too aristocratic for North China. "They don't like the cold," Ho observed. "This one is sick and can't gallop. But that one's all right—try him!"

I felt my reputation was at stake and mounted the big bay; it seemed a very long way up. I had meant to take him for a short gallop, but he took me for a long one. I brought him back at last, after a not very dazzling display of horsemanship, and Ho Lung looked on approvingly. His own horse was a tiny stallion from Yünnan, with beautiful points like a miniature Arab. Most of the Eighth Route Army mounts that I had seen so far had been hardy but nondescript: Ho Lung kept a better stable. This, too, was what one expected of the man who had organized the first cavalry in the Red Army.

We walked back to headquarters through the dusk. Every dozen yards, Ho would stop to exchange a few words with a soldier who saluted; I was told he knew almost every man in his division. One veteran with a grizzled beard passed, and the volatile commander smote him affectionately between the shoulders and inquired broadly about his private life. "Fifty-eight!" Ho said, holding up his fingers to show the man's age. "He's been with me for nine years."

Though the main strength of this division was drawn from Hunan and Hupeh, it had some more exotic representatives. As we passed an open doorway, Ho Lung suddenly plunged into the court shouting *"Man-tzu!"* (*Man-tzu* used colloquially means something like "southern barbarian.") A grinning youngster in uniform answered the call.

"*Man-tzu* comes from Tibet," Ho Lung informed us. "He joined us in Sikang on the Long March. He can sing and dance. Sing, *Man-tzu!*"

Man-tzu obligingly sang—a husky, quavering song that was punctuated by expressive grunts, and strangely conjured up visions of snow peaks and glaciers. Then he did a lama dance for us, and laboriously, with his tongue on one side of his mouth, inscribed some Tibetan characters with a Chinese brush. My own guess was that he had run away from a monastery.

Back at headquarters, I was dusting my typewriter in the presence of a curious throng of *hsiao kwei*, when "Gansky" broke into the room. "Radio!" he announced briefly. "English news!"

In a room near-by, a group had gathered around the loudspeaker. "We get the Tokyo broadcasts most clearly," the student operator told me apologetically. "There's too much Japanese interference on the southern stations, except Changsha. Tokyo gives news in English and Chinese."

It was something to be in touch with the outside world again, even if the news was likely to be unsympathetic. But I was hardly prepared for what came a moment later.

"At 2 o'clock this afternoon," a voice announced exultantly, "the Imperial Japanese Armies entered the walled city of Nanking, the capital of China. . . . Despite all obstacles, the Imperial Navy has advanced up the Yangtse and arrived off Nanking. . . . The fleeing Chinese troops, it is reported, left over sixty thousand dead behind them. . . ."

Wu translated the news briefly, and Kan shook his head. "The sixty thousand dead," he said, "will be *after* the Japanese have occupied the city." But it was a shrewd blow all the same.

"*That*," I said, indicating the loudspeaker, which had got on to something about the "cause of the Japanese success being the Imperial Virtue," "from its accent, should be a kind of Englishman." Ho Lung shrugged his shoulders as if in apology.

But after a short break, another voice took up the same argument in the authentic accents of Peiping.

"*Ma ti keh pi!*" Ho shouted. (This is a favorite Chinese expletive, and there is no polite English translation.) He shook his fist at the instrument. "Traitor!" It was hard to believe that a Chinese could be found to broadcast the news of the fall of his own capital from the capital of the enemy, but this was unquestionably a Chinese. The unctuous voice flowed smoothly on; with impassive face, the operator noted down the details of the broadcast. "Do you suppose it's true?" Wu asked me.

"Afraid so. This is an international broadcast—they must keep it more or less accurate."

Ho Lung was striding up and down the room. "*Nanking wan-la!*" he muttered. "Nanking is done for. But we'll get it back!"

A minute later, with frowning concentration, he was deep in a game of Chinese chess with one of his youngest recruits.

BY FIRE AND FLOOD

The life story of Ho Lung—which has already become a legend in a dozen provinces of China—is almost unknown abroad. Chu Teh studied in Europe; Mao Tse-tung has always had something of an international reputation. But Ho Lung, a leader of peasant armies long before there was a Chinese Communist Party, is an "ex-bandit" whose actual career is hardly less picturesque than the legend. It reads almost like a chapter from one of the old Chinese romances—the *Shui Hu Chuan,** for preference.

Here are a few episodes. Strung together, they form an outline picture of the Chinese revolution.

The early background is South China, before and during the first years of the Republic. Ho Lung was born just before the turn of the century; his family were poor peasants in Shangchih, in western Hunan—that most rebellious of Chinese provinces. Here the peasants suffered incessantly under the tyranny of the local *tuchun,* and a crippling burden of taxation (Ho's

---

* Translated by Pearl S. Buck under the title *All Men Are Brothers* (John Day Co., New York, 1933).

family had to pay five dollars a month in taxes; "middle" peasant families paid fifteen dollars). And here, at the age of eighteen, Ho Lung led his first peasant revolt.

This was in 1916, at a time when Yuan Shih-k'ai, that most ambitious of all Chinese politicians, was trying to make himself emperor. Ho organized the peasants and the local militia in his own district: in one day, they drove out the magistrates in eight *hsien*. Reinforced from neighboring districts, his army soon swelled to 150,000 men, armed for the most part with homemade guns, bigswords, and spears.

Against this peasant army, the northern warlords sent a force of ten thousand regulars. After a few days of desperate fighting, the peasants were routed, and the northerners took a terrible revenge. But in Shangchih, when they were about to set fire to Ho's own home, there was a sudden thunderstorm with heavy rain, and this "heavenly portent" so dismayed the superstitious northern officers that Ho Lung and his family escaped further penalty. (This incident was probably the beginning of Ho Lung's "supernatural" reputation among the peasants of South China.)

Now the Southwestern provinces combined against the North, and Ho became a commander in an independent peasant army. Many of his troops were still organized in the old Manchu style, with "green camps," and the most primitive and traditional of weapons. (In the mountains, they often fought the northern regulars by rolling heavy logs down from the heights.) But after several years of this irregular fighting, a truce was patched up, and the peasant army was disbanded. Ho went to Changsha, and was active for some time in political intrigues, working in close association with Sun Yat-sen's party. The air was thick with political plots and attempted assassinations: once Ho Lung, entrusted with the task of dispatching some northern delegates, called at the yamen in the disguise of a policeman, only to be recognized by some of his former troops. He was arrested for one week, but managed to escape and make his way back to western Hunan, where he organized some 300,000 peasants to declare their independence, and tried to form an army to occupy all Hunan.

But he was arrested again, and his army disappeared as if by magic. Some friends secured his release, and nothing daunted he determined to advance into Hupeh. In his own home he had ten rifles; he sent a few of his troops ahead with these, and remained in Hunan with only one boy with him. Ho and the boy were armed with kitchen knives; their first task was to secure some guns. They came upon an escort of eight soldiers who were guarding a deposed magistrate; two of the soldiers had fallen behind the rest. One was at a natural disadvantage, the other was eating. The boy attacked the former, Ho the latter, and so they got two rifles. Later they managed to get two more.

With these four guns, Ho Lung and his companions fought their way north through ten *hsien* and finally reached Hupeh. Once more Ho became an independent commander, fighting against the northern warlords. The alliances of military leaders at this time are bewildering enough even to the professional student of Chinese history; but in general, it is possible to distinguish throughout the southern faction who were "revolutionary" and supported Sun Yat-sen, and the northerners who were the "reactionaries" (at this time with the recognition and open support of the foreign powers).

Ho Lung, a rebel from his childhood, was always with the southerners, and was at this stage of his career "faithful to the ideas and doctrines of Sun Yat-sen." But he became convinced that the revolutionary armies should be directed by some political party, and felt that the Sun Yat-sen party was in many ways unsuitable for this task. In 1920 he read some of the writings of Chen Tu-hsiu, one of the founders of the Chinese Communist Party, in the periodical *Shengtao;* and describes this as a "turning point in his social thinking."

There followed three more years of fighting, when the Southwestern armies were combined in a "Bandit Suppression Alliance" against the northern warlords, Liu Hsiang and Wu Pei-fu. At this time, Ho was given the task of blockading the upper Yangtse. And here for the first time, in his own phrase, he became involved in "anti-Japanese activity."

The supply of ammunition on both sides was running low, when Ho Lung heard of the approach of a Japanese steamer with a cargo of bullets for the northerners; the steamer had anchored some ten miles down the Yangtse from his headquarters when Ho heard the news from a southern agent. He took a party of thirty soldiers, with a number of women; all disguised themselves as coolies, with pistols hidden beneath their shirts. In small boats, pretending to sell vegetables, they approached the steamer, and managed to get aboard.

Ho disposed his men at various points of vantage, and at a given signal they succeeded in capturing the ship, though not without wounding their own agent on board, who had sent them word of the vessel's approach. The latter showed them where the munitions were hidden, and Ho and his men departed, taking with them two Japanese officers. These two unfortunates Ho Lung held prisoner for two years, demanding a ransom of $200,000 from the Japanese government. Three Japanese consuls visited him at different times trying to negotiate the release of the captives, but Ho held out for the money, claiming that the Japanese had in fact been acting as agents of the northerners. In the end he got $100,000 and the permanent ill-will of the Japanese government.

From this time until the Northern Expedition of Chiang Kai-shek in 1926, Ho Lung followed the wars with varying fortunes; just before the expedition left Canton, he received a command in the National Revolutionary armies. Joining the revolutionaries at Wuhan, Ho took part in the expedition into Honan, and at this time had his first close working association with the communists. Later he took his troops to Kiangsi, and was a joint leader in the Nanchang Rising with Chu Teh, when the first Red Army was formed. The "left" revolutionary armies then marched south on Canton, and it was at this time that Ho Lung joined the Communist Party.

After the defeat in Kwangtung, with a group of some thirty revolutionaries he escaped to Hongkong, and then made his way to Shanghai. Several of the group, including Ho, were ordered to go to Soviet Russia for further military and political instruction. But at this period there was a very strained atmosphere between the Nanking government and the U. S. S. R.; diplomatic relations had been broken off, and there was no direct way from China into Russia. Some of the party suggested going via Japan, but at this Ho demurred: he was too well-known to the Japanese authorities, and had told the consuls who visited him on the Yangtse that if ever he went to Japan, "it would be with an army." So he suggested that he should go inland again to raise a Red Army in the regions he knew so well—central and western China.

Nineteen hundred and twenty-eight saw him in Wuhan again, where he got four rifles from the local communist organizer. This was enough for Ho; within a few months he had collected a band of irregulars, and was active in partisan warfare along the upper Yangtse. The troops he led here later became the Fourth Front Red Army; in the next year, working with Chou I-chun as political organizer, he raised another force in Hunan and Hupeh which became the Second Front Army, henceforth to be his own special command in the civil wars and on the "Long March" of the communists to the Northwest. (This army forms the basis of his present 120th Division.)

From the time he joined the Communist Party, Ho Lung's story is essentially the story of the Chinese Red Armies and the movement for Chinese Soviets which terminated in 1937 with the new "anti-Japanese" National United Front. But though this story has recently become better known abroad, many phases of it are still unfamiliar. The Central Chinese Soviet in Kiangsi and Fukien received publicity enough when Chiang Kai-shek was leading full-scale campaigns against it; but little is known of the Hunan-Hupeh Soviet, which existed for three years practically next-door to Wuhan. It was here that Ho Lung remained until 1934.

Again, one can only select a few episodes from a story that is certainly not lacking in dramatic interest. The Hunan-Hupeh Soviet centered around Hunghu (the "Red Lake"), and was frequently troubled by floods on the Yangtse; in 1931, the Soviet Government lived in boats moored to the beams of ruined houses. But this proximity to the water led to one surprising and little-known development: the formation of the first anti-Japanese "Red Navy" in China.

After the Japanese invasion of Manchuria, the Chinese Soviets had officially declared war on Japan, but their great difficulty was always to find some way to put this declaration into effect. The Kiangsi Soviet was blockaded in the mountains of the south, and could find no opportunity of making contact with the Japanese. But Ho Lung and the leaders of the Hunan Red Armies had captured some artillery, and they now formed a couple of shore batteries to fire on Japanese vessels passing up and down the Yangtse.

Unfortunately, from the shore they could not very easily distinguish the nationality of passing ships; so they decided to improvise a fleet of their own. They succeeded in capturing two steel freighters of the China Merchant Navigation Company, and fitted these out with guns. The *Lenin* and the *I-chun* (named after Ho Lung's former political associate, who had been killed in the fighting with the Kuomintang) then hoisted the red flag on the waters of the upper Yangtse, and the "Soviet Navy" had a brief but not inglorious history. The ships were finally abandoned when the Reds were forced to retreat to the south.

Another original development in Ho Lung's army was the first cavalry force organized by the Chinese Reds. In 1930, the Nanking troops attacked the Hunan Soviet with cavalry; Ho Lung and his men ambushed the attacking force, and assailed them with bigswords attached to the end of long poles. They captured nearly a thousand horses, and with these as a nucleus, built up a very efficient cavalry force of their own. The people of the Red Lake were skilled riders and could fight on horseback; according to Ho Lung, they could stand on their horses to fire, and were equally efficient with sabers. From this time on, every regiment in the Hunan-Hupeh Red Armies had a troop of cavalry, and they found them more than useful—once, when the main army was surrounded on both sides of the lake, the cavalry swam their horses across the water and attacked the enemy in the rear, saving an extremely critical situation.

In 1934-35, when the main Red Armies left Kiangsi and started on their "Long March" to the north, Ho Lung and his troops moved into Kweichow, where Ho first met Hsiao K'eh, his present second-in-command. From Kweichow they advanced through Yünnan, Szechwan, and Sikang, where they made contact with the First Front Army, and Ho renewed his direct association with Chu Teh. From Kweichow through Sikang, they marched every day for four months, and finally reached Kansu, where the "grand reunion" of the main Chinese Red Armies was effected in October, 1936. It was not until then that Ho Lung met Mao Tse-tung for the first time in North Shensi.

This is the outline of a career of twenty-five years of military activity, which at last has brought this natural leader of guerilla warfare to the "anti-Japanese front." It is the record of a lifetime of revolutionary struggle, though Ho Lung himself dates his career as a real revolutionary from the time when he joined the Communist Party. In any circumstances, he would probably have been a leader and a man of action, with his native genius for intrigue, and for organizing and commanding the "poor men" of China. But he found a natural place in the ten-year "agrarian revolution" led by the Chinese Red Army, where his independent command was allowed free play, and where, in his own words, he was "re-educated politically." The latest phase was of a piece with his whole career.

For here now Ho Lung, who had defied the Japanese so long before, had brought one army to the northern front; and was rapidly raising another. Over his "army district" at this time the lines ran open into Suiyuan, where another redoubtable guerilla leader, old Ma Chan-shan, was rallying his northern cavalry. And beyond that, the lines ran on into Manchuria, where a whole people only waited the signal for revolt. . . .

Not even Ho Lung could have asked for a better field to work in. "All my life," he told me with an expansive gesture, "I have wanted to fight the Japanese—and I never could get at them! *But now they have come to me....*"

THEATRICAL

A long room—perhaps it was once a barn, or the stables of some wealthy landlord—with open-timbered roof and wooden pillars; at one end, an improvised earthen stage, gay with streamers and colored slogans. The air, on this winter evening, is frozen, dust-dried, and blue with tobacco smoke. But nobody seems to mind. Densely packed on wooden benches or ranged against the walls, gray uniforms jostle the malodorous sheepskin coats of Shansi peasants. One has never seen so many children....

The "Soldiers' Club" is holding a gala night, to celebrate the formation of a local volunteer unit.

As we go in, the center of the picture is a glaring naphtha lamp, hung from a beam before the curtain. A black-uniformed mechanic, standing on a bench in the middle of the stage, dominates the scene; around him a circle of upturned faces, eager and expressive in the flickering light. They are the brown, universal faces of the Chinese peasant.

The lamp is giving trouble and burns dimly or bursts alarmingly into flame. From the entranced onlookers, helpful suggestions are not wanting. "Give her some more gas, comrade!" ... "That's a Japanese lamp you've got there"... *"Hsing-la!"* ("O.K.!") ... *"Weihsien!"* ("Danger!").

"Running-dog!" mutters the lamplighter under his breath, adjusting the refractory flame and amiably ignoring his critics. Then the light and his brow clear simultaneously. He claps on the shade to a chorus of cheers. "Ready! Start up."

Political Commissar "Gansky" takes the platform. He is a perfect master of ceremonies, with his round face and homely Hunan accent. "The meeting is open. Greetings to the anti-Japanese fighters! Special greetings to the peasant volunteers! Greetings to the two comrades from Mongolia!" He goes on to give a succinct report of the latest war news, condensing from radio reports. International developments—nothing here is simplified or glossed over. The soldiers' faces follow the news intently; the peasants, wonderingly at first, but with growing intelligence....

More speeches; a delegate from the newly-raised local troop. He is a burly figure in a rough-and-ready uniform, with the volunteer armband; the thick local dialect is almost unintelligible, but his own people listen with delight. Then one of the Mongols, in trailing sheepskin, tells of partisan fighting in Suiyuan. His round head gleams yellow in the lamplight.

The hall has filled to capacity; but through the press the local magistrate fights his way to the front, in a sudden burst of clapping. He adds a few words. Now several orchestras are tuning up at once; it is a medley of instruments, from the two-stringed Chinese fiddle to a mouth-organ band. *"Swallow over the Loft,"* says Wu beside me, recognizing a familiar air. The curtain sways ominously.

A whistle shrills, and the curtain is swept back with a flourish. The show begins.

As usual, the first item is a dance by the "Children's Group." These youngsters (their ages vary between ten and fifteen) are quite the most accomplished performers in the whole propaganda unit; many of them have made the "Long March" from the south with the Red Army. They have had several years of training, under one who studied in the home of modern ballet.

"International Dance." Imagine an interpretation in the manner of Lichine, scaled down for the performance of children to music that begins with a melancholy peasant air, and ends with the *Internationale*. These dancers (girls, you would say, in their short red dresses) have caught the real spirit of conflict; their young faces are tragic and intense. Nowhere else in China will you see modern dancing as original and expressive as this.

The first play is announced. The scene is Shanghai, in Chapei after the enemy occupation—a worker's family, with a number of friends who have gathered to talk over this crisis in their own lives. Should they fight, *can* they fight the invaders? The Japanese military police, accompanied by the inevitable Chinese traitor, arrive to search the house and its occupants; the eldest son is suspected of having been one of the Chinese irregulars. His mother loudly protests his innocence, and the audience shares the ironical knowledge that this is the one man in the group who has been counseling submission and non-resistance to the Japanese. Despite their protests, he is arrested and dragged away.

In the street, he breaks away from his guards, only to be recaptured, unmercifully beaten, and left for dead. His friends gather round the dying man, who still proclaims his innocence.

"I didn't fight—*but I should have!* Brothers, you must fight to avenge me." The workers seize their tools, make a start with the Chinese informer. Then they leave in a body to join the partisans. . . .

Crude, but effective propaganda. Lest anyone should have missed the meaning of the play, a political organizer makes a short explanatory speech to the peasants. This is the method of dramatic propaganda in this People's Army.

The children dance again. This is a livelier number—"Wedding of the Communist Party and the Kuomintang." Boys in charming little costumes of blue and white, "girls" in Chinese peasant dress with red kerchiefs. It is a dance of reconciliation, the climax to which is the entry of the "United Front" of "soldiers, peasants, merchants, and students"; and a tableau with two soldiers—one in the uniform of the Nanking armies, one a peasant guard with the red star on his cap. Together they level their rifles against the national invaders. It is keen political commentary, witty and apt, besides being an attractive "turn."

Perhaps this is too much modern fare for an unsophisticated audience, so now we have some more traditional items—Chinese conjuring, operatic singing in the old style of the Peiping drama, the popular Shensi "low-brow" drama, which is an approximation to music hall. In the intervals, there is community singing, and the room rocks with the sound.

Now another longish play. This is more topical, for its theme is the arming of the peasants into mobile units. The Japanese army is advancing, and the villagers have gathered to see what they can do about it. They have bought red candles to burn on the altar, and tell their troubles to the gods. Here is the old scholar, whose words are still heard with an exaggerated reverence; a few small artisans; but most of the group are peasants and farmers. They have gathered a few arms—bigswords and pikes; the old village headman arrives with a battered rifle. It is the only modern weapon among the group. Then the news that the Japanese troops are in the next village.

Again, the same question—*can they fight?* All the pros and cons are debated with salty peasant humor. Then a girl is brought in weeping, the victim of a Japanese assault. The tide of the argument turns suddenly and positively. "What use is this thing?" one peasant has just exclaimed, throwing down his spear. "I'll show you," now retorts the boldest spirit of the group. He tears down the red altar-cloth that was to have heard their prayers, improvises a flag. "We've got one gun, and our swords. We can attack at night—I'll show you a hidden path. We'll get our rifles from the Japanese dwarfs!" They form up and march off in a body....

There are several more plays, for a Chinese audience takes its theater in five-hour doses. And there are more peasant dances by the children, with one witty satire "Against Traitors," where the traitor is caricatured with something like genius by the star actor of the group (who was the son of a Shensi banker before he ran away to join the Red Army). It is all very good-humored, but the serious points are made vividly and effectively.

Tomorrow the "company" will leave for a neighboring town: they have been active all along this northern front. We walk back to headquarters under the immense sky. Someone is singing the song that I heard Lu Chi (the Rouget de Lisle of this later revolutionary war) sing, himself, in Yenan:

> *Wo men shih pei ya p'o ti min chu,*
> *Wo men shu yao chan cheng ...*

The words are an echo of the *Marseillaise,* but it is a rousing tune:

> *We are the people in oppression,*
> *We need to fight!*
> *Fight to break our chains,*
> *Fight to win peace ...*
> *Brothers! Arm yourselves, arise!*
> *On to Suiyuan, on to Taiyuan,*
> *On to Shantung, on to Hopei,*
> *To the front!*
> *Drive the fierce Japanese invaders*
> *Beyond our borders.*
> *With our own blood struggle for peace!*

TESTAMENT OF YOUTH

In those days at Ho Lung's headquarters, I became especially friendly with Hsiao K'eh, the young second-in-command of the division. Hsiao was an intriguing personality; he was certainly the most temperamental commander I had met in this army. But his mind was swift and incisive as a rapier, and he concealed an almost terrifying energy within his slight, girlish frame. He had a habit of disappearing into his own room with a pile of maps, and emerging hollow-eyed next morning with a plan for some complicated maneuver which would occupy the attention of his colleagues for days. Hsiao K'eh was one of the few communist commanders who kept a diary, and he had written a long account of his own experiences on the Long March which (Wu told me) was a literary masterpiece.

His bookish flair came out when I asked him for some details about his life. Such a request was always enough to launch Ho Lung into some amazing yarn about his "bandit days," which could only have found a place in a picaresque novel. But Hsiao took it—as he took any concrete proposal—very seriously indeed. "I will write you out an outline," he told me. Next day he handed me four or five sheets of dispatch forms, covered with minute, beautiful Chinese characters. "There is the story of my life," he said briefly. "I wanted it to be exact."

I reproduce that document here, without change; for besides being a typical communist credo, it is the story of a whole Chinese generation. Though few young men, even in China, where events follow swiftly in these days, can have packed as much into twenty-eight years as Hsiao K'eh.

"I was born in Chiaho *hsien,* in Hunan. Here, until 1921, my father was a small country gentleman *—every year, he usually held a minor position in the local government. During the wars between the North and South, the government raised money by forced levies and surtaxes, and the landlords and country gentry exploited the peasants very cruelly. For some

---

* *"Shen shih,"* the Chinese phrase, means one who has property, a good relation with the local officials, is perhaps an official himself.

years, the harvest was bad in Hunan, and the rural economy of the province was almost completely destroyed.

"There were some social changes. The poor farmers who had lost their land united in small bands of one or two hundred, to revolt against the government and plunder the rich families. Such primitive jacqueries had no advanced class leadership, but were favored by the general condition of social unrest, and often extended over several *hsien* at a time. My eldest brother was caught up in this wave of peasant revolt.

"The government sent troops to quell the rising in our district. The leaders of the farmers were bribed by the government and surrendered, so the rising failed. My brother was betrayed to the authorities, captured, and executed. My father was put in prison. In the next year (1922), government troops came four separate times to inspect our home. We lost more than half of what we possessed.

"With this, my second brother had to leave school; and in 1923, when my family became poorer, they asked me also to stop my studies. But I was firmly determined to get an education, and managed to continue at the local Normal School. It was a great struggle to pay my school fees; to save money, my clothes, socks, and shoes were made at home of the coarsest material. My private expenses were less than a dollar a year.

"Because my eldest brother had been killed, and the government troops had raided my home so often, I became bitterly hostile to the government and the powerful landlords. At this time there was a Student Movement in my school, of which I was one of the leaders. The government and the country gentry, as usual, supported the conservative teachers and suppressed the students. I believed then that there could not be one good man among all these landlords.

"In this period (1923-25), I had a cousin who was a student at Canton University. He often sent me books about the *San Min Chu I* and the theory of revolution. I read all the writings of Sun Yat-sen, *Marxism and Darwinism*, *The Life of the 72 Martyrs*, and the *Life of Sun Chiao-jen*.* From this time on,

---

* Sun Chiao-jen was an early revolutionary, killed by Yuan Shih-k'ai. The "72 Martyrs" led an abortive rising against the Manchus in Canton in 1910.

I had a firm and rational belief in Sun Yat-sen. Before this I had admired Dr. Sun, but with a somewhat blind and childish hero-worship.

"From 1921, I had had an ardent sympathy with the Canton Revolutionary Armies, and followed eagerly all their successes and failures. Sometimes I read the newspapers all night, and did not sleep, looking for news about them. In 1924, the tide of revolution swelled again in Canton, and I determined to go there and join the army. But I could not go until I had finished my school course.

"In January, 1926, I graduated at last. My school was 15 *li* away from my home; I did not tell my family of my intention, but borrowed seven dollars of small money, and set out for Canton alone. It was a very cold winter, and my clothes were thin; in my bag, I had only a pair of shoes and socks, and a few books. The books were, an *Outline of Educational Psychology*, the *Sun Sze* (an old Chinese book on military strategy), the *Yü Lu* (selections from the writings of the Ch'ing commanders, Cheng Kuo-fan and Hu Lin-yi), and the *Theory of Sun Yat-senism*. It took me nine days to get to Shaokwan, where I took the train for Canton. In Canton, I had hoped to enter the Whampoa Military Academy, but the time for regular entrance was past; so for the next five months I joined the People's Revolutionary Army.

"In June, 1926, the Northern Expedition under General Chiang Kai-shek started from Canton. The vanguard of the army rapidly took Changsha, and approached Wuhan. In March, 1927, I became an instructor in one platoon in Yeh T'ing's division at Wuhan. When the second northern expedition marched into Honan, I was a lieutenant. In the two months of this campaign, I studied the *ABC of Communism* and the *Plan of Communism* (I had already been a reader of the communist *Guardian* * for three years). At this time, I became a communist.

"Shortly after I returned to Wuhan, our division moved to Kiukiang and Nanchang. I judged the whole political position at this time from the communist standpoint; and later took part

---
* "*Shengtao*"—the same magazine which Ho Lung studied.

in the Nanchang Rising with Chu Teh. When our troops were defeated in Kwangtung, I escaped to Canton, and then returned to my home.

"I stayed at home for two or three weeks; this was just before the Chinese New Year. Two days before New Year's Day, I heard the news that Chu Teh had arrived with his army at Ichang, three days' distance from my home. I told my second brother, who like me was a communist; and left again without informing my parents. One day later, I arrived at the home of one of my best friends, who told me, 'Chu Teh is gone—no one knows where!' In despair, I returned home once more.

"My mother met me with tears in her eyes, and said, 'Last New Year you were not with us for the family celebration; and now that the New Year comes again, you again leave home!' She wept bitterly. But in my mind, I still thought always of Chu Teh and the army.

"After New Year's Day, I heard again news of Chu Teh. With two friends, I decided to leave and join up with him; we left two days later. After one day's travel, I arrived in the house of one of my father's best friends, a landlord named Hsiao. This landlord was very reactionary, but he did not suspect my views, and treated me well for my father's sake.

"In his home, I met several other big landlords who had been driven away from Ichang by the Red Army. I wore a black scholar's gown, and tried to get on friendly terms with them, for I knew that they would have the latest news about Chu Teh. I invented a story about myself, and said to Hsiao, 'Last year, when I was returning from Canton, I left part of my baggage in a shop in Ichang. Can I go and get it there now?'

" 'Wait a little,' said one of the other landlords, 'and my detective will return and give you all the news.' Soon this landlord's private agent arrived, and said that Chu Teh had retreated from Ichang; but he also made a detailed report on every movement of the 'communist bandits.' I said farewell to my host, and left; two days later, I found a village where the peasants had risen, and joined the revolt.

"After this experience, I began to train the mobile units, and fought against the landlord troops in that region. The unit I commanded, about fifty or sixty men, was very much trusted and supported by the local people, and we had a soviet government then that lasted for three months in south Hunan. In April, 1928, when the 'White' troops attacked, Chu Teh moved up into the Chingkang mountains. Our mobile unit did not get the order to withdraw, and was cut off by the enemy.

"We collected about 500 men, armed with all kinds of rifles and homemade guns, and struck up into the mountains for five or six days, hoping to connect with the main army. By great good fortune, we met Mao Tse-tung, who was returning with a regiment from the attack on Jucheng. This was a joyful union! We went on together into the mountains, and met Chu Teh's army. Henceforth, I became a subordinate and student of Chu and Mao. From them I learned the plan, theory, and method of revolution, not only for that time, but for the present and for the future.

"In the autumn of 1932, the Revolutionary Military Council appointed me to another soviet region—Hsiangkan (Hunan-Kiangsi). This was the first time that I worked independently. In 1933, our army defeated the troops of Wang Mao-teh, Chen Kwang-chung, Feng Wei-jen, and Li Chueh. Co-operating with the Central Red Army, we pulverized the Fourth Campaign of Chiang Kai-shek, and strengthened the Hsiangkan Soviet, making it a powerful left arm of the Central Soviet in Kiangsi.

"In January 1934, I was ordered to advance northwards, and our army was active for two months in Yuansui, Chinsui, and Hsinsui. When we returned, we defeated Wang Tung-yuan and Tao Kuang, and effectively defended the western front of the Soviet Government from attack.

"In August, I received another order, that the Sixth Military Group of the Red Army should leave Hsiangkan, and cross southern Hunan and eastern Kweichow to meet the Second Army Group under Comrade Ho Lung. We carried out the order, and in October not only united our forces in this barren area, but became the vanguard of the main army of Chu and Mao, which marched northwards at this time towards the anti-Japanese front.

"After the union of our armies, we marched into western

Hunan, defeated Chen Chu-chen (who had occupied western Hunan for years), and established the Hsiang-E-Chwan-Chien (Hunan-Hupeh-Szechwan-Yünnan) Soviet. Chiang Kai-shek then ordered all the armies of Hunan and Hupeh, and a part of the Central Armies, to attack this soviet area. But after six months' fighting, the campaign of the 'Whites' was smashed to pieces, and their armies retreated. This was the biggest success of the Red Armies since Chu and Mao crossed the Upper Yangtse, and wrote another glorious page in the history of the Chinese revolution.

"During this war, the Tangku Pact and the Ho-Umetsu Agreement were signed, and the Japanese invaders occupied Hopei and Chahar. The danger of complete national subjugation by Japanese imperialism became greater than ever, and our Second and Sixth Armies answered the call of the Central Committee to move north against the Japanese.

"On November 19, 1935, we left the soviet area in Hunan, and passing through western Hunan, Kweichow, southern Szechwan, and Yünnan, we crossed the Yangtse and met the Fourth Front Red Army in Sikang. Then we crossed the grasslands, and passing through southern Kansu, reached the borders of Shensi, Kansu, and Ninghsia, where we were present at the great meeting of the three main Chinese Red Armies in October 1936. Once more, we were under the direct instruction of the Central Committee, and the direct command of Chu and Mao. Now, in the new political situation, we are taking part in the glorious war of National Revolution.

"In the past ten years, I have done my work entirely under the plan and line of the Central Committee of the Communist Party. I am a complete 'internationalist'; and have an invincible belief in the principle and method of communism. In the ten years' struggle of the soviet movement in China, I was part of one great wave in the struggle. Because that wave was so mighty, my life and career became what they are.

"Ever since I first became loyal to the plan and line of the Communist Party, I wanted my life to become one with the life of the broad masses. I wished only to be one cog in the wheel that moves on the masses to ever greater struggle. Now,

THE NEW YEAR   227

as always, I desire only to be a thorough internationalist, to be a good student of Chu and Mao, and to join with the masses of our people in the great struggle for the liberation of our country."

THE NEW YEAR

That year which had opened so auspiciously for China, with the peaceful settlement of the brief but vivid drama at Sian, and a new promise of internal unity—drew to its close under dark and rolling clouds of war. From division headquarters in the hills of North Shansi, we watched as in a map the shadow of invasion spreading along the Yangtse Valley, north into Anhwei and south along the North China plain. Christmas Day, 1937—unlike that other Christmas a year before—was no time of general rejoicing in China.

In our own part of the world, the war situation had more or less settled down, at least for the time being. With their main offensive in Central China and along the Tsin-Pu * railway, the Japanese had withdrawn a considerable number of their troops from Shansi. They seemed to be content for the present to hold Taiyuan and continue with the work of widening the gauge of the Cheng-Tai railway, postponing the southward thrust that had been generally expected when I arrived in the province in November.

But—as I knew from the reports that daily reached our headquarters—they were finding the task of keeping open their communications to Taiyuan far from easy. North of the provincial capital, the Japanese held only a few of the main *hsien* cities; and though they could move between them along the main roads, it was at the continual risk of surprise attacks from the widely-scattered forces of the Eighth Route Army and the volunteer mobile units. These mobile units were becoming increasingly active: they had even been in the suburbs of Taiyuan, and their range extended northwards as far as Tatung and the borders of Mongolia. The Japanese might make sallies and "punitive expeditions" against them by daylight, but at nightfall they withdrew with some celerity inside their city walls,

* The Tientsin-Nanking line.

under cover of their heavy batteries. By now, they knew better than to continue their pursuit of these elusive "bandits" into the Shansi hills.

Meantime, at the turn of the year the news from the other fronts grew steadily worse. Hangchow, the capital of Chekiang, had fallen to the invaders, and there was already talk, over the Japanese radio, of the formation of a new "provisional government" of Kiangsu, Chekiang, and Anhwei. But though all this —as it was clearly intended to do—may have struck dismay into the hearts of the Chinese bourgeoisie in these rich central provinces, it had merely strengthened the will to resistance of the masses of the Chinese people. The "terrorist" tactics of the Japanese militarists, well examplified by the fate of Nanking and the surrounding districts, were having other results than those intended. For a taste of the Japanese methods in practice could do more to rouse the Chinese peasants against the invaders than any amount of "nationalist" propaganda from their own government.

And Shantung, that northern province directly in the zone of war which had so far unaccountably escaped any very serious fighting, was now getting its full measure of attention. The burning of the Japanese mills in Tsingtao (a step which may well be considered inevitable in the light of what the Japanese had been doing in other parts of the country) had provoked the attack and occupation of Tsinan, the Shantung capital; and it became clear that the immediate aim of the Japanese was to effect a junction of their forces along the Tsin-Pu railway. Around Hsüchow, the junction of the Tsin-Pu and Lung-Hai lines, Chiang Kai-shek had now concentrated the main body of his Central armies; and here, behind the Chinese "Hindenburg line" so laboriously prepared under the direction of German Staff experts, the heaviest fighting of the next months was to be expected.

But there was some more encouraging news to set against all this that sounded so disastrous for China. It appeared that the fall of Nanking had been the last necessary proof to the Chinese government of the futility of relying upon regular troops alone for the war of resistance. In the future, it was officially an-

THE NEW YEAR 229

nounced, partisan warfare would be much more widely developed, and the local people would themselves be armed and formed into self-defensive units. This was a complete change of attitude from the first months of the war; and even more decisively than any change of positions in the front, it marked the beginning of a new stage in the hostilities.

Then, too, it seemed clear that political changes were at last being seriously considered. Because these were of a nature that had been suggested from the start by the Chinese Communist Party, it was perhaps only natural that the Japanese should put them all down to the influence of the communists and of Soviet Russia. The general trend of political reorganization was twofold—first, in the direction of greater centralization of wartime government; secondly, towards a more fully representative popular system of government, and economic reforms that would improve the livelihood of the common people.

On January 1st, the first step in this political reorganization was announced with certain changes in the Kuomintang government. Chiang Kai-shek resigned from his position on the Executive Yuan, to be succeeded by H. H. Kung; a number of ministries were coalesced, and some of the most notoriously "pro-Japanese" officials resigned from office. At the same time, new appointments like that of Chang Chun (another "pro-Japanese" representative) under Dr. Kung, and of Chen Li-fu, one of the leaders of the reactionary "CC" clique,* to the Ministry of Education, showed that this was only a very mild purge indeed, and amounted to little more than the first step towards real reorganization. But it was a step in the right direction. Things seemed to be moving at last inside China. The measure of the immediate Japanese gains was also the measure of China's growing preparedness to continue the struggle on more realistic lines.

I had hoped to spend Christmas at the front; but at division headquarters, they insisted that we should stay for the New Year celebrations. To refuse an invitation to a feast is the height

---

* The "CC" is a current reference in China to a political group headed by the two brothers Chen Li-fu and Chen Kuo-fu, which has always played a very reactionary rôle within the Kuomintang.

of discourtesy in China (even in the Eighth Route Army, which has reduced the old formality to a minimum!). So I stayed on another week, with the best grace I could muster.

Already in the last days of the old year, our little mountain town was taking on an air of festival. Red paper streamers and arches of decorated greenery made their appearance in the streets; and I saw with some foreboding that we were in for a formidable series of banquets. I had grown accustomed to regular Chinese fare, but feast-dishes in China are a test of the hardiest foreign stomach.

The first three days of the new year were a general holiday, and many soldiers came in from outlying stations to join the revelry. This was apparently an auspicious season for Chinese weddings, and in addition to the New Year celebrations, we had several days of rural festivity, to the immelodious sounds of Chinese tabor and flute. The only unfortunate sequel to all this revelry was when one soldier (it was pleaded in his excuse that he had drunk three *chin* of *paika'rh,* which is an intolerable deal of any liquor) ran amok one night and shot up the town. No damage was done beyond some waste of ammunition and strong language; but the culprit was handed over to the political department for "discipline." It was the first—and remained the only—case of drunkenness I saw all the time I was with this army.

For my part, I soon lost count of the number of banquets we attended. The magistrate feasted us, and we feasted the magistrate; the same courtesies were exchanged with the head of the Army District. Headquarters Staff was entertained by the Supply Department, the Medical Corps, the Dramatic Group, and half a dozen others. Finally in return for all this, the Division Staff gave an immense banquet to which all and sundry were invited. When it was all over, Wu and I had consumed such quantities of white wine, yellow wine, red wine, scholar's wine, seaweed, lotus seeds, exotic fish, and other Chinese delicacies, that we felt in the poorest of form for a strenuous trip across country. It was as though the army had determined to make up for all their months of plain fare by three days of surfeit.

The New Year 231

"We need some fresh air," I pleaded to the chief-of-staff. "Can't we leave for the front tomorrow?"

"Surely," he responded. "We've made the arrangement with brigade headquarters. Horses will be ready tomorrow morning."

The little cavalcade gathered early for the start. We had an escort of six "express-riders," messenger-carriers for the division; they looked as though they could set a stiff enough pace. We carried our bedding on our saddles, and a few toilet things in saddlebags. It was traveling light—especially for that time of year.

"So long! And good luck."

"*Tsai chien!* We'll expect you back in time for the Chinese New Year!"

"Not if it means any more feasts," I made a private resolution. The ponies trotted along the narrow street, the icicles at their fetlocks tinkling like castanets. Outside the east gate stretched the frozen river; across the valley rose an unbroken range of hills. The horses' breath smoked like incense, and in the early morning the wind cut clean through our sheepskins.

We took the road up into the hills. At last we were on our way to the front.

CHAPTER EIGHT
THE FRONT OF WAR

PORTRAIT OF A WARLORD

Screened by a dark line of willows, it was almost impossible to detect the city from a distance. Only at one point the walls were visible, where they climbed the steep face of the hills beyond. And here a battlemented watchtower commanded the valley approaches, and the mountain pass.

We walked our tired ponies across the frozen river, into the shelter of the friendly willow trees. A blue haze of smoke from some hundreds of chimneys rose above the gray stone walls like an exhalation. The bare trees were noisy with the evening clamor of birds.

At the gate, a policeman on duty demanded my card. The simple action, the familiar black uniform and white-banded cap, were like reminders from a forgotten world of peace.

We found our way to the Eighth Route Army station, through a street where the Norwegian flag flew incongruously over a Chinese rooftop—a somewhat worldly invocation for the protection of an abandoned mission. Our quarters were in a schoolhouse, liberally decorated with Kuomintang blue. But the armed peasants at the gate, and a group of fifty or so volunteers drilling on the slope beyond, showed that here as elsewhere the organizers had not been wasting their time.

We had a friendly but unceremonious welcome from an overworked officer with the brusque manner of Hunan. *"Hsin k'u,"* he said briefly, meaning that we need not look for any special comforts. But he cleared room for us on the *k'ang*, and roared directions for the evening meal to the cook outside.

PORTRAIT OF A WARLORD 233

The city was garrisoned at this time by the First Shansi cavalry division, and I had a letter to General Chao Ch'engshou, their commander. There was just time to pay an evening call. "What's he like?" I asked the Eighth Route Army man. The latter shrugged.

"Old style! But much better than he was—he asked us to lend him some political instructors. Like most of the Shansi commanders, he's reorganizing his own troops. We get along very well together now."

I had not yet met any of the Shansi generals, so it was with a feeling of some uncertainty that Wu and I set out in search of General Chao. But on the way we were met by a messenger from his headquarters, who brought us with elaborate politeness to the lodgings of the division chief-of-staff. Here we remained, exchanging amiable nothings, until the great man was ready to receive us. This time we were escorted like emperors to an imposing gateway, guarded by half a dozen soldiers in black fur caps. And General Chao himself met us on the threshold with a magnificent salute.

He was certainly an impressive figure, and radiated geniality like a laughing Buddha. When he smiled—which was often—a little black mustache vanished in creases of prodigious good humor. His build was Falstaffian, approaching the Chinese ideal of prosperity and well-being. Irresistibly reminded of Chaucer, I could not help thinking, even in this wintry weather, what joy it would be to see him sweat.

His costume was as overwhelming as his courtesy. Cap and sleeves of his blue army tunic were of black astrakhan, and he wore the red-and-gold collar tabs of an army commander. Trousers of brown figured silk were stuffed into soft leather boots, secured at the sides (a discreet touch of modernism) by zip-fasteners. The whole effect was slightly *opera bouffe;* but undeniably picturesque.

Whatever his qualities as a soldier—and it was a little difficult to reconcile this well-nourished figure with hard campaigning—General Chao was a perfect host, in the traditional Chinese style. He led us into an overheated room and offered us flower tea. There was so much compliment and superfluous politeness in the atmosphere that I hardly dared broach the subject of the war. And when I did finally venture on some direct questions, it was not easy to make much of his replies.

The interview had become very one-sided, for I found myself doing all the talking. But on one point at least the general became serious; and this, I felt, was not without significance. "We have learned very much already from this war," he assured me. "I myself"—he laid one hand on his breast—"have become a changed man. We Chinese must change our old style of fighting, must learn the lessons of our own defeats. Now we have the new principle: not to defend different places with our troops alone, but to organize the local people to defend their own districts. This is what we are doing now in Shansi. We have learned much from the Eighth Route Army."

It was a very considerable admission from one who was so clearly of the old school. When we made our excuses and rose to go, the general was very much perturbed. "But, of course, you will stay here one more day, and let us offer you some hospitality?" I explained that we wanted to go on to the front as soon as possible, and had arranged to leave the next morning—perhaps we could stay over an extra day on the way back. The last suggestion had become a promise before we were allowed to depart.

Back at the army station, we had barely finished our simple meal when a deputation arrived, consisting of the magistrate and the local Mass Mobilization Committee. They came with the usual demand for news of the "international situation." However flattering it might seem to be considered an oracle on world affairs, it was difficult to give any interpretation of an extremely complicated and rapidly changing scene when one had to depend on scrappy and unverified radio reports. But I did the best I could for an hour or so, and at last the deputation took its leave, after singing a patriotic song.

It had been a long day, and we were unrolling our bedding on the *k'ang* when a uniformed messenger arrived with the surprising news that General Chao was coming to call. "Whatever for?" I groaned. "At this hour?" "Chinese courtesy," Wu informed me slyly. And sure enough, a few minutes later the

PORTRAIT OF A WARLORD 235

general arrived in person, to renew his request that we should "rest one more day" as his guests. Dismissing his escort, he removed his cap (in the Eighth Route Army, no one went hatless, indoors or out), and sat down on the best seat we could find for him—a wooden bench that creaked ominously beneath his weight.

In that poor room, where a foul-smelling wick in a dish of crude oil gave the only light, this well-dressed visitor seemed strangely out of place. But he put a brave front on it, and stayed for half an hour making polite conversation. Finally he presented us with a couple of tins of expensive cigarettes (which were more than welcome) and left after we had confirmed our promise to come and see him again. I felt, after all this, it would be the very least we could do.

Some three weeks later (to anticipate a little), we returned to the same city, after a strenuous mountain journey. And General Chao, delighted at this chance to redeem his reputation for hospitality, gave us a meal to remember.

We dined off a polished table with brass candlesticks—the most civilized thing I had seen for months. Every dish was perfectly cooked and served, and there were delicacies that had come from Canton and Szechwan. There was even fresh fish, though where the general got his fish from at that time of year remains a mystery. Our host was profuse in his apologies for what was unquestionably the best meal I had ever tasted in China—and Chinese cooking, when it is good, is probably the best in the world.

At the dinner table, General Chao was in his element, and reminisced about Yen Hsi-shan (a relative and boyhood associate); and the special house he himself had built for foreign guests at Tatung. After dinner, he talked about horse-breeding with a zest and an expert knowledge that had been missing from his conversation about the war. Finally, when he learned that we had sent back some of our horses (they were badly needed, I knew, at the front), he insisted on lending us a string of his best ponies, and a guard of cavalrymen for the last stage of our journey.

That night, we were brought back with lights to our lodging; I felt as though I had been acting in a scene from an old Chinese drama. "What's your impression of General Chao?" the political instructor asked me with a twinkle in his eye.

"He's perfect. But does he ever do any fighting?"

The Eighth Route Army man grinned. "Sometimes. They say he shot his third concubine after the Japanese took Tatung—said it was her fault. But his cavalry are all right; and he's 'improving' politically. We have all kinds in the United Front."

It was true enough, General Chao had shown by his action as well as by his words that he believed in the need for a change in the old-style Chinese armies. And that, after all, was something.

MOBILE UNIT

The first glow of a winter dawn was red on the walls of the city as we filed out of the east gate into a windswept river valley. Traveling in Shansi even in January is tolerable enough, so long as the wind keeps down; but if it blows hard, conditions can become extremely unpleasant. This was one of those days.

Much of our way lay over ice—there were innumerable river crossings, and often the melted snow had frozen along the track. The one Japanese cavalry horse we had with us (it had been provided especially for my benefit, but I had politely declined in favor of a neat little bay pony, who could find a track through snow with uncanny certainty) was continually in difficulties; at first he had refused to take the ice at all. The China ponies were infinitely safer: I believe they could have trotted across plate glass.

But it was cold going, and we were all thankful enough when we reached our destination—a little village in the hills where we were to stay with a local volunteer unit. The approaches were guarded by armed peasants, and along the cobbled street several figures in sheepskins with Chinese bigswords and automatic rifles stood before the different offices of this partisan base. We were welcomed at headquarters by the partisan commander, an Eighth Route Army instructor in a plain gray uniform and the close-fitting felt cap that was the regulation headgear of the Shansi volunteers. Headquarters, in a typical country farmhouse, were surprisingly comfortable.

By this time, the volunteer organization in North Shansi had reached a comparatively advanced stage; and now that we were in a war zone, I was not surprised to find a very high degree of departmental efficiency. *You chi tui* (volunteer mobile units) had been raised in many of the villages I had already passed through, and I had seen many of them drilling and practicing partisan tactics. But this was the first unit I had encountered that was actually in operation against the enemy, and had already been in action for some months.

I asked the local commander for details about volunteer organization in the district. He gave me a brief sketch of his own experience. "When our army first arrived here," he said, "the position was desperate. Many people had left their homes and fled, and the provincial organizations, like the 'League of Sacrifice' and the rest, had melted away. The Japanese had established 'Peace Maintenance Committees' in most of the *hsien* cities; but on the other hand, their troops had burned many villages and killed a great many of the local people. Those who remained were bitterly hostile to the Japanese, but they had no real organization, and no arms.

"In many cases, where the Japanese terror had been especially savage, the people themselves organized small bands of volunteers. They had a few arms, and managed to collect a number of bombs and hand grenades that had been left in the villages by troops of both sides. They themselves found out how to use these, and sometimes their tactics were quite skillful. For instance, near Fenyang, when a small troop of Japanese cavalry came to one village, the Shansi troops were afraid to attack them, and retreated; but the local volunteers surrounded the enemy billet at night, and climbed on to the roofs of the neighboring houses. They threw down their bombs into the Japanese quarters, and killed the officer and most of the troop."

"What is your method of organization now?"

"As soon as our army arrived in this district from Yenmenkwan, we began to co-ordinate the action of the volunteers, and improve their fighting methods. To begin with, we send organizers to every village, and hold mass meetings to explain the situation of the war. We show the people how our army is able to defeat the Japanese, always using a very small force against much larger enemy units. When they see for themselves that this is true, then many of the villagers are willing to form troops and begin independent action.

"Of course, some political reorganization is necessary. Where wealthy families still remain, we ask them for contributions of money and supplies. If the village headman is a landlord and does not assist in the work, we reform the system of village government, making it more democratic, and insisting that the people themselves should elect their own head. In this way we get a much greater political solidarity."

"How do you find the landlords, generally?" I asked. For my own brief experience of Shansi landlords and merchants had not been very encouraging.

"They vary a lot: some are patriotic and work very well with us. For example, there was one very wealthy old landlord near Kuohsien, who had been forced by the Japanese to become a member of the new puppet government. But really he sympathized with the Chinese resistance, and when we sent our organizers secretly at night to his village, he helped them very much. He showed them how to correct their southern speech, so that they could talk more like the Shansi people, and would be in less danger of discovery or betrayal.

"Then, when our troops came to his village, he himself wore a bigsword (he had once been a soldier), and wanted to go with them. But he was too old; so he sent his son to act as a messenger for the army and the volunteers. Later, his son was killed by the Japanese. When our troops brought his body back home, the old man did not weep, but said: 'This was a glorious death.'"

It was a good example of the practical working of the United Front. In this partisan base, there were more than a hundred volunteers organized. The room in which we slept was like a barrack, the walls hung with a strange assortment of arms. There were old homemade blunderbuses with bell mouths, and modern automatic rifles from the Taiyuan arsenal. One weapon which is especially common in Shansi is a short-barreled automatic of formidable bore, which takes forty cartridges in its magazine. It would not, I imagined, be very accurate; but it was well-designed for close-quarter fighting, and especially for night attacks—which was just the kind of action the volunteers preferred.

"How do you get on for ammunition?" I inquired.

"We get something, of course, from the regular armies. But we have also captured a lot from the Japanese. One mobile unit near here made a very good haul last November. A large quantity of ammunition had been left in the neighboring villages after the battle at Hsinkow, and the Japanese came to collect this. They put it all in trucks; but the volunteers attacked at night and captured the trucks. They handed over all they took to the Eighth Route Army—200,000 rounds of rifle ammunition and 7,000 shells! We used the shells later against the Japanese tanks."

With the whole of this northern district now organized and active in volunteer partisan warfare, I could understand something of the difficulties the Japanese would meet if they tried any further advance. The kind of "retaliation" practiced by the invaders against partisan action was always to burn more villages and slaughter more of their inhabitants—a measure which might have been designed to spur on the countryfolk to greater efforts and strengthen their determination to resist.

"When the Japanese first came," the instructor told me, "they always demanded money and chickens in every village, and often young girls. The villagers at first dared not resist; but now that they have more experience and confidence, they attack any troops that come with such demands. Here is one story that shows the real spirit of the Shansi people:

"A farmer called Li, who lived near Yuanping, had seen most of his family brutally killed by Mongol troops who came with the Japanese. He went secretly to the nearest Eighth Route Army base, and asked for five hand grenades. They showed him how to use them, and he went back to his home.

"At this time, the partisans were very active, and the Japanese wanted guides to show them the country so that they could make sallies against the Chinese forces. Li volunteered to guide one party, and made this arrangement with them. 'I will go first,' he said, 'and if I see any Chinese troops, I will make a sign with my hand—then you must all close up behind me to attack them.' The Japanese agreed to this, and they set out into the hills.

"At the top of the slope, Li made the sign with his hand, and the Japanese moved in behind him. Then he took the bombs, which he had hidden in his shirt, and threw them down from above. The Japanese thought they were being ambushed, and those who had not been killed fled."

"What happened to the guide?"

The partisan commander grinned. "He collected four thousand dollars from the dead Japanese, and a number of arms, and brought them to our brigade headquarters. Now he's a member of the Eighth Route Army."

These are episodes that do not figure in military reports. But they are typical of the kind of thing that is happening every day in the hills of North China. And because they are representative of the mood and action of the common Chinese people—not just of the regular troops—they are significant pointers for the future.

There is a saying among the peasants of Shansi now that originated with the first formation and growth of the mobile units: "*Jih lou hsi shan, pu hwei tou.*" It means, "The Sun has set in the Western Mountain, and will not rise again."

The "Western Mountain," of course, is Shansi; and the sun is the Rising Sun of Japan.

It may not prove to be just an idle word.

ALONG THE FRONT

Blanketed in mist, the little village looked unreal and ghostly when we left early the next morning. We watered the horses at a well fantastically wreathed in ice; they drank greedily from the freezing pails. These hills were in the iron grip of winter.

Ahead lay the range we had to cross that day. And an hour's march through the foothills brought us to the pass. Here our track led up the rocky bed of a stream, which rose ahead of us like a miniature glacier, with frozen waterfalls and green hanging icicles. For three hours we led our ponies along this mountain path before we came out again in a broad river valley beneath a pink-walled temple. It was smooth going from here to Taiyuan.

"Two hours," calculated the *pai chang* who was leader of our party, "and we can be at regimental headquarters."

The village nestled at the foot of loess hills, warm and friendly in the afternoon sunlight. The first thing that caught my eye was a decorated platform in the open air: "political mobilization," it seemed, had not been neglected here. We were only a few miles from the railway, and the main valley road that was the only Japanese communication between Taiyuan and the north.

"We've had four days of fighting this week," the political organizer of the regiment told me, as we sat around an open fire of logs, warming our hands. "The enemy are always trying to take this place, because it's so near the railway, and because we have been very active in guerilla warfare in this sector. But after four days they had had enough of it, and yesterday they retreated again."

He was a Kiangsi youth in his early twenties—the nearer one got to the front, as I was to discover in this army, the younger everyone seemed to be. This headquarters had the air of a cadet camp. But youth, in China, is no sign of immaturity. The regimental commander, I noticed, wore the ten-year star of the Red Army.

The Japanese had recently sent one division north from Taiyuan, they told us here—to "mop up the remnants of the Chinese forces," I supposed, remembering the favorite phrase of the Tokyo radio announcer. "By the way," I said, "there was a Japanese report just before we started out, that a 'communist' force of more than seven thousand men had been surprised and routed by Japanese troops near Yütze. Is there anything to it?"

The young officer roared with laughter. "Why," he said, "we haven't got as many as a thousand men together in one body anywhere along this front!" The regular fighting unit, at this time, was not even a company, but a platoon; the division I was with had a "front" of more than a thousand *li*. But now the Japanese were trying to fight the Eighth Route Army with their own partisan tactics, and it seemed as though there might be some action in the north, where we were going.

"Stay here for a day or two," they told me in this regiment, "and we'll take you to have a look at Taiyuan—from the hills!" But I had made arrangements to join the brigade in the north, and I knew that they were expecting us. We could only spend the night here.

We were lodged in the political center—a large room hung with slogans of the United Front. On the walls were black-and-white posters of the "big four" of the Chinese Communist Party —Chu Teh and P'eng Teh-huai, as army commanders; Mao Tsetung and Chou En-lai, as chairman and vice-chairman of the Military Committee. But over them, were the familiar portraits of Lenin and Stalin; and over these again, the portrait of Dr. Sun.

I had expected to find Spartan living conditions at the front, but had reckoned without my hosts. We were offered sweetened condensed milk before supper (only when one has been without milk and sugar for any length of time can one realize what these things mean to the average European!); and—an even greater marvel—English cigarettes. Both had come, of course, from the Japanese supplies; its proximity to the enemy lines of communication gave this regiment a distinct advantage. Every one at headquarters here, I noticed, had an excellent electric flashlamp with a supply of batteries in a leather case. "We captured two truckloads of these things," they told me.

Next day we turned north again, following the main line of the railway a few miles to the west, with a convenient range of foothills between us and the Japanese. "The peasants are very well organized here," the political organizer had told us; and he was not far wrong. Everywhere from now on to brigade headquarters, we met with the same eager co-operation that I learned to expect in Shenpei. Whenever we passed a village, the local volunteer unit would invite us in to drink tea; and there was never any fear of losing our way, with so many willing guides. Once we climbed a watershed between two river valleys, and from the hills it was possible to get a better idea of the country. To the west, the snowcapped peaks of the Yünchung Shan bounded one horizon, and to the north the high hills joined again. East we looked across the main valley where the railway ran, towards Wutai Shan—another wilderness of hills, where the Eighth Route Army has established their first "Provisional Government" behind the Japanese lines. Between these high ranges were innumerable lesser hills, intersected in every direction by a maze of valleys and frozen streams. It would be heartbreaking country for an invading enemy, for here there was no food supply except what was stored in the village farmhouses; and wherever the Japanese moved, the villagers decamped with their provender. For the most part, however, the invaders preferred to keep to the main valley, and not to risk their forces in such dangerous terrain.

After a day's easy traveling, we came out on a fertile plain enclosed by hills—it was the first real expanse of level ground that I had seen since leaving the south of the province. All this area had been fought over a few months before, as I realized when we passed the wreckage of a Japanese tank in the open fields. At first sight, it looked like easy country for tanks or cavalry; but the plain was crossed by several rivers, and there were dikes and ditches meandering in all directions. I began to understand how mobile infantry were able to hold it against the superior technical resources of the Japanese.

We spent that night with a company billeted in a prosperous-looking farmhouse. Apparently the owner was a Christian, for there were a number of colored oleographs in the Italian style pasted up on the walls. They were flanked, however, by some very pretty pieces of Chinese pornography, which rather destroyed the effect. I had been interested to notice obvious traces of mission activity throughout this district, and at the volunteer base where we had spent one night, the new recruit who brought us hot water had worn an immense brass cross over his padded jacket. He told us very solemnly that he was a Catholic, but it did not seem to interfere with his military duties.

This company commander, again, looked a mere boy; but he wore a Japanese automatic, and a Mongol fur cap with the yellow star of the Japanese North China armies. The ranking officer here was a political organizer—a tough Hunan peasant, with three fingers on one hand still frostbitten from the November campaigning at Yenmenkwan. "That was hard fighting," he told us with a certain grim relish. "For days we had almost nothing to eat, and no fire. But at that, it was nothing to the Long March."

Everywhere I heard this same tale. For the former Chinese Red Armies, fighting the Japanese in Shansi presented few difficulties comparable with those they had triumphantly surmounted in the past. Seldom, indeed, had they fought a campaign under more favorable conditions.

The company commander described for me one typical engagement of his unit. "At Huangtoupu, near Kuohsien," he said, "we attacked a column of a hundred Japanese trucks—we had only three platoons of infantry. We destroyed sixty trucks, killed about two hundred Japanese, and got forty rifles and two machine guns. One of them is a long-range machine gun for shooting at aircraft—come and have a look at it!"

He led me out into a courtyard where the gun was mounted on a terrace—as usual, a *hsiao kwei* was cleaning it industriously. "We had only twenty casualties in that action," the young captain added. "But the Japanese are getting much more cautious lately—we can't get them to advance at all! They always retreat to the fortified cities at night."

He took me to see another section of his men, all of whom were armed with Japanese rifles. The caliber ("thirty") is the same as the Chinese, which means that captured ammunition can always be used by either side. But in Shansi—or at least, in this part of it—there could be no question about who gained most from so convenient an arrangement.

This company had also taken part in the famous raid on the Japanese air base at Yangminpao, when they had destroyed twenty-four planes with hand grenades. In the first months of the fighting, only this army among all the Chinese forces had known how to make full use of that most valuable element of offense—surprise. It was a fair indication of the respect the Japanese had learned for their tactics, that while on other fronts they pushed forward their advance sometimes with amazing rapidity (even when opposed by numerically superior forces), in Shansi the invaders now moved with infinite caution, though they might be opposed only by a few dozen infantry with rifles and hand grenades.

"There's no need to be afraid of the Japanese," the political organizer assured me—as, no doubt, he had assured many mass meetings of Shansi peasants throughout this district—"if only you know how to fight them."

I could see what he meant.

WHERE THE BATTLE WAS

Next day, our road lay over Hsinkow, the main pass north of Taiyuan. In October of 1937, this had been the scene of the major battle of the North China campaign.

We chose our path with some care, keeping where possible to sunken roads, for these foothills might well be under observation from Japanese outposts. I was surprised that we could go through this stretch at all by daylight, but our new escort from the company that had entertained us the night before were supremely confident. According to them, the enemy were anything but aggressive in this sector—they had had some unfortunate experiences there in the last few weeks.

As we climbed a spur of the hills, I noticed what seemed to be newly-dug trenches and earthworks: in this crisp mountain air, the frozen ground kept the marks of a pick fresh for a winter. We were passing over the field of battle. "When we arrived here," the troop commander told me, "there were still hundreds of dead bodies all through these hills. We collected them and burned them."

The toll of the Hsinkow fighting had been more than thirty thousand killed, fairly evenly distributed between the Chinese and the Japanese. The battle is noteworthy, not only because of the heavy losses on both sides, but also because here for the first time in North China, the Japanese received a decisive check in a battle of positions, and had on the whole the worst of the fighting.

In the last week of September, 1937, one part of the invading Japanese armies had suffered their first serious reverse at Pinhsingkwan. That was a mobile action in the hills, but it opened a new phase in the Chinese war of resistance, where for the first time the defending armies took the initiative, and developed offensive action against the Japanese. And in October, the Chinese high command, with a special order from Chiang Kai-shek, and actively supported by Yen Hsi-shan and General Wei Li-huang (the Central commander-in-chief in Shansi), had determined on a policy of prolonged and serious resistance in the north.

The new policy, the first immediate result of which was a really united command of the Chinese armies, both Central and provincial, found notable expression at Hsinkow.

The vanguard of the Japanese advance had already occupied Kuohsien, when in the first week of October hostilities began around the pass itself. At first, this was again mobile warfare; but when the Chinese concentrated their troops on both sides of the valley, it soon developed into a positional battle, with the Eighth Route Army carrying on guerilla operations in the rear and on the flanks of the Japanese. The degree of co-operation reached at this time between all the Chinese units was unprecedented.

The defenders had massed something in the neighborhood of 100,000 troops at Hsinkow, the backbone of which was Wei Li-huang's 14th Army. In addition, there were General Hao Mon-lin with two Central divisions, and a number of Shansi commanders. The fighting quality of the Shansi troops was decidedly inferior to that of the Nanking armies, but here for the first time they too put up a very good showing. The Japanese had two divisions and one brigade—in all, about 60,000 troops, with, of course, very much better equipment than the defending Chinese force. But for three weeks they made no headway whatever; and before long, found themselves caught in a very difficult position.

The part of the Eighth Route Army had been to attack and if possible sever the Japanese lines of communication. They succeeded in doing this on three main routes; only the road through Yenmenkwan remained open, and it was subject to constant attacks. (Several times the Chinese partisans re-occupied the pass at Yenmenkwan, but were unable to hold it.) The Japanese brought up supplies and reinforcements only with the greatest difficulty, and at one stage were obliged to bring in their ammunition by plane.

Under these conditions, and with serious losses in the actual fighting at Hsinkow, the invading forces found themselves meeting with the most stubborn resistance they had yet encountered in the north. In effect, it was a stalemate, with the odds generally favorable to the Chinese, for the country suited their style of fighting, and for the first time the main command was beginning to make successful use of flank attack.

What saved the situation for the Japanese, in the end, was the rapid drive of another part of their armies along the Cheng-Tai railway, and the immediate threat to Taiyuan. Wei Li-huang had made a gallant stand, and it was not his fault that the mixed Chinese troops defending the eastern approaches to Taiyuan failed to hold their positions, and fell back with such alarming precipitancy. The main Chinese defense was withdrawn from Hsinkow on November 3rd, in a desperate attempt to save Taiyuan. But the eastern front had crumpled so badly that there was no longer any hope of defending the provincial capital.

It is futile to speculate on the "if's" of military history, and to suppose what the position might have been in Shansi if Niangtzekwan—the key pass in the east—had been more resolutely defended. But what is worthy of notice here is the significance, both military and political, of the battle of Hsinkow.

Not only did it teach the Japanese—who, at this stage, were supremely confident in North China, believing that the only serious Chinese resistance was to be expected in the central provinces—a most salutary lesson about the fighting quality of the northern armies at their best; but also it gave invaluable encouragement to the people of North China. Three weeks or so is not very long for a battle to last in modern warfare, but it must be emphasized that the Chinese armies abandoned Hsinkow on their own initiative, and that the withdrawal was carried out in a regular and orderly manner, with singularly few casualties, at least in its first stages. (It was only later, when some of the Shansi armies got out of control, that scenes of disorder, such as I had witnessed on the road to the south that November, became common.)

This check to the Japanese advance increased the confidence of the regular armies, and stimulated immensely the growth of the volunteers and mobile units. These latter had been able to do very useful work while the main resistance held, and they had very soon learned that the Japanese were not invulnerable. Politically, the position at this time improved enormously, with a real United Front in the military command and the volunteer organizations. Even the disheartening loss of Taiyuan could not efface these valuable lessons.

The Chinese had suffered heavily, but in all ranks—General Hao Mon-lin, for example, an army commander, had been killed in the front line. The troops knew that at least they were not being sold out, as the 29th Route Army had been in Peiping, by their own command. And they had also the knowledge that, heavy though their losses had been, the enemy had suffered if anything even more severely.

Hsinkow—while it lasted—was the high-water mark of Chinese resistance in North China, and a very significant omen for the future. If Taierhchwang, in April of 1938, was the first major Chinese victory of the war, Hsinkow was the try-out that laid the pattern for it.

Crossing these loess hills honeycombed with dugouts and trenches, and still littered with fragments of shell and odd hand grenades, one had little difficulty in reconstructing the main outlines of the conflict. And—with the exception of the great plain—North China is a land of hills, with many other positions equally favorable for defense. With strengthening of the Chinese armies that the present crisis was only hastening, such episodes as Hsinkow might well be repeated in the not-so-distant future.

We kept to the hill tracks, which lengthened our route considerably; but often there was a view of the main valley, with the towns and the highway occupied by the Japanese. It was almost nightfall when at last we reached a village where the Chinese flag flew bravely over the office of the local volunteers. Unaccountably—it seemed to me—we were expected, but the grapevine news service was pretty efficient in Shansi.

We were welcomed eagerly in a courtyard where new weapons were being assembled from a most curious assortment of old iron and rifle barrels. Here were peasant girls joining in the work of mobilization with characteristic energy. (The general position of women in Shansi is very backward, but under the influence of the invasion of girl students from the north, with other more "emancipated" members of their sex, the Shansi womenfolk seemed to be coming pretty effectively out of their traditional retirement.) I was greeted eloquently in English by a young Peiping intellectual who wore the uniform of the peasant guards.

That night our whole party slept on a single *k'ang*, in a smoky farmhouse that had been loud with the sounds of a Chinese orchestra when we arrived. It was a "lucky day," and there had been a wedding in the village—in the main street we had passed the groom in his decorated chair, borne in front of the closed red litter where his bride was concealed. But now at last quiet had been restored, and only the occasional challenge of the peasant patrols outside broke the silence, before the village slept.

ACROSS THE JAPANESE LINES

That morning, the troop commander woke us with disturbing news. A force of two thousand Japanese were moving west from Yuanping, and the brigade headquarters we were making for had been shifted that night—no one knew precisely where. Traveling now was likely to be dangerous.

"What do we do?" The *pai chang* shrugged his broad shoulders. "Go on till we meet some of our own men, and find where the brigade commander is." The fact that we might meet the Japanese first did not seem to trouble him.

The Eighth Route Army never has a fixed front, and in view of the new Japanese activity in the north (which we had heard of three days before) there was likely to be quite a lot of movement in this district. It lent a touch of zest to our expedition, which so far had met with no greater hazards than a frozen river crossing. We set out rather earlier than usual, with a guide from the local volunteers to show us the way to the next village. A troop of a dozen horsemen makes a fair enough mark, and we moved carefully, keeping in the shelter of the loess foothills. The peasant guide knew every short cut and hill path; we should have been helpless enough without him, in this maze of ravines and watercourses.

Before long we began to meet refugees coming from the east—pathetic little family groups, a woman and a couple of children on a donkey, with perhaps one man following with a sack of grain. Most of them knew little more than that the "dwarfs" were coming. And that news had been enough for them.

The first large village we reached seemed peaceful enough, with a group of peasants sitting in the sun smoking their long Shansi pipes. "Where is the Eighth Route Army?" we demanded. One spokesman grunted, and waved his pipestem vaguely in the direction of the north. But although one of them offered to guide us there, he did not seem very sure of the position. Perhaps, he suggested, there were "two or three soldiers" in a near-by village. We had gone barely half a mile, before we met a group of refugees who assured us positively that the Japanese were in the village we were making for.

In China, one gets used to contradictory reports. Our guide stood waiting patiently until we should make up our minds to go on; this new announcement left him unmoved. "What do you think?" Wu asked me. "Shall we risk it?"

Anything, I felt, was better than turning back; it was difficult going among these hills, and I was determined not to retrace what painful progress we had made already. "*Ta mati!*" said the *pai chang* abusively, "we'll try it!" With our hill ponies, we should always be able to make a prompt getaway in the event of any untoward encounter.

Carbines were wiped and loaded, Mausers filled and cocked;

Across the Japanese Lines 251

it was all, I thought, absurdly like a scene from a film. Then, with our guide and a couple of scouts in front, we moved on eastward.

It was a clear winter morning, and the peaks of Wutai Shan were a soft blue line across the horizon. Cautiously working our way over the crest of a hill, we came out directly above the railway. In front stretched the broad plain; we could see Yuanping, a dark cluster of trees and houses; and a dozen other villages, compact within their clay walls. But some of these were charred and blackened, and the blue haze of smoke that hung above them was more than could ever come from a score or so of modest hearths.

The Japanese, in fact, were burning the villages for several *li* on either side of the main road; and it was from these that the stream of fugitives we had passed were coming. From where we were, the white outbuildings of a railway station were within easy range; here, almost certainly, there would be Japanese troops. But though the *pai chang* swore under his breath, we could not stay too long to investigate.

Our phlegmatic peasant guide brought us over the hills to the famous village. Here there were no signs of military occupation of any sort; only a few children sliding on the ice and the inevitable pigs and chickens in undisputed possession of the little street. But as we turned the stone archway we were challenged sharply, and a soldier in a blue greatcoat with fixed rifle appeared suddenly from a doorway. We had found the Eighth Route Army.

The guide had been right. Here there was only an outpost of the brigade, but at least they could direct us to headquarters. And as we struck up into the hills again, another soldier from a high rock (where he had been keeping a watch on the valley) waved us towards the path.

Now it was straightforward enough, for our scouts could read the way from telltale signs hidden among the rocks and grasses. (This army, I had discovered, had its own direction signals, as subtle as any gypsy bent twig or fern.) The going was more difficult than ever, but at any rate we were no longer traveling blind.

I had been riding in a daydream, when suddenly the troop commander beckoned from ahead. "Hurry!" We kicked our ponies into a gallop, and crossed the mouth of a valley, to come out fair upon the railway track. Southward, these rails ran direct to Taiyuan; Japanese outposts were less than a mile away. We were right against the enemy lines.

For a while, we rode north along the railway, which for a considerable stretch had been demolished by the Eighth Route Army and the volunteers. The sleepers had been torn out and burned, and the rails were twisted and in some cases thrown aside. It was not a very thorough job, perhaps, but it served its purpose. The westward loop of the Tung-Pu railway, between Yuanping and Hsohsien, was at this time entirely in the hands of the Chinese.

Riding along the track, my pony gave me a good deal more trouble than the Japanese. He was always skittish, and had certainly never seen a railway before: he shied at every twisted rail and signal post. But at last we came clear of the embankment, on to a stony hill path that was very much more difficult going, but which he accepted as part of a familiar world. We all breathed a little more easily, for now we were back in friendly territory.

Brigade headquarters we found at last in a tiny village, at the foot of towering cliffs: it was like a scene among the Dolomites. The rock face had natural tints of pink and blue, and now—in the soft glow of evening—the hills were fantastically beautiful. This mountain fastness, resolutely defended, looked secure from any attack.

Outside one farmhouse a sentry stood on guard, with the brigade standard beside him. We entered the little courtyard, where a wizened peasant was feeding a mixed flock of sheep and goats. All livestock had to be brought indoors in this January weather; it was a hard time for the lambs, some of them even younger than the new year. But I had hardly expected to find our brigadier in such a rustic setting.

Then, in a moment, we found ourselves in the center of a welcoming throng. "Comrade Wang Chen"—the brigade commander—was a slim, hawk-faced southerner, with shrewd eyes and a lithe grace of movement. "Liu Tze-ch'i, chief of staff." Wu was enthusiastically greeting a couple of old student friends from Peiping, who had found work in this army unit. One was a girl with short hair, in the blue cotton uniform of the Eighth Route Army.

"You chose a fine time to come," the brigade commander informed us cheerfully. "We sent out a party to meet you, but you must have gone different ways. Didn't you know there was fighting on the road today and yesterday?"

Briefly he told us what had happened. The day we passed Hsinkow, the Japanese had begun an attack; as usual, the Chinese had withdrawn at first, trying to tempt the enemy up into the hills. But the Japanese, after burning a few villages, had moved back again to the main road. Then—that same morning, about the time we had crossed the hills above Yuanping—a force of several hundred Japanese had set out on another sally. They had been surprised and completely defeated by a newly-raised Chinese platoon.

"This time," Brigadier Wang told us, "we went to meet them. Our troops were raw, with only three months' training; but they wore peasant clothes, and carried pistols and hand grenades under their coats. The leader was one of our company commanders—he pretended to be a merchant. They got within a hundred yards of the Japanese without being suspected, and then suddenly opened fire.

"The Japanese were taken completely by surprise, and the whole action lasted less than an hour. We must have killed and wounded about a hundred of the enemy—they took off the bodies in three trucks. We had one platoon commander killed, and six men wounded."

It was a rousing welcome to the 359th Brigade.

CHAPTER NINE
PARTISAN

BRIGADE HEADQUARTERS

I stayed for a week with the brigade, and every day there was fighting along the front—small skirmishes, for the most part, but very wearing for the Japanese, and excellent training for the new Shansi recruits. The stretch of road between Kuohsien and Yuanping was the usual theater of war. The Japanese had several thousand troops in each of these towns, and at Tienkiachwang, a small village midway between the two, they were at this time busy constructing another fortress protected by heavy artillery. Every night, raids were staged by the Chinese volunteers; and generally the Japanese were on the defensive. It was hardly the pleasant picture of "mopping up the Chinese remnants" that had been painted by the Tokyo radio announcer.

The 359th Brigade, as its commander lost no time in informing me, had a history. Originally it had been formed, in the year of the "Great Revolution," from peasants of Hunan, Hupeh, and Kiangsi, with a stiffening of workers from Changsha and Wuhan, and a political cadre of revolutionaries who had escaped the "White Terror" in Hankow. It had begun as an irregular mobile unit, operating along the borders of these three southern provinces, and its first experience had been in just the kind of partisan fighting in which it was now engaged.

"We were directly under the command of Chu-Mao," Brigadier Wang told me, "but at that time we had very poor arms, and no fixed army base. Whenever we captured rifles from the White troops, we sent them on to the main Red Army. It was not until 1930, when Chu and Mao went to Changsha, that we became part of the regular Red forces. Then this unit became an independent division, with a fixed base in the mountains and more complete equipment.

"After the Changsha fighting, we stayed between the Fourth Front Army and Ho Lung, co-operating with these larger forces. We fought in all five of the major campaigns waged by Chiang Kai-shek against the Red Armies, and gained very much valuable experience. We corrected any loose and romantic ideas we might have had at first; and because ours was a real working-class division, under the direction of the Central Committee, we were able to assist in the defeat of the four first campaigns against the Chinese Soviets."

When the Chinese Communists issued their "Anti-Japanese Manifesto" of 1934, and the Red armies prepared to march north, Wang Chen's division became part of the 6th Military Group, under the command of Hsiao K'eh. This group had been the vanguard of the Long March.

"The first thing the main armies had to do," Wang told me, "was to break the blockade around the main Soviet District in Kiangsi. The Nanking troops had built their 'iron ring' around the soviets, and every kind of road—even the smallest track— was held by the Whites. So the Red armies marched where there was no road at all!

"We had been ordered to begin the advance, and had reached Kwangsi when we got an order from headquarters to return and connect with Ho Lung's army. We marched 7,000 *li* (more than 2,000 miles) in a hundred days—sometimes we covered over 150 *li* a day; on other days, when there was fighting, we advanced less than 10 *li*. But we met Ho Lung on time, on the borders of Szechwan.

"On the Long March itself, we were under Jen Pi-shih and Hsiao K'eh. We started in August 1935, and covered more than 20,000 *li* before we met the main armies in Kansu over a year later. We crossed *Ta Hsueh Shan* ('Big Snow Mountain') *

---

* This mountain—difficult to locate because of the general term of reference— has been identified by some travelers as "*Ta Hsueh Pao*," on the western border of Szechwan and the eastern fringe of Tibet. It is shown marked on recent maps as "Mt. Stubbs."

in Sikang, where we spent more than four months—and that was cold; I tell you, Shansi is nothing to it! Since we arrived in the Northwest, we have been taking part in the United Front movement, and directly in the war of resistance against Japan."

Retelling the story, Wang grew as excited as a boy; and at one stage he left the room abruptly, to return with a paper-backed volume in one hand. It was a copy of Barbusse's *Stalin*, which served as an improvised photograph album. He turned the leaves to show me stained and smudged photographs of various army commanders, and odd Red Army groups, in all kinds of costume, in half a dozen Chinese provinces.

"This was on the Long March...." "You were all a lot thinner then! What's this?" "Crossing the Yellow River. That's Ho Lung in the grass hat." It was a fascinating record; among these faded snapshots I recognized, sometimes with considerable difficulty, commanders and political organizers whom I had met (looking very much sprucer now!) in these last months in Shansi. With such varied experience as this, it was not surprising that the Eighth Route Army had found less difficulty than some other Chinese forces in adapting itself to the new conditions of fighting against the Japanese. There was probably no other army in the world, at that time, that could claim a record of ten years' continuous fighting—certainly there was none in the Far East.

"After the settlement of the Sian affair," Wang went on, "we had a period of six months' rest and training, with special study of the theory of the United Front, and co-operation with the other Chinese armies. It is a good indication of the political solidarity of our troops, that even after this ten-year war, not a single soldier wanted to leave the army and return home!"

In the communist style with which I was now familiar, he summed up the history of his brigade for me. "Because this brigade has a strong revolutionary theory, because commanders and soldiers alike have a high degree of political consciousness, we can develop a revolutionary spirit and solidarity in the most difficult circumstances, and overcome all obstacles we meet. Because we have always been a people's army, and have fought for the benefit and liberation of the Chinese masses, we have always had the people's support, and wherever we went could always get food, and new recruits when we wanted them.

"Since this brigade was first formed as a mobile unit in Hunan, we have continued with our political training. When we became a unit in the regular army, we always had a political department and never neglected this side of our activity. With this combination of military experience and political training, we have become a real revolutionary army, dedicating ourselves to the great struggle for our national liberation."

Wang Chen himself, I felt, was a good representative of his own theory. This thirty-five-year-old commander had begun working on the railway at the age of twelve, shoveling coal on the Hankow-Changsha line. At fifteen, he had become a member of the railway workers' union; and in 1925 had received his first military training at Changsha. After the break with the Kuomintang, he had returned to the railway to do political work, and had been the original political instructor and organizer of his present brigade. From that time on, he told me, he had never left the brigade except when he was wounded.

It was not an unusual history in the Eighth Route Army. But it meant that, whatever hazards this present war might have in store for the 359th Brigade, there would be nothing irresolute or half-hearted about its leadership.

Wang himself wore the faded blue cotton uniform of his whole command; but he had—rather incongruously, it seemed to me—a magnificent fur-lined overcoat of civilian cut, in which I had noticed the label of a Peiping tailor. Once I passed a comment on this splendid garment, and he told me its story. It had belonged—like most of the rare traces of luxury to be seen among these troops—to one of those curious phenomena of Chinese society curtly described as a "traitor." These were the new domestic enemies that had taken the place of the landlords formerly opposed by the Chinese Red Armies.

Mr. Ti Huai-ching had formerly been the "first gentleman" of Kuohsien. Once an official in the Peiping government, he was a returned student from Japan, and had always belonged to the pro-Japanese party in North China. A native of Shansi, he had returned to his own district on retiring from office, and had found a new occupation in telling everybody how weak the Chinese really were, and how strong they might become with the friendship and co-operation of Japan.

When hostilities broke out in 1937, he had continued along this line with new ardor; and because he was a man of some standing, had had considerable influence on the local population. The Eighth Route Army organizers, when they reached Kuohsien, challenged him publicly, and proposed a new slogan which later became a popular proverb—"Our people *are* poor, yet they have strength enough to resist the invaders!" But Mr. Ti had retained his own views; and after the Japanese advance into Shansi, began to prepare the people of Kuohsien to welcome them. At this point, Wang broke off the story.

"What happened to him?" I asked, feeling that it was a delicate question.

The brigade commander raised his eyebrows for a moment. "He was a traitor. He was shot." He looked at me directly. "Afterward, we found that he had just paid $200,000 into his bank account...."

GUERILLA WARFARE

I was familiar enough with the general strategy and tactics of the Eighth Route Army, but here at the front it was possible to get some first-hand information about their actual experience in the present war, and the method of fighting that they had developed. The experience of this brigade was typical.

Their mobility could be judged from the ground they had already covered. Arriving in Shansi early in September, they had been ordered first into Hopei, to carry on partisan warfare along the Ping-Han railway. But when they reached Hopei, the Japanese had already occupied Paotingfu, and were beginning their advance into Shansi through the main pass at Yenmenkwan.

Leaving a number of scattered units on the Hopei border, the brigade marched west again, covering more than 100 *li* each day. One regiment went north to Yenmenkwan, which at this time was twice reoccupied by the Eighth Route Army; the other began operations on the flank of the main Japanese army north of Hsinkow, where the Chinese were at this time making their major stand in North Shansi. Since then, they had been moving continuously, with the double object of keeping up an incessant attack on the enemy lines of communication, and of organizing volunteers and new army units from the local people wherever they went.

"At Yenmenkwan," the brigade commander told me frankly, "we were not entirely successful, because we could not break the enemy communications completely. As you know, Pinhsingkwan and the railway were at this time blockaded by our troops, and the road through Yenmenkwan was the only Japanese route to the north. If we could have cut this, the invading force would have been completely isolated. But we arrived at Yenmenkwan a little too late."

(It is only fair here, perhaps, to point out that the Shansi provincial armies, which had been entrusted with the task of defending these northern passes, had not proved very resolute. The classic example is that of General Li Fu-ying, who had been ordered by Yen Hsi-shan to hold Tienchen, the strategic approach to Tatung. General Li had only waited to hear the sound of the Japanese guns before he beat a hasty retreat; afterward he was shot by Yen for neglect of orders.)

"The Japanese were able to fortify the main peaks," Wang went on, "and to hold them with a heavy garrison and artillery. So, although we destroyed many bridges and attacked every Japanese column and convoy that came along the main road, we could not entirely prevent them getting through.

"Meantime, the Chinese resistance at Hsinkow had proved very effective indeed; and General Chiang Kai-shek gave the order that there was to be no retreat. This was the time when General Hao Mon-lin was killed at Hsinkow; the morale of the Chinese troops was very good, and we were all much encouraged by their new spirit. Our units along the main road north of Hsinkow redoubled their efforts, attacking every day; and for a while we had perfect co-operation between the regular armies in fixed positions, and our own troops in partisan action. This successful fighting at Hsinkow is a good example of what the Chinese armies can do with a united command and real co-operation."

In such talks as these with Wang Chen and Liu Tze-ch'i, I managed to form a clear picture of the methods of fighting of their troops. What was especially interesting was the way in which they had developed effective tactics against the very much superior Japanese technique.

It must be remembered that while some units of the former Chinese Red Armies had had experience against comparatively modern armaments in the campaigns of the civil war, many of these peasant soldiers had never seen a tank—some had never seen a motor truck until they arrived in Shansi. The first part of their training, in the present hostilities, had been to familiarize themselves with the methods of the Japanese advance. This was orthodox modern war practice—to begin, if there was any concentration of troops ahead, with aerial and artillery bombardment; and to follow this up with an advance of troops preceded by tanks and armored cars, with cavalry on the wings.

The Eighth Route Army had devised many stratagems against this superior equipment. For a start, they never massed their own lightly armed troops, but kept them in small roving bands, attacking always on the flank and in the rear, preferably when the enemy was in motion. They had no artillery or guns that could be effective against tanks, so they began by burying shells in the roadway (often these were shells captured from the Japanese). With detonators attached, these shells were exploded by any heavy weight; and by this means, a number of tanks were destroyed. But the Japanese reply had been to compel Chinese farmers and peasants to go before their columns in heavy oxcarts to test the road—a barbarous procedure which resulted in the death of many innocent victims.

At that, the Chinese guerillas changed their tactics, and instead of using shells, buried a number of large bombs which could be exploded by a lanyard from a concealed position beside the road. (They had, of course, no modern explosives or "sapping" equipment.) This was more accurate, and effective in hill country, where the main road was the only possible approach for mechanized units.

With the withdrawal of the regular Chinese forces from Hsinkow and the Japanese occupation of Taiyuan, the picture was somewhat changed in North Shansi. The Japanese made no serious further advance, but contented themselves with consolidating their positions. More recently, they had been sending troops north from Taiyuan to try and meet the Eighth Route Army and the partisans at their own game, seldom using more than one or two thousand men in a unit. These were the "bandit-suppression" tactics of the Kwantung army in Manchuria; but so far (as I had seen for myself) they had met with singularly little success. In fact, most of the offensive action of the Japanese in Shansi had been effectively paralyzed.

"Here is one example," the brigade chief-of-staff told me. "We built what looked like heavy fortifications halfway up a mountain. The Japanese scouting planes noticed this, and for several days bombed the mountain very heavily. We left a few troops nearby, with orders to scatter as if in flight; no doubt the Japanese airmen reported that the 'Chinese defenses' had been destroyed, and our troops routed! So the enemy sent a large cavalry force to come and clean up the remnants.

"Meantime, our main forces had been waiting in ambush at the foot of the hills—very much nearer the Japanese than the latter suspected. We surprised their cavalry when they advanced, attacking from short range with machine guns and hand grenades; and inflicted very heavy losses on them before they retreated."

The invaders had only one reply to such tactics—this was to burn all the neighboring villages within reach. It was a measure of their own impotence, and did nothing to convince the local population of Japan's "peaceful intentions" towards the Chinese people.

The favorite weapon of the Chinese partisans, I found, was not the rifle, but hand grenades. Every soldier in the Eighth Route Army carried several of these, usually of the "potato-masher" variety—primitive enough, but deadly at close quarters. One advantage of these grenades was that their use could be very quickly taught to the peasant volunteers.

Often, I was told, a small group would set out on a raid with nothing but hand grenades. Half a dozen men could carry forty or so of them, which was quite enough for their purpose.

The Japanese troops, if they had them, usually threw their bombs too early—sometimes forgetting to take out the pin, so that the bombs fell harmlessly; or, if they were using contact bombs, often letting them fall in soft ground where they failed to explode. All such enemy trophies, of course, were eagerly collected by the partisans.

Everywhere in the Eighth Route Army, I heard the same story—that the Japanese infantry were weak at close-quarter fighting. Their rifle fire was reasonably accurate at long range, but they could offer little resistance if attacked suddenly and by surprise. And their artillery was not much use against an enemy that never massed, and was seldom to be found where the Japanese supposed them to be.

"The chief hope of the invaders now," Wang told me, "is to occupy the larger towns and the fertile valley lands, and drive us back into the hills, where they suppose we will be short of food, and unable to get many new recruits. But in fact, they hold only the main cities; and every night the volunteers come out on the plain and approach the main road. Often a single man, in peasant clothes, will take a couple of bombs, and hide near the road. Then, when a Japanese truck passes, he can throw a bomb high, so that it falls inside the truck (which is probably moving fast). He has plenty of time to get away."

Such tactics as these, of course, needed resolute and skillful fighters; and a high degree of initiative on the part of the soldiers and partisan leaders, as well as the general command. But these necessary qualities were not lacking, and the Shansi peasants were proving that they could do their part. The brigade commander summed up the position for me succinctly:

"We have shown clearly, already, that partisan warfare is effective even against a modern army. It is especially effective, of course, in co-operation with our own main forces; but it can be carried on independently.

"By our methods of fighting in this army, we have shown the people of North China that they *can* resist the Japanese successfully, and without heavy losses—for we always use a very few men against a much larger enemy force. We have shown that arms are not everything, and need not be the decisive instrument of warfare in such country as this.

"Moreover, we have proved to the peasants that they can get a supply of weapons and ammunition from the enemy, if they are resourceful; so that if need be, they can operate on their own initiative entirely, and the lack of arms need not restrict the scope of their action.

"More important still"—and here he nodded cheerfully across at the brigade political organizer—"in the course of five months' fighting, we have been able to organize many thousands of the Chinese people, to encourage them in their efforts, and enlarge the war of national resistance. And this, after all, must be the final factor in the struggle against Japanese imperialism."

PORTRAIT OF A HERO

Life in this little village under the shadow of the mountains did not lack variety. The bugles woke us in the early morning, vibrant in the frozen air. They were the signal for the soldiers to turn out for exercise; and before long the street outside would echo with the thud of soft Chinese shoes, and the heavy breathing of new recruits.

Always, it seemed, there was someone singing. It might be the hoarse staccato of marching troops, or a single voice raised in some peasant air of Hunan or Kiangsi. In the evenings, one heard often the plaintive tremolo of a Chinese flute.

We took our meals with the brigade staff—special food, I knew, prepared for my benefit, with rice that had been captured from the Japanese supplies. There were always solicitous inquiries about my digestion, but I found that I flourished on two good Chinese meals a day.

In the morning we would talk with soldiers, or pay a visit to the children's Theater Group. These *hsiao kwei*, as ever, fascinated me; the youngest of them was eleven, and he had come from Kweichow with the army. They rehearsed their dances solemnly under the direction of a seventeen-year-old girl student, who had left a middle school in Peiping to join the Eighth Route Army.

Then we might drop in at the Propaganda Department, where

a young returned student from Japan was generally busy sorting out propaganda leaflets printed in Japanese, that would be taken by peasants (perhaps with a present of fruit) inside the towns occupied by the enemy. At night, we listened to the radio broadcasts on an excellent American wireless set. Like the rice, it was an involuntary contribution from the Japanese army.

Among all these active, friendly people, there was one who moved always, I fancied, with a certain detachment. This was Liu Tze-ch'i, the brigade chief of staff. He was not aloof, for his natural manner was friendly and direct, and the *hsiao kwei* obviously worshiped him. One of them had told me earnestly that he was "very brave."

This young officer (he was just thirty) with the build and scarred features of a Roman gladiator, made a curiously distinct and powerful impression. There was something hypnotic about his gaze, which even indoors seemed turned into the far distance. He had the natural dignity of the Chinese peasant, but with it an unusual seriousness.

Liu had come into my room one day, without removing the Mongol cavalry cap that he wore like a helmet. Only Wu was there with me, and on a sudden impulse I asked him to tell me how he had joined the army. Liu nodded, without any of the conventional demurs of Chinese politeness, and told the story very simply and directly.

He had been born in a very poor peasant family in eastern Hunan, and at the age of nine had spent seven months at school —all the formal education he ever got. At twelve, he was apprenticed to a shoemaker in his native village, and after three years at this trade made shoes himself. In 1926, he had joined in the revolutionary movement, and became an inspector in a labor union. After the break of the Communist Party and the Kuomintang, he had escaped the terror and made his way to Canton. Here, he said, he had his training—"among workers."

He was one of the organizers of that fatal and bloody insurrection, the Canton Commune; and the experience of those three days made him a revolutionary for life. When the commune was defeated, he went to Hunan again, dodging the reactionary landlords who knew and hated him. Here he joined the mobile unit that later became the 359th Brigade.

After a brief military training, he was sent back to his own district to do secret political work, and raise another mobile unit. He had no arms; and with great difficulty, secured a couple of Chinese bigswords from the house of a local official. Starting with these, he armed the poor peasants, and formed a unit that continued active for more than two years. Their best weapons, he said, were homemade guns and improvised bombs.

Liu smiled grimly remembering those years. "For a month at a time," he said, "I did not take off my cartridge belt; we never had the chance to change our clothes. Once we spent three months in the mountains in midwinter, sleeping in the open—we would wake to find our bedding covered with snow. Five separate times, the Kuomintang issued orders for my arrest, with a high reward—anyone who knew me might have turned informer. But I was never betrayed."

Later, he had a more important command, with ninety rifles under him in the "Red Defense Corps." Then successively he became company commander, regimental commander, and finally chief-of-staff of a division in the main Red Armies under P'eng Teh-huai. On the Long March, he commanded a regiment in Chu Teh's army corps. "Once," he told me in a casual aside, "we lived for fifteen days on grass."

When at last the Red Armies reached the northwest, Liu took a course at the Military Academy—it should have been a year's advanced training, but the demand for experienced officers at the front cut it short at eight months. With the usual "school" in the Red Army, he had learned to read and write comparatively young; but his course at *"Hungta"* was the longest period of formal instruction he had ever had.

About his experiences in the present war, he was reluctant to speak. But I gathered a few details from other informants. Near Yenmenkwan, he had personally led a party to blow up an important mountain bridge; for three days, he and his men had sheltered in the hills, without food, until they succeeded in achieving their object. There were other stories, too, but the picture is already complete.

He had been wounded seven times—in the head, both legs, and in the back. One bullet had entered one cheekbone and gone out the other, so that now he breathed with difficulty through one nostril. Another time, wounded in the thigh and crippled, he had walked six miles before getting any attention. "I used to be very strong," he said earnestly (and, looking at his superb physique, I could well believe it), "but I can't run fast uphill now." It seemed to be his only real regret.

In any other army in the world, such a record would have earned a galaxy of stripes and ribbons. But the only "decoration" Liu wore (not without pride) was the five-pointed star of ten years' service in the Red Armies. "I was praised by the army command," he said, "for my endurance, and for my ability to lead small bodies of men." It was the nearest I had ever heard him come to boasting.

I choose the story of Liu Tze-ch'i, not to single out one man at the expense of the rest; and certainly not with the idea of glorifying war in any of its phases. But there is a necessary distinction to be made, I think, between the general beastliness of war, and the human qualities that war can breed. Courage informed by the intelligence must still be considered a virtue: it is rare, and in these days it is mostly revolutionary. Liu Tze-ch'i seemed to me a good example of it; and he was one, among many, who happened to look the part. Like the hero of a Malraux novel, he might have been a communist *"par dignité."*

If I thought Liu Tze-ch'i would ever be able to read these pages, I should owe him an apology. But Liu was no linguist. He too, like Wang Chen, had his own little private album—a discreet, black-bound volume which he once handed over for my inspection. "Can you read this?" he asked, turning up some unpasted pages.

I found the title, and blinked; it was *De Urbanitate*, a treatise "for the use of the clergy" compiled by a disciple of one Jean de la Fosse. "I think so," I replied, and began to mouth the high-sounding Latin phrases:

Above, peasants of Shansi.
Below, soldiers of the Eighth Route Army with antitank gun captured from the Japanese.

"*Corpus servare mundum non contentus, sive emungas, sive tussias, sive spuas, sive sternuas, ita haec age ut nulli adstantium sis incommodo. Ideo tussiendo vel sternuendo, linteolum seu sudarium aut manum contra os applicabis, non salivam, invitus quidem sed illepidus, in faciem conversantium expellas....*"

It was a curious find in this army, some of whose habits would have scandalized the reverend author. "What's it about?" Liu demanded.

"It teaches you," I said diplomatically, "how to improve your table manners."

"French?"

"Old French," I said; it was the best description I could give.

"Ah," grunted Liu, and spat expertly out of the doorway. "Well, so long." He gathered up *De Urbanitate* and departed into the night, his square shoulders silhouetted against the mist. In the distance, I could hear him singing:

Chi lai, pu yuan tso nu li ti jen men! ...

Arise, all you who would not be slaves!
With our own flesh and blood we will build our new
Great Wall....

The plangent bugle blew "Lights Out."

THEY CALL IT PEACE

"'That's Kuohsien over there," said the brigade commander, "with the big wall." He handed me the glasses—once they had belonged to a Japanese officer—for a closer inspection.

Beneath us, the plain stretched wide and luminous in the winter haze. The regular division of fields marked it like a chess board; here and there were the clustered square compounds of villages. Fringed by a dark line of willows, the main road ran to the south, beyond the winding streak of white that was the Hutou river.

"If you had a very good rifle," I said ("telescopic sights" was too much for my elementary Chinese), "you could do some good sniping from here." I illustrated what I meant by pantomime: through the field glasses, one could clearly distinguish figures going in and out of the city gates, and the khaki uniforms of sentinels.

The brigadier nodded. "The Japanese rifles are better than ours," he said. "Now we are picking out our own best shots, and arming them with captured guns." From the cover of these hills, concealed rifle men could be very dangerous to enemy troops moving across the open plain.

Peaceful as the scene appeared, some of these village walls—if one turned the glasses on them—contained nothing but blackened ruins of houses. They had not been destroyed in the fighting, but burned out by the Japanese troops in revenge for the night raids of the partisans. "That's where we are going," Wang said, pointing out one large village. "Our troops are there, and we have volunteer units scattered all over the plain." He completed his careful examination of the roads. "Ready? We can go."

The horses were waiting at the foot of the hill; I had a big black Japanese cavalry mount which could probably (it was some reassurance) outrun anything we were likely to meet on the plain. For we were moving by daylight in what the enemy, at least, considered their territory.

Before long we had reached the army outpost, where we had a rousing reception. The clay walls were daubed on every side with Chinese slogans, and there were even some colored paper streamers which said, "Welcome to the foreign friends of China!" and "Long live the International Peace Front!" We rode on into the plain, past fields that were bare of crops (for there had been little sowing last autumn in this war-torn region). Flocks of sheep and goats were grazing peacefully on what they could find of nourishment, watched for the most part by small boys. Children and old men, I had noticed, were almost all that seemed to be left of the local population.

But peasants with the volunteer armband, ancient rifles slung across their shoulders, guarded the approaches to the village we were making for. And here, behind walls freshly pierced with

They Call It Peace 269

loop-holes, I read the unmistakable signature of Japan's "civilizing mission" in North China.

A few houses had been spared—not by goodwill, for even these had charred doorposts where the fire had failed to catch. But for the rest, this once prosperous village was a desert of crumbling walls and blackened rafters. Only a pile of stones and ashes remained of each pathetic little household. The school had been burned. The temple had been burned. There had been no discrimination in the hand of this incendiary.

There was no need to ask those villagers who remained what they thought of the Japanese. They clustered around us in the street, smudge-faced children and old men clutching empty tobacco pouches. One gray-haired peasant opened his rags to show us the scars made by Mongol bayonets. He had been lucky, for he had escaped with his life, though it was not easy to see what life held for him now.

He told us, in halting sentences, of old men of seventy who had been tortured, their fingers severed by the sword of the samurai. A favorite method of the Japanese was disembowelment; only when this traditional rite had been performed on the wretched victim, was he put out of his misery by a kindly bullet. In most cases, it seemed, these horrors had followed an unsuccessful demand for money or for young girls—a demand which, in all probability, these Shansi villagers had barely understood (for though the Mongolian troops spoke Chinese, it was with a villainous accent that was unintelligible even in this neighboring province).

Every war brings its crop of "atrocities," and a disillusioned western world tends nowadays to discount most of these as propaganda made by either side. But I cannot believe that these subtleties were appreciated by simple Shansi peasants, standing in the ruins of their own homes. These tales bore the tragic accent of sincerity.

Any men—whatever the color of their skin—who have been caught up in the maelstrom of modern war, are capable of horrors. But there is a peculiarly cold-blooded kind of cruelty that is characteristic of the thing called fascism; and the Japanese, even among oriental nations, have a notable contempt for human life. A combination of these factors, perhaps, had wrought this havoc.

For the Japanese military command, which has deliberately chosen the tactic of terrorism, which has ordered the bombing of open towns in China and earned itself a reputation internationally which will be very difficult to live down, has clearly fascist traits. Too little is known still of the methods the Japanese militarists practiced for years in Manchuria, the policy of "devastation" which they had found from experience to be the only effective counter to partisan warfare waged against them. When I was in Japan shortly before the outbreak of the present hostilities, I found some of the things I recounted about Manchuria—which I had heard on unimpeachable authority—greeted with polite disbelief by my friendly Japanese hosts. "Our army," they said smilingly, "could not do these things." *

But it can. And now the same method of wholesale reprisals that had already graced the "rising young Empire" of "Manchukuo" is being widely put into effect in many parts of China.

This policy is, briefly, to clear the countryside of "hostile elements" by burning them out. The "bandits" are seldom directly affected, for they have usually taken to the hills long before the Japanese punitive expedition arrives. But whole villages are razed, so that they cannot serve as a future base for partisan activity. And the victims are almost always the most innocent and helpless members of the community.

Here in these villages near Kuohsien, we heard of many old people who had taken to the hills to avoid the marauders, and had perished of cold or starvation. The able-bodied peasants had since joined the mobile units almost to a man. Never until now had I heard such bitter resentment expressed against the invaders, with the unrehearsed eloquence of pure passion. Those who have lost everything are the ones who have the most to win. "If we can keep the land," one peasant said, "our houses don't matter." And that they were going to fight for their fields was only too evident.

In this district, because of the activity of the volunteers, the villages had been demolished for many miles along the highway.

* See, for example, T. A. Bisson's scholarly volume, *Japan in China*, Chapter XII.

Surveying the wreckage, I thought grimly of the smooth voice of the Tokyo radio announcer who described the "peace and order" returning to North Shansi. They make a desert, and call it peace.

We rode back to the army station, where a meal had been prepared in our honor in an open courtyard. Here on the plain it was almost warm in the sunshine, even in mid-January. The peasants had brought food in gargantuan portions—not even the Japanese could kill all the pigs and chickens in Shansi. But near Hsinkow, where the invading armies had stayed for a month, I was told that all the cattle and sheep had been slaughtered. The people were especially bitter about this, for these are the livestock in China that are most difficult to replace.

What will be the results of the Japanese policy in North China? Already, perhaps, they have restored a semblance of order along the railways, and in the main cities have found a number of those whose property was too valuable to be abandoned, and who will serve for a while as their puppets and lackeys. But the nature of Japanese economy is such that these new imperialists are driven to the most ruthless and heavy-handed methods of exploitation. They must have quick returns, or they perish: this is the gigantic gamble which the rulers of modern Japan are playing with their own nation. And methods such as these will spare no class or section of the people in the occupied areas. Before long—as in Manchuria—even the merchants and landlords who now give their support to the conquerors will realize what they are up against.

And the common people—the *lao pai hsing* of China, whose livelihood was poor enough even before they were stripped of their few belongings and the torch set to their roof-trees—how are they likely to respond to this new situation? The political backwardness of the North China peasants was once a byword, but war—under these conditions, at least—is a great educator. It is the common people of China who so far have borne the brunt of the present hostilities; already they have been forced by their new rulers to undertake the repair of roads and railways, to provide some of the manpower that helps to drive the Japanese military machine.

The Chinese peasant may be illiterate, but he is not slow to appreciate any new factors that affect his own life so profoundly. In Manchuria, three provinces were taken by surprise in the first sudden onslaught, and only by painful experience have the common people learned what their fate was henceforward to become. Yet in spite of their unpreparedness, the Manchurian volunteers have carried on the struggle for five years against overwhelming odds.

In North China, there is this striking difference from 1931 —that now, in many districts, the peasants are organized and armed, have already established their partisan bases. And there are two hundred million of them. From what I had seen in North Shansi, it seemed to me that even the Japanese apologists would have some difficulty in maintaining for long this fiction of "peace."

CHINA'S NEW GREAT WALL

The brigade commander was leaving headquarters to inspect some new recruits under training, and Wu and I left with him on the first stage of our return journey. We were going back by a shorter and more direct route through the hills, and this recruiting base was on our way.

Snow had been threatening for two or three days, and it was under a slate-gray sky that we arrived at length at a little mountain town, sheltering in a river valley under the main range. It looked desolate enough from a distance, but the Drama Group came to welcome us as we walked our tired horses across the river bed, and we made something like a triumphal entry, preceded by a juvenile bugle band with flying banners. Several girls in uniform marched among the group.

In the open square that served as a parade ground, more than a thousand new recruits were drawn up in ranks—they made a smart enough showing, in regulation army greatcoats, though as yet they had no rifles. Their commander called them to attention, and the brigadier mounted a rickety wooden table to deliver a long address.

This, I thought again—watching the rows of brown, weather-beaten faces, following every word with frowning concentration

—was the immense reserve of China in the present war. In normal times, these Shansi peasants and petty artisans would have led quiet and uneventful lives among their native hills. But those times were out of joint; and the vast rumor of war, rumbling southwards with the invading Japanese armies, had sounded a new call to action.

What was the life they would lead in the months ahead? It would be strenuous enough, in all likelihood, but physical hardship was nothing new to these Chinese peasants. There would be danger, but danger now was unavoidable, and not least if they should choose to return to their villages to taste the first fruits of Japanese "civilization." All this, they knew well enough.

But there would be certain compensations. For in this army, they would learn many things besides the technique of partisan fighting. Every Eighth Route Army unit—even those at the front—had two hours a day of "class work." This included one hour of political study, and one hour of "cultural" education. Those who could not read and write would be taught, first in "Latinhua," the new romanized script that the Chinese Communists had early adopted for elementary education; later in the old Chinese characters. They would make their first acquaintance, perhaps, with other countries of the world; and their mental horizon, once bounded by the Shansi hills, would be extended to take in the whole international scene.

They would learn to see their own struggle, not as one desperate local effort, but as part of a world struggle. They would learn the historical significance of the Chinese revolution in the whole world progress. Their comrades in the ranks would be not only old companions, but others—peasants and workers like themselves—from every province of China. Meeting these southerners who had crossed the Yangtze to come north to the anti-Japanese front, they would become aware, perhaps for the first time, of the common interests of all their own countrymen.

And in the soldiers' clubs that were another regular feature of this army, they could take part in a dozen other activities besides the main one for which they had been mobilized. Here they would find musical groups, athletic groups, the ever-popular wall newspaper, the theater, and many things besides, all opening up fresh perspectives. They would soon discover that, in this army, there were no social distinctions between officers and men, and that they would share alike in all their campaigning with their own commanders.

All this (which, baldly stated in English, sounds like so much crude recruiting propaganda) has a special meaning if one remembers how barren the lives of these people had always been in the past; and the traditional Chinese contempt for soldiering—once commonly regarded as the last resort of a scoundrel.* The Japanese invasion, of course, had changed all that. But even so, there was no other Chinese army at this time which could offer so much to its new recruits. The pay was small, but it was a good life.

That afternoon, we were invited to an outdoor performance by the Drama Group. For three hours or so, we sat in the open, in the beginning of a snowstorm, to watch the show.

The chilly weather did not deter this massed audience of soldiers and peasants. We all squatted on the ground before the open stage that is to be found in the center of most Chinese towns and larger villages, and that is normally used for official meetings and by old-style traveling companies. In the "wings," a large wood fire had been provided for the performers, for after all they had the worst of it.

As usual, the star turns were given by the children, and their dancing—which, under these conditions, certainly deserved it—earned hearty roars of approval. I was interested to see that the choice of plays had been carefully suited to this country audience; it was a definitely "lowbrow" performance. The Japanese officer who figured so frequently always had his face painted white like the conventional Chinese villain; all the pieces were short, full of action, and intelligible even to the fur-capped village children who swarmed around the front of the stage, or perched precariously in the bare branches of neighboring trees. It was first-class entertainment, and no political point was allowed to be lost.

* One may quote again the well-worn Chinese proverb—"One does not make good iron into nails, or good men into soldiers."

The finale—and again, this was characteristic—was a "Beggars' Dance" to an old Chinese folk-song that is universally known: *Lien Hwa Lou*, "The Falling of the Lotus." It has a catchy tune that you may hear sung anywhere in the streets of North China:

Wo-men t'ou shih mei-fan-ch'ih-ti ch'eng p'eng-yu is the opening solo line, and the chorus joins in a refrain. In a free English rendering, with the repetitions, it runs something like this:

We are all poor friends together, without food to eat,
Poor friends picking one flower blossoming, a single lotus flower!
We walk together along the road, the road of hunger and cold,
Walk together, two flowers blossoming; the flower opens and the lotus falls.

But new words had been found for the old song, and the audience was not slow to take them up.

Those who want to fight the invaders, set your hands to work! the leader would sing. And the chorus was deafening: *All the Japanese robbers together cannot stop our iron fist!* An hour later, everyone in the town was singing the song, to the new words.

The snow was a nuisance; but the wind kept down, and next day we set out on the return journey. There were the usual reports of *shanping* on the roads, but our cavalry escort should be able to deal with them. Brigadier Wang and Liu came with us to the end of the town; ahead loomed the high range of the Yünchung Shan we had to cross that day. It was a world of glittering white, and there was more snow coming.

"You won't stay on a few more days?"

"Nothing we'd like better. But now I've got to get out of here—back to Hankow, Hong Kong. Perhaps back to Europe."

"You'll tell the other countries about us, about China?"

"I'll try. That was what I came here for...."

What *did* they know about this war abroad, I wondered again, looking at these eager brown faces, the little mountain town with its peasant soldiers, the laughing *hsiao kwei* playing in the snow with the local children? On the face of it everything seemed to be going so badly for China. Peiping, Shanghai, Nanking—all that the foreigner knew best of this country was already in the hands of the invader.

But where was the real strength of the Chinese people? Not in the big coastal cities, not in the provincial capitals. Surely it was here, in the villages and district towns, here among the peasantry who at last—after so many years of ignorance and civil strife—were being welded into an organic whole, with one conscious and increasing purpose.

The social unit of China is still the village; and it was the village that would become the real center of the war of resistance in the future. This much was already plain. And, knowing the superb vitality of these people, knowing them to be aroused as never before in their history, I had little doubt of the ultimate result. Out of the storm and stress of the present crisis a new China would emerge, and it would be a very different China.

CHAPTER TEN
UNITED FRONT

THE RETURN

It was on our return journey to the south—nearly a month of steady travel through the Shansi hills—that I felt at last I was beginning to know North China.

One may live for years in a land of exile or adoption without belonging to it; only too many Europeans in China remain forever strangers to the land and the people. But forced marches through winter snows, nights in buried villages, the start at dawn and the life of the road, bring one closer to a country than all the books in the world. One day was very much like the next, in its common routine of march and bivouac; but each day added its touch to build up a fuller picture. Complete, the picture is one that will not easily fade from memory.

I own to a feeling for North China that I find difficult to explain, even to myself. The beauty of these barren hills has a greater charm, perhaps, for the foreigner than for the Chinese connoisseur: it is a Wordsworth kind of country, and one would need to borrow the language of the *Prelude* to do justice to it. If you ask a Chinese (one who knows all China) what he finds most beautiful in his own land, he will almost certainly think first of Soochow or Hangchow—some melting southern landscape, pagoda by the lake, willows green with spring. What is harsh is forgotten. Rock and stone in Chinese painting become crags of fantasy—softened by the painter's brush, they are turned to dream mountains afloat in space. The most cherished quality of all Chinese art is its *serenity*.

Serenity is gone from China now; Soochow and Hangchow, that "paradise on earth," is a paradise defiled; few cities north or south have escaped the terror from the air. But it was in the hills of the north that the Chinese people first developed their own war against the invaders, and the very wildness of this northern setting seemed to me the natural expression of the mood and temper of a people under arms. North China is a hard country, with its extremes of heat and cold, with its clear, dry air and its great winds that sweep out of Mongolia, laden with dust or snow. You must see this land in winter to know it, when rocks thrust up dark against the snow, and the clear sunlight ranges over leagues of frozen loess. Then there is a beauty in these firmly-molded hills, with their strict treeless line, that I had never found in the warm south.

And as for the people of North China, who have been abused so often for their lack of spirit and their apparent indifference to the nature of their rulers—one can only say that the Japanese invasion and occupation has changed all that. It was true in the past that the northern provinces were badly governed and politically backward, that the yielding character of their people seemed strangely at variance with their magnificent physique and ancient military traditions. But the experience of a year of war has shown how swiftly this people will respond to a resolute and determined leadership; and the criminally brutal (from their own point of view, incredibly short-sighted) methods of the Japanese have played right into the hands of the Eighth Route Army and its political organizers.

In the cities, by the free use of machine guns and the executioner's sword, the Japanese may have succeeded in holding under a cowed and sullen populace. But the country tells a different tale.

I remember we came one night to a tiny village deep in the hills, sheltering amid heavy snowdrifts. The sun had dropped out of sight, and it was almost nightfall. The troop halted by the little shrine that guarded this mountain valley, and our commander asked to see the head of the village: we needed billets for the night. The headman appeared at last, a wizened scarecrow of a man with drooping gray mustaches, fumbling the inevitable brass pipe and tobacco pouch. This was a poor village, he protested without much conviction in his voice:

there was no fit accommodation, the town was only forty *li* down the valley. Then, wide-eyed, he gazed with astonishment at my big black cavalry mount. What sort of a horse was that anyway? He had never seen such a horse.... Behind him a group of children, gathered from nowhere, made similar noises of incredulity.

The troop commander pressed his advantage. "That's a Japanese horse, old comrade—our army has captured many such horses from the invaders of our country. We come from the front, where every day our soldiers fight against the enemy. All we ask is a bed and shelter for the night. We will pay for everything...."

Already the old man had dropped the mask of indifference, and was clearly friendly. Something could probably be arranged. He shuffled off in the snow.

Half an hour later we were all established in one little farmhouse, our horses in the barn, soldiers in the loft above. The fire was lighted again for the evening meal, and we gathered around a steaming cauldron as two young peasants, keeping up a running conversation, dexterously rolled pancakes of *yü mien.** It was not long before half the village had drifted into the courtyard.

"What do the Japanese devils look like?" one young villager asked timidly. "Are they giants, like their horses?" The troop commander began on a long and complicated answer, and soon we were in the middle of a political meeting. The soldiers described the burning of villages in the north by the Japanese, mass executions, forced-labor gangs.... There were other stories that went even deeper home; stories of deliberate outrage perpetrated by the invaders that struck at the very roots of the Chinese sense of family decency. Through these simple words, the full horror of war broke perhaps for the first time in this village that so far had escaped war's devastations.

Early next morning, before we left, the old headman came round to see the troop commander; he brought with him a bronzed young peasant in a fur cap who seemed prepared for

---

* A coarse flour made from a kind of maize, which is the staple food of the poor peasants in Shansi.

a journey. "We need a self-defense corps here in the valley," the old man said. "We ask the Eighth Route Army to help us. This is my grandson; he will go with you as guide, and he wants to join the army. If you will send someone to teach us how to fight...."

So it goes on, day in and day out, through all the hills and valleys of North China.

Back at division headquarters, Ho Lung and Hsiao K'eh were both away at military conferences in the south. Ho Lung returned the day before we left; he had ridden fast, and was in the highest of spirits. "I saw Chiang Kai-shek at Loyang," he told us, "and he was fine." Ho thrust up one thumb in the Chinese gesture of superlative praise. "*Shih fen hao*—one hundred per cent a patriot! You should have heard his address to the commanders...." Over the New Year, in a supreme effort to make up for the disaster of Nanking, a remarkable unanimity had appeared among the military authorities. Political co-operation was not yet as complete as it might have been, but here too there was steady progress.

Two items of news from the south caused special excitement. "Wang Ming is back," was the first announcement I heard at headquarters; Wang Ming, long regarded as one of the best theorists among the Chinese communists, had been for some years in Moscow as Chinese representative in the Comintern. His appearance in Hankow at this stage was certainly significant. But still more encouraging to this division in the northern hills was the first direct confirmation of the arrival of Russian planes and pilots inside China.

We had heard a good deal about those Russian planes already, especially over the radio from Tokyo. Japanese emotions on this subject were mixed: Tokyo, it seemed, was deeply shocked that the planes should be there at all, and at the same time exultant about their "poor performance." But Ho Lung showed me with pride photographs of a Russian fighter, and of a big four-motored Soviet bomber. "This is the fastest plane in China today. And that one can carry forty men! Now at last we shall be able to do something against the Japanese in the air!"

THE RETURN 281

There has been a good deal of misunderstanding about the nature and extent of "Russian aid" to China in her war against Japan. The Soviet planes in Hankow and the small group of Russian fliers and instructors with them were a concrete fact. But there were American, British, and Italian machines in the Chinese Air Force, and from the first there had been one group of foreign pilots which included Americans, French, British, and Central Europeans. The foreign personnel, in all cases, was only a stop-gap until the Chinese could train more aviators of their own: their first line of trained pilots had been almost entirely eliminated by the end of 1937. The most considerable element of "foreign assistance" to the Chinese Government in the conduct of the war at this time was still the group of German military advisors, headed by General von Falkenhausen, who had been working with Chiang Kai-shek for some years before the war began.

In supplying planes and technicians to the Chinese government (on a purely commercial basis) the Soviet Union was playing no more than the part of a friendly neighbor, and was in no way exceeding her rights under international law. And the extent to which Russian war supplies were coming into China was absurdly exaggerated. A favorite claim of the Japanese propagandists (it was echoed by several "neutral" foreign commentators who should have known better) was to the effect that the "Chinese communist armies" in particular had been "sovietized," and were freely equipped with Russian planes, Russian tanks, and Russian staff officers.

I had been nearly five months with the Eighth Route Army, with a good many different units; and I had not seen a single Russian rifle or machine gun, let alone big guns, tanks, planes, or the trace of a Russian whisker. The plain fact was that this army had been left to fend for itself; any new equipment it got was from the Japanese. It was with the same battered rifles they had used to fight their way half across China, with the same primitive home-built hand grenades, that Lin Piao's and Ho Lung's men had checked the Japanese advance in Shansi. If anything, this army was being starved of military supplies; all new equipment imported from abroad by the Government went straight to Hankow, and was distributed among various forces on the main central front.

But one thing the Eighth Route Army did get from the Soviet Union (and this might have been more difficult for the Japanese to understand) was the sense of solidarity in a world struggle, even if it might not immediately be implemented by vast Soviet armaments. Something else that Ho Lung had brought back from the south he showed me almost furtively, his voice lowered to a confidential whisper. "See," he said, "Wang Ming brought four of these from Moscow—he gave me one." I held the little button up to the light.

It was the badge of the Twentieth Anniversary of the founding of the Soviet Union, a tiny gold-leaf hammer and sickle, with the dates "1917—1937," inlaid in ruby glass. What it must mean to an "old Bolshevik" like Ho Lung I could easily guess; I knew how these communist commanders valued their own ten-year Red Army star. This glass trinket was a symbol of all that had been built up in the New Russia over twenty difficult years. To Chinese communists it was also a sign of the "socialist fatherland." And the faith and confidence they had in the Soviet Union never wavered, even though their own army should be the last to benefit directly from the Soviet war supplies.

Ho Lung—this man whose reckless courage had long been a byword in China—now eyed his little red button with infinite regret. "The devil of it is," he sighed, "that I don't even dare to wear the thing! It would be the only one in this division, and too many other comrades would be jealous of me." It was the first time I had seen the morale of the Eighth Route Army seriously threatened.

CHRISTIANS AND COMMUNISTS

"Spring" comes to China, by an immemorial convention, after the Chinese New Year.* And there was a breath of spring in the air as we traveled south through the Shansi country-side, where a pale sun had begun to melt the February snows, to

---

* This is a shifting date, determined by the old Chinese calendar. The "New Year" usually falls early in February.

soften the frozen profile of the hills. Children gathered in the open before doorways still gay with the colored New Year scrolls; work was beginning in the fields; the winter landscape was coming to life. And not even the shadow of war over half this province could entirely darken the joy of living, the resurgence of the human spirit that comes with the slow awakening of the yellow earth.

It was a real spring morning when I returned to Army Headquarters, riding in a battered truck with P'eng Teh-huai. That indefatigable commander had filled in most of the drive with a detailed analysis of the international situation, elaborating a theory that the conflicting interests of the "fascist powers"—Germany, Italy, and Japan—in the Far East would never allow real co-operation between them, so far as China was concerned. "In Europe, yes, the fascists can work together. But not here. Italy wants Japan to move south, to embarrass Britain and France. Germany wants Japan to be strong in the north, to attack the Soviet Union—the Germans are very afraid of a Japanese defeat in central China, and afraid, too, that they may lose their growing China trade to Japan. These contradictions in material interests may prove stronger than all their 'Anti-Comintern alliances.'..."

We came to the village at last; P'eng leaped down and led the way to headquarters through streets that seemed decked for festival. On every hand there were banners of welcome, slogans in English, French, German. "You know," P'eng told me briefly, "there are a lot of foreigners here now."

It was the first I had heard of it. Foreigners with the Eighth Route Army were not so common: I ran through all the names I knew. Agnes Smedley was back in Hankow; Anna Louise Strong—that veteran friend of China and the Chinese Revolution—had returned from Moscow to renew some old associations, and had made one visit to Shansi. But she too had already returned to the south. The only remaining foreigner I knew of was a venturesome American officer, Major Evans F. Carlson, who had made a long trip as military observer with units of this army in the east. But Carlson—from whom fragmentary wireless messages had been heard from time to time—should still be up in Wutai Shan. The mystery deepened.

Either the Eighth Route Army had been making new friends, or this must be the "Russian advisors" at last. My curiosity was already sufficiently aroused as we entered a stone-flagged courtyard, where Tso Chuan called an eager greeting from an open doorway. Behind him was a big man—a foreigner—in rough tweeds and a leather jacket; his granite features looked as though they had weathered all the storms in the Arctic.

"This is a Russian comrade," Tso Chuan told me. I looked for a political commissar at the least; but the stranger heaved his great bulk through the doorway, and introduced himself in Russian: "Skvortsov—*Press-Tass!*"

It was only another journalist. But in the main room I caught a glimpse of a sturdy and familiar back, at the head of a conference table. "Who is with Chu Teh?" I wanted to know. "The other *yang-jen?*"

Tso Chuan nodded; he seemed to be enjoying a private joke. I entered the dark room to pay my respects to the commander-in-chief, and found myself being introduced to his guests. Seated around this "conference table" were—a Swiss woman-journalist, an American tourist, a white-haired Anglican deaconess, a lecturer from a mission college in Wuchang, and the daughter of the Bishop of Hankow!

It was a goodwill delegation from Hankow's foreign colony to the Eighth Route Army. And they had come not just to see that army for themselves, but to bring a substantial contribution of money, warm clothing, and medical supplies for the relief of the partisans in the Shansi hills.

That was a gala day at headquarters. The arrival of the "foreign friends" was itself an occasion; but such a group as this, which had come bearing concrete evidence of sympathy, and had braved the hazards of railway travel in wartime to visit an army that for ten years had been outlawed by Church and State, was assured of more than an ordinary welcome. The "International Peace Front" was building up at last in China, my guard told me with great satisfaction.

"What do you think about the Christians now?" I asked Tso Chuan, when we had finished a ceremonial lunch, and stood around the improvised athletic field waiting for the afternoon "welcome meeting." It was a pleasant village scene, this open square lined with Shansi peasants come to watch the strange spectacle of an army that played football with the local children. Skvortsov, fresh from Moscow, was a keen soccer player, and was passing on some of the finer points of the game to the less initiated. His neat heading and powerful shots at goal drew appreciative shouts of *"hao!"* from the onlookers.

Near by a basket-ball game was in progress, where Chu Teh was getting in his daily two hours of exercise. A canny player, Chu was respected by the crack army team (despite his fifty-some years) as a strategist, and the delight that flashed across his dark, homely features when one of his maneuvers met with success was justly famous. An army commander in his shirt-sleeves scuffling in a dusty field with village children is not perhaps a common sight, but it was familiar enough around Eighth Route Army headquarters.

"These are very good people, these friends from Hankow," the young chief of staff responded to my question. "We have had many different experiences with missionaries in China, and sometimes in the past they were not very happy ones. How much better it is now, when Christian friends can come to visit us, and see for themselves what the terrible 'Red Army' is like!"

Tso went on to tell me of an incident which had recently occurred in the fighting in western Hopei. In Laiyuan, a *hsien* city, Italian Catholics had a mission station. In their first advance the Japanese had occupied this city, and had proceeded to set up the usual "Peace Maintenance Commission," composed of wealthy Chinese renegades; the Italians, whose relations with the Japanese were very good, had co-operated in this enterprise. Later Laiyuan was reoccupied by a unit of the Eighth Route Army, whose first task, of course, had been an attempt to round up the Chinese "traitors." The latter sought sanctuary in the mission church, and the Italian priests had refused to surrender them.

"Did you bring them out by force?" I inquired. Tso shook

his head very seriously. "We knew the Italians were working with the Japanese," he said. "But if we had forced our way into a foreign mission, the story would have been used again to discredit the 'communist bandits.' We reported the affair to the National Government, which lodged a protest with the Italian consul. We left the mission undisturbed."

This case was exceptional. The great majority of mission workers in China, appalled by the suffering the war had brought to the Chinese people, were hardly less indignant at the invaders than the Chinese themselves. And while it was no part of their duty to bless the banners of either army, few Christian missionaries in China, whatever their own affiliation, could consider themselves "above the battle."

"How about the Catholics in this village?" I asked. Above the tiled roofs beyond the playing field rose the spire of a large parish church. "Oh, *they're* all right," Tso assured me. The parish priest was a Belgian who had taken Chinese citizenship. "They have invited us to come to Mass tomorrow."

"Are you going?"

"Chu Teh has accepted on behalf of the army."

Just then a bugle call sounded "assembly." The basketball game broke up; Chu Teh hastily donned his tunic, and straightened his old cloth cap. He led the way to the mass meeting.

Inside a large courtyard that made a natural outdoor theater, the welcome meeting was held. The court itself was packed with soldiers, and guards armed with rifles lined the roofs on three sides. The money from Hankow—it was some forty thousand dollars, all in one-dollar bills—made an impressive pile on a little wooden table, surrounded by bundles of woollen socks, toothbrushes, and medical supplies.

All the foreign visitors made speeches, including the deaconess, who spoke in perfect Hunan dialect and was greeted with tumultuous applause. Finally Miss Frances Roots, in the name of the Relief Committee in Hankow, made the official presentation of money and supplies. In acknowledging the gifts, Chu Teh replied not in the name of the Eighth Route Army, but of the Northwestern Partisans.

"Our army now," he said, "is supported by the National Government, and we have no special need of food or clothing. But all through the north of this province, the peasant volunteers, many of whom have lost their homes, are continuing the day-to-day struggle against the invaders. It is for them that we are happy to acknowledge these contributions from friends in Hankow. For these fighters and their families, this money will mean food, clothing, shoes, the most necessary things of life.... The people of North China will continue the struggle; they will know now that they do not stand alone...."

An episode of the war, that may seem slight enough in the telling. But the implications of that little meeting were not small. To these peasant soldiers of China, at least, it meant one thing. Whatever foreign governments might do, the *peoples* of the democratic countries were their friends.

FIFTH COLUMN

At Tungkwan, the wounded were crossing the Yellow River.

This crooked elbow of treacherous water, where three provinces meet, is one of the strategic points of China: there is a time-honored proverb, "He who holds Tungkwan is master of the Middle Kingdom." The city lies on the south bank of the river, flanked by rising hills; through Tungkwan the east-west Lung-Hai railway runs on into Shensi, following the Wei River through a bottleneck pass. North is Shansi, south is Honan. There is no bridge across the river.

Ankle-deep in sand, we stood and watched the heavy junks heading upstream with the wind, or beating back against it beneath the loess cliffs. Many of them flew a Red Cross pennant, and carried bales of medical supplies on their return journey to the Shansi side. Hundreds of refugees stood patiently waiting for a place in the ferry; they were continually joined by little parties who came trudging over the sand dunes, their faces set towards the south. As each junk was filled and poled off from the shallows until the current caught it, another worked in to take its place.

Our army pass secured us a passage on one of the hospital boats. I found myself seated next to a boy in muddied uniform, who had been shot through the groin. His face was drawn and dark with pain, but he lay against the mast in silence, eyes narrowed against the bitter wind. A friend, his head bound with a filthy rag of bandage, went over to talk to him.

"How is it, comrade?" White teeth shone for an instant in the flicker of a smile. *"Tsou ko-la!* The wind is cold." Without a word, the other passed across a cotton blanket.

How is one to write of the Chinese wounded? This batch—they were Fu Tso-yi's men, from the 35th Division—had come halfway across a province before they could get more than a dressing for their wounds. No morphine, no anti-tetanus serum. ... One could imagine the journey that must have been a nightmare for this peasant boy who gazed through sunken eyes at the Honan shore; for him and for thousands like him. Some lived through it.

The Chinese Army Medical Corps was so understaffed and ill-equipped that it had more than enough to do looking after the Central divisions on the main front. The provincial armies were virtually without surgeons, and it was an open secret that during this first year of the war, army authorities had in many cases followed the principle of letting the seriously wounded die as soon as possible.

It was less trouble in the long run. A soldier's life was cheap; there were plenty of replacements....

That policy was slowly changing. In the north, the Eighth Route Army had set a different example—from the old Red Army days, it had always placed the highest possible value on the life of each individual fighter. With deplorably inadequate means, somehow this army managed to tend its wounded. Local peasants would lend a hand, acting as stretcher-bearers, or nursing wounded men in concealed villages until they were able to be moved. The keynote of it all was co-operation; and that was something this war was beginning to teach the Chinese people as a whole.

There has always been co-operation of a sort in China. But until these last years, traditionally this has rested upon some community of local interest: it has been co-operation between members of a family, or of a village clan, and rarely more than

Fifth Column 289

this (except, perhaps, during the brief period of labor union activity in the revolutionary years up to 1927). The traditional co-operation of the poor against the rich is something different: that has been real enough, as the communists found in the ten-year Soviet movement. But now for the first time a new sense of unity, of identity of interest, was growing among all sections and classes of China. It was being proved in action at the front, where the need was most urgent; but gradually—all too slowly —it was extending to the rear as well. To anyone who knew "old China," every single instance of this new spirit of co-operation was more to be prized than military victories.

Passenger trains were still running to schedule along the Lung-Hai railway; we were lucky to get out before the spring offensive brought the Japanese flying columns to the north bank of the Yellow River. The main Chinese concentration at this time was around Hsüchow, junction of the Lung-Hai and the Tsin-Pu lines, where the "final battle of the war" (according to the Tokyo radio announcer, who must have had many disappointments) was then preparing. Much was to happen, including a major defeat of their armies, before the Japanese took Hsüchow; and the tenacity with which the Chinese held the Lung-Hai railway was to prove a further surprise.

At this time, we traveled comfortably enough in a third-class carriage to Chengchow, junction for Hankow; and put up in a top-floor room in a Chinese hotel near the station. This seemed to me an unhealthy neighborhood, but Chengchow hitherto had unaccountably escaped bombing, and we felt we might take a chance. I went off to visit a friend in the American Baptist Mission, whose hospital compound was a refuge for hundreds of wounded soldiers and civilians. Skvortsov departed mysteriously in search of a colleague from *Tass*.

But when we foregathered that night, the Russian journalist was insistent that we should take the first train for Hankow. He gave his reasons in two words: *Fifth Column*.

Chengchow, it seemed, had been the center of the Japanese Intelligence Service in Central China, and had escaped bombing so long only because the spy network in this strategic railway junction was so extensive and so valuable to the enemy that they could not afford to jeopardize it. The careful plans Japan had made for her China conquests included an elaborate underground information service: this had functioned so well, with the assistance of a small army of Chinese agents, that the Japanese had news well in advance of every significant Chinese move. Chinese counter-espionage got off to a slow start; now, in Chengchow at least, it had begun to assert itself.

For on the day that we arrived there, the police had drawn their net. No less than fifty secret agents had been arrested, several of them found to be in possession of radio transmitting sets. The evidence was overwhelming, and the haul—which had been prepared for several weeks in advance—was pretty nearly complete.

It had broken Japan's "Fifth Column" along the Lung-Hai, for the time being at least. But the news would leak out, and the Japanese retaliation would be swift. We were well advised to take the Hankow train; the morning after we left, Chengchow was so thoroughly bombed that every building around the station was leveled. This was only the beginning of an attack that was to leave Chengchow a ruin, before the Yellow River floods saved it again.

It has often been asked, how the Japanese can find Chinese agents to work for them in such numbers; and the answer generally given has not been one complimentary to the Chinese. But though men may sell their souls, they do not generally throw away their lives for money. The thing is much more subtle than that.

When the Chinese planes were returning one evening to their base, after a very successful bombing raid on Japanese positions, a hand grenade was thrown at the first plane to land; the explosion wrecked the plane and seriously injured two fliers. That bomb was thrown by a *Chinese*, who had not one chance in a thousand of escaping with his life (he did not escape). There is only one possible explanation for such a suicidal action, and it is the explanation why Chinese soldiers from Manchuria will wear a Japanese uniform, and carry arms—though not very resolutely—against their fellow-countrymen. For every conscript in the armies of "Manchukuo" is guaranteed not only by his own family, but by a number of individual guarantors, whose lives are forfeit if he should ever desert or fail to obey orders from his Japanese commander. And in the same way, there are probably few reliable Chinese agents of Japan who are not bound by the same threat to family relatives. There is no tie stronger, for the average Chinese, than the ties of family; to set against this a dawning conception of nationhood, is to fight with new ideas against ideas that are hallowed by centuries. In many cases, it has been an unequal battle, and the old loyalties have won out.

But not always; and one of the most interesting developments of this war in China, to the casual observer as to the sociologist, has been the conflict set up by changed conditions between old systems of thought and new. Probably the first considerable body of Chinese to set an idea above family were the communists; it has often been argued that for this one reason alone, communism can never succeed in China. That is a question—posed in this form—that only the future can decide, and any discussion of it is irrelevant here. But at least the communists have demonstrated, by their own leadership and often enough by the response of their rank and file, that devotion to an ideal can be strong enough in China to cut through older and more familiar loyalties. And one great question before the Chinese people today is whether this new idea of national freedom, of national independence, can finally assert its power over a complex of conflicting and negative emotions inherited from the past.

The familiar definition of China as "a tray of loose sand" no longer holds; part of that sand, at least, has already become concrete. The idea begins to express a reality, and there can only be one end to this process. Either the reality must be established, and China emerge from these critical years a conscious nation; or else the defeat of the idea must seal the relapse of many of her people into the slumber of centuries.

HANKOW SYMPHONY

The "three cities" of Wuhan—Hankow, Hanyang, and Wuchang—which sprawl across both banks of the Yangtze where the Han River joins it, represent the second commercial and industrial center of China after Shanghai. American journalists are fond of referring to Hankow as "the Chicago of China," though the comparison is not very apt—perhaps the common possession of a factory district facing a waterway is what suggested it. But the relative importance of Hankow to Shanghai is not badly indicated by the relation of Chicago to New York.

Like Shanghai and Tientsin, Hankow—as one of the three Chinese cities most completely dominated by foreign capital—has a comparatively "modern" look. Along the Bund, off which the cruisers of five nations might anchor when the river was running high, banks and offices, warehouses, villas and consulates, all built in western style, are a monument to the commercial enterprise of the West in the last century. Hankow once had its full quota of foreign concessions; of these, only the French and the Japanese remained effective at the outbreak of war in 1937. Japanese nationals were early evacuated, and the Chinese took over the Japanese Concession, which they used as a convenient military base during wartime.

We ran into Hankow through a wilderness of railway tracks, littered with ancient rolling-stock—everything on wheels had been mobilized for the war crisis. The station was heavily guarded, but the city was calm and everyday life—including air raid precautions—seemed to be remarkably well-organized. First impressions of Hankow were definitely reassuring. This city was really the war capital of China, for though a number of senior government officials had removed up the Yangtze to Chungking, Hankow remained the executive center for both military and political organization. Here the Generalissimo had his Headquarters, and here many heads of departments, deprived of the spacious offices they had once occupied at Nanking, dwelt uneasily in obscure tenements, often behind locked doors.

Accommodation was a real problem, for the city was as overcrowded as Moscow. I might have fared badly without the generous hospitality of the American Episcopal Mission; Bishop Roots, whose daughter we had seen so recently in Shansi, made me welcome in a household which included at this time a number of foreign volunteer doctors, and Agnes Smedley—now thoroughly immersed in the endless problem of medical and civilian relief. The liberal nature of these arrangements, which gathered all schools of thought under one roof in the common cause of aid to China, was another sign of the times. At Bishops House, H. H. Kung or Chou En-lai might be equally likely to drop in to tea: and this atmosphere of a friendly interchange of views, under the mellow Christian influence of a liberal churchman, was something that had been lacking in China all too long.

To be in a modern city again after months in the hills was at first immensely stimulating. Hankow had a fine dash of martial spirit in those days: everywhere on the streets one encountered military uniforms, cafés and cabarets were filled, and money flowed like the champagne of some of the foreign fliers (the Russians, by contrast, kept strictly to themselves, and were never to be seen in public). It was an artificial atmosphere, of course, built up around the war tension, and the uncertainty as to how long Hankow could be held. But the situation in Hankow had infinite possibilities, if they only could be realized.

The communists at this time had already worked out a plan for the defense of Hankow, which involved direct arming of the city's industrial workers (the largest Chinese proletariat outside of Shanghai), and envisaged Hankow becoming another Madrid. This plan was still opposed by certain Kuomintang officials, and there was little immediate likelihood of its being adopted. Though the Chinese Communist Party had its own open organization in Hankow and published its own newspaper, it was still subject to frequent attacks, and several times the Generalissimo had intervened to prevent overt friction. But the United Front held triumphantly through all this; and only those who knew the full story of internal intrigue and the difficulties to be surmounted, could appreciate the strength of this achievement.

Meantime, the outer drama of the war went on; and one side of it was well illustrated by the struggle for control of the air. Here the parallel with Spain is so striking that it deserves to be quoted.

Unlike the Spanish government, China had not been completely unprepared for the first attack in the air: she had a small but fairly efficient first line of fighters and light bombers, and a small force of first-line pilots. But the Japanese superiority in planes was at first so overwhelming, and the tactical use of the Chinese aviation so poor, that the balance of air power swung steadily against China. The first months of aerial warfare proved that, as combat-fliers, the Chinese were probably superior to the Japanese; but they were rash to the point of recklessness, had a dangerous tendency to break formation, and lost a great many of their best planes by bad handling on the ground. By the end of 1937, the Chinese air force was reduced practically to insignificance; and the Japanese were making bombing flights as far inland as Kansu with impunity.

In this period of breakdown, the Chinese government, like the Loyalists in Spain, was forced for a time to rely on foreign mercenaries. The foreign fliers in the Chinese air force—notably the famous "Fourteenth Bombing Squadron"—were probably all sympathetic to the Chinese cause, and their record in the air, both for courage and efficiency, was magnificent. But there were obvious drawbacks to such a system, and it was impossible to keep this group of foreign pilots under military discipline. (In Spain, the Government had at first met with the same difficulty.) The turning point, in Hankow as at Madrid, was the arrival of the Soviet planes.

This meant not merely a substantial addition to the fighting strength of the Chinese air force: it brought too the beginnings of an adequate staff of technicians, and a group of fliers who were authentic volunteers. The Russians lived and slept with their planes, so that they were always able to take them up at a moment's notice in any emergency. Until the Chinese (who had established their big new aviation school in Yünnan) were able to train a new first line of pilots, the reorganized air force could at least hold the key cities. And by a significant change of tactics, the offensive power of the Chinese aviation was now used almost entirely along the Japanese front. To the Chinese troops, it meant that for the first time they had the support of their own planes in the actual fighting.

In Hankow, Japanese raids had been coming almost daily. One heard the first warning, and before long it would be followed by the roar of the Chinese planes as they took the air. But this was still cut-and-run tactics; for long enough, the Chinese had not dared to try conclusions with a strong Japanese raiding force. One day brought a dramatic change.

"Do you want to take a bet?" a Canadian nurse had asked me the night before. This girl, I knew, had friends among the foreign fliers.

"Which way?"

"If the Japanese planes come over tomorrow, that we bring down at least ten." I hoped she was right, though I did not share her confidence. But it was a good inside tip.

The warning sounded just after noon. It found me on my way to the British Consulate; and from the upper windows of this useful sanctuary we had a grandstand view.

When the second warning went, the Chinese planes were already in the air, climbing steeply from the field. This time they did not turn and run. Circling steadily, more than thirty of them held their positions above the city, and vanished among the clouds. They were going to fight.

"There come the bombers," someone said: twelve big Japanese planes in formation were bearing down from the east. They flew at a great height, but above them their escort was already engaged with the Chinese pursuit. For once, the Japanese had miscalculated: their fighters were outnumbered three to two.

Anti-aircraft batteries were coming into action, and the explosions were almost continuous. Chinese gunfire seems to be either very good or very bad; now some of the puffs of gray smoke came dangerously near the slow-flying enemy formation, but the Japanese kept high and were taking no chances. Of the fighting planes, nothing was visible except a gnat-like dance of tiny black objects in the void. Then a gleam of silver wings, and one plane was falling swiftly, a dark pencil of smoke against the clouds....

The bombers had circled the airport. We watched for the bombs, but the land batteries drowned any separate explosion. Then the whole house rocked suddenly, though the aerodrome was a couple of miles away: all the bombs had gone together. The raiding squadron, obviously unprepared for such a reception, continued its progress eastwards and out of sight. "That's all for the day, I think," said the gray-haired consul. "What about some lunch?"

That evening we had the report. Jean won her bet: fifteen Japanese planes were down, including one bomber. The Chinese lost three of their pursuit planes. But they had regained control of the air in this sector, and for some months after that the Japanese tried only night raids on Hankow. The Chinese air force, heartened by the Hankow battle, daily extended its activities, which were climaxed in this period by the daring and successful raid on Formosa—the first time, in the history of the Empire, that Japanese territory had been bombarded.

Soon after this, the Fourteenth Squadron was disbanded. Slowly, under almost inconceivable handicaps, China was beginning to find her own strength.

Before leaving Hankow I paid a final visit to the Eighth Route Army office—it was my own farewell to these people with whom I had traveled for nearly half a year. The office was located, appropriately enough, in the heart of the Japanese Concession. My last view of Chou En-lai was of that versatile spokesman of the Communist Party sitting on a *tatami* mat, with a handsome *kakimono* on the wall behind him. Chou must have got very little sleep in those strenuous Hankow days, for he was always busied in momentous negotiations; but his manner was suave and diplomatic as ever.

He was very optimistic about the "concrete political progress" that had been made in Hankow, and felt that any crisis which might occur in the future (there were several already in sight) could never be so serious for China as that which had followed the loss of Nanking. "Nanking was the turning point," he told me. "The last real chance of a compromise. Now even if we lose Hankow, it will never be so bad again."

One thing troubled Chou En-lai more than the rest, and that was the equivocal attitude of the "democratic powers" in the Far East. "It's you people they're afraid of," I suggested. "The British haven't forgotten Hankow ten years ago." But Chou insisted that the foreign policy of his own party was identical with that of the Kuomintang.

"This is not true just for today," he added. "We are not opportunists. We believe that China must continue for a long time in her fight against Japanese imperialism before she is successful. In this period, it is very important for us to have every possible assistance from friendly foreign powers. And if in the end we do gain the victory, we shall need all the more the economic and technical assistance of more highly developed foreign countries to rebuild China after the war.

"Any questions that are still outstanding, such as extraterritoriality and the unequal treaties, can then be settled by peaceful agreement. We shall continue to welcome foreign capital investment and foreign enterprise in China."

Chou repudiated any suggestion that the communists were seeking control of the National Government, or hoping to establish a soviet system in any part of China. "We want to continue in the United Front, not only during the war period, but after it as well." The communist view was that the political and economic condition of China was favorable for the establishment of a democratic republic, but not yet for anything more than this. It was clear that any threat to continued political unity would not come from their side.

Ten years before, the communists had been openly established in Hankow; and their presence had been anything but reassuring to foreign interests in that city. Now—and it was not surprising, after the experience of Shanghai—there were many foreigners who would rather have the communists there than the Japanese. The choice before foreign interests in China was not perhaps, to their way of thinking, an enviable one. But by co-operating with a progressive Chinese government, they might keep China's goodwill and something of their old privileged position. By cooperating with Japan, they were certain to lose both.

Outside the Eighth Route Army station I parted from my bodyguard, who had accompanied me faithfully on all my wanderings since I left Yenan. Wang was returning to his native mountains, resplendent in a brand-new leather belt, with a fine red silk tassel on his Mauser. Country-born, he had enjoyed the brief excitement of the city, but he was obviously happy to be going back. "Hankow is all right," he told me, "but we can fight the Japanese better in the hills."

I shook his hand and wished him well; it was hard to realize that I should not be seeing his familiar figure again. "You don't want to come to England with me?" I asked him; this was something we had often talked of in lighter moments.

As usual, he grinned and hitched up his deplorably baggy trousers. "You'll take me with you?"

"Surely."

He scratched one ear, and thought it all out again from the beginning. Finally he shook his head. "I can't go to England now...."

"You're afraid of the boat?" The most water Wang had ever seen in his life was the Yangtze; to him the sea was still a mystery.

He drew himself up in all the affronted dignity of his seventeen years. "I'm not afraid! But now we have to defend North China, and we'll all be needed. *Every man*..."

HONG KONG DISCORDS

Through the parted clouds, a glimpse of wind-darkened sea: these lonely billows roll on unchecked as far as the Philippines. The cloud bank shuts again, and the big Junker is dropping fast. In the next seat, the former Chinese Minister to Japan stirs uneasily and delicately fingers his eardrums. He is a charming old gentleman in a heavy silk gown, with drooping mustaches and the air of a distinguished mannequin. All the way from Hankow he has been sitting with a pad on his knees, idly sketching Chinese characters.

"*K'uai tao-la*," says the ambassador's secretary, reverently gathering up the written sheets (the old man was a celebrated calligrapher). "We'll soon be there."

The clouds are thinning now, those clouds that wreathe the mountains of South China for half the year. Beyond their verge a dark pile of rock thrusts suddenly, a shoulder of green. The Peak. The plane sweeps out in brilliant sunlight across a deep-blue harbor, shut between the hills of the mainland and the island fortress. The roadstead is dotted with scores of ships at anchor, crossed and recrossed by the yellow sails of junks. Off the naval moorings, where the lean cruisers hold the port, a submarine supply ship rides the water as squatly as a duck, surrounded by her ugly brood.

Kowloon, on the mainland, is flat as a barrack-square: beyond, the green of rice fields, red earth, and pasture of the Leased Territories. It is a patchwork of light and color, all under the shadow of the Rock. This is Hong Kong, Britain's foothold in East Asia, the Gibraltar of the China Seas. . . .

The peculiar significance of Hong Kong and the fact of its being a British Crown Colony (things, like the British Empire, usually taken for granted) took on an added value after Japan launched her major drive against China. This strategic island base, casually acquired by its present rulers in an era of licensed banditry, became with the war one of the key factors in an increasingly complicated situation. Hong Kong proprietors, even more unaccustomed than the taipans of Shanghai to take any thought for the morrow, realized with a thrill of genuine excitement both their present opportunity and their very uncertain future. The present was pure gain, but the future would hardly bear thinking about.

In these last years, when Japan has made all the running in the Far East, we are inclined to forget what British imperialism could do in its heyday. Lord Palmerston as Foreign Secretary spoke a very different language from Lord Halifax; British statesmen, in that generous nineteenth century, knew what they wanted and usually got it. Hong Kong, regarded by many at the time of its acquisition as the dubious spoils of a very dubious war, proved one of the most solid investments Britain has ever made. Gateway to the South China trade, with the best deepwater harbor on the whole China coast, it was not long before this barren rock became a thriving colony, the greatest *entrepôt* port in the East.

Only twice, in its long and prosperous history of nearly a hundred years under the Union Jack, has Hong Kong been seriously threatened. The first time was in the years of China's "Great Revolution," when the shipping strikes directed from Canton tied up the British port for months on end, and turned its busy docks into a desert. But the revolutionary wave passed on, and Hong Kong breathed again.... The second challenge, less widely known because less publicized, was unveiled—again from Canton—in 1936, with the decision of the Chinese Government to build a deep-water harbor up the Pearl River at Whampoa. British and Chinese officials paid each other smiling compliments across the banquet table when this decision was announced. But the former knew well enough that, had it ever gone into effect, Hong Kong's very *raison d'être* was gone.

Next year, Hong Kong was saved by the war. But *for how long?*

That was a question the Japanese high command must have been asking themselves pretty frequently of late, I reflected, as we drove past the Kowloon railhead to the ferry. Line upon line of canvas-shrouded cars filled the railway sidings; the outline of the canvas told its own tale. Huge packing cases awaited transport, many of them ingenuously marked "Farm Machinery." Hundreds of motor-truck chassis stood around in vacant areas: in factories not far away, men were working double shifts to build bodies for them. Near the coal wharf an immense floating crane, recently shipped out from Belfast by the Chinese Government, had just finished unloading twenty-four locomotives.

The port of Hong Kong took on a new lease of life when the Japanese guns spoke out at Lukowchiao. The Whampoa project was already dead; Shanghai was blockaded; Japanese cruisers patrolled the China coast. But Hong Kong was British still, and there were guns on the Peak (though not so many, perhaps, as the Colony might have wished). Without a declaration of war,

HONG KONG DISCORDS 301

Japan did not yet dare to enforce a blockade of foreign shipping. From the late summer of 1937 armaments, machinery, war supplies of every kind flowed in a steadily increasing stream through Hong Kong into China. In the first months, by a pleasing touch of irony, the largest contribution by far came from Japan's European "allies." Armament manufacturers—especially when there is a chance to get rid of surplus stocks—are very internationally-minded.

Hong Kong boomed. While Japanese bombs systematically wrecked the industrial areas of Shanghai, the British port became the only part of China that was doing well out of the war. And by this accident of history that made it an open channel of war supplies, a British Hong Kong became for the first time useful to the Chinese people. The Rock, whose threatening profile had frowned so long across South China as a symbol of foreign domination, suddenly took on a friendlier aspect. Thus the whirligig of time (and international war markets) brings in its revenges. . . .

It was not to be supposed, of course, that Hong Kong had changed its very nature overnight. The extent of British aid to China was still to be measured strictly by the profits of trading companies: sentiment has little to do with business policies in the Far East, as is shown by the way British capital came to terms with the Japanese in Shanghai. And the last thing the Hong Kong authorities wanted was any revival of political activity among the Chinese of the Colony. In the first months of the war, when the Seamen's Union (remembering perhaps the strength it had in other days) tried to carry through a boycott of Japanese shipping, the Government wasted no time in debate: the Union was declared illegal and dissolved. Strikes for higher wages in several factories in Hong Kong (where rents had soared and provision prices rocketed as a result of the war boom and the influx of refugees) were settled just as promptly as Indian police could do the job. Hong Kong had not forgotten 1925.

But there was one specter at this feast of war profits and colonial prosperity which was really disturbing. *What if Japan should decide to do something about Hong Kong?* This was something which agitated even the somewhat unreceptive minds of Hong Kong's olympian Peak-dwellers, and had become a kind of nightmare to responsible British officials. For the plain truth of the matter was that Hong Kong could not be defended. And nobody knew that better than the Colony itself.

Frenzied last-minute war preparations were very much in evidence during that spring. New guns were being mounted in the old forts, the Volunteer Defense Corps was increasingly popular, and a spirited call was made upon the "patriotic" sympathies of the local Chinese. An aircraft carrier arrived, and a new flotilla of submarines. Blackouts were staged at night in the best traditions of A.R.P.—that is, most ineffectively—and extensive maneuvers were held in which an "attack" on the island, with two "enemy" landing parties, was successfully "repulsed." An Indian regiment took up its quarters in Kowloon to guard the boundaries of the Leased Territories; in Hong Kong itself British regulars became more and more conspicuous. On the face of things, this Far Eastern Gibraltar looked far from defenseless.

But that Hong Kong could ever stand up against a full Japanese attack, no one for a moment pretended to believe. The British Prime Minister admitted as much in a speech on Imperial Defense, when he conceded that in the event of a large-scale war, "certain outlying portions" of the Empire might have to be "temporarily" abandoned. The phrase was heard in Hong Kong without enthusiasm. It was evident that Hong Kong was lost without a battle fleet at Singapore; and there would be no battle fleet. Moreover, it would not even be necessary for Japan to attack Hong Kong—by naval blockade, and a landing party on the mainland, the port could be isolated and starved out in a few weeks.

Such was the situation of this Gibraltar of the East—an island fortress as vulnerable as Gibraltar itself has become in these last years, and a far more tempting bait to the aggressor. Inevitably this focal point of the rich South China trade must become—sooner rather than later—the center of an impending clash of rival imperialist interests. And the only way in which Hong Kong *could* ever be defended—that is, by the full co-operation

HONG KONG DISCORDS 303

of the American Navy—has probably been thrown away since the British Government adopted its newly-chosen principle of *parcere superbis et debellare subjectos.* The sun may never set upon the British Empire, but over some parts of it a new Sun has risen. That Sun is hostile, and its rays strike fairly on the Peak. . . .

Long a haven for defeated warlords and turncoat politicians, Hong Kong has sheltered in its time the best and worst of Chinese exiles. In the war months, it had become a preferred sanctuary for wealthy refugees. Here Shanghai merchants and bankers came to rest for a little in the suites of de luxe hotels, as they strove to recoup their shattered fortunes. Local millionaires, blandly ignoring the war, went ahead designing newer and more fantastic castles. Watching some of these well-dressed figures stepping into limousines, I thought of the peasant soldiers I had left lying in northern villages, raw cotton from the fields the only dressing for their wounds. Theirs was another China. . . .

But the war had brought some surprising changes. One day in Hong Kong I encountered by chance the Al Capone of Shanghai—an opium racketeer whose former holdings had been fabulous. This king of the underworld had suddenly discovered that he was a patriot: in his field, as in so many others, the Japanese had shown a supreme contempt for the Open Door. He had now turned over his whole organization to the volunteer movement, and was directing operations from Hong Kong while his erstwhile thugs (whose marksmanship was always admirable) had become Shanghai's most redoubtable terrorists. A good many doubtful reputations had been similarly redeemed by the war.

It was in Hong Kong, even more than in Hankow, that I realized again how much of China's future depended on the strengtening and consolidation of the United Front. All these widely differing classes and elements of a uniquely hybrid society had one thing in common: their interests, directly or indirectly, were threatened by Japan. Not all of them had yet realized it, as I found in talking to one comfortable middle-aged Chinese official in the British Customs. It was very sad about Hankow and Canton, he agreed, but what could he do? There were too many

Chinese soldiers anyway, and his sons were at the British university.

"And if the Japanese should attack Hong Kong?" I wanted to know. He smiled serenely. "Britain will protect us...."

But Britain will not, nor will France, nor America. It took the Chinese people a year of war to learn this bitter lesson (the lesson of Spain): that there was only one foreign government, and one with no formal obligation, upon which they could rely in any weather for assistance.

"We have learned not to expect very much from Britain," Madame Sun Yat-sen told me one morning in Hong Kong, with a tinge of irony that was entirely without bitterness. "Or from America, or from any of the western democracies. China may have to make her fight alone, and we are not afraid to do it. But this we do ask of your governments—*not to help our enemy.*"

I looked out across the bay, beyond the tangled masts to the blue crest of Lion Mountain. Over there was Canton, towards which—perhaps at this moment—Japanese armadas of death were winging their way, American-built planes flown on American oil. North was Shanghai, where British bankers were sitting down with Japanese generals to work out plans for "co-operation" and the "return to normalcy." So it is that empires in their last days help to destroy themselves....

The widow of China's greatest patriot, this gentle, sensitive woman in whom his spirit burns with a clear flame, spoke now like the widow of all of China's dead.

"We are strong, if we can find our true strength. China is united now, and is at last a nation. It is what my husband always wished, and what he gave his life for.

"In the end we shall win, and we shall win through our own suffering...."

EPILOGUE
THE BLIND INVADER

SECOND SPRING

It was cherry-blossom time in Dairen when I returned again to the north, in a freighter bound for America. I was leaving China, and fate as well as fortune had decreed that it should be a modest exit, avoiding the war-torn area of Shanghai.

Wisdom advised against setting foot once more on Japanese soil, after some of the company I had been keeping; and I had looked for nothing more than a glimpse of Japanese coastline to speed me on my way. But fate intervened again in Dairen. It was thanks to the movements of the Imperial Army that I was presented once more with an opportunity to revisit North China and Japan, retracing my steps over the same route I had traveled —nearly a year before—in the last peaceful spring China had known.

For the narrow basin of this artificial northern harbor was chock-a-block with army transports, and there was a long line of nearly twenty vessels at anchor in the roads. It would be a week at least before we could dock, the skipper told us blasphemously; and another week before the cargo could be shipped. He advised going ashore and putting up at the Yamato Hotel. Some of the girls at the *Perroquet* were not bad-looking....

It was cherry-blossom time in Dairen, and the lanterns were ablaze along the half-mile of beach front where nostalgic Japanese officials came in these spring nights to drink *saké* underneath the petaled boughs, and watch the *geisha* dance. April is the cruelest month, in wartime: I wondered how many of these young soldiers, now lying back at ease along the cool turf, before next spring might lie beneath it. The lines of a German poem haunted me as I watched them:

> Ein Tännlein grünet wo,
> Wer weiss, im Walde,
> Ein Rosenstrauch, wer sagt
> In welchem Garten?
> Sie sind erlesen schon,
> Denk es, o Seele!
> Auf deinem Grab zu wurzeln
> Und zu wachsen...

And it was not just the thought that many of these revelers were marked for death; but of what war would do to the rest of them, to the unluckier ones who survived. There is something so contradictory between the Japanese love of flowers and the Japanese love of killing that some onlookers, who take only the tourist view of Japan and are delighted with the former taste, find it difficult to believe in the second at all. It would seem ungrateful to remind them that these young recruits, fresh from home, with the open sunbrowned faces of peasants, were being sent to a country where they would carry out, under orders, things that a Nazi storm-trooper might shrink from.

This, and other points related to terrorism in wartime, I discussed later on with a publicity man from the South Manchuria Railway (for now that I was ashore after all, official contacts were to be sought rather than avoided; and it is to the S. M. R. that all visiting journalists in Manchuria must address themselves). He was a young American whose father had worked for many years with the Japanese government, and who had himself married a Japanese wife and absorbed pretty thoroughly the Japanese point of view. It was interesting to meet a foreigner who could speak so openly for an unpopular cause; he did his best to convince me, I have no doubt with complete sincerity, that most of my own ideas about Japan were all wrong.

We dined together one night in company with a Japanese police official—this is an arrangement not uncommon in totali-

SECOND SPRING   307

tarian states, for it provides a kind of protection for both sides if controversial topics are raised. And we talked about the "China Incident" with surprising freedom.

I heard here an explanation of the outrages which followed the Japanese occupation of Nanking that has been given a wide circulation in the Far East: the troops who first entered the Chinese capital, it was claimed, were third and fourth class reservists, middle-aged men who were "more likely to get out of hand with women" than youngsters. [If this explanation is found convincing, it is surely a strange commentary upon Japanese family life.] But the major charge against the Japanese military command in China is not the disorders incidental to invasion, but the regulation army procedure of mass execution and terrorization of the civilian populace that is now well attested by a mass of evidence. And this cannot be explained away by counter-accusations.

"What the Chinese have done," I was told, "is so much worse...." Followed details of the impaling of Japanese women on wooden stakes, of the torture of Japanese soldiers, and the like.... "Whatever is said of *our* army, we know a Japanese soldier would never do things like that."

This had a familiar ring. When it comes to atrocities, I suppose, one must believe the things that one has seen, or for which the evidence is overwhelming: there will be horror stories told on both sides of any war. But in this war, it was the Japanese troops who had been given unlimited opportunity. And there is a clear distinction to be drawn between isolated acts of violence (the "Tungchow massacre" is one of the few of these in which the Chinese are accused that is well authenticated), and a deliberate policy of terrorism and mass murder. It is the difference between killing in the fury of passion, and killing in cold blood. I have heard Chinese officials deplore certain of the events at Tungchow, and had seen for myself the policy of the Chinese command towards prisoners of war. Japan has expressed no regrets for what happened at Nanking; and for the slaughter of thousands of Chinese civilians in captured towns, a Japanese army commander (who no doubt is devoted to peonies) must take full responsibility.

But though we could not agree about many things, this encounter was to prove useful in a number of ways. A feeler I had put out about a quick trip to Peiping was heartily seconded —much to my surprise—by the S. M. R. "We can give you a pass on the railways," the publicity man told me.

"Are there any strings tied to it?"

He shrugged. "We give it to any accredited foreign journalist. All we ask is that you write the truth about what you see." It was obvious that he was hoping the Japanese occupation of Peiping might make a good impression.

This was a chance I had not dreamed of. My visa for Manchukuo would automatically be taken care of, and I should be able to travel back by rail through Korea to Japan, and rejoin my ship at Yokohama. Some sacrifice of the ethics of professional journalism was likely to be involved: I knew I should be expected to give this trip a favorable write-up. But professional ethics may be sacrificed more easily than the truth.

"Thanks," I said with complete sincerity. "I'd be delighted to make the trip...."

So it was that I found myself, still feeling slightly guilty, very comfortably installed in a first-class compartment in the Mukden Express. In the same car was traveling an Italian Fascist Mission on its way to Hsinking: the Marquis Paulucci and his friends went through the whole elaborate business of an official Japanese farewell with a poor grace, for they were visibly dropping from lack of sleep. Higher up on the same platform a troop of White Russian guards were taking their orders from a Japanese officer. In the picturesque uniform of the Intervention, with long hair sticking out like straw beneath their forage caps, they looked like caricatures of counter-revolutionaries from a Soviet play of the civil war. They did not seem to relish their present position, I fancied; but probably they had little enough choice in the matter. And they were better fighting material for Japan's army than the Manchurians were ever likely to be.

I could not avoid the feeling that I was traveling in an enemy country. A Japanese officer in the next seat to mine unstrapped his pistol and hung it up in the corner; I remembered trying

SECOND SPRING 309

out that same model of automatic with a young commander of the Eighth Route Army, when we had been going over some spoils of war. Its performance had been unimpressive, and we had decided that a Mauser was much better. Now, I found myself wanting to tell this new traveling companion what I thought of his gun. . . .

There was military activity all along the line to Mukden. The Kwantung Army is an army of occupation, and it is kept on the job. But many signs here pointed to more than the routine "bandit suppression." All bridges along the railway were being duplicated, new telegraph posts mounted, new lines of track laid. And all these lines ran on to the borders of the Soviet Union. In the midst of one war, Japan was already preparing for the next.

But not altogether smoothly. I had been cautious about talking Chinese to anybody on this trip, for foreigners in Manchukuo are very conspicuous. But in Mukden I found a communicative porter, and a quiet spot near the baggage room. I asked him what news came from China these days, how the war was going. And I used an impolite phrase for the Japanese armies to make my meaning clear.

He was a big, round-shouldered fellow with a heavy face, and at my question his whole expression altered: surprise fought with suspicion. Yes, he answered guardedly, he had heard the Japanese had suffered a big defeat. In Shantung. "Taierhchwang?" I asked.

"*Tai—erh—chwang* . . ." His voice dwelt lovingly on the throaty syllables, the name of this little town that meant now for the Chinese what Guadalajara or Teruel or the Ebro meant to the people of Spain. And then he talked rapidly, throwing all caution to the winds. Sure, they had heard about it; not in the newspapers though—they only printed stories of Japanese victories. He was a "Shantung man" himself, and one of the best bits of news he had heard in years was the execution of Han Fu-ch'u. Shantung was a good place to fight, and the Shantung men were good fighters—if they had arms . . .

"And *here*?" I wanted to know. He shook his head; here it was bad, here the Chinese "ate bitterness." Then suddenly he remembered something, and his face became as eager as a child's. Did I know about the big fire in the airplane factory last week?

"In Mukden?" I had heard some garbled reports in Dairen of a mutiny in the army that had just been suppressed in time, and of a destructive fire at Mukden in which more than forty planes had been burned. The origin of the fire, it seemed, was a mystery.

My Manchurian porter looked up and down the deserted platform before he confided: *"Yeh shih wo-men ti..."* "That was our people too."

PEIPING IN SHADOW

At Shanhaikwan, where the Great Wall runs down to meet the sea, I made my first direct acquaintance with the "Provisional Government of the Republic of China." Several members of the Peiping puppet regime boarded the train, on a triumphal tour to the old capital. They established themselves in a private car, strongly guarded by Japanese troops.

I began to feel a little uneasy; if my friends the guerillas were active in these parts, this might not prove to be the safest of trains to travel in. For our progress to Peiping was marked by a full local turn-out at every sizable station. We would draw in at high speed to the excruciating strains of a bugle band, past a platform lined by (unarmed) Chinese police. Beyond these again were usually rows of school-children, each one clutching a paper flag—the five-barred flag of Manchukuo that had become the emblem of the new Peiping administration. The train halted only briefly; at some stations, it merely slowed down long enough to allow one of the silk-gowned puppet dignitaries to show his venerable whiskers at the window. Then he ducked back again to safety, and the train gathered speed before the bored-looking children had their cue to wave their flags and cheer.

Demonstrations can be made to order; but it is hard to manufacture enthusiasm. And the extreme reluctance of the Chinese officials to appear in public, while understandable enough, did nothing to encourage the illusion that they were being welcomed by a grateful populace. The general impression left by these sketchy ceremonies was a melancholy one. The only participants who can possibly have enjoyed themselves were the buglers, for most Chinese are happy when they are making a noise. But at least we could be sure of getting in to Peiping on time; it would have been really dangerous for that train after nightfall.

I have never returned to Peiping without the familiar thrill, the reawakening of astonishment at the enduring beauty of this dusty old capital. Some Chinese have maintained that they would rather have seen Peiping in ruins than in the hands of the Japanese: this is the language of revolt, and a language long foreign to the North. A year before, it would have seemed meaningless in Peiping itself.

But here, too, so much had changed. I had left a city stunned by the swiftness of its own downfall, even though in many ways it had invited conquest. I came back to a city wise and sly as ever; but no longer a city without hope. Even in this dry air of disillusion enthusiasm had renewed itself. And in Peiping in those later days a single phrase was on every tongue: it ran like a whisper through the markets, dropped with inimitable nonchalance from beggars at street corners. *"The guerillas..."*

For the Chinese troops had returned after the first collapse, and now there were guerilla bands in the Western Hills, in the mountains of Jehol, along the highway to Tientsin. That April, when the Japanese had rushed reinforcements down to Shantung after the defeat at Taierhchwang, Peiping was held by a garrison of barely three hundred men. It is almost certain that the Chinese, if they had wished, might have recaptured the city. But they could not have held it for long, and the threat of these mobile forces circling the city walls was perhaps greater than the effect of any direct attack could have been. It kept Peiping, and not only the Japanese, in a state of prolonged suspense.

"What worries me," the head of one foreign embassy told me, "is what the Chinese troops are going to do to *us*, if they do retake the city. They've no reason to love us, after all that's happened." He went on to summarize. "You know, after the battle at Taierhchwang, General Sugiyama * flew across here, and made a full tour of all the fronts. He decided that the situa-

---
* Then, Japanese Minister of War in the Konoye Cabinet.

tion in the rear—all this guerilla stuff, and partisan mobilization in Hopei and Chahar—was so dangerous that any further Japanese advance must be postponed until they had made a thorough job of consolidation. He went back and reported as much to Tokyo.

"But the Army's blood was up: Taierhchwang had to be avenged. So Sugiyama went out of the Cabinet, and Itagaki came in his place. The drive on Hsüchow, and on to Hankow, went ahead. Now the Japanese garrisons are cut down to the barest minimum all over the North, and the area they control has been steadily shrinking. It's a magnificent opportunity, of course, for the guerillas—not so much to counter-attack, as to re-establish and strengthen their bases. And there will be no chance of a campaign against them now before the winter."

There was ample confirmation for his story. I met one American journalist in Peiping who had just returned from a trip to the largest Chinese-controlled area in this northern region—the "Border District of Hopei, Shansi, and Chahar," with its capital at Fuping. He described a Chinese "popular front" government which had been welcomed by the people of Hopei as the best they had ever known—a government which was extending its cadres, originally units of the Eighth Route Army, into an efficient mobile fighting force; was developing a *Tze Wei Chün*, or "Self-Defense Corps," on a generous scale; was operating its own factories and arsenals, communications, newspapers, hospitals and village co-operatives.... After the first Japanese invasion and the collapse of the regular defense, the people of North China had recovered their nerve and their ancient spirit. Now they were preparing a new kind of resistance—a defense based upon mass mobilization, with a strength and flexibility the old provincial armies had never possessed. And the reconquest of the North, if the Japanese ever got around to it, was likely to prove a much more formidable task than anything they had encountered in the summer of 1937.

This, then, was the picture of North China after a year of war: a countryside armed and resolute, where the invaders held only a few key cities, with a doubtful control over the railways that linked them. One of the first tasks the Japanese had set

PEIPING IN SHADOW 313

themselves after their initial victories was the completion of a new railway from Peiping to Jehol, which would no doubt prove very useful for bringing in reinforcements from Manchuria if they were needed. The new line had been officially opened just before my arrival. (One of the things about this opening which was especially appreciated in newspaper circles in Peiping, was the fact that the only two foreign journalists who had gone through on the first train—a British writer who was notoriously pro-Japanese, and an Italian fascist—had both been shut up by the Japanese commander in Jehol on charges of "espionage.") But already stories were circulating that the new line had been cut by Chinese troops; and in the months that followed, it was found quite impossible to maintain a regular service along it. Before long, even the main line to Mukden by which I had traveled was to be seriously interrupted.

And in the center of all this was Peiping, capital of a "Provisional Government" whose writ ran only a few miles outside its city walls. The capital itself was quiet enough: here there had been no terror, for it was generally where they encountered stiff resistance that the Japanese had found "strong measures" necessary for pacification purposes. But there was an air of make-believe about the new government and all its ways that left no remaining doubt as to what would become of it without the aid of Japanese bayonets.

The contempt expressed on every hand for the personnel of the new puppet régime was so withering that one felt it would have been simpler for the Japanese to drop even the pretense of "Chinese rule." For the Japanese military alone, along with hatred might have gone a certain grudging respect. These obscure relics of a vanished era who had been resurrected to lend a façade of dignity and scholarship to the new régime, were so bankrupt in both that they made the "Government" a mere laughing-stock. Politically, they were worse than negligible; for most of them had been associated with the old Anfu clique, and the people of Hopei and Chahar had not forgotten the most corrupt government North China had ever known.

No single index, indeed, affords more striking proof of the political and diplomatic failure of the Japanese in China, than the quality of the Chinese they have got to work for them in the occupied areas. In the first months, when the new Peiping régime was being formed, Japanese agents were hard at work trying to win over some better material. Their first choice in North China was Wu Pei-fu, a reactionary old warlord who once headed a strong Northern coalition, had been a protégé of the British, and was unquestionably a man of real ability and character. Old Wu was living peacefully in retirement when the storm broke, and seems to have made no effort to avoid it. But his reply to the first Japanese overtures directed towards him is classic.

"Tell the Japanese," he said, "that I shall be very glad to head such a government as you propose—on two conditions. *First,* that all Japanese troops are withdrawn from Chinese territory. *Second,* that Generalissimo Chiang Kai-shek approves the appointment!"

Not many years before, Chiang Kai-shek had been Wu Pei-fu's bitterest enemy; they had fought many campaigns before the final triumph of the Nationalists. But now Chiang Kai-shek, forced back up the Yangtze from what had been his own local stronghold in the provinces of Kiangsu, Chekiang, and Anhwei, was the leader of a united China even to a northern warlord whose power Chiang himself had broken. This phenomenon of old-style Chinese officials holding out against all the most tempting sweets of office (something which the Japanese had encountered in Shanghai and Canton as well as in the North) was perhaps the most unexpected of all the surprises this strange new China held in store for them.

A very few days were enough to show me all I wanted to see in Peiping. There could be no question but that here—where conditions were probably more favorable for the creation of an "autonomous government" than anywhere else in China, where a greater moderation had characterized the actions of the Japanese military command, and where national consciousness had formerly been at the lowest possible ebb—the invaders had signally failed to put across anything convincing in the way of a political movement or an independent system. Regimentation there had been, and a certain amount of surface organization.

PEIPING IN SHADOW 315

Impressive schemes for the "economic reconstruction" and "exploitation" of North China had been drawn up on paper: but Japan had not the capital to finance them, and did not control the countryside where they were to be put into effect. Altogether, the outlook for the new "reformed" Government of China was not very promising.

Meanwhile Peiping lived on—as it had lived so many years in the past—under the shadow of an alien rule. Its time was not yet. The impassive faces of coolies and rickshaw-men in the streets told no tale of mounting passion, betrayed nothing of the new resolution they had learned from the armed men in the hills. But the hope was there, and a new kind of confidence very different from the old false self-confidence of the days of Lukowchiao. Their time would come. . . .

On my last night in Peiping, I was listening in with a friend on the short-wave radio (all Chinese broadcasting stations are on the short wave, so that possession of a set of this nature is now a criminal offense in the Japanese-controlled areas). We had been trying to break through the barrage of local interference to the hidden interior that was China. And at last we heard a Chinese voice, speaking low but very urgently.

"Hullo, hullo!" it was calling; and then, in a tone almost of despair, *"I can't hear you.* Hullo, hullo, hullo . . ."

At last the answer must have come, for the announcer's voice rose exultingly. "Hullo, I can hear you now! Come back, all clear; *come back . . ."*

It was a ground station calling to a missing Chinese plane; for a moment the curtain had lifted on the vast drama of war that was going on back there. My friend looked at me across the radio, and in her eyes was the same gratitude that had been in the voice of the radio announcer.

"That used to be the worst part of it here: that we were cut off from the war, and it all went on beyond us. Now we have our contacts again. Peiping *may* be a ruin before our armies take it, but at least it will be China . . ."

Her words died, on the sound of muffled firing somewhere out in the Western Hills.

THE ARCHITECTS OF EMPIRE

What had been happening to the "Continental Plan" of the Japanese Army during a year of war? The journey back across Manchuria and Korea to Japan at this critical stage of the whole China campaign gave one a good deal of food for reflection on this all-important question. A number of facts emerged with startling distinctness.

Manchuria—first fruits of the real continental invasion that began in earnest in 1931—is the recognized stronghold of the Japanese Kwantung Army, a force with a peacetime strength of some 150,000 men. This army, the spearhead of invasion in the North, is the most experienced, the best-equipped, and the best-staffed at the disposal of the Imperial Command. Up to 1937 it had consistently held to its own semi-independent policy, which may be summarized as consolidation of Japan's military supremacy in North China and Inner Mongolia, in preparation for the coming struggle with the Soviet Union.

The first phase of war in 1937 was entirely to the liking of the Kwantung staff, and some of their best divisions took part in it, including Itagaki's, and Doihara's celebrated "flying column," which was the first to reach the north bank of the Yellow River. But apart from these picked mobile units, the main strength of the Kwantung Army was kept in Manchuria, and was steadily reinforced by the best of the younger recruits who were called to the colors. For the heavy work in Central China (up to the battle of Taierhchwang in April, 1938) Japan used mainly second-line reserves; and by this time some 300,000 troops, the finest offensive force Japan could muster, was concentrated inside the borders of Manchukuo.

The general Japanese strategy was clear. It was still hoped that a smashing victory in Central China might lead to a quick settlement of the China campaign (with a minimum of losses to Japan's fighting strength); and then, with full mobilization at home and all her industry geared to wartime production, Japan might swing into action with the vaunted "lightning-attack" on Siberia and the Maritime Provinces. This, at any rate, was the opinion of a number of foreign military observers early in 1938; and the spring of that year was generally favored as the time already chosen in advance for these daring new operations.

It may seem incredible that in the middle of one large-scale campaign, Japanese army leaders should be seriously considering so immense a task as an attack on the Soviet Union. But it must not be forgotten that Japan was very slow in realizing that the chance she had missed for a quick settlement of the China campaign at the time of the capture of Nanking might not soon repeat itself. The way in which the Chinese defense had crumpled after Shanghai was so encouraging to the Japanese command that there can be little doubt they expected a similar débâcle at Hsüchow, Chengchow, and Hankow. Moreover, Japanese army circles were convinced that prolonged political troubles in Russia, and the resultant "purges" in the Red Army, had seriously weakened the latter's fighting strength.

Up to the spring of 1938, then, an extension of the Far Eastern hostilities to include the Soviet Union seemed by no means unlikely. There can be no other explanation to account for the preponderant Japanese strength accumulated at this time in Manchuria. But the events of that spring completely altered the picture.

In general, the first phase of the China campaign—up to the fall of Nanking—had gone decisively in Japan's favor. But the Chinese not only survived the collapse of Nanking, but rallied so magnificently that within four months they were in a position to counter-attack on the main front. And the battle of Taierhchwang—the worst defeat the Japanese armies have ever sustained in all their history—ushered in an entirely new phase of the war. The virtual annihilation of two of their best divisions, and the immediate subsequent retreat along a wide front, at last convinced the Japanese command that there would be no "quick victory" in China. More troops, and good troops, were badly needed in Central China; and they could only come from the North. The decision taken—apparently against the advice of the War Ministry—to "avenge Taierhchwang" and launch a large-scale drive in Central China, meant that for the first time Japan was drawing upon the reserves hitherto kept for action against the U. S. S. R. Any attack on Russia must now be abandoned, probably for the duration of the China war.

This was the position when I traveled across Manchuria in April. Several divisions had already left for the south, and first-line troops were being called in from the northern frontiers to join the major offensive against Hsüchow. The feelings of the Kwantung Army at this changed state of affairs can well be imagined. For it was dead against their line of policy to allow any weakening of military strength in the North, and now whole armies were plunging into the quicksands of Central China on inevitably costly and probably inconclusive expeditions. With the conquest of North China only half completed, Japan was preparing to throw something like her full strength into an invasion of the central (and even southern) provinces. The Continental Plan, in fact, was now a chaos; and it was highly problematical if even North China could be saved from the wreck.

For the major problem of the North—the direct overland connection of the northwestern provinces with the Soviet Union —remained unsolved. And this most cherished dream of the Kwantung Army, the driving of a wedge westwards from Suiyuan across the "Red Northwest," seemed now frustrated.

Very little was heard, during the first months of the war when Japan's immediate objectives in North China were fairly well-defined, about operations in Inner Mongolia. It is worth recalling here that the first Japanese drive along the Ping-Sui railway took their columns further west than they have been at any time since. On two later occasions—in the autumn of 1937, and the early spring of 1938—successive drives were launched against the Northwest, though not on a major scale. The second of these succeeded briefly in crossing the Yellow River into northern Shensi, but it was soon turned back.

Why did not Japan press these thrusts against a vital strategic area? One answer, of course, is that there were not enough troops to spare for the job. Another—and one which the Kwantung

THE ARCHITECTS OF EMPIRE 319

Army in particular appreciated—was the role of the People's Republic of Outer Mongolia. Every time that Japanese forces have threatened this northwestern zone, things have happened in Outer Mongolia. All through the autumn of 1937, Mongolian cavalry and mechanized divisions stood by on the borders of Suiyuan. And, as if that hint were not enough, when the Japanese at one stage moved against Paotow (still held by the Chinese forces), Outer Mongolian troops came down as far as Pailingmiao. The Japanese column was very rapidly withdrawn.

Outer Mongolia, which is a Soviet Republic though not an integral part of the Union, is perhaps one of the least-known, certainly one of the least-visited parts of the modern world. But the military relations between Urga and Moscow are sufficiently understood, and the Japanese at least have no illusions about the military resources of this sparsely populated state. Urga has a modern and well-trained air force, equipped with Russian-built planes; and if this should be brought into operation (as it could be, without committing the U. S. S. R. to war) the Japanese would be faced with an entirely new factor in North China: a serious challenge to their undisputed control of the air.

Some consideration of these factors is enough to show the serious danger to which a general invasion of China has exposed the whole structure of Japan's continental empire. On an orderly plan, it might have proved possible to consolidate the North, isolate the Northwest, and only by further stages proceed to the reduction of the Yangtze area and South China. But no single one of these necessary preliminary objectives has been attained. Instead, Japan has set herself the impossible task of delivering a knockout blow to an antagonist whose real strength, never accurately gauged, is now only beginning to appear.

It is both dangerous and misleading to attempt to consider the Far Eastern war in isolation: it seems likely enough now that, long before a final decision has been reached in China, this conflict will already be merged in a greater one. But it is hard to avoid the conclusion that China, given her geographical situation, her protected sources of supply, and the new unity and spirit of her four hundred million people, cannot be defeated. If it were China alone against Japan alone, there could be little risk in prophecy about the ultimate outcome. But the situation is not as simple as that.

There are certain world forces whose chief concern, in the Far East, is to prevent at all costs one by no means unlikely result: the total defeat of Japan. These are the forces whose influence has already come into play in restricting foreign assistance to China; in other circumstances, that influence might well be transformed into active support for Japan. There is not much chance of China becoming another Ethiopia; there is a very fair chance that the attempt will be made to assign to her the fate of Czechoslovakia.

That attempt will fail. For China is already fighting, and her people know what they are fighting for. No compromise settlement can ever be acceptable now to a responsible Chinese government. And when a whole people are roused to arms as the Chinese people are today, they may lose every battle but the last.

MAY DAY IN TOKYO

At first, I did not think it could be true. The same shabby suit, the same kindly, short-sighted eyes.... But it was indeed my old friend the Passport Officer, looking more lugubrious and absent-minded than ever. I reminded him of our last meeting the year before.

"You have been in China since then?" he asked with mild curiosity. I told him Hong Kong, which seemed a safe answer.

"So?" He sighed deeply, and began to enter up the details of my passport with the old conscientiousness. He did not want to talk about the war, even when I asked what he thought about it. "This is a difficult time for Japan, we must all make great sacrifices," was what his few comments amounted to.

"And how is it now in Japan?"

Perhaps he misunderstood the question; surely there was no guile behind his naïve enthusiasm. "Ah, in Japan it is beautiful now! But it is too bad—again you will miss the cherry

MAY DAY IN TOKYO 321

blossom...." He made a careful note of my mother's maiden name, and offered to show me the way to the train.

Japan *was* beautiful to look at in late April, as we followed that curving track along the Inland Sea that is one of the most delightful train journeys in the world. The hillsides were bright with flowering shrubs, yellow and red and smoky blue; and the air was heavy with the spring. Pale oranges glowed through their dark leaves; in the well-tended fields, vegetables were dressed for market in almost military array. This was a country at peace, and not at war.

It was beautiful, and my heart rose in me against it. For instead of these tranquil hills, I saw another country—ravaged fields where no crops would ripen this year, the blackened beams of ruined villages, cities where the dead lay piled beside the river banks. It was not a pleasant picture, though it was the work of Japanese artists, some of whom were proud of it. Would they sit so placidly, these well-fed passengers, I wondered, if they looked out from their windows not on quiet towns and sunny orchards but on a depopulated countryside, haunted by the shapes of grossly-fattened dogs (only the dogs fed well in China, these days), while thirty million people fled westwards to escape those "friendly" armies? I wanted to bring this picture into that crowded railway carriage—the real picture of the war.

But people in Japan saw only another picture, as I realized when I took up some of the illustrated magazines from the tourist car. Here were colored photographs of Soochow and Hangchow, Japanese officers sailing on the lake, Japanese soldiers feeding sweets to children, Chinese peasants waving the flag of the Rising Sun to greet their conquerors.... It was a lie, just as the tranquil and prosperous air of these islands was a lie. But how many Japanese knew that?

I arrived in Tokyo on the Emperor's birthday. The occasion was celebrated by a mass review of troops, and by a flight of nearly a hundred bombers over the capital. (On that same day, fifty warplanes raided Hankow, to commemorate the Mikado in another fashion.) The streets of Tokyo were decorated with army and navy flags, and I looked for something like the hectic atmosphere I had known here the year before, when the war was only brewing. But to my amazement no crowds thronged the streets to watch the marching units; not even the children raised their eyes to watch the passage of the dark formations overhead. Tokyo, under a rising wind, went about its business with a sullen and studied indifference. This city was trying hard to forget the war, and wanted no bombing planes as reminders....

Even the newspapers, I found, were playing down events in China as far as possible: the public wasn't interested in war stories, and there had been no victories to report for some time. And I realized then one of the difficulties of the Japanese propaganda—a difficulty that must confront any government which tries to represent a full-scale campaign as a mere "incident." Officially, Japan was not even at war, and none of the normal slogans for such a situation—the danger to the Fatherland, safety of the Empire at stake, and so forth—could be considered appropriate. Instead, there was this troublesome "China Incident," which had lasted so long already; and Japan was only trying to befriend the Chinese people, and in a month or so it would all come out right.... *That* was what the Japanese people were still being told; and there were still many who, for their own peace of mind, wanted to believe it.

Up to Taierhchwang, the illusion had held. But now, just when the strain of war was really beginning to tell, that strain could never be admitted. Many expedients were adopted to conceal the real state of affairs. I found that the families of soldiers killed in China were forbidden to publish the news, even to their friends. Severely wounded men were being sent to Formosa or Manchuria or Korea, rarely to Japan. But still the war went on: more and more men were needed, more and more deaths had to be announced. It is not easy to deceive the masses of a nation indefinitely, and already the dilemma of the Japanese Government was becoming embarrassing. Either they must tell their people the truth; or they must continue a fiction that by now was wearing dangerously thin.

May Day in Tokyo   323

On May Day, I went to visit the War Exhibition in Ueno Park. Here at least, I thought, Tokyo must come to grips with the real situation. The very scale of operations in China must surely emerge from any pictorial record of the war.

And indeed, an effort had been made at reality. Here were the famous bombers that had raided Nanking, their fuselage riddled with shrapnel; and beside them, the wreckage of Chinese planes. War relics and trophies had been gathered together rather aimlessly. There was a series of carefully staged tableaux of the highlights of the war—the battle of Nankow Pass, the Shanghai fighting, triumphal entry into Nanking, the landing at Tsingtao. Lighting and sound effects were ingeniously applied.

But it did not work, any more than the birthday parade. The thousands of visitors who wandered through the grounds were more interested in the trade exhibits, the amusement park, in boating on the lake, than they were in this display of the prowess of the Imperial Army. And the political flavor of the exhibition, it seemed to me, was equally wasted. Everywhere the Rising Sun flag was draped with the swastika and the flag of Italy: portraits of Hitler and Mussolini frowned gloomily from every pavilion. But of enthusiasm for "our gallant allies," I could find no trace. I stood for a considerable time as the solitary student of an immense wall-chart illustrating the "Sovietization" of Chiang Kai-shek's regime. One part of it showed Russian battle planes rising from Moscow, painted a fine revolutionary red, changing their color in mid-flight, and arriving at Hankow blue, with the white Kuomintang sun on their wings....

With all their flair for exhibitions, the Japanese could not put over the China war so long as it remained a mere victory march. And—because the Imperial Armies can never be defeated—that was all that was allowed to appear. Only too obviously, the public was getting a little tired of it.

What effects had the war brought inside Japan? There were few indications on the surface, beyond the rationing of motor fuel, the curtailment of luxuries, the attempt to close down certain forms of entertainment. To the casual traveler, this country—or the cities, at least—might appear a little subdued, perhaps, but in other ways normal. Japan was organized for war with an efficiency only possible in so compact a country, and the Japanese are masters of the organization of poverty. There were no obvious signs as yet of that crack-up of the national economy that some people had confidently expected to see in Japan within a few months of the outbreak of war.

But I remembered how Mao Tse-tung (who was probably as well-informed about the internal situation of Japan as most people) had spoken a warning against any underestimation of Japan's power of endurance under war conditions, so long as no economic sanctions were made effective against her by foreign powers. The old analysis of Japan's greatest weakness holds good: her almost complete dependence on foreign countries for war materials and supplies. On this point, Japan remains as vulnerable as ever, but so long as she is able to have free access to raw materials abroad, and somehow to obtain her foreign credits, that vulnerability will not be exposed. Mao had estimated that in the most unfavorable conditions, Japan could hold out for a minimum of two years. Premature economic collapse was a miracle the Chinese no longer hoped for.

But the steady wearing-down of the morale of the Japanese people was a factor more easily calculable. I talked of this with one foreigner who had lived for many years in Japan. "It is true," he said, "that one year of war has not made much noticeable difference, on the surface. Regimentation, of course; the National Mobilization Act; tightening-up politically. But the weakest link is still the peasantry. These are the group who suffer first, with their fixed market prices, from a rising cost of living. The city workers are not so badly off, for the time being.

"Then the manufacturers are far from happy, with Japan's foreign trade falling off, and limitation of all imports except war materials. There's a good deal of tension between different groups, behind the scenes—hence this confusion of foreign policy. But if inflation comes—and it must, if the war goes on—there may be panic.

"And that will be the dangerous moment for all of us. For if there *is* a crisis at home, the military leaders are capable of almost anything, looking for a way out. That's what Britain is afraid of, with good reason."

"And revolution in Japan?"

He shook his head. "The peasants and workers can't get together. Here inside Japan the government has all the brakes on. But there's one place where it might come: *inside the Army*. And if the Army once goes, Japan is finished...."

If the Army goes.... At the Tokyo Railway Station I watched a draft of reservists, called up to join their units, leaving for China. Young men in mufti wearing colored silken sashes.

It was the saddest of leave-takings. Each recruit stood with bowed head in the center of a little circle of friends, while these sang an interminable farewell song that echoed like a dirge. Several I saw broke down and left before the song was through. There were no bands, no flags, no cheering....

I remembered how these platforms had looked in July, 1937. Many things may happen between the beginning and end of a war.

THE UNCONQUERED

The ship moved slowly out past the army transports into the open waters of Yokohama bay. We were clear of Japan, but not yet clear of her last attentions. A police boat chugged noisily by, binoculars trained on our almost deserted decks. High against luminous clouds, a squadron of seaplanes circled overhead, the sun flashing silver upon wings that scared the gulls. Fuji, the Mountain of Harmony, had hidden her flawless cone in mist....

We were leaving an unhappy country—a country its rulers had first made mad, and then bound in madness. I had seen how unwillingly this people was swept into war, and I knew with what reluctance some, at least, of them regarded the desperate adventure that darkened the years ahead. "We keep our thoughts," one young student in Tokyo had said, "locked up in our hearts. While this war lasts, we are dumb." And the tragedy of it was that for Japan, now, there could be no turning back: those who were not blind to the risks were powerless.

The risks are great, but so is the goal Japan has set herself. If Japan could win in China, could break the spirit of the Chinese people and build for herself an empire of five hundred million subjects in Eastern Asia, then indeed the world might stand within the level of her dreams. From her own Pacific fortress, *Dai Nippon* might watch with gleeful expectancy the disintegration of Europe, accumulating in the meantime reserves of trained manpower that might well prove invincible. It is a prospect to dazzle the eyes of any conqueror.

Nor is it all illusion. Those who flatter themselves that Japan has come too late into the field of empire to overtake her established rivals, forget that this is the age not of the division, but of the re-division of the world. At any time in the nineteenth century, Britain or France or Tsarist Russia might have been eager enough to attempt the dismemberment and subjugation of China—if they had ever been given the opportunity. Nor is there reason to suppose that their methods in doing it would have been so very different from Japan's. What General Matsui's troops did in Nanking was on a more heroic scale, perhaps, but pretty much on the same pattern, as what Lord Elgin's troops or Count Waldensee's did before them in Peiping.

But the nineteenth-century balance of power, which was quite as real in the Far East as in Europe and effectively prevented any single nation from dominating the rich resources of a vulnerable China, has been shattered in the twentieth century. Japan, profiting by the preoccupation of the Western powers with an "unbalanced" Europe, has for more than a decade been left a free hand in Asia. With nothing more to fear than protests from those powers whose interests in China she so directly threatens, she is forging ahead in her empire-building with a fine disregard of other nations' feelings. And this apparent recklessness is well calculated. If nothing short of foreign intervention could stop Japan in China, her military leaders would have very little to worry about.

But there remains one factor, and that the most obvious one, which all Japan's plans have overlooked: the continued resistance of the Chinese people. Japan can succeed only when China abandons the struggle. *And the Chinese people will fight on.*

No one could have said that with utter confidence before 1937: it can be said today with increasing emphasis for every city and town occupied by Japanese troops. And it is the knowledge of this new temper in their antagonist that has driven the Japanese command to such furious efforts to shorten the period of the war by rapid occupation of key strategic centers. It is not so difficult for the Japanese armies to take a city; the more difficult thing for them is to hold it, and turn it to any use. And the fantastic notion of conquering all China and holding it against a hostile populace is something not even a Japanese commander can contemplate with equanimity.

In China and in Spain, it is the same war—the defense of popular freedom against fascist aggression. This greatest issue of our time was first raised openly in 1931, when historically China became the first front in a developing world struggle that was to take in, within less than a decade, Ethiopia, Spain, Austria, Czechoslovakia. On three of those successive fronts the battle has already been lost to the aggressor. Only in Spain and in China the struggle goes on. Against heartbreaking military odds, the Spanish people have held the fascist offensive in Europe; though if the odds should be still further weighted against them they may yet prove overwhelming. What of China, and the fate of her millions who are only beginning to know the meaning of democracy?

The future may seem gloomy enough, to those of us who look on from across half the world. With all her coastline and all her principal cities now in the hands of the invader, China is fighting at last with her back to the wall. But that wall is not, as it is for the Spanish people, a hostile and blockaded ocean. It is the immense hinterland of Asia, a region that over centuries has been the birthplace of mighty empires, rich in natural resources that have hardly begun to be tapped. China today has turned back upon her ancient boundaries, the mountains of Tibet and the deserts of Turkestan, renewing in her hour of need her oldest historical communications with the outer world. Those communications can be made secure against any attack; and one at least of them can ensure for the future a permanent source of military supplies. For China—it is her greatest advantage over Spain—has direct contact with the one world power she can count on to stand by her.

With the few changes, then, of an unfamiliar scene, the picture in the Far East today is essentially the same picture that we have seen only too often a good deal nearer home: the struggle between the principles of independence and popular government, and forces that are the negation of these. Though Japanese invasion has brought disaster and suffering to China on a scale that appalls the imagination, at the same time this purge of blood and fire has released inside Chinese society progressive forces which, if they are allowed free play, may transform that suffering country into something like the free democratic republic that was the ideal of Sun Yat-sen. For the people of Japan this war holds out no such hope: only a vision of further conquest that will demand a further sacrifice. And China's strongest ally in the years ahead may well prove to be this growing disillusionment of the Japanese people, and of the rank and file of the Japanese armies.

Between the beginning and the end of a war... It is where we all stand, in these days when democracy is on the defensive in three continents, when only the enemies of peace seem able to combine successfully. And the common people of China, could we of the West but realize it, are fighting our battle. Efforts have been made to betray them by "friendly governments," as the people of Spain have been betrayed by governments in Europe that called themselves democratic. But the Chinese people —and it is one of the few beacon fires of hope upon the international horizon—are still unconquered.

They have found at last the way of resistance, and the way to freedom. And it is to China the world must look today for the fullest expression of that spirit of human endeavor which never yet, over the longest years, has known defeat:

The Unconquered

To suffer woes which hope thinks infinite,
To forgive wrongs darker than death or night,
To defy Power, which seems omnipotent;
To live and bear, to hope till Hope creates
From its own wreck the thing it contemplates,
Neither to change, nor falter, nor repent . . .

This is China's destiny, and she has the power to achieve it. For in the bare northern hills, along the green Yangtze valley, through the rice fields and rain-drenched mountains of the south, a whole people in arms is slowly finding its own leadership. And against the full strength of a resurgent China any armies in the world must break and fall.

It was Japan that was blind, I felt, as our ship rounded the last cape and I watched the islands sinking out of sight. The seaplanes had returned to their base. Two weeks away was America, over a fog-bound northern sea.

REFERENCE LIST

OF NAMES, EVENTS, AND PHRASES COMMONLY USED

AMAU DOCTRINE: Warning issued through Japanese spokesman to Western powers (April, 1934) amounting to a "hands off China."

ARAKI, GENERAL SADAO: Outstanding leader of Japanese military extremists; became Minister of Education in Konoye Cabinet.

BABA, EIICHI: Former Finance Minister in Japan; extreme type of Japanese capitalist; died late in 1937.

BLUECHER, MARSHAL VASSILY: Commander of Soviet "Red Banner Far Eastern Army"; former Soviet military adviser to Chinese Nationalists under name of GALEN.

CHANG CH'ING-YU: Commandant of the Chinese Police (*paoantui*) in the East Hopei "Autonomous Government." Led rising at Tungchow, July, 1937.

CHANG CHUN: Former Foreign Minister in Chinese National Government; commonly considered "pro-Japanese"; later became vice-premier under H. H. Kung.

CHANG HSUEH-LIANG: The "Young Marshal," son of Manchurian warlord Chang Tso-lin; led Sian Coup, 1936, to protest against Nanking Government's "policy of surrender to Japan." Since the release of Chiang Kai-shek, the Young Marshal has remained virtually a prisoner, and has been kept out of any active part in the war.

CHANG TZE-CHUNG: "Pro-Japanese" Mayor of Tientsin at outbreak of war; took over in Peiping after Sung Cheh-yuan departed; later deserted the Japanese to rejoin his troops in Shantung.

Chao Ch'eng-shou: Commander of First Shansi Cavalry Division; old-style Chinese commander and associate of Marshal Yen Hsi-shan.

Chao Teng-yu: Commander of 132nd Division of 29th Route Army under Sung Cheh-yuan; killed in action at Nanyuan during Japanese attack on Peiping.

Chen Chih-hua: Young Communist organizer of the mass movement in Shansi.

Chen Li-fu and Chen Kuo-fu: Two brothers, leaders of "CC" clique within the Kuomintang; very reactionary and consistently "anti-communist."

Chiang Kai-shek: Generalissimo of the Chinese forces and "Leader" (*Chu Tsai*) of the Chinese National Government; formerly Commander of the Northern Expedition from Canton which resulted in establishment of the Nanking Government and outlawing of Chinese Communists; since 1937, recognized head of a United Front Government including all parties in China.

Chou En-lai: Influential spokesman and representative of Chinese Communist Party; since 1938 vice-chairman of Political Training Department of the National Armies.

Chu Teh: "Red Napoleon"; former commander-in-chief of the Chinese Red Army; now commander of the Eighth Route Army of the National Revolutionary Forces.

"Continental Plan": The plan for Japanese expansion on the Asiatic continent, which has been favored by Japanese Army leaders, especially by the Kwantung Army; military events in the present China war have shown a radical departure from the lines laid down by the Kwantung Army strategists.

"Democracy": An independent English-language journal published in Peiping from May 1937 up to the Japanese occupation.

Doihara, General Kenji: The "Lawrence of Manchuria," one of the most brilliant and restless of Japanese empire-builders; discredited after failure of his "North China Autonomy" scheme of 1935; but led a Japanese unit with dash and vigor in the present China campaign.

REFERENCE LIST 333

EIGHTH ROUTE ARMY: The most common form of reference to the reorganized Chinese Red Army, now operating under Chu Teh over several provinces of North China; in addition to the Eighth Route Army in the North, there is another communist force, the "Newly Organized Fourth Army," now active in Chekiang, Anhwei, and Kiangsi.

FENG CHIH-AN: Second-in-command (under Sung Cheh-yuan) of the 29th Route Army, and Chairman of Hopei at the time of the Japanese invasion in 1937.

FENG YU-HSIANG: The "Christian General," former leader of the Kuominchun, later a member of the Nanking Government. Now an active supporter of the United Front, more engaged in political than in military work.

GINZA: Main shopping and amusement thoroughfare of Tokyo.

HAN FU-CHU: Former warlord of Shantung province; obstructed Chinese resistance to Japan in present campaign and was shot for "neglect of orders."

HAO MON-LIN: Commander of a Central Division at the battle of Hsinkow, where he was killed in action (October, 1937).

HAYASHI, GENERAL SENJURO: Japanese Army leader, premier for a difficult term of office early in 1937; later gave way to the government headed by Prince Konoye.

HIROTA, KOKI: Prominent Japanese politician, former premier and perennial Foreign Minister under several governments; his "Three Points" of 1936 outlined an aggressive Japanese policy towards China.

HO LUNG: Celebrated Chinese guerilla leader; took part in Nanchang Rising of 1927 when Chinese Red Army was formed; now commander of 120th Division of the Eighth Route Army.

HO-UMETSU AGREEMENT: The secret treaty signed in June, 1935, between General Ho Ying-chin, Chinese Minister of War, and General Yoshijiro Umetsu, Commander of the Japanese North China Garrison; it specified considerable Chinese concessions to Japan in North China, beyond the demilitarized zone established by the Tangku Truce of 1933.

HOPEI-CHAHAR POLITICAL COUNCIL: The anomalous body, semi-independent but owing allegiance to Chiang Kai-shek, which emerged at Peiping in 1935 under the chairmanship of General Sung Cheh-yuan.

HSIAO K'EH: Young Communist commander associated with Ho Lung; now second-in-command of the 120th Division of the Eighth Route Army.

"HSIAO KWEI": Literally, "small devil"; a member of the Young Vanguard of the Eighth Route Army.

HSU HSIANG-CH'IEN: Former commander of the Fourth Front Red Army; now second-in-command of the 129th Division of the Eighth Route Army.

"IRON CRUSADERS": An organization of vulgar White Russian elements recruited and employed by the Japanese for terrorist work inside foreign concessions at Tientsin, Shanghai, etc.

ITAGAKI, GENERAL SEISHIRO: Formerly chief-of-staff of the Kwantung Army; an active field commander in the early months of the present China campaign; later replaced General Sugiyama as War Minister in the Konoye Cabinet.

JEN PI-SHIH: Head of the Political Training Department of the Eighth Route Army.

KAN SZE-CH'I: Political Commissar to Ho Lung in the 120th Division.

KAO KWEI-TZE: Commander of the 88th Division of the Chinese National forces.

KO LAO HUI: The "Elder Brothers" society; one of the oldest and most influential of Chinese secret societies, generally non-political but now resolutely anti-Japanese.

KONOYE, PRINCE FUMIMARO: Former political protégé of Prince Saionji (sole surviving, or *Genro*, Elder Statesman, of Japan); succeeded to General Hayashi in June, 1937, as Japanese Premier, still with the reputation of a liberal; now leader of a War Cabinet that is committed to the "defeat of the Chiang Kai-shek régime."

KUNG, DR. H. H.: Finance Minister of the Chinese National Government, and since 1938 President of the Executive Yuan.

REFERENCE LIST 335

KUNGCH'ANTANG: The "Share-the-wealth Party"; name of the Chinese Communist Party since its inception, retained within the present United Front.

KUOMINTANG: The "Nationalist Party," founded by Sun Yat-sen as the *Tung Meng Hui;* the dominant party in the Chinese National Government since 1927; since 1937 cooperating with the Chinese Communists and other party groups.

KWAN HSIANG-YING: Political Commissar to Ho Lung in the 120th Division of the Eighth Route Army.

KWANTUNG ARMY: The Japanese "army of occupation" in Manchuria, with its headquarters in the Kwantung Peninsula; this army has often held a policy at variance with that of the Tokyo General Staff and the North China Garrison; it looks always towards a war with the Soviet Union.

"LAO PAI HSING": The "old hundred names" of the Chinese people; a common expression (especially used in the armies) to connote the common people, "the masses."

LATTIMORE, OWEN: Editor of *Pacific Affairs;* author of many well-known books on Mongolia and the Far East.

LIN PIAO: Youthful President of the Red Military Academy in China; commander of the 115th Division of the Eighth Route Army; seriously wounded in the fighting in Shansi, February, 1938.

LIN PAI-CH'U: Veteran communist leader in China; former Finance Commissar to the Chinese Soviets; now a political leader in the United Front.

LO FU: Foreign-trained Secretary to the Central Executive Committee of the Chinese Communist Party.

LO HSUEH-CHING: Dean of the "Anti-Japanese Military Academy" in Yenan.

"LONG MARCH": The epic trek of the Chinese Red Armies from their southern base to their new base in the Northwest, 1934-36. Their route reached as far west as Tibet, and covered more than 20,000 *li* (over 6,000 miles).

LIU HSIANG: Reactionary warlord who for many years had dominated the southwestern province of Szechwan; in 1937 affirmed his loyalty to Chiang Kai-shek, came to Hankow, and died there the same winter.

LIU PEI-CH'ENG: Young communist general, commander of the 129th Division of the Eighth Route Army.

LIU TZE-CH'I: Chief-of-staff of the 359th Brigade of the Eighth Route Army.

LU CHI: Famous Chinese musician, composer of many of the best known songs of "National Salvation."

MA CHAN-SHAN: Veteran Manchurian commander; led the resistance against the Japanese in Tsitsihar after the Mukden Incident; duped the Manchukuo Government, and has since been noted for his "anti-Japanese activity." Now commanding Chinese cavalry forces in Inner Mongolia.

"MAFOO": Chinese groom or horse-attendant.

MALRAUX, ANDRÉ: French revolutionary writer; author of two novels of the Chinese Revolution: *Les Conquérants,* and *La Condition Humaine.*

MAO TSE-TUNG: "Chinese Lenin," former Chairman of the Chinese Soviets, joint leader (with Chu Teh) for ten years of the Chinese Red Armies; retains his leading position in the Chinese Communist party, but holds now a position in the National Government.

MARUNOUCHI: The business district of Tokyo.

MEIJI SHRINE: The central monument in Tokyo, shrine of the Emperor Meiji who gave Japan a constitution in 1867, and is generally regarded as the "Founder of Modern Japan."

MINAMI, GENERAL JIRO: Leading Japanese Army extremist, prime mover in the Mukden Incident of September 18, 1931.

MITSUI and MITSUBISHI: Two of the largest monopoly trusts in Japan, whose interests (especially Mitsui's) cover banking, heavy industry, mining, shipping, etc.; though challenged recently by the spectacular growth of the Aikawa interests, Mitsui and Mitsubishi still have a stranglehold over Japan's economic life.

NANCHANG RISING: The rising led by Chu Teh and Ho Lung at Nanchang, Kiangsi province, in the summer of 1927, when the first Chinese Red Army was formed.

REFERENCE LIST 337

NIEH JUNG-CHEN: Vice-commander (under Lin Piao) of the 115th Division of the Eighth Route Army; most active organizer in the formation of the Chinese-controlled partisan area known as the "Border District of Hopei, Chahar, and Shansi."

PAI CHUNG-HSI: Formerly chief-of-staff to Chiang Kai-shek on the Northern Expedition; later quarreled with Chiang, and withdrew to his local stronghold in Kwangsi province; since 1936 reconciled to Chiang Kai-shek, and now Field Commander of the National Armies on the Central fronts.

"PAI KA'RH": A strong Chinese spirit distilled from rice and other grain, very commonly drunk in the North.

PAOANTUI: "Peace Preservation Corps," a Chinese gendarmerie or special police, armed with rifles and machine guns.

PAULUCCI, MARQUIS: Leader of the Italian Fascist Mission which visited Japan and Manchukuo in the spring of 1938.

P'ENG TEH-HUAI: Vice-commander of the Eighth Route Army under Chu Teh; former commander of First Front Red Army.

RAILWAYS: The current reference for different lines is generally used, as follows: *Cheng-Tai,* from Shihkiachwang to Taiyuan; *Lung-Hai,* from Haichow (on the coast) inland beyond Sian; *Ping-Han,* Peiping-Hankow; *Ping-Sui,* Peiping-Suiyuan; *Tsin-Pu,* Tientsin-Pukow (Nanking); *Tung-Pu,* Tatung-Puchow (across the Yellow River from Tungkwan).

RONIN: Literally "wave-men," a feudal term indicating "masterless samurai," traditionally one of the unruliest elements in Japan; now applied loosely to Japanese agents and racketeers in China and elsewhere, who are active in smuggling, dope-traffic, etc.

SATO, NAOTAKE: Japanese diplomat and statesman of moderate views; Foreign Minister in the Hayashi Cabinet of early 1937.

"SHANPING": Deserters who break away from the Chinese armies, often turn bandit, and form a serious problem in restoring order in the war zones.

SHEN HUNG-LIEH, ADMIRAL: Former Mayor of the Municipality of Tsingtao; permitted the destruction of Japanese property by Chinese irregulars; Shen later joined the guerillas in Shantung, and now holds the title of Governor of that province in place of Han Fu-chu.

SHENPEI: "North Shensi," a term often loosely used to refer to the Special (Communist) District of Shensi, Kansu, and Ningsia.

SIAN COUP: The arrest of Generalissimo Chiang Kai-shek on December 12, 1936, by Marshal Chang Hsueh-liang and a number of radical elements, in co-operation with General Yang Hu-ch'eng; the reconciliation of the Kuomintang and the Chinese Communist Party dates from the settlement of the Sian affair.

SMEDLEY, AGNES: American leftist writer, author of several books on the Chinese Revolution; lately active in the organization of medical and civilian relief in Hankow and South China.

"S.M.R.": The South Manchuria Railway Company, one of the largest organizations of its kind in the world; the S.M.R. has dominated the development of Manchukuo, and bids fair to do the same with North China.

SNOW, EDGAR: American writer and newspaperman; China correspondent of the London *Daily Herald*; author of several books of which the most recent, *Red Star Over China*, describes his pioneer visit to the Chinese soviet regions.

SOCIAL MASS PARTY: The *Shakai Taishuto*, only approximation to a Labor Party in Japan, led by the veteran Social-Democrat Dr. Isoo Abe; since the war, the Social Mass Party has gone over to the right.

STUDENT UNION: The old "Peiping and Tientsin Student Union" was one of the few active political organizations in North China in the years before the war, and was fanatically nationalist and "anti-Japanese."

SUGIYAMA, GENERAL GEN: Japanese military leader whose influence, since the outbreak of the China war, has been perhaps a moderating one: resigned from the Konoye

REFERENCE LIST 339

Cabinet when his advice about North China was disregarded.

SUN YAT-SEN: "Founder of the Chinese Republic"; led the revolution which overthrew the Manchus, established the Kuomintang Party, and died just before the successful launching of the Northern Expedition.

SUN YAT-SEN, MADAME: The widow of Dr. Sun, inheritor of the revolutionary tradition of the Left Kuomintang and driven into exile after the split between Right and Left in 1927; a leader of the National Salvation Movement, Mme. Sun is an ardent supporter of the United Front.

SUNG CHEH-YUAN: Formerly Chairman of the Hopei-Chahar Political Council at Peiping, and commander of the 29th Route Army; "Defender" of Peiping against the Japanese attack in July 1937.

TAIERHCHWANG: The great Chinese victory in southern Shantung in the first week of April, 1938.

TANGKU TRUCE: The agreement signed in May, 1933, after hostilities in Manchuria, Shanghai, and the North, by which the Chinese armies withdrew into southern Hopei and a "demilitarized zone" was set up in Hopei and Chahar. The terms were kept secret for many months.

TASHIRO, GENERAL KANICHIRO: Appointed commander of the Japanese North China Garrison in 1936; regarded as a "moderate," but died of brain fever, July, 1937.

TSO CHUAN: Acting chief-of-staff of the Eighth Route Army, in North China. (The titular chief-of-staff, General Yeh-Chien-ying, was largely occupied in Canton and the South.)

TUNG LIN-KEH: Vice-commander of the 132nd Division of the 29th Route Army, killed in the first Japanese attack on Peiping.

UTLEY, FREDA: British economist and writer, author of *Japan's Feet of Clay*, *Japan's Gamble in China*, and other works exposing the weakness of Japanese economy.

WANG CHEN: Commander of the 359th Brigade of the Eighth Route Army.

WANG CHING-WEI: Prominent Chinese politician and veteran member of the Kuomintang; commonly regarded as having been "pro-Japanese." Now "Vice-Leader" (under Chiang Kai-shek) of the National Government, but with little political influence.

WEI LI-HUANG: General commanding the Shansi front under Yen Hsi-shan; commander of the 14th Central Army.

WHAMPOA ACADEMY: The training school for military cadets of the Nationalist Army near Canton, where Chiang Kai-shek (the first President) made his reputation, and many of the leading Chinese generals were trained under Galen.

WU LIANG-P'ING: Young Communist official, formerly Foreign Affairs Commissar of the Chinese Soviets.

WU PEI-FU: Veteran North China warlord; candidate for office in puppet Peiping Administration under the Japanese.

YEN HSI-SHAN: Once known as the "Model Governor" of Shansi; established in his province for forty years until the Japanese drove him out; made commander of the Second War Area at the outbreak of the fighting, but did not emerge with very great credit from it.

YIN JU-KENG: Japanese "Puppet" in the East Hopei Anti-Communist Autonomous Government; escaped the Tungchow massacre only to be imprisoned by the Japanese.

YU HSUEH-CHUNG: A former associate of the "Young Marshal," active during the Sian coup; in command in Shantung during the present war.